Tickling the Bear

OTHER BOOKS AND FILMS BY DAVID WANN

BOOKS

Log Rhythms, a book of poetry

Superbia: 31 Ways to Create Sustainable Neighborhoods

Biologic: Designing with Nature to Protect the Environment

Affluenza, the All-Consuming Epidemic

Reinventing Community: Stories from the Walkways of Cohousing

Simple Prosperity, Finding Real Wealth in a Sustainable Lifestyle

The New Normal, an Agenda for Responsible Living

The Zen of Gardening in the High and Arid West

TV DOCUMENTARIES

Sustaining America's Agriculture: High-Tech and Horse Sense

Beyond Business as Usual: Meeting the Challenge of Hazardous Waste

Transportation 2000: Moving Beyond Auto America

Mega-Cities: Innovations for Urban Life

Placemakers: Bringing Back our Neighborhoods

Designing a Great Neighborhood: Behind the Scenes at Holiday

Raptors at Risk

tickling the
BEAR

HOW TO STAY SAFE IN THE UNIVERSE

A NOVEL BY

DAVID WANN

Chokecherry Press
Golden, Colorado
www.DaveWann.net

Editing: Aysha Griffin
Book design: Anne Clark
Cover images: Getty Images, iStock

Library of Congress Cataloging-in-Publication Data
Wann, David
Tickling the Bear: How to Stay Safe in the Universe 1st edition

ISBN: 978-1-7368391-0-2
1. Fiction/Family/Life.   2. Fiction/Nature & the Environment.

Published by Chokecherry Press
1015 Cottonwood Circle
Golden, CO 80401

Visit *www.DaveWann.net*

We need something bigger than we are
to be awed by and to commit ourselves to.

—Abraham Maslow

Contents

Acknowledgments

Although my writing and filmmaking career has centered on non-fiction books and documentary programs, I decided five years ago to "have a little fun" fictionalizing the kinds of people I'd written about, admired, or interviewed. I wanted to reveal the heart behind their ideas and paint impressionistic portraits of everyday heroes who are gracefully and bravely changing humanity's place in the world, just in time. I didn't know back then that the creation of a fictional world can become a rabbit hole about the size of the Grand Canyon.

Throughout the project's evolution, I'd poke my head out of my office, excitedly bouncing plot twists and character traits off my very creative wife, Anne. Shaking her head, she'd comment, "He wouldn't say it that way," and I would then go back and urge him to say it differently. For the most part undaunted, I was certain I was crafting a story that brims with adventure, whimsy, bravery, romance, and satire. Sure, I battled the usual challenges—procrastination, self-doubt, and a busy calendar—to produce endless versions of this playfully earnest story. And I know one thing: I would never have had the energy, patience and courage to keep working without Anne's steady support.

In the homestretch, I imagined readers laughing out loud, crying on the sly, and pondering themselves silly! The Great American novel. Then, enter the editor I wish I'd discovered years ago, Aysha Griffin. This talented, intuitive woman told me, gently, that while the book had potential, it was by no means done. "The reader knows what he looks like, but how does he *feel*?" So in my final months in the rabbit holes of Denver, Northern California, and the island of Borneo, I chased away the rabbits and spent ten-hour days digging deeper emotionally, cleaning up the mess that used to be a manuscript.

Thank you, Anne and Aysha!

Thanks to Katie Schnack for educating me about Facebook, hash tags and strategic publicity, and to Margie Baxley who revitalized my long dormant website, *davewann.net*. And a huge thank you to the readers of early drafts—neighbors and friends who sometimes connected with my characters and urged me to keep going. They often remained mercifully silent about rambling descriptions that Anne and Aysha later tossed in the compost pile.

While this "first novel" has been a life-changing experience, at this point I'm not certain there will be a second novel. Unless the world begs me for it, and maybe not even then! So enjoy this one, and if you have a chance, please contact me to let me know how much you loved it. Otherwise I'll probably assume you didn't because I'm a writer and most of us become shell-shocked and a little demented. But one thing is certain: it feels so good when you get a book just the way you want it ("Hey, that's pretty good!") and the project is done!

Tickling the Bear

One

Passport Expired?

Eight days after being told he could be dead within a year, Marcus Blake was slowly re-emerging from the numbness. The disease known as the Q virus wasn't contagious but was almost always fatal. Medical data set his chances at five percent or less.

Like many people, Marc had wrapped life's daily activities around himself, choosing to believe that death only happened to others or was at least a long way off. After enduring the prolonged death of his wife a few years earlier, maybe he assumed he'd already paid his dues. But here he was again, sorting death's details:

Which doctors have expertise with this virus? Should I bet on conventional medicine or also look at natural alternatives? Have I made promises I haven't kept?

I'm sure other people ask themselves these same jittery questions when death starts knocking. With a dull-toothache kind of feeling, we wonder, "Have I loved enough? Have I been kind and generous enough? My financial bank account may be in decent shape, but what about my relationship bank account?"

I guess I'm going to find out.

He had a deep bond with his daughter Lisa, who lived with her husband in the Denver metro area, as he did. He wouldn't want to impose on her, though. He hoped he would have the energy in the months ahead to support her in whatever way he could. His brother Rocket, a small-acre organic farmer and woodworker in Northern California, had been a lifelong gold anchor. The brothers had an unshakable emotional contract, well-proven over the years. Marc also adored Rocket's unpretentious wife, Ellen, but they lived a thousand miles away.

He was confident that his closest friends, Kai and May, could help him keep his balance, and he had other good friends, too, some of whom he'd supported when *they* needed help. *But these friends and family members have challenges of their own. They're active people, trying to manage their daily routines and also stay sane in these uneasy times.* Lisa, for example, put in long hours in her imported-craft business in Boulder, where she depended on a strong economy and a craft market that sometimes wobbled. Rocket's small farm could support him and his wife Ellen only if the non-farm work continued to pay half the bills. Kai and May were very unselfish people, but both were busy making changes in their work lives. Kai's parents, Yukio and Michiko, were close friends and mentors, too, but they were in their eighties, patiently trying to convince Kai to become a full partner and then take over the family's herbal healing business.

Clearly, Marc would need to rely on his own tenacity and resilience. Given these strong qualities, it was conceivable he *would* survive, but if his time were short, what were the most meaningful and satisfying things he should be doing? He mused, *If my whole life flashes before when I die, will it even hold my interest?* Truthfully, his angst was not just about his own mortality but also the last gasps of a teetering civilization. This anthropology professor fervently hoped his species would somehow *stop bickering* and rely on evolution's most valuable assets: cooperation, empathy, and fairness.

In his early years, right out of Berkeley's doctoral program, Marc had grabbed a promising teaching assignment at the University of Denver, where he'd stoked the aspirations and self-confidence of many students. He loved the work! From the front of his auditorium-style classroom, he'd bark amiably, "You don't have to think like me, but dammit, you do have to *think*!" Students never knew what to expect in his classes. If the topic was Islamic culture, the professor might show up in a Bedouin robe. Or when discussing over-consumption in the U.S., he might instruct each student to carry all unrecyclable trash *everywhere they went* for a full week, then write an essay about the discussions they'd had with strangers, or how large and odiferous the collection had become. Well-liked by students because he wasn't stuffy or dusty with his material, Marc loved to encourage students to produce papers and projects that crackled with insight and originality. He often acted as an agent and promoter, linking students with work opportunities or passing research papers to journal editors.

The Future Studies program he'd designed at DU, quickly replicated at other universities, provided Marc and his students a virtual time machine to the past as well as the hypothetical future. The professor firmly believed that the most fruitful innovations would be a blend of social, ethical, and scientific breakthroughs, so he and his student-colleagues explored the historical patterns of human behavior, probing civilizations that had changed directions spontaneously, like a sky full of migrating Sandhill cranes.

Marc wasn't the least bit ready to call it quits. "If I was an orange," he told his daughter, "I'd still be full of juice." But it was time to tell his closest friends the vexing news, and he'd arranged a lunch with Kai Sakata, a level-headed, trusted friend. Probably Sakata would have a valuable thought or two about what to think and do in a situation like this. Of course, if Marc had assumed a tough-guy persona like many American men, his response to the virus would be largely opaque. He would have to appear strong even when he didn't *feel* strong...appear decisive and invulnerable even while keeping the migraines or ulcers to himself. Under the influence of scriptwriters who mold personalities and fathers who model opacity, that tough guy would treat his illness like a wrestling match. But how do you wrestle an invisible opponent? *Man up, no emotion, get through it.*

But Marc had never been that kind of a man. He knew it would take far more than bluster and machismo to defeat a virus capable of eating

5

him alive. It would take a realistic understanding of the disease, a science-based strategy for healing, and a resilient desire to be here. He wasn't one to smother his fears and pray the disease would just disappear, but he wasn't going to let fear dominate his life, either. He would draw on a lifetime of insights, try to keep his sense of humor, and if he could, outwit this frickin' Q virus.

As he put breakfast dishes in the dishwasher, Marc glanced at the refrigerator. As was his habit, he started pondering the *significance* of the standard American fridge-front, with all its Post-its and memorabilia. In a sense these spaces were static Facebook sites, crammed with visual clues about a household's hopes and high times. Vacation pictures were often indicators of personal vitality: were the vacationers hiking up a mountain trail or scarfing foot-long hot dogs in Atlantic City, with splotches of mustard in the corners of their grinning mouths? Currently featured on Marc's fridge were a few images with apparent squatter's rights, mounted several years earlier. A time-curled photo showed Karen and their college age daughter, Lisa, at a book signing for Karen's well regarded sci-fi book, *Earth Rising*. Next to it was a shot of a fairytale backpacking trip that Marc and Karen had taken with their best friends May and Kai—from Aspen over Conundrum Pass to the incomparably gnomish mountain town of Crested Butte. Snapped by a passing hiker, the photo immortalized a playful Karen threatening to dump a pot of icy stream water down Marc's back. He could still recall the way that very peaceful weekend had felt. The pitch and timeless splash of the creek seemed to be coaching mindfulness: "Here, this is it, right here."

A third image, neatly displayed in a transparent sleeve, documented Marc's come-from-behind victory in a Chess Federation match. With an exhausted, exhilarated smile, he gestured humbly toward the valiant chess pieces that had done the real work: crushing his highly-ranked opponent and thereafter good friend, Robert Hillman. A few clips of bumper sticker wisdom owned space by the handle. *"Be yourself, everyone else is already taken,"* counseled Dr. Seuss. Warned a second post, by Jesse Stoner, *"Worse than failure is succeeding at something that doesn't really matter."* And a third quote, now slipped partly crooked, satirized America's misguided social priorities: *"Currently, more money is spent on breast implants and Viagra than on Alzheimer's research. So in the very near future there should be a large elderly population with impressive breasts and magnificent erections, but no recollection of what to do with them."*

—Sally Feldman

Swinging a leg over the saddle of his well-used road bike, Marc glanced around the neighborhood, a place he knew well after twenty-seven years...twenty-four of them with Karen. Many of his neighbors were also long-term residents with whom he'd spent many fine moments in one front yard or another, chatting about raising children, which shrub would thrive in a high-plains desert, or which political candidate might do the least harm.

Marc had always put a lot of faith in the potential of neighborhoods to create trust and build social capital—a form of wealth the value of which increases the more you spend. In a DU course he'd called *Habitat*, students had explored the re-visioning of neighborhoods, especially in suburbs and inner cities that don't effectively meet human needs. Any residential neighborhood, anywhere, could become an extended family, sharing tools, information and support. A cooperatively-purchased house could serve as a community center, with a shared pickup truck and a large community garden in backyards-without-fences.

As Marc pedaled through his own familiar neighborhood, he reflected on what might lie ahead if this creepy virus had its way. *Dying might be even more grueling than being born. We scream in the beginning and we often scream at the end too, in each case wrapped in blankets so we'll just, please, shut up! But while we're here, look what we get: orange blossoms, romance, symphonies and sunsets, gypsy rhythms and emotional epiphanies!* When facing an end to such riches, humans invariably delve deeper into the meaning of life. *They ask themselves, "Will traveling to Bali or Brazil or Baltimore help me understand and accept that life is miraculous—whether or not I'm here? Can sweaty, heavy-breathing sex deliver the vivid existential connection I crave? Will reading an 880-page history of the world help clarify what exactly I'm doing here?"*

Ten minutes later, Marc and Kai Sakata sat outside a cafe in Denver's Washington Park, a brick-solid neighborhood known both for its vitality and sky-high house values. Marc would normally have been delighted, *ecstatic*, on this first really warm day of summer with its fragrant scents and sudden influx of oxygen. But things felt so different now. After he and Kai ordered free-range burgers, Marc skipped the casual banter and just dropped the bomb. "I have some news that really...*sucks!*" His hazel eyes meeting Kai's brown ones squarely, Marc continued with a gulp, "In my annual checkup, the doctors *found* something: a virus similar to Lyme disease that's really, really hard to kick. The typical course this 'Q virus' takes is to steadily destroy white blood cells. The immune system checks out, and then, within a year or so..." He snapped his fingers to complete the thought, "Passport expired."

"Well, unless you renew it, right?"

Marc ignored Kai's words for the moment. "Thankfully, it doesn't spread from person to person, just insect to person. Probably a tick, but they haven't figured that out yet..." Though Marc had tried to shift gears after the diagnosis, they were still grinding like an old Mustang transmission. He was stunned, as anyone would be. For only the second time in his life he felt betrayed, the recipient of a blunt tweet from the universe: "#Fuck You." Though he delivered his stark news like a camper stepping carefully over a friend's sleeping bag, the words seemed to kick Kai right in the forehead.

Each man was strong in his way: Marc a quietly confident man of knowledge who'd always taken care of his own health and supported the success of others. He modestly downplayed the PhD after his name, focused on the work itself rather than the status. He'd discovered along the way that the biggest, most reliable reward was often in the doing.

And Kai Sakata? A grateful dropout from the Wall Street world of high-risk, high-return investment, seeking personal enlightenment while working part-time in the family business, Kibo—the Japanese word for hope. The 35-year enterprise marketed herbal cures as well as the design of meditative Zen landscapes. Though less commanding in stature than Marc, Kai was more intense, more focused. Physically toned, he was a gentle person with a strong core. Since his early years he'd advocated for peace, civil rights, and the environment. Although he'd accepted a lucrative job offer in his mid-forties from Lehman Brothers in New York City, he'd finally bailed out of this profit-obsessed trade in search of something more holistic. With a vehement mandate from his Japanese family and its culture to do his very best in all things, he'd returned nine years earlier to Denver to rediscover himself, and the word "useful" was high on his list of life goals.

"Shit!" Kai said. He reached across the table to grab his friend's arm, offering spontaneously, "There must be natural cures for this. Herbs, superfoods, meditation...acupuncture?"

"Sure, they're all part of the strategy. And of course I've already gotten prescriptions for conventional drugs, even though I'm...skeptical." Mocking the TV ads, he said, "May cause internal bleeding, bloating, belching, and ugly lesions in the shape of New Jersey...Anyway, I just wanted to let you know what's up, in case this is my last...*inning*, or whatever." He knew how trite this must sound to anyone not yet on the cosmic shit list, but having endured his wife's early passing, he knew death personally, knew in his bones that it sometimes has its way like a flash flood in a desert arroyo, or a hailstorm right before the harvest.

Kai admired Marc's dispassionate cool, even though both men knew it was partly a façade at this early stage. "You've told Lisa, of course?" Lisa was Marc's high-energy, very analytical daughter, thirty-three and strongly aligned with her Dad. Working through Karen's illness together had permanently cemented their bond. "Of course. She's offering great support. She's really on me to get going with my prescriptions." He proudly thought about Lisa and her easy-going husband Brad, entrepreneurs on Boulder's Pearl Street Mall. Although they couldn't afford to live in Boulder's chronic real estate bubble, they'd bought a more reasonably priced house in nearby Louisville, getting together with Marc at least two or three times a month.

There was another pause as Marc reached for his glass of iced tea—cool to the touch with a few drips of condensation. He took a long, thirsty guzzle, marveling how vivid the world becomes when life may be in short supply. Always the anthropologist, Marc pondered if this heightening of the senses was an evolved strategy to help share useful information or to take care of critical details before the jig is up. He also mused, *maybe a clear acknowledgment of mortality actually makes life richer: we let go of the compulsion to control everything, and in a way, we inherit a very ingenious universe—a damn good trade.*

Setting his glass down emphatically, the professor's silence invited Kai to speak. Kai now scrambled for a useful thought, the muscles in his jaw bulging. A man of action as well as empathy, Sakata quickly pivoted from off-balance to black-belt aikido. "For starters I'm going to ask Dad what natural treatments can zap this kind of virus." Acknowledging Kai's growing commitment to natural cures, Marc raised his eyebrows and nodded appreciatively. "Okay, thanks, man." Then Marc leaned forward, unashamed of his vulnerability. "What would you do in my shoes?"

"I'd fight it!" Kai said without any hesitation. He was a man of action, literally grounded in his gardening, bicycling, skiing, and relationships. Throughout his twenties, he'd been a firefighter on a hotshot crew that was dispatched wherever needed. Slight burn scars on his neck and right jaw were an indelible reminder of a hellish day near Chico, California when he'd saved an elderly couple's lives as well as their horses, but just about paid the full price. To Marc, these barely noticeable scars had always seemed heroic, but to Kai, they were simply a reminder of who he was, inside. After a thoughtful pause, Kai continued, "If I absolutely knew I was going to die—which you *don't* know—I'd see what contributions I could make before my time was up. I'd drill deeper into things I already felt passionate about, rather than chasing some 'bucket list' of fantasies." The edge in Kai's voice was evidence he'd much rather talk about Marc's return to health than some grim voyage into the sunset. It was also a cultural trait of Kai's upbringing. As the only child in a Japanese family, Kai had been taught to avoid dramatizing one's own challenges or accomplishments. You just did what you were supposed to do, out of pride, respect, honor, and duty.

"Go with the things that make you happy, man. I mean, you love teaching and inspiring students about cultures, you keep up with politics... gardening, skiing, your Scrabble and chess competitions, the softball league—you're going to keep doing that, right?" Marc was player-coach of a co-ed softball team. The first scheduled game was in a few weeks, and the first practice, in a few days. "I may play, but I'm going to find somebody else to do the managing."

Kai's comments about passions reminded Marc of a dream the two had long shared. "If I beat this, we'll do that cycling trip through Tuscany." Only a week after his diagnosis, Marc's words seemed to explore an uncertain future as if he were gripping a flashlight with a sputtering beam.

"Sure. Let's plan on it! Maybe this fall, who knows?" After a pause, Kai added, "You know, I've always been amazed by the commitment you bring to all your interests. You are *present*." "Thanks, Kai. But the question is, which pieces of that *busy*ness really matter? And by the way, my garden's just a potted plant compared to the Sakata compound!"

Kai and his parents shared a large Zen inspired landscape in the yards of two adjacent houses, one of them on a double lot, in Denver's lively Highlands neighborhood. When Kai had returned home with a stash of ethically questionable Wall Street money, he'd signed mortgages for both houses with large down payments, an action that challenged his parents' sense of authority but at the same time made them extremely proud. Together Kai and his parents had torn down rickety cedar fencing between the two yards to create the large contemplative garden that had become a neighborhood landmark, even catching the attention of a local TV station and a national magazine. Both yards, including the greenhouse behind the parents' house—were abundant with fruits, vegetables, ornamental and medicinal plants—some with names like shisito, bok choy and mizuna.

Yukio and Michiko were second generation immigrants whose ethics were still firmly rooted in Japanese culture, including Zen Buddhism and Shintoism—a reverence for the shimmering magic of nature. Their healing practice was a blend of traditional techniques and Western methods, using a computer data base to track patient feedback. Yukio believed that for some ailments, conventional medicine could be a better choice. Still, with good success in alleviating pain and supporting well-being, several of his traditional formulations had gained a foothold in both the Asian community and the healthy-lifestyles crowd. Many of Yukio Sakata's clients respectfully regarded him as a *sensei* despite his hybridized approach.

More than anything, the father wanted continuity. Wouldn't it fulfill and perpetuate his sense of service if his son finally agreed to follow in his footsteps?

Kai knew that Marc would always carry the loss of Karen as if it were a backpack filled with stones. *It must be hard to be in Marc's shoes right now, without a partner,* he thought. Kai and May had also been very close with Karen. The two couples sometimes vacationed together in beautiful places like Costa Rica or British Columbia. Karen and May frequently ran or skied together, and the two men liked to explore the rural areas of Colorado on their bikes, or just walk and talk. Occasionally they got out their compound archery bows and set up a target in Marc's large backyard. Or sat down at a chess board with a pitcher of locally brewed beer.

One of Marc's fondest memories of Karen was the first time he met her. At the time she was an ambitious young author. They'd met during intermission at a small-venue play and by the end of a short, electric conversation, they were anticipating the other's thoughts and exchanging contact info. At that point in her early career she'd already published a story in *Harper's* magazine and interned in Seattle as an editorial assistant for *YES!* Magazine. She was the prototypical starving artist who oozed creativity—intently talking and listening about writing, art, health, nature, music, politics, wordplay and wittiness. Though she didn't feel the need to be glamorous or cover-girl skinny, she was at ease with herself. Her energy was radiant but subtle, like a partly cloudy dawn with shafts of vivid blue peeking through. Her dark eyes glowed mysteriously when they met Marc's, conveying something far beyond words. (What might she have sensed about her fated illness even back then?)

They'd gone on several walks in Washington Park and the foothills near Denver, then Marc spent a Saturday morning helping her move into a new apartment near the Botanic Gardens—closer to his house. With every date the barriers came down as the magnetism between them grew. After three or four dates he confessed that he sometimes felt woozy standing next to her, and she was opening up to him, too. Tilting her head adorably one day, she joked, "When I haven't worked on a story or chapter for a few days, I can imagine my poor characters pacing back and forth impatiently, looking at their watches, asking each other, 'Where the hell is she? What are we supposed to do NOW?'" Her facial expressions were so animated, so very cute that he wanted to kiss the expressions formed by that pretty mouth.

Marc, whose own writing was mostly for scientific journals, asked her if a fiction writer's life was a little like a casino. "Good analogy. Every time you sit down to write you're working the slot machines. And if you're a writer with integrity whose work finds an audience, it's not just money that comes out, but something even more valuable: a deep satisfaction that you brought something into the world that wasn't there before." Marc was intrigued by another of her metaphors: writing a novel was like launching a space probe to Jupiter. There was no way of knowing if it would successfully go into exploratory orbit when and if it arrived, years later. The writer can't predict what may come up in her personal life to distract or derail the project. She also can't foresee what will happen in the world that makes the story more compelling, or less.

"But I do know one thing: the mission damn sure won't succeed unless you launch it. I realized back in high school that it was easier to write than fret about not writing," she said with a smile he had already come to adore. With a disciplined focus that Marc admired, Karen's writing had indeed become a successful mission. Her science fiction novel, *Earth Rising*, gained a cult following and was still selling well fifteen years after its publication. Another book, *A Forest at the Edge of Life*, had won an Independent Publishers Award for best fantasy fiction of 2014.

What a difference between the Karen of the early days and the Karen who ended up uncertain who she even was..., Marc thought. Their marriage had been his richest slice of life, no contest. He wouldn't call it perfect. After all, they each had their opinions and passions about how to construct, demolish, and reconstruct relationships. She was the playful, spontaneous writer whose next move was often a surprise; he was the droll, soft-spoken academic, nice looking and comfortable in his body. Really, not a bad match at all.

Kai Sakata and May Hansen had been married for nine years, also a very happy union. She was a remarkably attractive Danish woman with fairly short silver-blonde hair and a trim physique. Coincidentally, Marc had also known and dated May many years before. In fact, in those relatively carefree years almost forty years earlier, Marc and May were considering moving in together when her mother got sick, compelling May to move back to Denmark. Their long-distance relationship continued for close to a year, and several times they'd each crossed the 5,000-mile chasm that separated them. But Marc wanted more than a long distance romance and May's return date was uncertain. She'd implied that she might actually stay in Denmark, so why didn't he move there to be with her? Meanwhile, and very unexpectedly, Marc had been swept away by Karen, a fascinating woman who, happily, lived just a few miles away. He delivered this news to May on a very awkward phone call.

However, Marc hadn't seen the last of May, not by any means. When her mother died a few long years later, she returned to her much-loved Colorado to continue working in non-profit activism. After quietly confirming through mutual friends that Marc had indeed married Karen, May dated a series of men without a lot of magic, until finally crossing paths with Kai— a man a few years younger than she whom she'd met at Boulder's Conference on World Affairs. Kai and Marc also knew each other in overlapping social circles, and one step at a time, the two couples became an extended family— along with Lisa and her husband Brad, and Kai's parents. This little band of progressive thinkers got together often for dinners, book and movie discussions or short hikes and picnics in the mountains.

A cherished memory: on one camping trip Karen and Marc had taken with Kai and May, the two men sat leisurely on a creek bank, their fishing lines dangling in the water. Neither was much of a fisherman but they'd miraculously reeled in two mid-size trout and baked them in tin foil with lemon and thyme—probably the most delicious and energizing food Marc would ever eat. That night, invigorated by the hike, the fish, fresh air, bright stars, companionship, vodka and pot, his lovemaking with Karen seemed to reach a new height of intimacy. The melodic, lilting music of the two women's laughter the next morning—folding tents and drinking the last of their coffee—still brought a sense of gratitude. Recalling that trip, Marc would remind himself, "By God, I've *done* some things. Real things."

Throughout his life, all his mentors and scholastic tests concurred: Marc should be a communicator, a guide, an innovator. And he had been. Still, though the customs stamps on his passport filled half a dozen booklets and his knowledge of human behavior was just short of encyclopedic, he had to admit that the times were wearing him down, even before the virus invaded. Karen's passing and the invasion of idiots like Trump & his cronies were taking a toll on his optimism. Suddenly, even wealthy Americans were insecure refugees, huddling near Wi-Fi hot spots, seeking peace of mind but not really finding it. Though Marc's career goal had always been to envision positive futures, his cynical side sometimes broke out—a little like the concentric, purplish rash that now erupted and retreated on his right thigh—a graphic symptom of the Q virus.

Psychologically, Marc was more solid than many. His parents had been there for both Marc and his brother Dennis (soon to be known as Rocket) in their formative years. Their mother, a nurse, and their father, a book-loving library director, each had a strong ethic of fairness which they passed along to their boys. Though two years apart in age, Marc and Dennis were often seen together, trying to make sense of the world. In pre-teen years Dennis, the elder, had diplomatically intervened when a few of the tougher sixth graders had targeted Marc as a "teacher's pet." Returning to his old elementary school at lunch, Dennis pulled several of the hecklers aside. Strategically passing out Snickers bars, he said, "Let's talk," walking them over behind the fence so Marc wouldn't even see he was there. Dennis explained that everybody was good at something but no one was good at everything. "My brother Marc is smart, that's what he's good at. He's also pretty damn good at baseball and soccer, but he's not going to brag about it."

He invited one of the kids to name something he was good at. "Building model airplanes," the boy said, unwrapping the candy bar. "Right, and does anybody tease you about that?" The boy shook his head. "You just want to do what *you* like to do, and so does Marc. You know what? He may be able to help you guys with your homework if you treat him with a little more respect." This little band of not-so-bad bullies was so stunned by Dennis's directness and unthreatening approach that they actually did back off. In fact, one of them later joined Marc's circle of nerdy high school friends, and they became teammates on the golf team.

The Blake boys grew up immersed in sports. Though Rocket excelled at both baseball and football, Marc stuck with baseball, golf, and chess. He wasn't going to get his bones crunched for gridiron glory! Even in their late teens, the Blake brothers were notorious throughout Ohio for their baseball prowess. Several minor league teams tried to sign each of them right out of college. In fact, with nothing more pressing at the time, Rocket tried a season with the Indianapolis Indians—then a Cincinnati Reds farm club. He had strategically—and in his mind, *heroically*—dodged the 1972 draft by convincing a medical student to perforate one of his eardrums, permanently affecting his hearing but not his convictions.

He'd done okay with the Indians—a skillful young shortstop with major league potential—but at that time the pay scale required minor leaguers to have part-time jobs or else be damn good gamblers. Although he cherished the game, the collective angst of teammates scrapping to make it to the majors didn't feel right. When he didn't get called up after a season in the minors, he quit. The stronger pulls were independence and romance. He packed a vanload of possessions and moved to northern California to be with his future wife, Ellen.

When Marc graduated a few years later, he took a different escape route from the military. Wary the draft would be reinstated, Marc successfully applied for Conscientious Objector status, serving two years with a health-related non-profit in Rhodesia (later Zimbabwe). After that he found another internship in Ghana, finally settling back in Berkeley to complete his doctorate in anthropology. He was a self-starter, fueled by genuine curiosity and an earnest desire to accomplish something important.

Together, the Blake brothers exemplified many of their generation's formative maxims and mottos: question authority, be here now, make love, not war, you are what you eat, do your own thing, freedom now, and even— in Rocket's case—turn on, tune in, and drop out.

Two

Living the Dream

I n the space of forty-five seconds, four minor yet telling events occurred at the Blake homestead, where Marc's brother Rocket lived. 1. Rocket's wife Ellen cornered a plump, clucking hen, grabbed the bird by the neck and expertly swung it 180 degrees, instantly ending its life—the first step in a chicken dinner for that evening. 2. Their thirty-four-year-old daughter Sara, living at home while she searched for a job in architecture, hung several brightly-colored tank tops and lingerie on the clothesline, sneaking glances across the ravine at the neighbor's house. Secretively, the neighbor, John, watched from his living room, wishing Sara would warm to his advances. 3. Sara's six-year-old son Zak, after squandering nearly a whole bag of organic dog treats, finally succeeded in getting Widget, the smaller of the household's two West Highland terriers, to rise up on her haunches and beg, proving that she now grasped the benefits of Pavlov's work. (The other terrier, Wilhelmina, aka Willie, had already mastered the trick.) 4. Rocket fumbled with the ignition key of the pickup truck borrowed from John, suddenly questioning his own well-proven mechanical abilities.

It was Saturday morning, June 6, a sunny day full of promise except for the mechanical *glitch* that had Rocket flummoxed. Since his own pickup was in the shop, he was borrowing John's to make the nine-mile run to the hardware store for oyster shells and organic grain as supplements for the chickens, rock phosphate for the root crops, work gloves so Sara and Zak could help harvest fruits and vegetables (enough with the excuses!) and a sharp, high-quality chisel for his woodcarving project. Rocket had

19

been hired by the elementary school to carve two totem poles from massive Douglas fir trunks.

He tried the key upside down, then tried wiggling it back and forth while also rotating the steering wheel and pleading, "C'mon, Baby!" The key fit the slot but just wouldn't turn. Fumbling his iPhone from the tattered pocket of his work jacket, he auto-dialed John's number. "So what's the trick to starting this rig?"

"Morning, neighbor!" John replied. "No trick. No problem, I'll come out."

Rocket thought, "John's got plenty of money, why doesn't he just get the damn thing fixed?" With a lengthy to-do list—most notably a looming deadline on the wood-carving project—Rocket felt edgy. He was normally easy-going but his day was getting off to a slow start. John emerged from his recently completed Mediterranean-style house wearing comfortable fleece pants and a rumpled orange T-shirt, gripping a mug of coffee. The two men had a bond of camaraderie after all the work they'd done together. A few years earlier John had hired Rocket to oversee the excavation, framing, roofing, and much of the stone and tile work on his spare-no-expenses home—a project that had won praise in the *San Francisco Chronicle* for its efficient and elegant design.

Opening the truck door, Rocket looked up at John, shaking his head and shrugging his shoulders. "I can't figure this frickin' thing out, man, your key must be slightly bent or something, it just won't turn." John poked his head into the cab and laughed. "To get the truck started, ding-dong, I suggest you dig into your pocket, find *my* key, and start her up. THAT'S NOT MY KEY."

Rocket was stunned. He'd forgotten that when he got into the truck, Ellie's keys were in his shirt pocket. He'd been absentmindedly trying to start John's truck with his wife's SUV key. Doh! He didn't try to cover his embarrassment but just laughed it off, although once again wondering why John always seemed to be one step ahead. Of everybody, really. With a meticulous sense of organization and a self-assured, quick wit, John often made Rocket feel slightly inadequate even though he was twenty years older (and supposedly wiser) than John. Was it John's financial success and take-charge attitude or just the boyish good-looks and amiable nature that made him such a stand-out? Rocket sometimes thought John should run for political office. It wasn't hard to imagine him as a California congressman riding his entrepreneurial success all the way to DC.

"Hey, thanks for lending me your truck, man. I'm going to run my errands after I grab some breakfast, you need anything from town?"

"No, nothing I can think of, thanks. And you're welcome to borrow the truck any time," John said. Then, unable to resist needling his foreman and close friend, he added, "Maybe just leave my keys right in the ignition to prevent further confusion?" Rocket playfully gave him the finger as he walked away, as if they were a couple of college fraternity brothers.

The nickname 'Rocket' had first surfaced way back in eighth grade, after he'd become the only kid in his grade to smack a baseball over the tall chain-link right field fence separating the playground from the neighbor's yard. "Did you *see* that?" his classmates buzzed when gym class was over, scuffling unwillingly back into the building. "That ball flew over the fence like a rocket," said one, who—as if destined—later became a Boston area sportscaster.

Rocket had shunned his given name, Dennis, finding the nickname more...swashbuckling, but in a way the given name was a good fit with his younger self—definitely a 'Dennis the Menace' type. He'd always had a streak of independence, questioning authority even as they cut the umbilical cord. He wasn't beyond a useful fib or borrowed homework in grade school and junior high, and at 13 he was caught swiping chocolate bars at the Corner Store for himself and a few friends—a premeditated crime he considered both risky and, well...generous. At 16 he was scolded by the gym teacher for smoking cigarettes out behind the bleachers, and that same year, Miss Gatyas, the totalitarian typing teacher, slapped him on the wrist for looking at the keyboard—an action that erased any willingness to master touch-typing, ever.

He went on to set records for cutting high school classes in his senior year, an achievement he was quite proud of. Because of his standing among many as a cool guy—(a little like The Fonz in the vintage sitcom, *Happy Days*) he could borrow friends' cars for the day to go in search of a *real* education, either alone or with his girlfriend. A few times they'd started early in the day, driving from the Columbus suburbs to Cincinnati to watch the Reds take on the Braves or Phillies. There were few things that Rocket loved as much as baseball, but even just walking along the railroad tracks to the bridge while others sat powerlessly at their desks made him feel like a judo master finessing his opponent—the System. Somehow, he'd avoided being expelled or even sent to the principal's office, but one day his friends told him what Mr. Daly had said in English Comp class: "It's Friday, so I guess we won't be seeing Dennis today." In a less intellectual way than his brother Marc, Rocket could spot holes in the collective American psyche, and it may have been his natural ability to write a gutsy, probing essay on the subject that prompted Daly to give him an unofficial pass.

In high school and college, psychedelic drugs anchored by marijuana were an occasional weekend recreation, which of course required knowing the right/wrong people in the counterculture black market. Marc clearly remembered getting a phone call from Rocket, asking for help—unusual for his self-reliant older brother. He'd taken LSD and his friend had wandered off somewhere. Rocket wasn't "freaked out" but just a little unsettled. Could Marc come get him? They found Rocket's friend staring at the lights on an outdoor Christmas tree, completely hypnotized. After dropping him off at home, the two brothers drove around in the family car as Rocket intently explained to Marc, "If you listen carefully, the world is humming and it's all woven together, sort of like...a fuzzy...fisherman's sweater." (And maybe that was true).

A few years later at college, Rocket's solid presence as a Red Hawk shortstop/slugger at Miami of Ohio necessitated going easy on drugs of any kind. He wanted to give his best on the diamond, where he felt immune to America's standard procedures and obstructions. At ball practice and in games, things clicked: he was in the flow. His brother also played baseball at Antioch, and the brothers liked to talk on the phone about how the season was going and whether the manager knew what the hell he was doing. Rocket's year with the Indians gave him time to ponder his future, and the prize that kept floating up in his ponderings was to be his own boss—maybe on a piece of fertile farmland. Really, it was the lingering '60s dream of 'Back to the Land' that took him to Mendocino County, California where his college girlfriend Ellen had grown up. At first they stayed at her parents' ranch, where Ellie's open-minded folks were supportive of the kids' relationship, even providing spaces where Rocket could learn to grow fruits and vegetables and have access to a small woodworking shop.

Rocket may have carried his baseball nickname into later life like a rebellious tattoo, but he had to woefully wonder, at the age of thirty-three, if he shouldn't also tattoo a "B" (for bankruptcy) on his forehead. He and Ellen couldn't have predicted in the early years that they'd lose their small, rundown farm outside Ukiah in the late 1970s. They never imagined that their primary source of income, the pear tree orchard, would be wiped out by fire blight, a bacteria that turns leaves and branches as black as bankruptcy itself. The wine grapes would be a bust, too, mostly from drought-complicated inexperience. When they couldn't make the payments on the farm and Rocket couldn't find a job related to his woodworking talents, he at first settled for construction work as a laborer. Meanwhile, Ellen valiantly went after a Master's degree in psychology, driving three hours to University of California at Chico half of each week to attend classes and stay with friends.

Did their failure out of the gate finish them as a team? No way. They'd come through those lean years all the more determined to successfully steer clear of mainstream America, with its cluttered, overpopulated landscape and prune-faced, rigid rules. Rocket's two-year stint at a camouflaged marijuana farm was step one in their slow-motion financial comeback. In their notorious home county, growers prided themselves on cultivating some of the finest, most potent organic pot in the world. Living in a tiny box of a house in Ukiah, Rocket and Ellie settled into the Mendocino lifestyle, where local self-reliance was a dominant ethic. You'd never find anything but locally-produced Mendocino Chardonnay or locally-saved heirloom vegetable seeds on this couple's shelves. They steadily learned to grow, can and store the fruits and vegetables that symbolized their commitment to the planet's well-being.

When the couple first crossed paths with John Bechard at a friend's party, they recognized a kindred spirit. Their friend had told them he was a successful and 'conscious' Silicon Valley dropout, and they walked into the room just as John was saying, "The loss of species from careless development, and the complete lack of direction in America's moldy mainstream has brought us to this environmental crossroad." This computer savant was anxious to bail out of the Bay area and live a more rural, self-sufficient lifestyle. And he had the money to do it. A Silicon Valley prodigy who'd helped propel Apple to the top, he risked his savings and credit rating to start his own small software company after leaving Apple, designing apps for the burgeoning digital revolution. The business was a quick success—right place, right time, right guy. Within a few years he'd amassed the capital to buy a prime chunk of real estate, then spent a few years designing and dreaming about his new-age home. He was looking for someone to help him build this super-efficient, super-cool house near Willits, in Little Lake Valley. Did they know of anyone?

Well, yes, they *did* know someone! Now it was Rocket's and Ellie's turn to be in the right place, right time. They took to the idea of working with John like a couple of hungry 'coons at a Whole Foods dumpster. Rocket became the foreman of John's avant-garde project, applying some skills he already had and learning everything else as he went. (The aphorism "Fake it 'til you make it" matched Rocket's personality well, or closer still, "Feel the fear and do it anyway"). Within two and a half years, John's 2,400 square-foot and off-grid home—what Ellie kiddingly called the "Manor house"—was built out, overlooking a lush, permaculture-inspired homestead, surrounded by row crops, vineyard, pasture, and forest.

John rented the existing, funky little cabin to Rocket and Ellen so they could oversee the construction project 24-7. Then, after they'd proven their abilities and become John's trusted friends, the younger man offered to sell them the cabin and six fertile acres at a good price. Although Rocket and Ellen signed a mortgage with John for the land, they still rented the cabin until they could afford to buy it, though John insisted that when they felt ready to buy, the rent they'd paid would go toward purchase of the house. Rocket immediately laid a new hardwood floor in the little cabin and converted the cute little red storage barn into a woodworking studio and greenhouse for starting seedlings. They leased solar energy from a company that paid up-front costs as part of the contract. It was a comeback moment for them to be off the grid at last! Ellie put herself in charge of managing the couple's second-chance homestead, supervising the construction of huge garden beds for market gardening, a root cellar, and a large, well-protected chicken yard. At farm auctions, they acquired the equipment they'd need to grow and market produce and cut flowers. At the same auctions and in classified ads, Rocket outfitted his woodworking studio with sturdy vintage equipment.

John stayed in a rented house in Willits as the house project began, then as the construction neared completion, he moved into its garden level, looking onto the courtyard's newly-planted flower and shrub garden. Next to the bedroom on that sunlit floor was John's office, equipped with a four-foot-square computer screen, where the small business owner could oversee the progress of apps his staff designed remotely. At age forty-four, John had the self-assurance of an astronaut whose first mission had been a success. You could see signs of family heritage right on his face: the prominent nose of a Frenchman and the ruddy cheeks and blond hair of a Scotsman. Undeniably an eligible bachelor, he co-starred in a real life 'rom-com'—the attempted wooing of Sara, Rocket's and Ellen's daughter. Despite being ten years older than her, John was determined to win this strong-willed, sometimes brooding brunette, back in the singles market despite her insistence that she was in no hurry to find Mr. Right—if there *were* such a person.

Nobody respected (and feared) Sara's temperament more than her parents. Raising her had been a roller coaster ride that would probably never end. But they'd always been proud of her spirit, her convictions, and in recent years, her devotion to her son Zak, a six-year-old with a very inquisitive mind. Now back in the unconditional comfort of her family, Sara was opening up. With every passing week she seemed to have less of an *attitude*. She wasn't exactly "sweet" (never that!) but progressively less sour. Sara preferred being outside the box, much like her father. After getting a full scholarship and completing a year at the NewSchool of Architecture in San Diego, she'd abruptly chosen to spend a full year sailing with her boyfriend in the Sea of Cortez, then up and down the coast of California and Oregon. When she'd finally completed her degree at the age of 27, she'd further stunned her parents with *more* adventures ("drifting," in her mother's words), including eight months surf-bumming and waitressing in New Zealand. Most recently, she'd spent six years as a well-paid model in Los Angeles, doing magazine and TV ads and sharing the parenting of Zak with his father Greg—soon to be known in some circles as "the asshole."

Sara was stunningly pretty—gorgeous would not be too strong. A fashion designer had commented in Elle magazine that "Even a burlap bag would look great on Sara Blake." Ellen saved the clipping Sara mailed, a little worried that her daughter might become an 'it' girl in the hopped-up LA celebrity scene. But Sara got bored with the skin-deep world of modeling and decided to follow through with architecture after all. Her youthful worldliness and beauty charmed John to the core, prompting him to move a little too fast for Sara's comfort. They'd had dinner together a few times at his impressive new house, ridden horses, and walked together several times since her arrival. Despite her subdued response, John had confided to Rocket and Ellen that he intended to win Sara's heart and marry her. In an impulsive, California-casual kind of way, he was seeking their blessing, which definitely got a reaction from Rocket. "We'll see, eh, John? You know your way around, no question, but she's got her own mind..." Both parents thought highly of John though his pre-proposal sentiments seemed way early in the game. Later, when they were alone, Ellen joked, "God, does this mean we'll finally be able to hand her off to someone we actually trust?"

Before heading into town for supplies, Rocket wanted to grab a cup of strong tea and a plate of eggs and potatoes at home. He walked vigorously on the path around the gently-sloping ravine. He could have jumped in the truck and been home in less than a minute, but he never got tired of looking at the beautifully productive landscape he'd helped create: the ravine with its terraced gardens, orchard, and pastured animals—mostly overseen by apprentices. He took a deep breath of clean morning air, grateful that his farmer-fantasy had finally come true after years of blood, sweat and tears— and the leverage of a generous young millionaire. Having overseen the excavation of the ravine, Rocket knew each feature of it. About a third the length of a football field and also thirty yards across, this sculpted feature was twenty feet deeper at the bottom than the two homes that perched over it. The ravine was designed around the oval shape of the small pond at the bottom. Rocket's grandson Zak had quickly discovered that the pond had bass in it and he loved to kneel on the redwood dock and study their dark, waggling shapes and sudden splashes as they harvested striders on the surface.

On top of the ravine, near John's circular driveway, was a wooden gate with wrought iron crosspieces that Rocket had crafted, framed by two simple stone pillars. The relatively level six-acre pasture beyond was currently occupied by nineteen blissful alpacas, two horses, and a dairy cow—the latter on loan from a friend who was out of the country for a year. Sometimes one or both of their little Westie terriers would trot into the pasture with Rocket, who joked that the dogs' furry heads looked very much like the alpacas' except without the long necks. Even the dogs seemed to acknowledge the resemblance, standing a bit taller in that grassy open space.

John's house featured walls of poured concrete with embedded, creamy-white pigment, framed by third-growth redwood. The roof's red tiles had integrated solar cells, and the neutral, stucco-like exterior paid homage to architecture John had loved when he'd spent a summer in Tuscany. Next to the house were four seventy-five-foot rows of grapes on sturdy trellises. And hidden in a thicket of oak trees, manzanita and pepperwood—a few hundred feet from John's house—was a small yurt, typically the home of three or four interns on a property Ellen liked to call the 'farmette.' After-hours, their little camp, complete with a computer-controlled compost toilet and a brick oven—perfect for making pizza or sourdough bread—often delighted one's senses with wisps of marijuana, incense, and garlic and onion-based stir fry made from fresh garden produce. The flawed, lilting flute tones or reggae guitar beats announced from a distance that life was in progress, and that it should never be complicated.

On Rocket's and Ellen's side of the ravine were long swaths of terraced garden beds, tucked into the ravine's slope—accessible by pathways of hardy clover for wheelbarrows, carts, a tiller, and even a small Caterpillar tractor. A solar-powered lift on iron rails very slowly delivered harvested vegetables, fruit, and cut flowers up to the barn—when batteries were fully charged—where Rocket, Ellen, and the interns would prepare them for market or set them aside for household use. Along the length of the little barn was a small greenhouse built from recycled lumber and re-used skylights. An artist friend from the food co-op had traded Rocket and Ellen two beautiful stained glass panels for a tall bookshelf built by Rocket. These vividly colorful pieces graced either side of the greenhouse entry: two brightly-colored depictions of the garden beds, the two houses, and the small pond at sunrise and sunset.

Behind the couple's small cabin, built in the 1950s, were a small orchard, a mini-vineyard, a series of long, rectangular garden beds, and eight bee hives. Zak's favorite place of all was the large treehouse he and his mom slept in. Attached to the sturdy trunks of four living white oak trees, the treehouse had a circular staircase woven through several of the supporting trees and their sturdy branches. On its finely-sanded oak deck were two-

and-a-half miniature rooms equipped with cozy beds, deck chairs and various built-in storage boxes. What more could a six-year-old kid want? And from the shady deck of this overlook, Sara loved peering northwest over the rolling hills; on clear days, she could make out Anthony Peak— at 7,000 feet the county's tallest mountain. She also claimed she could smell the ocean, thirty-five miles to the west.

Three

Earth Life!

Absorbed in their café conversation in which life and death danced right on the table, Marc and Kai didn't notice that most of the lunch customers were gone. Marc asserted, "Here's the way I look at it: Life's a little like a game of Scrabble. You make your best words with the letters you get and the skills you've gained, but if the right letters don't show up, maybe you make the most of the time you have left." He shrugged his shoulders. "It is what it is. But don't get me wrong—I'm going to fight this in my own way."

Kai took a deep breath, then exhaled slowly, choosing his words. "Look, I know you're a Scrabble champ and all, but what are you saying? If you don't get the Z you give it less than 110 percent? I see it differently: life isn't happening to us, *we're happening to life*. When the chips are down, you get up and you get more chips." He knew he sounded abrasive, but he wouldn't buy into Marc's metaphor of life as a fatalistic game of Scrabble.

Now Marc was a little peeved at Kai for his safe and unthreatened position in life. "Easy for you to say, dude. But hey, I'm kind of in a corner here. I don't think you've ever been told you may be *dying?*"

"Touché."

"Look, as you can imagine, after a week here on *death row* I've been thinking a lot about the 'meaning of life.' Although it's drummed into us that we're alone in the world—that Death waits for us like some drooling, deranged monster—I believe that we humans, and plants, and even the bacteria in our guts, are in it *together*. Earth life is a single, co-evolving organism. Nobody's alone! So when I die, I continue because the rest of me continues." Looking at Kai intently, he concluded, "So, I'm...safe in the universe, whether I'm alive or dead." Then he sat silent as if his words had just checkmated fear itself.

"Interesting thoughts, and I agree with you—you know that. To me, it's as if we each have billions of eyes, but we're designed and even *trained* to see only through the eyes in our own slightly deranged heads. But philosophy aside, life needs you here, as YOU, for a few more decades. Got that?! So would you mind putting your energy into *living*, please?"

"I'm gonna give it my best shot, man." Then, opting for straight-up honesty, Marc admitted, "The truth is, I'd be so grateful for a solid connection like yours, with a clear thinking, energetic woman like May. But how can I expect that?" In a wounded tone of voice—maybe the first time Kai had ever heard Marc whine—he said, "I may be a dead man walking..."

"Oh, bullshit, you'll beat the odds and live to be 100, still teaching your Future Studies courses."

Shaking off the shadows, Marc forced himself to relax, changing to a lighter subject. "I know I've told you about some of my dating disasters. Did I ever tell you about Alice? A highly caffeinated, very endearing woman on a whirlwind tour of single men—having dated a very impressive *twenty-one* of them before me." Kai listened with a slight smile, nodding his head.

"We went out eight or ten times, and she would always assure me that I was well above average, in intelligence and...other things. But really, her first love was her career, working with military vets. One day I emailed her, probably a little impulsively, that I'd like to be able to see her more than 1.5 times a week, *on average*. I gave her a good-natured ultimatum, kind of meant as a joke: 'Play me or trade me.'" Marc paused for effect.

"What happened?"

"She traded me."

"Next!" Kai said, laughing.

"Then there was the very funny redhead, the one I let 'get away.' You remember Carla, who kind of kept me in the game after Karen's death, then went back to her old boyfriend, Les?"

32

"Sure. She *was* funny. Very cute, too." Marc reprised his standard Carla punchline, mostly reserved for male friends: "Yeah...I guess she was screwing Les but enjoying it more."

"Sounds like a country song to me! Hey, you'll find the right one, I know you will."

Even as he sang the blues, Marc was furtively studying the faces and gestures of three attractive women at a nearby table. Apparently in their 50s and 60s, they were talking comfortably, laughing and being so...*female*. He played the inevitable bachelor game—which was the One today? He tried not to be obvious but really, after several long years as a widower, an inner voice countered, *Why* not *look—politely? I am interested.*

As if a cartoon light bulb had magically appeared over his head, Kai suddenly straightened in his chair. Catching Marc checking out the women, he'd had a mischievous inspiration: "Think about this, Marcus Blake: for women who don't want the commitment of a long-term relationship, *you're the man*." Whether or not it was meant as a joke, the idea immediately amused Marc. It actually made sense, in a roguish kind of way: rather than be just an earnest, nerdy professor with a potentially terminal illness, he could deliberately morph into the mythical Bond, James Bond. Suavely irresistible, scoring one beautiful woman after another, like sexy sports cars queued up at a gas pump. He had to admit it would be a kick, in a twisted sort of way, to retrace his steps; that is, to sleep with single, unattached women of all ages: someone in her thirties, forties, fifties, and sixties; and okay, even a healthy yoga nerd in her seventies. (Even though at sixty-three he was on the road to seventy himself, in his still-boyish self-concept he was always eight or ten years younger.) But really, how could this fantasy be fulfilling, or even *possible*? A man who'd never once cheated on a steady girlfriend or spouse, Marc replied to Kai's suggestion with exaggerated disdain. "What kind of woman is that? Airhead chick, just out for the thrills? Can she even name her U.S. Senators? Is she needy underneath all that moisture cream and makeup?"

"No, not needy at all. She's just got her own life. She's already done the marriage thing. Now she wants to be creative and...indulgent with her time. She wants a coterie of girlfriends to travel with, drink lattes with, and talk about menopause with. *Then* she wants a man, after the pause." Marc snorted, and Kai added, "You'll be the poet, the soulful guy who's *deeper* than these other superficial clowns. Of course the women want you, you're empathetic, and you have that *je ne sais quoi*."

"Okay, you sold me, send 'em over, The gigolo's in." Meanwhile, with well-concealed guilt, he was at that very moment breaking one of the Ten Commandments (ouch) as he secretively coveted Kai's wife, his own girlfriend way back in the day. Even in friendship, May scented Marc's life like a fresh sprig of rosemary. But he knew forbidden thoughts like these need to be quickly squelched.

"Good, it's settled, you're the Stud Muffin. Better get a naked-babe calendar for your bulletin board, yeah, baby! So, what *else* do you want in the upcoming year—and of course, the dozens of years beyond it?" Marc responded playfully, "What do I want this year? Enlightenment and boundless ecstasy! That's all."

"You could go back to...where was it...Borneo?—with all the undiscovered species, and the hunter-gatherers?"

"Yeah, it was the huge island of Borneo, a part of Malaysia. I met some of the gentlest, most pure-hearted people there—the Penan tribe—still hunting game with poison darts, but at the same time trying to figure out how to stop the high-tech clearcutting of their homeland by greedy capitalists."

"Do you think that's where you originally caught the virus?" Kai asked, with sudden curiosity. He knew how useful it could be to know the geographic origin of the disease. Maybe a vector-specific folk cure could be found. "I don't know," Marc responded, lifting his eyebrows. Even the doctors were uncertain about ground zero for this bug. They only knew the virus—with its telltale concentric purple rings—had a very nasty reputation.

"I sometimes wonder why I'm retiring when so much of my energy has gone into teaching. But I can't leave the department hanging halfway through a semester if I'm too sick to continue." Kai was troubled by Marc's decision to stop teaching. "Keep the door open, man. As you said, a lot of your connections and activities are at DU. Besides, you're kind of a legend over there."

"Yeah, right."

A friend of Kai's was sitting down at another table and waved. "Excuse me for a minute, guy. I want to say hi to Roger over there, I'll be right back."

Marc thought about Kai's advice to stay at the University. *I could call the Dean back...*he thought, as if scanning his future to see if teaching was still in it. Although he was about ninety percent in favor of retiring to better his odds against the virus, he *was* having a hard time imagining life without the structure of work. He wasn't one for extreme "sports" like intensive Facebook grazing or binge-watching Netflix series. Shopping malls made him dizzy, sometimes even a little nauseous—too many colors, too many chemicals in the products, and too many parking spaces to lose your car in.

*You just whistle your way through it, like a dark alley, right? Finish some articles, take a trip somewhere, maybe Hawaii, play some softball, ride my bike more, hang out more with friends...*Then the truth popped his soap bubble again: if the virus persisted, he'd probably end up counting the days left like a man at the end of a treasured vacation. Was he the kind of person to make fighting death his way of life? Sure, he had the strength, but it sounded kind of desperate, kind of self-centered to be obsessing about white blood cells and immune systems.

If I stay at DU for its familiar routine, will that help me recover? But how can familiar *be* bold *enough? In this chapter of my life, why shouldn't I get myself arrested for a cause like climate change, like May did? Hell, it doesn't matter anymore if I have a criminal record so why not dress up in some wacky dinosaur costume, notify the news channels, and chain myself to a 100-ton railroad car full of prehistoric coal, squealing and moaning down the track? Or set myself on fire on the 16th Street mall to protest airstrikes that are killing civilians in Syria? But no...I can't quite picture myself as a human fireball even if it might 'go viral' if I filmed it. Let's leave that one for the Buddhist monks. Plus, I'd probably have to breathe carcinogenic plastic fumes from my sneakers and high-tech shirts, so forget that."*

Besides, wasn't suicide the easy way out? Wasn't there something in each day to be grateful for? A joke. A brilliant string of jazz songs on the radio. A sudden visit from Aunt Kathy, or as a prank, maybe a friend shows up at the front door disguised as the Pope. Or maybe it really is the Pope... it could happen—he may have heard about my flagrant irreverence and come to give me a private sermon...A trip back to the old neighborhood. A breeze wafting the scent of linden or lilac right to my Adirondack lawn chair in the backyard, where I'm rereading War and Peace. *Moments like these might be included in an ironically upbeat book I could title,* Ten Things to Try before Suicide. But he knew he wouldn't really have time to write a book, not if he wanted to be a good father, brother, friend, uncle, and responsible citizen, possibly all in the space of a single year. The words of a woman with terminal cancer crossed his mind. She'd moved to Oregon to arrange a physician-assisted death and in the process spurred a death-with-dignity movement. Her last advice was direct, and poignant: "The world is a beautiful place. Spread good energy. Pay it forward," she'd written before downing her suicide cocktail. Marc decided he'd rather be instantly offed by an asteroid from another galaxy—small enough not to kill anybody else, of course. *What a cosmic way to go,* he thought. On a more pressing level, he wondered, *what would be* my *last and best advice?*

Kai came back to the table and sat down, suggesting that the two of them go out and have some fun. He wanted to get Marc's mind off the Grim Reaper—maybe they could dress the Reaper up as Dolly Parton or Mr. Rogers. "You know what sounds like a good idea to me? Let's go get drunk. I haven't done that in a long time. I have some really good Scotch at home, you want to put down a few Scotch sours?"

"Let's go," Kai said, standing up.

Marc paid the bill and the two men rode bikes back to Marc's place. Their café conversation had come through a fog and both were pretending, at least for a while, that this specter of death was a mere inconvenience. In the shady comfort of Marc's backyard, they each drank two and a half very strong drinks, trying rather comically to land their arrows on or near the tripod-mounted target. Inevitably, their slurred conversation came around to May. They each sat down on the lawn. Marc noticed that his house was at an angle, but it didn't worry him a bit.

"She wants to help lift up some of Denver's most distressed neighborhoods, and she wrote a guest column for The Denver Post. Unfortunately it didn't sit well with the local Black Lives Matter organization. She was quoted on TV news saying that neighborhood violence could be reduced with pedestrian police officers and background checks."

"What's wrong with that?"

"Nothing really, but neighborhood leaders said they need jobs and grocery stores, not just friendly cops and promises."

"How's she taking the blowback?"

"She feels really bad. She told me, 'I wish I had run the column past my Director first, she would have given the piece more...relevance.' Really, all May wants to do is help these neighborhoods be better places."

"Is she getting heat from the Director, too?"

"Yep."

"Anything I can do to help?"

"No. She just needs to mend some fences. Don't tell her I told you about this, okay? She's embarrassed."

"You got it."

This was the first time Marc had heard anything negative about May's high-energy work. He knew her as an organizer and connector whose living room was often filled with spontaneous laughter and passionate voices discussing state-wide strategies for climate change, urban agriculture, or neighborhood empowerment. Marc remembered that her father had been a Social Democrat in Denmark's parliament when May was growing up, and that she'd carried her father's environmental convictions to the U.S. where she became a student leader at Smith College. But it was May's and Kai's 'urban homestead' lifestyle he knew best. When the two had first met, they recognized each other's convictions: May an activist and Kai an investor in municipal bonds and the stocks of regional companies. He loved supporting projects he could point to with pride and also collect a moderate income from: wind farms, light rail projects, small business incubators, and museums.

Together, they'd discovered that living sustainably was the opposite of sacrifice if you just shifted your identity. "Sustainability is not just what you do, it's who you are," May liked to say. "Not just created by the world, but *creators* of a new world." If the attention to health, connections with people, and creative space made you happy, who needed a high-stress job and all the consumer junk? (As a guy who drove an old still-efficient Toyota even though he could afford a new car, Marc could relate.) The pressure-cooker lifestyle of Wall Street had taught Kai about the benefits of unashamed moderation, and May had adopted it quite willingly.

As a frequent guest at the couple's meatless Monday or Grilled-salmon Sunday parties, Marc had marveled at jars of canned and pickled produce, and herbs hanging from kitchen beams to dry. Kai and May had created an unpretentious life together: a little travel, lots of gardening and cooking, a variety of personal interests, and good times with friends. They'd worked at keeping their romance alive dancing tango on Wednesday nights or Texas two-stepping at The Grizzly Rose on Saturday nights. From a distance, Marc had watched what May's life had become, sometimes wishing—after Karen's passing—that he'd stuck with her years earlier, long before she'd met Kai. It was obvious that she was happy. When she spoke passionately about nature or climate change, her cheeks flushed with color and her sky blue eyes sparkled confidently. And Marc admired Kai's ability to be May's unchallenged equal, radiating his own sense of quiet confidence. But secretly, Marc had to admit that he was mildly irritated—as well as jealous—about his friends' gusto-filled lifestyle.

Even so, Kai and Marc respected and understood each other. Kai ignored Marc's past history and rapport with May, and each man loved having a close friend he could laugh with, bike with, and sometimes even get a little drunk with. When the archery match started up again, neither man came close to the bull's-eye, but fortunately, none of the arrows landed on the neighbors' back porch or killed a beloved cat.

Four

At Home on the Homestead

When Rocket walked into the cabin for a quick breakfast, Ellen was at the side-counter gutting the chicken she'd already plucked, an activity that made her look so much the "Earth Mother" some of her friends kiddingly called her. Of the two, Ellen was the more pragmatic and detail-oriented, while Rocket was the big-picture guy, often less sequential in his thoughts than her. On a Myers-Briggs table of personality types, they had a similar framework—introverted and empathetic—but when it came to organization and straight-up logic, there was a gap that sometimes seemed like the Grand Canyon. They'd learned to effectively fuse their traits to enable successful teamwork, not to say there was never tension or misunderstanding. But they had mutual admiration and respect. To an enduring degree, they had each other's backs.

Rocket, still amused about his battle with the wrong key for John's truck, confessed playfully, "I'm a loser, aren't I?"

"Well, you're not perfect, but you're probably about the best I could have done." She looked up from her work and said, deadpan, "I settled for you." He ignored her "so-called humor"—a term she sometimes used for his own wandering whimsy, which he defended as "two percent funny"—better than no humor at all.

"No, I mean I *lose* things, like in a magic trick. One minute, a piece of paper is in my hands—the deed to our land, say—and the next minute, it's gone, poof! Somehow it reappears the next day on the living room coffee table—under a stack of catalogs and last year's Christmas cards. I never *studied* magic, but..." Rocket had lost items such as cell phones, car registrations and once, a passport, but it wasn't just *things* he excelled at losing, he also tended to lose passwords, calendar events, and sometimes even the names of two friends he was introducing to each other. (What a relief, when they introduced themselves, covering for a fellow Boomer.)

"Well, you're sixty-five and I'll cut you *some* slack for that..." Ellen was a few years younger than Rocket. Glamor was not her thing, though her health and self-assurance were very attractive. Her arms had lifted many crates of organic produce and her legs had carried her many miles—on memorable hikes and also back and forth to the garden and the fields where they raised cut flowers. Or to the yurt behind John's house where the crew of volunteer interns stayed. An early-riser on busy mornings, she sometimes rousted them out of their little yurt just after sunrise when a crop was ready to be harvested or a bed prepped for planting.

"You're a space cadet, Rock," she continued, shaking her head and waggling her hand back and forth in an aerial slap. "Maybe if you cut back a little on the pot..."

"I haven't smoked anything in a couple of days."

"Well, it's probably too late anyway, your brain cells are already fried. But you could be a little more organized, couldn't you? Then you wouldn't lose things so often."

"Here's the deal though," he explained, as if patiently. "If I never lost things then I'd never have the pleasure of *finding* them, would I? Finding things is so much fun that it's almost worth losing them," he insisted. She rolled her eyes. "I know, you'll probably tell me I'm too much like messy Marc."

"At least he has a valid excuse, now."

"Maybe I should ask you or Sara, or even Zak, to *hide* my wallet—but not *too* far out of sight—so I could have that wonderful feeling of relief, that gratitude of finding it by accident and not having to call credit card companies and motor vehicle offices..."

"Careful what you ask for, my dear. I'll hide one little tool after another, right when you need it, and whole days will become frantic scavenger hunts."

"Oh, please," he said, hugging her from behind, as chicken juice dripped from her knife. "That would be so much fun." He glanced again at the recently-sacrificed hen on the counter, feeling a sense of abundance and rightness. They'd treated this organically grown hen quite well when it was alive, right up until it stopped laying eggs. (They knew the hen's time had come when its comb feathers had lost their sheen). Then the hen had made a final if involuntary contribution to the homestead's overall wellness. Rocket and Ellen were damn proud of being about three-quarters self-reliant, an outcome they considered more valuable than money.

"What are we having with the chicken?"

"How about peas? There are lots more to be harvested ASAP. Hopefully, Sara will pick another wheelbarrow full today, which we can take to the co-op tomorrow. Then we'll can and freeze some for ourselves, later this week. Let's have a salad, too, okay? Would you have time to pick a big bowl of salad greens, radishes and early carrots?"

"Sure, I'll do that when I get back," he answered, dipping a bag of green tea in and out of his cup and crunching on a toasted bagel with homemade grape jam. "Oh, and we also have chocolate cake for dessert. Maybe we could have John over for some cake."

"*Oops*," Rocket thought, feeling a twinge of guilt that he didn't dare confess: he knew that under the old-fashioned metal cover right behind her, the cake had already been "sampled," first by some anonymous, messy opportunist (Zak) then later, by *him*. Rocket had cleaned up the pile of crumbs, and what the heck, there was still enough cake left for everyone, if they were small pieces....

"Well, John may have other plans," Rocket said, covering. "Besides, don't we want to keep it for ourselves?" There was silence as Ellen immersed the cleansed chicken in a pot of boiling water. After parboiling, she planned to roast the meat in the oven, inserting a few whole, perforated lemons in the cavity to flavor it and keep the meat moist.

"Keep what for ourselves?" Sara asked, walking barefoot into the tile-floored kitchen with an empty laundry basket in one hand. "Your mother wants to invite John over for dessert tonight." The father and daughter exchanged a look of concern—for different reasons—as Ellie teased, "Or maybe you'd rather spend alone-time with John?"

"Alone time? For what?" Sara answered, a wrinkle of puzzlement on her forehead. Feeling conspiratorial heat from her parents, she blurted recent thoughts, "It seems like John always has to be the big shot. His house will prevent climate change, all by itself. His software company donates ten percent or whatever of the profits to save species...He's kind of a walking bumper sticker, isn't he? It seems like every time I hang out with him, he does all the talking. Can you imagine *living* with a guy like that?"

"He's probably just trying to impress you, Sara," Rocket said, knowing that to be true. The father was also very familiar with the complexities of his daughter's psyche. His hunch was that the castle wall she'd built around herself probably had a secret entry she hoped someone like John would find. "John can't help it if he's successful, can he?" her father continued, too obviously a front man. "I know, personally, that his shine can be a little intimidating, but you know what? He's a really good man."

"A woman could do far worse..." Ellen said, trying to sound impartial but like Rocket, missing the mark. "He's definitely interested, and after seeing him in action for the few years we've known him, I know he always does what he says he'll do...."

"Oh, I don't know," she said, walking out of the room, in complete control. He may have committed but she had not, and she didn't *have* to, despite all the pressure. Even Zak called John her boyfriend. "There are plenty of great guys out there..." she said over her shoulder, like a strutting Siamese cat with its tail aloft. Rocket and Ellen looked at each other in amusement as she left the room, both of them entertained by the ongoing drama. Rocket wondered protectively what sort of men she'd met and dated in her largely out-of-touch LA years before she married Greg, Zak's father. Maybe better not to think about that, he told himself. If those men were anything like her anger-challenged husband had been, they weren't worth much.

Still facing the kitchen counter, Ellen asked in a carefully neutral tone, "When are you planning to finish the totems?"

"Well you've seen that they're almost done," he answered, hoping to leave the house before the topic of money came up again. For several years, Rocket's work on John's house had been a financial boon for them but with that work mostly done, things were getting tighter. Trying to skirt the issue, he asked, "What do you think—are they going to like them?" He felt pretty good about how the carvings had turned out, but it had sure drained his energies along the way.

"Yeah, they're beautiful! Do you think you'll finish them in the next few weeks? We could sure use the money." Rocket got his wide-brimmed hat off the hook—a cross between a cowboy and ranger hat—and strode toward the door. "I'm doin' my best."

"We're having that PTA fundraiser in early July, and Ted wants to have the poles in place for that. He's excited." Rocket knew she was just taking care of business, but it felt like she was taking care of *his* business. He didn't want to deliver the poles until he was completely satisfied with them, until each of the figures jumped out at you, telling a vivid little story. "The target date for completion is June 20—summer solstice. I'll make it—you can tell Ted that if you talk to him. That's what coffee's for..." Besides the deadline, Rocket was worried about the phone call he'd gotten a week earlier from Marc about the virus. As the older brother, he'd always felt protective. Even more stress came from his commitment to build an oak dining table for a couple in Ukiah. And all the tilling, planting, and harvesting really couldn't wait, either. Then, too, he was feeling a little inexperienced as a grandfather. Was this really the good life?

Ellen's schedule was also crammed. Although school wasn't currently in session—she was a part-time psychologist there—she'd been scrambling to harvest and box up the early produce—radishes, garlic, turnips, kale, chard, spinach, snow peas and snapdragons. The eggs from thirty-five chickens (usually one egg daily per bird) had to be gathered, washed, and packed, and winter squash seedlings had to be planted. Whenever she commented that things were piling up, it felt to Rocket like she was implying that he was doing the piling. And couldn't he be neater? The other night she'd sarcastically called him "the guy I wipe up after in the kitchen." Naturally, he aspired to a higher station in life than that.

Five

The Last Exams

With a stack of final exams under his left arm and a too-full cup of Sencha green tea in his right hand, Marc was relieved when he set them both down on his backyard table without spilling tea on the papers. Though bird calls were now a full-throated, joyful chorus rather than solo performers chirping the winter blues, it still felt chilly—typical unpredictable Colorado spring weather. When a sudden warmish breeze cut through the chill, it caught the corners of the top few essays and whisked one onto the patio bricks. As he jumped up to retrieve them, the tea sloshed a little, but didn't land on any of the exams. *This may be a lucky day,* he thought.

His plan was to get through five of the remaining fifteen exams, then walk to his office and finish the rest, since they were due to the department administrator by noon the next day. He'd turn them in early since he'd be in the office anyway that afternoon, boxing up the contents of his office—and his career.

In the exams he'd graded so far, he loved student responses to his deliberately provocative question: *In what specific ways is conventionally grown, typical supermarket food unfit for human consumption?*

He scooped up the fallen exam and was glad it was written by Tom Bridger, an especially bright senior. Settling into his well-cushioned chair (how many backyard daydreams and birdsong symphonies right here, over the years?) he took a gulp of tea and read:

"The 1970s slogan, 'You are what you eat' was not addressed just to people but to any organism which eats: animals, microbes, and plants throughout the global food web. Humans and all other species are codependent with enzymes, proteins, and minerals that have evolved in healthy soil. Yet industrial food, which occupies most of a typical supermarket's shelf space, is unfamiliar to our bodies. During its growth, transportation, and processing, conventionally produced food acquires traits that often make it unpalatable—even to pests. For example, in one experiment, when offered a choice between a bin of organically grown grain and a second bin of genetically modified and synthetically fertilized grain, lab rats chose the organic pile eighty-three percent of the time..."

Marc was impressed by the young man's knowledge as well as his earnestness. The professor often commented that at least half of his best insights came from his students. After a few pages of discussion about the nutritional value of food, Bridger went into its *social* nutrients—what Marc called the anthropology of food (also the name of the course). The student quoted 'slow food' activist Alice Waters:

"When we eat fast-food meals alone in our cars we swallow the values and assumptions of the corporations that manufacture them. According to those values, eating is no more important than fueling up, and should be done quickly and anonymously..."

At the end of the exam, Bridger summarized, *"Refugees from the global, industrialized food system are hungry for alternatives that can deliver a sense of community, craft, flavor, vitality, sustainable methods of agriculture, and climate change prevention in every bite. It's my generation's challenge to turn the current healthy food 'trend' into a widely accepted way of life. Isn't it time to stop asking why healthy food is so expensive and start asking instead why junk food is so cheap?"*

On the half-blank final page, Bridger had scrawled, *"Marc, I just want to thank you for your great course on the anthropology of food! You've really made me think about how out of tune our food system currently is! Keep up your great, mind-bending teaching, and I hope we can stay in touch.*" Marc felt a flush of pride, both for the quality of the paper and the student's gratitude. He also felt a little guilty that he hadn't told this year's 261 students that he'd be retiring. *The returning students will find out in the fall,* he thought, *I wish I'd been able to tell them more directly, but I hadn't gotten the bad news yet when classes ended...*

Throughout his years as an instructor, Marc fought the trend toward digitized cram-for-the-exam by occasionally inviting students to his house for dinner and discussion, sometimes asking musicians, actors or dancers among them to perform for the group. He momentarily considered that option: maybe invite the A students over and grill some fish and vegetables or shish kabob. "But then I'd have to do a massive house cleanup," he thought. He wasn't ready for that level of neatness, not yet. Really, he hadn't been ready for that kind of neatness in several years. After all, he had other priorities: saving the world takes focus. Truthfully, he'd defaulted to that trite bachelor's oath, "Wash windows and vacuum at least every six months, whether needed or not..." At least the kitchen was in decent shape, due to a renewed interest in mastering a few great recipes—especially Nepalese and Indian. But don't look on the bottom shelf of the fridge, where crimson pasta sauce had spawned emerald isles.

When it came to house cleaning, he tried to rationalize that his house—in its current state of decomposition—was really more like a campsite, so no worries. Hadn't he seen lots of grass huts and corrugated metal yurts that were far less immaculate? But if he were honest, he *did* feel a bit subhuman, a bit like the Incredible Hulk, skulking around the house vowing to get after the cleanup, *soon.* (With that green skin, Marc pondered, can the Hulk photosynthesize? Why shouldn't we genetically engineer tiny botanical solar collectors into our skin?)

He ascribed to another element in the bachelor code of ethics: Never let the house get worse than three days' worth of sweaty, god-awful, superficial remediation. Yet, even with that intensive effort, the neatness would still be largely an illusion, wouldn't it, because visitors could neither see nor imagine the chaos in drawers, file cabinets, and boxes throughout the house and garage. But wasn't this really a Standard American Practice (SAP)—shove it in the drawers to at least maintain the *appearance* of orderliness? Maybe he shouldn't feel such shame for being interested in other, more pressing things...Well, actually, *anything* rather than cleaning. Leap from a passenger train? No problem. Eat fried beetles? Done. Sing, *These Are a Few of My Favorite Things* (tone deaf) at an anthropology conference? All preferable to sorting, wiping and scrubbing. Who was he, Cinderella? In this bachelor phase of Marc's life, the term "domestiphobia" might apply—fear of the time and energy required to maintain a flawless household.

When Karen was alive, he'd been so much more attentive. She didn't buy into Marc's false ineptitude with appliances and cleaners, and she once threatened to show Kai's mother Michiko—a meticulous Japanese matron—what Marc's home office looked like. "Now that'll light a fire under you!" Karen had told him. But her domestic expectations were nothing compared with Marc's own mother! He remembered thinking when his mom went blind that the sole benefit was never again having to see his house, never again having to urge him, with pleading, religious fervor, to get out the Dirt Devil (whatever that was) and *use* it...every single day!

Marc observed how Americans were now seeking shelter inside the walls of their warmly humming desktop computers. Websites and social media (he hated that term) had now replaced nature and camaraderie as points of refuge. To be a loyal member of this digital dreamland and demonstrate extreme bravery, who would not boldly click a selfie on a slick promontory overlooking a majestic, thundering waterfall?

Would the simple, good life of his youth ever be seen again or had it been swiped away by billions of selfies grinning from billions of screens, in some cases seconds before death? Grins become grimaces when a lethal plunge or unseen projectile completes the story. In Russia's Ural Mountains, two hikers got a last, coolest photo of themselves holding a live grenade which somehow did not destroy the phone. Another fun-loving vacationer hung in there during the Running of the Bulls, snapping a close-up of spike-sharp horns irrevocably in search of his trachea. But let's be honest; when it comes to getting that certain, wacky Facebook shot—preferably taken on a good hair day—no risk is too great.

On every metro senior's daily to-do list: update Netflix queue, then dispatch a continuous stream of emails, texts and tweets, reporting what we're doing *right now* (pretty much nothing). At desks and in coffee shops teeming with tapping laptoppers, Americans continually risked being scolded and humiliated by their own devices for typing incorrect passwords or failing to save critical documents-in-progress. ("Ha ha," mocks Bart Simpson's nemesis, Nelson). Adroitly ducking through news briefs on their phones, these once-serene citizens become ninja warriors trained to vaporize popup ads in less than a second, darting under fire to the next morsel of pop culture. Risking personal meltdown when a computer's response time is slower than a blink, they ignore the fact that one dark day they'll experience gut-wrenching, emotional upheaval when the computer they thought was their best friend...crashes! No-o-ooo-o! Taking data, images, bookmarks, their *lives*—down, like a sinking ship.

"To life!" Marc mentally toasted with his mug of green tea. "Because we can't be idiots without it!" Four more exams read and emptying the last gulp of tea, Marc reentered his den of disorganization with peaceful resolve to continue ignoring the mess.

Stuffing a folder with the last exams into his pack, he recalled a final exam he had taken in his own undergraduate years. On a Philosophy and Religion final, he'd pondered the professor's enigmatic question, "Why?" for a full fifteen minutes before scribbling, "Why not?" and walking out of the classroom. Fortunately, the professor had given him a B in the course after a specially arranged oral exam.

He headed over towards his longtime office, feeling a very pleasant warmth in the air. As he had for the past three decades when he was in town, he left his house unlocked; he'd rather put trust into the world than fear. (By the luck of the innocent he hadn't yet lost his collection of folk art and craft.) Walking onto the campus 25 minutes later, he felt strangely intrigued by the unfamiliar insights and realizations playing out inside him. For one, he was gradually letting go of the responsibility he'd always felt for co-creating an eleventh-hour strategy for humankind. *(Now that's a load off...)* Maybe it was time to pass the baton now, and maybe he wouldn't have any choice anyway. *This is the exact place where I was interviewed by the 60 Minutes crew about daily life 200 years from now. In the sunlit hallways of that building I remember spontaneous, pivotal conversations with very bright and hopeful students. And what about that potentially catastrophic department skirmish, which, of course, I diplomatically smoothed over...*

Over the years, Marc's assigned office at DU had become larger and brighter. As a newly-hired instructor back in the day, he'd been assigned a dark cubicle near the lunchroom, where both the giddy laughter of overworked adjunct professors and the droning, snickering voices of the comfortably-tenured-ten invariably stole his focus. But steadily, as his perceived value increased, so did the square footage of his office. After a decade or so, he'd become a confident, bright-star professor who didn't want or need to be dean but did aspire to be a damn fine instructor. In the decade beyond that, he'd matured into one of the university's elite—the inspiration and traction behind a pioneering new department.

He remembered how hard he'd scrambled before finding the DU position. In the years between his undergraduate and graduate years, he'd filled out dozens of job applications with virtually no luck. His overall objective was to retain deed to his soul and still make a decent living, but to get there, you had to be belittled and slapped around like one of the Three Stooges. He'd observed a few similarities in the various application forms—intriguing to a guy with an anthropology degree. For example, there was always a *Reason for Leaving* box, about the size of a paper clip, below each previous job. You were supposed to summarize your life story in these tiny boxes, explaining why you'd left each job or why it had left you. But wouldn't you need a whole *book* to explain why you craved work that was inspiring? A job where fellow employees and employers were not only friendly but committed to doing quality work as a team? In no way did the applications provide enough space to write, "We need jobs that accomplish something useful and socially beneficial; that don't strip our dignity, and that provide a living wage—not just 0.02 percent of the CEO's salary. Workplaces where our voices are heard and our creativity tested but not used up. Jobs that make us feel vital, empowered, unique, and appreciated."

What would be Marc's reason for leaving early from his current job—*life*? At an existential level he really couldn't say. Maybe just call it the "luck of the draw," and even that probably wouldn't have fit into the tiny box.

As he unlocked his office door, the jangling keys reminded him he'd soon need to turn them in. He would be keyless after packing up all the books, posters, and office knick-knacks. Walking into a room he knew by heart and by its vintage campus-building smell, he glanced out the large window at the spacious quad with its walkway-lining maple trees, scurrying students and sculptures of various heroes, some of whom later became villains...or just as ingloriously, were totally forgotten. As he sat down, an unfamiliar sharp pain shot through his chest. He had no idea what caused it, but he arched his back and shrugged it off. No big deal, probably the salsa on his breakfast eggs. Still, with a nagging sense of anxiety, he came to grips with the notion that he might not spend the upcoming year in some cozy, carefree café, lovingly reserved for those who might be dying. Like everyone else, he'd have to deal with auto emission tests, daily meal prep, drug prescriptions, license renewals, mouse-in-the-wall house maintenance, two-hundred-dollar sacks of groceries, and all the rest. But maybe he could set aside half an hour each day for meditatively dying in peace. Like yoga, only dying.

He clicked the start button on the Bluetooth speaker on his desk and scrolled through his playlist, searching for favorite, comfortable gems of the '60s and '70s—Beatles, Joni Mitchell, Paul Simon, Paul Winter, Otis Redding...Another stray memory floated up as he scanned the list. *I'm eighteen with a driver's license; she's seventeen and lives right on my block. As we drive down East Fifth Avenue in Columbus, the sky starts to spray little droplets of rain/sleet onto the windshield. After flipping on the wipers I reach over, laying a sweaty, doubtful hand over hers. The Beach Boys' "Heroes and Villains" booms out of the speakers, and miraculously, she doesn't pull away.*

With his cherished archive of music as background, Marc's spirits began to muddle out of the swamp, only to be sucked back by a blog on his desk that he'd written right before getting his bad news.

"In the midst of a civilization-wide meltdown, we're trying to do the right things with the wrong instructions. Ours is a society that uses *more* and *more* of what we have less and less of—resources—yet steadily uses *less* of what we have more and more of: humans, reproducing like jackrabbits, desperate to find meaningful work. We turn up our air conditioners, making the world ever hotter, and evidently believe we can teach other nations how not to kill by killing them. For the sake of convenience, we attempt to forestall biological collapse with technical solutions, rarely considering reliable, time-honored changes in behavior. Need water? Dig deeper wells, their pipes sucking air like straws in a near-empty glass. Short on fish? Subsidize longer nets, satellite imagery and sonar to scrape the bottom of the seafood barrel. Hunt down that last sea bass and cook it up! Yum, even though its tissue may cause cancer, neural damage and insane laughing fits."

He felt relieved that he hadn't posted the grumpy blog, though he knew it was all too true. It was clear to Marc that the footloose free market, as it operated in the new millennium, could more appropriately be called a freak market. Why were we spending ten times more for fossil fuel subsidies than for education? If all the dysfunctional aspects of the U.S. economy—cancer from crappy air, forest fires from freakish weather, fake news, single use products—were subtracted from the GDP, would economists still be able to say the economy was actually growing? On balance, he wondered, do the daily ticks and tremors of the stock market measure productivity or destructivity?

Gandhi had it right, Marc thought: there's far more to life than increasing its speed—especially if you're traveling in the wrong direction. Marc's deepest, purest hope was that we DO know—way down in these crazy, twisted genes—when to change the itinerary. He thought, *So many rewards are waiting if we just take the more scenic trail, just embrace a different, slower way of living. Like retrievers after a cool, refreshing swim, we could shake off the collective paranoia about not having enough, or* being *enough. Why not go down in history as proud cultural game-changers instead of yammering, subservient sock puppets?*

Six

The Great Chocolate Cake Robbery

From guy talk at The Pub's Wednesday night happy hours, Rocket heard a lot of grumbling about wives and girlfriends—talk he steered clear of, suspecting that sometimes the men were just dissatisfied with themselves and their work, or often the lack of it. Despite the bumps, he cherished his relationship with Ellie, a tough cookie who'd stuck with him even through the whitewater rapids of bankruptcy; a woman who'd learned to manage construction projects and household finances like a pro. Their lovemaking was damn good most of the time, although there were occasional lapses, such as the dry spell they'd seen for the past few weeks. Maybe he needed to apologize, even though he wasn't exactly sure what he'd done. As they were getting into bed the previous night, she'd called him a "pathetic, pathological...proctologist"—a description with just enough edgy alliterative humor to make them both break out laughing. Sensing further verbal warfare, Rocket said, "I have the right to remain silent. Anything I say can and will be used against me." Then he'd added, "You know what? I'm gonna tell your mother on you—ask her what she did when you got naughty like this as a kid."

"She'd hold a halo over my head, of course," Ellen said in angelic self-defense. They were like a couple of six year olds—their grandson's peer group—trying to one-up each other. How much of their mutual hissy fit was just venting? Why didn't they just drive a few miles down Canyon Road, get out of the truck and scream at the stars? Now, with two more mouths to feed and clean up after, it seemed like a few new wrinkles had snaked onto Ellie's forehead, and Rocket's, too. Since she handled the bill paying he didn't know exactly how they stood financially, but judging by her anxiety he was pretty sure he didn't *want* to know. It was a time of transition. Didn't she see that he'd been the primary breadwinner for the last few years and was just shifting back into his woodworking and woodcarving?

"I'll do better," he said, a small percentage of him wishing a quick kiss on the cheek could temporarily turn her to stone so he could escape to do his errands. "I do appreciate you, you know."

"And I appreciate you, too," she answered, looking at him with a dim yet recognizable morning-sparkle of romance in her eyes and a slight, white-flag smile around her mouth. He made sure he had John's truck keys, his wallet and cell phone, certain he was forgetting something...then headed out the door. Houdini himself would have been impressed with the escape.

Seeing Zak down at the pond Rocket called, "You want to come to town with me?"

"No thanks, Grampa. I'm catching tadpoles and crawdads."

"All right, don't fall in, okay?"

"Can you get me a carton of that chocolate milk?"

"If I see it. See you in a while." Rocket loved getting to know his grandson. In the month since Sara and Zak arrived, he'd watched them both downshift from the inevitable speed and tension of L.A. life to a more relaxed pace. She'd increased the length of her daily run to two or three miles, commenting how "soft" the air felt in her lungs and how it gave her way more energy. For Zak, just being outside was something new and liberating. The tiny scorched lawn and daily life at the LA condo were just not that wonderful, except for one thing: a heartfelt, kindergarten crush on his nanny! When they'd first arrived in Willits, video games were life itself to Zak, the rest was only waiting. And for the first few weeks, he was like a young sugar addict twitching with agitation until the school bell rings. Now, he was winding down and letting his senses and curiosity carry him, challenging himself and feeling proud of this new independence. "This is my favorite summer," he'd told his Grampa a few days earlier, even though the summer really had just begun. Rocket had responded, "Mine too, Zak."

The boy hung out at the pond under the remote but eagle-eye of his mom. He threw pebbles and stones of various sizes into the water, studying the "plink" sound of the pebbles and the "kaplosh" of the larger stones, whose splashes sent concentric circles all the way across the pond. He was hoping John might have some time that afternoon to take him horseback riding, though he hadn't seen that cool neighbor in a few days. He felt pretty lucky, though: already, he had helped Grampa carve a rough, two-foot-long totem pole, seen a bald eagle soaring over the pasture scanning for rabbits and mice, watched coyotes slinking into the forest on the road to Willits, and stood under one of the tallest trees on Earth with his mom, over by Fort Bragg. He'd ridden around the property in an ATV, which John had let him steer if he promised never to tell anyone, and ridden horses with John and his Mom. He'd acted out Harry Potter scenes with another boy his age at the elementary school playground, vacant in the summer months. He'd helped gather the eggs almost every morning with Gramma, who showed him how she cooked breakfast burritos. He'd picked and munched crunchy fresh peas, gone to craft night at the library where he'd made a cloth lightning bug with a tiny, blinking LED light. He'd learned from Grampa how to barter at the farmer's market, caught a bass in the pond about the size of a small zucchini, climbed oak trees and even *lived* in a cool tree house! He'd built a solar-powered Lego car with John, and explored for butterflies and weird bugs by himself. Life on the farm was way better than life in LA!

Rocket was happy that John had become a hero to Zak, although beneath the surface there was an unspoken, friendly competition for his grandson's attention. Of course, from John's perspective, there was strategic value if Sara saw him as a perfect stepfather. But it was also easy to see that both John and Rocket were kids at heart. They loved to climb right into the mind of this high energy six-year-old to co-design cardboard forts in the living room or perform puppet shows for tiny but wildly appreciative audiences.

However, Rocket thought with some degree of envy, *very few people have their own airplane, and horses! Not everybody has an awesome tunnel/ wine cellar in their house with walls of solid, naturally-occurring rock...* Still, the tree house was in Rocket's column, and this Grampa-in-training made a mental note to schedule an overnight fishing and bird-watching trip for just him and Zak.

A winding gravel driveway about two hundred yards long connected the two houses with the main road to Willits. At the intersection was a little hamlet of several vintage cabins, a general store with a large wooden deck, an adjoining café open for breakfast and lunch only—except on Saturday nights when dinner was served—and a wooden fruit and vegetable stand, mostly used in harvest months. Then, down the road was a neighborhood of several dozen houses where some of Rocket's and Ellen's friends lived, and a few of John's too.

As he pulled onto Route 20, Rocket saw a good friend, Will, a guy he'd hunted and drank beer with for years. They each pulled over in the restaurant's empty lot, vehicles pointing in opposite directions as the men talked through truck windows. Rocket told him about the return of his daughter and grandson and the crops they'd already planted, and listened to his friend's bulletins about a sick heifer and an upcoming fishing trip to Alaska. Then, feeling the heat of his work deadline, Rocket politely cut the conversation short. As he drove, his mind was still occupied by challenges on the home front. How could he make sure that he and Ellie didn't take that low, mucky road through the portals of hell, where he typically employed semi-cynical humor posing as cheerful and she groused about not being *heard*? The inevitable result was a grumbling stomach, and he didn't want to go there. Rocket had noticed that the two women in his life didn't always see eye to eye, either. Sometimes Ellie tried a little too hard, which in turn made Sara push her mother even further away. He also wondered about getting Zak enrolled in school. Would he go to Brookside Elementary, or would Sara and Zak move out before school started? He hoped not.

Regarding marriages, he concluded that whether you're right or wrong in a given discussion or debate, sometimes you just go along. Smoothing the rough edges of a marriage was like signing a contract for an online software purchase: you don't have time to read and analyze the six tiny-font pages they throw at you, so you just click "agree" and you're on your way. *Oh hell,* he thought, accelerating on the empty road, *it'll work itself out, it always does.* He tuned in KMKX, the local classic-rock station: Bob Dylan was singing *Positively Fourth Street.*

In town, he checked off his list of errands one at a time, diagonally parking in front of the florist's shop to tell Wanda, the shop owner, that the snapdragons would be at their peak in the next few days. "If Tommy can come over and harvest some of our snaps, we'll give you a screaming deal per bundle." It was common practice in this town of 5,000 that you bought each other's products or suffered the social consequences. If Ellen forgot to tell the editor of *The Willits News* when the Blake's snapdragons were in, Wanda would probably do it, adding that the new Asian vases in the flower shop were also on sale. As he climbed back in John's truck, he saw a few people he knew, way down the street in front of the diner. He waved and one waved back but the others maybe couldn't figure out who was driving John's truck. After gathering tools and feed at the hardware store and chocolate milk for Zak, he headed for home, but at the edge of town did a hasty U-turn, going back for a bottle of Ellie's favorite wine. He was hoping he'd win some points for that personal touch, maybe even score later that night.

Rocket loved the way a small town enfolds rather than isolates its residents. He'd traveled in the U.S. enough to know that great little towns were withering on the vine, especially near metro areas. These days, if urbanites wanted to experience the pace and feel of Main Street the way it was back in the day, they just about had to travel to Disney World's faux communities, where smiling shopkeepers and Fourth of July parades were nostalgic reminders that communities once felt leisurely and secure.

Rocket wondered how Disney designers would portray current life in an older metro-area suburb. Would they create background ambience with sounds of highway traffic, beeping garbage trucks, and maybe a gun shot from the meth lab at the edge of town? Would they portray gridlock with bumper-to-bumper cars, complete with Disney smart phones so riders could let family members know they'd be late for the next ride? Would they hire actors to play the beleaguered suburbanites who can't drive—the elderly, disabled, and low-income residents, peeking out from behind stage-set living room curtains?

Rocket was 110 percent behind the regeneration of local, living economies, where a person could participate and help make critical decisions. At the local scale, you could help organize a music festival, spearhead a local ban on fracking, encourage traditional architecture, mentor new farmers, and enjoy pancake breakfasts hosted by firefighters you've known for years. Many residents of Willits and its surroundings had attended open-house gatherings at the Blake/Bechard homestead, always marveling at John's beautiful house, the small farmette, and the ever-popular treehouse. Small town life wasn't perfect, Rocket knew that. Judging by demographics, lots of humans either needed or wanted to be in cities, but Rocket knew he'd avoided a lot of commute-and-consume stress by living in rural Mendocino County, and he'd do it again in a heartbeat.

Later that evening, Ellen, Rocket, Sara and Zak sat at the long, sturdy oak dinner table Rocket had crafted with pegs and glue rather than screws. Dinner included roasted chicken, a huge bowl of garden salad with orange and red nasturtium blossoms on top, and fresh peas with red onions—all as local as you could get. The adults were drinking the wine Rocket had picked up, but Zak had a different meal altogether. After whispering to his Mom that he couldn't eat one of the chickens that was friends with—he just *couldn't*—Sara suggested that maybe they should let Zak have his way this time rather than making a big deal. Ellen agreed but Rocket didn't, although he kept his mouth shut. "I have an idea," Ellen said, "Let's make you a bowl of alphabet soup, your favorite, right? We're thinking of playing Scrabble after dinner, so maybe you can get some practice spelling." Rocket noticed the warmth and kindness she was sending Zak's way. Why couldn't he have some of that? "Alphabet soup!" Zak said, excitedly, with a six-year-old sigh of relief. In the minds of many his age, meat should always come straight from cellophane packages, and *never* be seen legs-in-the-air on a platter, especially if the meat had recently been known as Goldie.

"I talked to a guy named Bill Wheeler today, an architect in Ukiah," Sara reported. Ellen and Rocket both stopped eating to listen. "He said I could stop by and talk with him, although he doesn't have any starting positions right now. He gave me the names of a few of his colleagues in Santa Rosa, though. I'm going to call them tomorrow."

"Terrific!" Rocket said, relieved that she was moving ahead with her plans. Since they'd arrived, Sara had read lots of books, spent a little time with John, took dozens of nature photographs, and hung around with Zak, *however*...He thought it was admirable that she'd insisted on paying rent for household expenses, gas, and their treehouse perch, but he was anxious for her to find interesting work. She wasn't a kid anymore.

"How's that alphabet soup, Zak?" Ellen asked. "Did you make any words yet?" Zak had fished four soggy letters out of his soup and lined them up on his plate. "Yup," he said. "leaf: L-E-E-F."

"Almost," Rocket said. "Leaf is L-E-A-F."

"Oh."

"Do you have an A in there?" Sara asked, paddling around in the soup with her spoon. "I don't see an A, but I do see a K!" she said. "What does that spell? In fact you might have some of this in your soup right now. L-E-E-K, you know, kind of like an onion."

"Or like when a boat is leaking," the boy said, to demonstrate his intelligence. "No, a different kind of leek," Sara said, wishing she'd dredged an A instead. "Spelling can be complicated but don't worry, you're such a smart boy, you'll learn fast!" Ellen smiled adoringly at her grandson. She got up to start clearing the table, and Rocket stood up to help, holding his breath as Ellen put dishes in the sink and took a step toward...the scene of the crime.

"Look what we have for dessert!" she announced. Then, in a halting, puzzled voice, she said, "*What the...?*" Holding the metal cake cover in one hand, she turned to confront the thieves. She had the look of a bomb with a fuse the length of a strike-anywhere match. "I made that cake so I could have at least a piece for my Dad—it's his *birthday* tomorrow! And I told you that!" Striding toward the table, she glared at Zak, suddenly noticing a detail she hadn't seen before: in the corner of his mouth, smudged onto his upper lip, was evidence enough to send the boy up the river for life: a tiny particle of dried and forgotten chocolate. Reaching over impulsively, she scraped the chocolate off Zak's lip with her fingernail, dangling it triumphantly right in front of his eyes, which tracked the fearsome finger back and forth hypnotically. "It was YOU!" she squawked. "That cake was to share with my father!" she repeated in case Zak (and the birds and rabbits outside) hadn't gotten that yet. "But look how much cake you ate!" she said, looking over at the counter.

"Well I..." Zak began, and ended. With sharp, angular movements, Ellen glared at Sara, then Rocket—each of them lowering their eyes. As the meltdown continued, the suspects were wondering, frankly, if Ellen had lost her marbles. *Her anger is not really about the cake,* Rocket thought, *She just needs to vent.* Ellen was trapped in the heat of her emotional release—a mama cat who'd run up a tree and couldn't get back down. She looked again at Rocket's face, frozen in a would-be amiable grin, halfway expecting to find another chocolate smudge on *his* lip. "And it was you, too!" she said with narrowed cat's-eyes and that accusatory finger demanding confession. Rocket was stunned. He hadn't expected *this* much of a reaction. Still, refusing to repent on command, he effectively pleaded the Fifth. "It's not that big of a deal, Ellie," he told her, reaching out for her arm. "We really appreciate that you made it, and we're really sorry that we snitched a little of that *delicious* cake...Let's get your Dad something from Roland's Bakery. I'll get it." Ellen brushed his arm away. "A little?! You ate almost the whole thing!"

Now Rocket was on the stand at a military tribunal, facing a very stern looking judge. "Well, I took a peek at it earlier and..."—he thought about the evidence already in the court record—"someone had already eaten a *little* bit of the cake, and I thought it was okay just to have a little slice, too. It tasted so good that I had another, just *little* piece," he said, demonstrating the tininess of the slice with his thumb and forefinger. However, looking at the cake over on the counter, he could now see that his raid had not been the final one! There were, at that point, maybe two pieces left.

"But I didn't take *that* much," he said, shaking his head in vehement denial. And with a brave little smile, Sara then fearfully confessed. "It's really good cake, Mom." Ellen shook her head, incredulous at the scale of the crime. Though she did have the shadow of a steely smile on her face, she also felt cornered. It was a conspiracy and she was the victim. Plus, she was pissed *she* wouldn't get much of the cake, after all the work she'd put into it. And really, here was the crux of the issue: Work. They were freeloading while she did the work. Day after day, from her perspective, they were off at the redwoods, or napping, or smoking pot in the workshop.... She went silent for an instant, looking at the floor and realizing how impossible it would be to explain the whole context of her eruption.

Rocket saw an opportunity for gallantry. "We understand," he said, speaking on behalf of the whole gap-toothed band of rogues. "We love you, Ellie, and we know it's about more than the cake." After a pause he said sincerely, "What kind of help do you need? What do you need us to do to share the work more evenly?" A few tears welled up in Ellen's eyes as she regained her composure. Her outbreak had let off some steam, but more importantly, maybe now they'd listen to her. She mentally assembled the priorities and gave orders—an Admiral scrambling to save the ship. "We need to finish picking the peas. If the pods get much bigger, they're not marketable, you know that. We need to harvest the snapdragons, with the stems all the same length—bundle them up and ship 'em off well before they reach peak bloom...And we need to butcher and freeze a few more hens this week," she said, looking straight at Zak as if to say, *That's the way life works, little man.* Out loud, she told him, "If the hens aren't laying, they need to contribute in other ways."

She continued scrolling down her list. "We need to sit down with the current intern crew and let them know what we expect from each of them: thirty hours of work a week." (She emphatically tapped the edge of one hand onto the palm of the other). "And how, in return, they'll learn how to start their own operations, or postpone getting a job, or whatever." Looking at Rocket, she said, a little more gently now, "Rock, you need to finish your totems...And do you think you could help get the rest of the winter squash planted, and the Yukon Gold potatoes?" Captain Rocket Blake nodded as Tom Hanks might have in *Saving Private Ryan.* "And do you think you could be the one to talk with the interns? They seem to like you." Blake nodded again, then went down the chain of command to Seaman Zachary Blake. "Can we count on you to collect all the eggs *every morning*—that's about thirty or thirty-five eggs—and take them into the barn to be cleaned and packed into cartons? That's an important job."

"Yes!" Zak said earnestly, relieved that he might not be punished.

Ellen, still standing, put a hand on Zak's shoulder, saying, "That would be a big help. And I'm sorry I yelled at you for eating some of the cake. Maybe you didn't know we wanted to save some for my Dad's birthday." Then, looking directly at Rocket, she said, "But YOU did." Rocket sat helplessly now, as if gagged and strapped to his chair.

Then Ellen looked at Sara, once again waggling the ominous finger. "And so did YOU." She took a deep breath and added, "Baby, you need to do some cooking around here, and help us with the farm work—that's how we make our living...this isn't a vacation..." She looked back at Sara after the last statement, to see how her daughter had taken it. Sara nodded, apparently not just obediently but with respect—as if relieved to see her mother rising up and taking charge. Then Ellen cut to the chase with a gulp: "And, we may need to ask John if he can wait a bit on this month's rent and land payments."

Uh-oh. Now Rocket got it. He hadn't thought the finances were this dire, but it was clear now that everyone needed to pull their weight. Sara looked down at the table, embarrassed, and Zak appeared uncomfortable, too, retreating into the safety of his bowl of soup. Trying to relieve the tension, the boy shouted heroically, "Look at this, you guys: ZAK!" Like the slowly emerging message on a toy crystal ball, the Z had floated sideways to the surface. Then he'd borrowed the K from the word "leek," mushed an H into kind of an A with his fork, and voila: Z-H-K.

"I think you're ready for a game of Scrabble!" Rocket told the boy, standing up and putting his arm around Ellen. Then he leaned in and whispered in her ear, "We got this."

Seven

Why Not?

Sitting at his desk, determined to finish grading his last exams and start packing things up, Marc's thoughts were interrupted by an assertive knock on his office door. "C'mon in, it's open." With flawless synchronicity, as the door swung open, the opening note of an iconic 60s tune—a piercing, whining, dive-bombing note—exploded from the cylindrical speaker on his desk. Then the words, "WILD THING, YOU MAKE MY HEART SING" announced the entry of Kerrie Winfield, a one-time student and assistant, now 28 and fully in blossom. Their eyes locked and they both laughed at how perfectly the song had announced her entry. "I just keep the song queued up for whoever comes along," he joked over the volume of the song. "The dean, the custodian, Donald Trump—whoever."

Instead of a predictable "Hi, Marc," she playfully did a few dance moves in time to the music, her hips undulating in one direction and her upper body somehow gliding in the other. (What is it about female anatomy?) Then she stopped, with an unpretentious, radiant smile on her face. However, when Marc stood up and began moving back and forth in front of his desk (at first a little like the Tin Man) Kerrie's shoulders and hips were back in motion. In that very first instant, each acknowledged a chemistry they'd known six years earlier as teacher and teaching assistant. Such feelings were completely off the table then. He was happily married, she was a student. But now their body language announced a completely different message: availability, even a fortuitous *inevitability*.

The wide gap in their ages was suddenly irrelevant, as was the taboo of teacher/student trysts. He wasn't a teacher anymore and she wasn't a student. They knew in an instant they'd soon be doing what humans do out in the hayloft—even though, since the semester they'd co-taught, they'd seen each other only a handful of times—at noisy campus mixers or the supermarket. Now, in a pagan late-spring celebration, they danced like a pair of prairie chickens in heat, smiling involuntarily as they strutted. The energy between them was the rough equivalent of the shifting flux between a powerful magnet and a shiny ball bearing.

The stage was irrevocably set: bright young, attractive woman alone in a room with the teacher she'd always put on a pedestal, at a moment in her life that wasn't cluttered with immature, unworthy males. (She'd recently cleared the deck by breaking up with a guy she thought she could love, who was, in the end, "only capable of loving himself.") And Marc? At that moment, he might have told you he was just some widower—a pretty decent fellow who'd been told he might be dying, and who now craved the relief of connection...to something, *anything*, but especially this. Well aware that Kerrie knew him from earlier and more energetic days, he quickly mobilized to reprise that younger, more charismatic self. As they laughed again, each a little disoriented, Marc transformed himself into a beaming, uniformed Richard Gere in *An Officer and a Gentleman*, confident he would sweep this young damsel off her feet and carry her away from all the small town indignities. As the song ended, he reached for her arm, saying with a bashful smile, "I always knew you were a Wild Thing."

"I take that as a compliment. And you're no slouch, either, maestro," she said, looking directly into his eyes. Marc wasn't positive he was truly a maestro in the English sense of the word, but he loved the way she said it. "What are you up to, anyway? Where are you working now?" he asked, meanwhile feeling a full body swoon he hadn't felt for months or even years. She dazzled him. With some deep-rooted, primordial magic powered by physics and biochemistry, she'd flipped a switch in him. (Was she feeling the same?) Despite the recent strikeouts with women, he was going to go for it. The two were standing close enough to feel each other's body heat, their breathing heavy from the dancing and the rush of this serendipitous opportunity. Marc was stunned by the ingenuous beauty of her pearl white smile, the way her fragrant strawberry-blond hair swished onto her shoulders and the delightful visual access her sleeveless tight-knit dress allowed.

For her part, she took in his steadiness and status. This was a world-class harbor whose deep waters she revered and trusted. Impulsively, he gave her a quick hug. What else could he do? Though still experimental, the hug crunched through long-time barriers like an Arctic icebreaker. As she opened the ornate iron gates of a wondrous secret garden, he rode in like a heroic if nerdy professor in slightly dented armor.

A silver necklace with a sapphire pendant sparkled on her graceful, youthful neck, and to Marc, Kerrie's outfit was far more than flattering, it was exhilarating. It seemed to trumpet, "Summer is here, and so am I!" If any further doubt remained, her active endocrine system sent a sensual pink blush to her face, along with a genuine, so-sexy smile. He reciprocated, radiating a primal sense of confidence and seasoning, which she could feel when his hand quickly caressed her neck. At a basic level, what Kerrie craved was to be grown up, at last, to be acknowledged as an attractive, capable, remarkable woman. Marc had always thought of her as a good looking girl, but now she was so worldly! Her Celtic complexion featured a little batch of light-colored freckles on her nose and cheeks—like tiny chocolate chip cookies, he thought. Drawn into the clarity and mystery of her eyes, he noted that the tiny speckles in her hazel-green irises were a close and very hypnotic match with the freckles. In Marc's own eyes, and the slight puffiness under them, Kerrie noticed unfamiliar shadows from events that had occurred since she'd studied and worked with him. But she also felt his passion and hunger, lots of it.

With the certainty of intimacy already established, the two came temporarily back to Earth, each slightly ruffled but standing their ground.

"What am I up to?" she asked, with a lilt in her voice and her hand loosely gripping one of Marc's arms. "Well, I'm working at the Denver Art Museum, in the acquisitions department."

"Really? Wow!" Marc leaned over impulsively and kissed her cheek, as if to officially congratulate her success.

"You'd like some of the Incan art and craft we've just gotten in from Peru and Ecuador." He answered, "I'm sure I would!" as the two continued to meet each other's gaze. "Do you speak Quechua?" he asked nonsensically, his thoughts scrambled by her youthful radiance. "No, but I speak fluent Spanish," she answered with raised eyebrows that seemed to say, "I'm smart." But Marc already knew that. They'd worked together to orchestrate the course he'd called *Not Your Father's Facebook*, about the future of Artificial Intelligence. Her work performance had been extremely impressive. She'd led a break-out team whose final report ("Convenience or Insanity?") had been excerpted in various blogs. Standing before him was a polished gem, and he craved an exchange—even of non-sexual energy—with this youthful diva. The early afternoon sunlight streaming through the window backlit her hair, lustrous and stylishly in place except for the one rebellious curl springing just slightly toward her cheek. Whether it was the faintest hint of perfume or youthful pheromones, her fragrance and nearness made him feel like a kid whose Christmas wish list had come true. Standing right in front of him was Santa's irresistible daughter.

Recovering just a little, he suggested flirtatiously, "Tal vez deberiamos bailar otra vez?" (Maybe we should dance again?)

"Me la gustaria," (I would like that), she said confidently. "O, tal vez tu deberias darme una leccion." (Or maybe you should give me a lesson).

Marc gulped, in joyous, mischievous disbelief. He heard a distant bugle and a Field Marshall's command: "CHARGE!" Strategically, he made note of the full-length zipper down the back of her dress. It was easy to imagine how a slow, tantalizing unzip would leave her almost naked, except for her underwear (no doubt bright and silky) and those spare, sexy sandals. She had the slender, muscular legs of a onetime track athlete, and he wanted to feel the heat and power in those muscles.

"Que classe de leccion?" (What kind of lesson?)

"Ya sabes," (You already know) she said with a sultry assurance that matched or exceeded his.

"Hay que cerrar las cortinas de la ventana?" he asked, with a smile. (Should we close the window blinds?)

"Si, absolutamente," she responded, her shoulders coming forward as she leaned in to be kissed on the mouth. Now, the blush of her skin was unmistakable. He ran his hand along the inside of her warm, sleeveless arm. Any remaining caution signs disappeared into mechanical slots like metal pop-up targets in a carnival shooting gallery. They kissed passionately, oblivious to the world outside. Immediately, she felt acknowledged as a desirable, intelligent adult, while he experienced the rapid thawing of a soul-sized chunk of ice.

She tucked the wayward curl behind her ear and released the Venetian blinds with a clatter while he quickly locked the office door. They were complicit in a high-adrenaline caper, and it felt so liberating! Moving eagerly back to the now-empty dance floor, they fell into the warm, exciting embrace that life and luck had granted them. As they kissed, he slow-danced her toward the cracked, frumpy leather couch across from the window, where he stood behind her, luxuriously unzipping her dress. Each of them cooed gratefully, as if every kiss, every stroke scratched an existential itch. Then, while Kerrie perched enticingly on one arm of the couch, Marc quickly found an album of Debussy music on his phone and sent it through the speaker on his desk. He moved back toward the couch, his underwear still on, awkwardly hopping on one foot as he pulled a sock off the other.

"I've always had a crush on you," she told him between kisses. "Who, me?" he asked, as if shyly. Then he changed the subject, not wanting to waste time assessing or confessing his earlier taboo feelings for her. "I can't believe how lucky we are, right at this moment, right on this very planet," he said in a low voice, brushing the back of his wrist against her breast, as if by accident but really from magnetic attraction. "I was so sorry to hear about your wife," she said, interrupting their sex play and temporarily fire-hosing Marc's passion. "Thank you, Kerrie," he said, his hand now harvesting the glow of her smooth cheek. "That was a long time ago..." He was intent on kissing her neck and nuzzling through the fragrant softness of her lustrous hair. But she continued, "You know, I didn't come here to seduce you. I came to see if you still have the file for that project we worked on."

"You didn't seduce me," he said in a sex-muffled voice. He was busy, he didn't want to talk anymore. "It was *fate* that seduced us," he concluded, well aware that any dying-but-horny old con artist might recite a line like this. Now his hand was between her parted legs, seeking and finding the warmth of her inner thighs and the receptive moistness of her excitement. "Mmm, I'm so glad you were in," she said, in a low, husky voice, now equally eager for passionate silence. There may have been an occasional footstep in the hardwood-floored hallway outside the door, and ongoing comments by birds and squirrels on the other side of the curtained window, but for these two, there was really only one thing.

When they resurfaced, they knew each other in a far different way. What had happened, and the *way* that it had happened, had bulldozed a permanent, secret chamber in the universe—one that was theirs alone. He watched as she stood up like a lingerie model, pulling on her panties then refastening her bra—first fastening it in front, then pulling it around her body into place. She seemed to be posing for him alone. Pushing her arms through the stylish dress, she requested, "Can you zip me up?"

"Of course, although it's a shame to cover up that smooth, beautiful skin." He couldn't resist studying her tall, graceful frame and inhaling the sight, smell, and touch of her. He hugged her from behind, caressing her hipbones gratefully before reluctantly zipping her dress in a long, slow zip. "Who helped you when you put the dress ON?" he asked, not with dread but just curiosity. "My housemate," she answered. Not wanting, for the moment, to examine the stature of this housemate, he asked, "Where do you live?"

"We live in a Lodo apartment, three of us," she said, turning around to talk directly to him (Those eyes! That skin..!) "And you're still in your house on South Gaylord?"

"Yeah, I'll probably die in that house," he said automatically, forgetting for an instant that he very well *could* die in that house, sooner rather than later. He wasn't sure what the next step should be, with Kerrie. Typically, isn't there at least a temporary assumption of continuity? But what would she say when he told her he was not only retiring, but possibly...expiring? Did he sense Kerrie's iron garden gates slowly swinging shut, as if she routinely had casual sex and this was no big deal (even though he suspected that was not true)? Maybe her sudden inwardness was deference to his seniority? Maybe he really *was* the Maestro...

As Marc got dressed, Kerrie noticed for the first time the purplish, geometric rash on one leg, but embarrassed, didn't say anything about it. Overall she saw an extremely interesting man who had just released something very significant in her. She didn't have an ounce of regret, and neither did he. If the truth be known, the word "score" was prominent in each person's grateful psyche. "Do you want to get something to eat? Are you hungry? Or, we could grab an ice cream cone at Bonnie Brae." In a joking tone, he added, "Or we could just go over to the County building and get married—maybe get a street guy to be a witness?" They both smiled at his little joke, and she threw a mischievous grenade, "What if I get pregnant?"

"Ain't gonna happen...vasectomy years ago." They each smiled. An awkward moment. Then he remembered why she'd originally come to his office. "What kind of info do you need? What did we call that class?"

"*Not Your Father's Facebook*," she said instantly, in a way revealing that the class had been a milestone for her. "My group's project was *Convenience or Insanity*. Remember? All our needs are artificially provided by corporations, just like in a Memory Care facility. I just need the dates of the project and maybe your assessment of my role in the class? I'm applying for a grant for the museum, and it'll be great to include it." As she spoke, Marc went to his computer to search for the class files. Over his shoulder, he teased, "So really, you were just making sure I'd give you a good assessment?"

"A blowjob for the teacher," she boldly confirmed, continuing his joke. As she looked through the now-bright window, she saw a few Ultimate Frisbee players winging strikes back and forth on the quad. The athlete in her wanted to join them, sprinting and stretching to catch the spinning saucer. "Here's the file," he said, relieved that he didn't have to root around for it—way too clumsy for a knight. "Do you want a hard copy, or do you want me to just email it to you?"

"I already had a hard copy," she punned, though she wished she hadn't—it was already a stale joke. "An email would be great, thank you!"

He gathered his papers and they walked to her car, floating in a gilded carriage yet trying—a little too politely—to have a conversation. The world was such a confusing place, even for a seasoned geezer or a world-conquering young lady, and it was magical to conspire intimately with another person. A little awkwardness was fine, wasn't it? They drove over to Wash Park where Marc routinely rode his bike, typically completing both the inner and outer loops for a quick five miles of riding. As they walked past the boathouse, well known as the hundred-year-old Park's most scenic and romantic location, he explained, "The Park was partly funded by a philanthropist, the 'unsinkable' Molly Brown, who survived the Titanic disaster." (Suddenly, he'd become a museum docent to cover his schoolkid shyness.) "And down the path about half a mile is a bloom-for-bloom replica of Martha Washington's perennial garden at Mount Vernon."

"You are One with this park."

He wanted to put his arm around her and kiss her as they walked, but instead opted for propriety. Seeing the two of them frolicking on the path, would some colleague gossip to people who knew him? But, what could they do anyway, now that he was retiring? Still, what would *strangers* think?

Despite his anything-goes medical condition, he was still a hostage of his culture. She was oblivious to the way it looked, other than her confidence that she was completely the man's equal—not his protégé.

They went over to the same bistro where Marc and Kai had eaten the day before. Sitting outside, they continued to blossom in the mild weather and warm glow of their adventure. He asked about her current relationship status, and when he could see her again. "I'd like that," she said with hesitation. "I'm... not seeing anyone else right now...But maybe we shouldn't have expectations, or 'sexpectations' of a rendezvous every other night, do you think? I mean..."

"I wouldn't see the harm in it," he responded with a roguish smile, still feeling a virile exhilaration. "But I know what you mean. Boundaries are good." He realized as he spoke that he needed to be upfront about his own situation. When she asked about *his* personal life, he kind of fell apart. "Well, I'm not seeing anyone either...and...I've never cheated on anyone, but...given my circumstances, you may not have to worry about extended sexpectations." He was amused by the term, it was fun to say it, even in this very vulnerable moment.

"What do you mean, your circumstances?" she asked, smiling cautiously, trying to read his body language. As he retold his story, her completely open, youthful face fell like an overinflated angel food cake. He saw genuine tears in her eyes. By the looks of things, the alarming news only seemed to heighten his appeal. (Or was he just hoping?) He gratefully cupped her hand as they talked. Ironically, to him the unlikeliness of a real relationship seemed to make their encounter even more tantalizing.

"I need to go grade papers, they're due tomorrow," he said as they finished their celebratory desserts. Can you give me your number?" She reached into her very earthy-looking leather bag and fished out a colorful, well-designed business card. (She was so *cute*, successfully making her way in the world!) "I should go back to work, too. I can drop you off if you want." She paused, then said sincerely, "I really enjoyed getting together with you, well, you know what I mean...it meant so much to me." (Was that another blush?)

"It ain't over yet," he answered in a reassuring tone, confidently assuming—or at least hoping like hell—that he could now drink from this feminine fountain of youth whenever he so desired.

When they pulled up in front of his house, he said with innuendo, "Thanks for your visit." They looked into each other's eyes like they'd just shared a roundtrip hot air balloon ride to Munchkin Land. He kissed her quickly but passionately, and she matched his energy, confirming her feelings. (*That'll get the neighbors talking,* he thought.) She even said, "We're going to fight your Q virus," like they'd be side-by-side every step of the way, now that she was his Wild Thing.

"You're terrific," he said, leaning through the open car window, one hand on the window frame. "So are you," she responded, running her smooth, warm hand over his.

As her Subaru pulled away, he laughed, knowing that Kai would never believe what had just happened a day after their chatter about women.

He floated through his house into the kitchen, setting his day pack down, along with a motley stack of mail. On the kitchen counter was a sumptuous, fragrant surprise: a freshly baked pie with a note beside it! As he read, he immediately sank a fork into the still-warm pie. The note was from May and the pie was raspberry—no doubt from the raspberry patch in one corner of their fertile front yard. *"My dear friend, I'm so sorry to hear your news. I came over to tell you that we are here for you, whatever you might need. Kai is positive you will beat this. We want to have you over for dinner soon. Can you let us know some good times for you?"*

Despite "getting lucky" that day, Marc felt a full suite of emotions, including an unexpected shiver of loneliness, as if unpacking one set of feelings let out all the others. He should get in touch with Lisa the next day, he thought—that would help. She'd told him she wanted to spend a day with him to help make his house more comfortable and organized. He welcomed any time with his much-adored daughter.

When DU was in session—and when he wasn't dying—loneliness had never been an issue. But Kerrie's cute phrase, "no sexpectations," stung a little, feeling too much like "no genuine connection." And the note and pie from May made him feel supported, yes, but also a little like an outcast from the smiley-faced universe of happy couples with heart-shaped emojis pasted all over their lives.

He finished grading his exams (the last ones ever!) and drove over to the after-hours box at the University to drop them off, along with the always-dramatic final grades. Then he went back and warmed some leftovers, followed by *three* rewarmed pieces of pie and a glass of rice milk. He watched the opening gallery of robberies, rapes and political rumors on the 10 o'clock news as he got ready for bed, still experiencing a whirlwind of emotions. But he had to admit, there *was* a certain new feeling inside, some fresh little sparkle that had put an involuntary schoolkid grin on his face. For the moment, despite the fountain of emotions, he was living in the present. Screw future studies of *any* description.

Eight

Top Ten Reasons

Marc and his daughter had arranged a time to give his house a makeover—no small challenge! The house was stuffed with items ranging from totally worthless to nearly priceless, but overall it was a home sorely in need of decongesting. Although Marc had been raised in the post-War consumer fever of "affluenza," he felt he was more immune than many in his generation. In his childhood home in Ohio, he'd witnessed the birth of the kwik n' easy, press-1-and-you're-done lifestyle, and like all Americans, he'd absorbed the ads' dire warnings: "don't broadcast bad breath;" don't be *humiliated* by "ring around the collar." He was a veteran of the ever-inflating American myth, having been there when the great schism first arose between Tupperware tops and bottoms. How did these refugees get away, and...where did they go?)

The anthropology of new-millennium America was a common backdrop in the courses Marc taught. He felt as guilty as the next guy for dicing the world into microscopic bits of asphalt, plastic, glyphosate and other mystery-molecules, but objectively, he was at least an A- on green living, all except in the energy-intensive travel column. Student trips, cultural research and international volunteer work had made him a familiar face at airline ticket counters.

Despite his house's current dusty disarray, it was uniquely durable and "all natural." The bedroom and stairway were carpeted with wool (though much to the delight of moths), the first floor was a blend of brick, tile, and hardwood, and the kitchenware was stainless steel and ceramic. Copper pans hung classically over a deep-set sink. This was a household well known for its many objects and images from other cultures and eras, most of them conceived and produced Before Plastic (BP). The intrinsic value of these arts and crafts evidenced the many years Marc and Karen had spent together, at home and in their travels. The front entry was a sunny brick-floored atrium with a wall-mounted, seeping fountain and miniature rainforest. Walking into the living room, the first thing you saw was a pair of cherished photos in simple black frames: Karen standing, awestruck, with Margaret Atwood—author of *The Handmaid's Tale*—at a fundraiser for Bill Clinton's second presidential campaign, and a black and white shot of Marc and his brother Rocket with wide high-school grins on their faces, standing at home plate shoulder-to-shoulder with baseball's shadowy legend Pete Rose, in Cincinnati's Riverfront Stadium.

The living room decor combined Karen's passion for fine art and Marc's for traditional crafts. A few large-framed prints of Miro, Gauguin and Klee shared space with several brightly colored masks and textile wall hangings—an unusual combination celebrating a diversity of cultures. In the hallway to the kitchen, a mini-museum of hunting, cooking and farming implements still in use in traditional cultures was housed in a glass-door cherry bookcase: a rattan shrimp trap from the rice paddies of Vietnam, a lashed wooden hoe from Guatemala, and a small bow and arrow from the Uruguayan rainforest. It was no accident that Lisa had gone into the import business. She'd always treasured artifacts like these and researched their back stories. She'd recently urged her father to have these treasures reappraised and reinsured, as she and Brad had done in their Boulder shop.

When Lisa arrived and called out to her dad, he was staring in the mirror in the study, giving himself a quick glance of affirmation. He wanted to be 100 percent *present* with Lisa, his deepest and most valued connection. She was a high-energy, independent and ambitious young woman on whom he'd bet in just about any situation. And not just because she was family. Her appearance owed nothing to style or pretense, but rather to authenticity, comfort, and openness. She wasn't glamorous but down to earth and full of life. With Lisa, what you saw was what you got. And what *did* Marc foresee that day? A potential scolding. Really, wasn't cleaning the house her excuse to lecture him about the urgent need to start taking his prescriptions? She was going to lay down the law, he knew it. He loved her for it, but he just wasn't certain he wanted to ingest those shiny red, white and blue capsules— The Joker that could suddenly turn on you, mowing down your immune system with tiny semi-automatic granules. He needed to get more firsthand information about the success and side effects of the drugs, he would tell her that, assure her that of course survival was his highest priority. As they stood in the living room that was so familiar to both, he could picture her jump-roping or practicing ballet here, filling out college and job applications there at the dining room table, and a few years later bringing Brad home to meet the parents. Life had been lived well here, no question. But then death had taken a ransom.

"Where do you want to begin?" she asked, hopeful that he had a plan or at least a commitment to the task. Lisa's strategy was to be light and conversational at first, then go in for the Full Nelson. She wanted to get some momentum going, breathe some life back into both the house and her father. "Do we have to begin?" he asked, a warm smile on his face. He sensed that things were going well for his girl. She seemed confident, relaxed, and energetic. "Why don't we go outside and have a cup of tea and a bagel first? It's a beautiful morning!"

"Okay," she said, thinking this might be a good opportunity to badger him about the drugs as well as surprise him with a new development in her life. "Do you have some of that loose-leaf Oolong tea?" she asked. "Orchid oolong? Yeah, I still have a little sack of that."

Out in the backyard she began with, "How's the match.com world treating you?" He always became so animated and comedic talking about his matchbox misadventures that they usually had a pretty good laugh together. Although Marc didn't plan to reveal his most recent, ego-boosting adventure with Kerrie, he did want to share an email conversation he'd had with a woman quite a few months earlier, which he thought was especially clever. While Lisa basked in the morning sun, he brought out the three-page transcript and handed it to her. She turned her chair away from the morning glare as he checked on his little garden patch. She quickly began to see several slightly devious strategies at play in the dialog, which had apparently taken place over the span of a few weeks.

Dear Marc,

Thank you for your email, and for making me one of your "favorites." I must confess that you are a bit out of my age bracket. Yes, age is just a number, but for some reason, I seem to end up dating men a few years younger than myself. It may not be a deal breaker, but I am a straight shooter, and I just need to be honest about that.

You sound like a fun person. Not sure where to take this...

Melissa

---------- ---------- ----------

In his follow-up email, Marc had gone with flattery and satire, gently making sport of her wish-list of ideal qualities in a mate. Lisa laughed as she read.

Hi Melissa,

Yes, seeing your desired age range, I knew I was a little outside your bracket, but what else is new? I've always been outside one bracket or another. You just seem so natural and full of life that I said to myself, *Why not see just how flexible this delightful lady's bracket might be?* And now that I see there might be SOME flexibility,

I have no idea what to do next, either. I'm just flattered that such a young, attractive, humorous lady responded to my email.

Maybe that had something to do with the immaturity she's come across in this platoon of air-headed young bucks she's dated recently, with enough consumer debt among them to make Wall Street bankers salivate. She must be tired of these poor saps who THINK they've mastered the art of kissing but still have so much to learn; who are all too often dishonest, guarded, and insincere. She must be so ready for an older, more seasoned gentleman— a James Bond sort of guy—suave and quick-witted, who drives an Aston-Martin and vacations in Monte Carlo.

Of course, I don't know where exactly she'd find a guy like that, but I do know where she could find a guy with the heart of a poet and a damn good tool kit.
Marc

---------- ---------- ----------

Not hearing back in the next few days, Marc had pulled out his uncharacteristically self-promoting "Top Ten Reasons" list, which he'd mentioned to Lisa back when he first wrote it. Lisa knew that persistence was one of her Dad's strongest (and sometimes most annoying) assets, so it didn't surprise her that he wasn't giving up on this interesting, slightly younger woman. In the email, the strategy was to exemplify two desirable male traits on any Match-woman's wish list: creativity and confidence.

Hi again Melissa,
I love your user name, *allnatural*. And you are totally in MY preferred age bracket, so at least one of us is covered on that. I really think we could make each other laugh, just judging by your

profile, and by a few of your intentionally goofy photos. (The one with the wacky glasses that magnify your eyes is so sexy). I can imagine you and me running down an idyllic beach in Spain at sunset with your hair trailing in the breeze, pausing to sip Mojitos at a beach cabana. Then, at last...finger painting together, planting our easels and toes firmly in the warm sand, our fingers artfully, passionately tracing the intensity of our mutual desire. Doesn't that sound unbelievably romantic?

No? Well, what about this, then: ten pretty decent reasons to begin *obsessing* over me. On your mark, get set, obsess!

TOP 10 REASONS TO GRAB MARC BLAKE BEFORE SOMEONE ELSE DOES

1. He knows the euphoria of romance, and OMG does he want that feeling again—who doesn't?
2. He's funny in a divergent, quirky way but also has a soulful, romantic (not sad) side.
3. He's a widower, a professor and creative type who understands and respects the creativity in each of us. (Why does Jackson Pollock paint? Ask Marc).
4. He's taken care of his health; he's never once taken a prescription drug except antibiotics, which never work on a bad cold or flu anyway. He's probably walked, run, and pedaled the equivalent of a trip around the home planet, and in fact aspires to soon experience another long walk like Hadrian's Wall in England or the Camino de Santiago in Spain/France. He's looking for a playful, no-drama travel mate, know of anyone?
5. He does love to travel, and has studied and taught about cultures on six of the seven continents, (including occasional summer semesters with students in Asia and Central America)

but also loves being at home. He loves being with interesting people but also loves being in his own more or less comfortable skin.

6. He has very little debt, emotionally or financially. In fact, it's statistically correct to say he's "made it" financially. (Whew! wasn't always easy...)

7. Damn good Scrabble player, and chess player too. Loves to ride bikes. Not much of a skier, can't throw a javelin to save his soul.

8. He's sexy, especially in the growing season when he eats fruits & vegetables picked the same day from his own small garden and his good friends' large garden.

9. Being an Eagle Scout (after constant hounding by his dad) he's trustworthy, loyal, helpful, friendly, courteous, kind, obedient (?) cheerful, thrifty, brave, clean, and reverent (depending), with some understandable exceptions, lapses, holidays, and variances.

10. He's got Juice: if he didn't, how could he turn down an offer from a pro baseball team, survive decades in academia, have a long, delightful if now-poignant marriage; raise a wonderful daughter; write a bunch of boring articles for journals; travel to 30 different countries; and be in contact (?) with a remarkable woman like you?

So, come on, forget about those arrogant young knuckleheads who aren't worth your time, and *go for the gold*!

Cheers, and with fingers crossed,
Marc

```
  _o
 _ \<,
(_)/ (_)
```
---------- ---------- ----------

Melissa had apparently been impressed with this over-the-top Top Ten List. As Lisa read on, she thought, "Oh my god, maybe he's snowed her." Melissa's quick response to his list had been,

Wow, Marc.....
You should be a politician! Lol!
That was a pretty persuasive essay!
Let's meet for a cup of tea sometime before Christmas.
I work every weekend, and have Tuesdays and Wednesdays off.

Sensing possible victory, Marc responded the next day:

Here's a little dating game for you, based on Maya Angelou's poetic wisdom: She wrote that you can tell a lot about a person by the way she/he handles these three things: a rainy day, lost luggage, and tangled Christmas tree lights.
Ciao for now, Marc

```
  _o
 _ \<,
(_)/ (_)
```

---------- ---------- ----------

Melissa wrote:

I love Maya Angelou—I could listen to her recite the dictionary. Here are my responses:
Rainy days......great for cuddling, reading a book, or baking cookies.
Lost luggage.....depends where you are. Tahiti.....just get a new toothbrush....isn't that all you need to bring? Syria? Better find a bulletproof vest and construction helmet and stay inside.
Christmas tree lights......I am a master at untangling necklaces and lights.

What about you?

Have a great Christmas, and I hope we can meet early in the New Year.

---------- ---------- ----------

Marc wrote:

Melissa, somehow I knew you'd be a champ at dating games and also a fan of people like MA. Btw, have you ever heard Billy Collins recite his poetry? Check out *The Lanyard* on YouTube. It's a hoot!

Here's my own top-of-my-head list:

Rainy days: Cuddling, absolutely, but alas! Despite the drizzle, no one is available today...Still, rain is great for going to the museum, feeling good about the moisture your garden is getting; reading/writing/procrastinating; eating cookies (chocolate chip, yes, please: warm, chewy, and chocolaty on the inside and crunchy on the outside!)

Lost luggage: A lesson in Buddhist thinking. In Belize, I bought a pair of cheesy shorts and a T-shirt from Chinese sweat shops and called it good until my luggage finally showed up two days later. Eastern Shore of Virginia, I had picked up the wrong bag and, when I opened it, found a goofy, plaid 1950s style sports jacket. United Airlines sent a courier 3 hours one-way, so thank god the guy had his jacket in time for his presentation. In Kuala Lumpur... don't get me started. The luggage never came. I had to traipse into the Borneo rainforest with the wrong gear.

Untangling: Getting better, but with ten thumbs, I sometimes resort to wire cutters. Without a doubt, it would be a relief to have someone around who's a master.

Marc

---------- ---------- ----------

So, it was looking pretty good, Lisa concluded. Marc had then pressed forward with a light, flattering email titled, here's what I liked about our phone conversation:

Pretty much everything. In particular, I liked our back & forth bursts of passion about small, mundane topics like life and death, good and evil, past relationships, and aspirations. I like that you have definite opinions about what's right for you, and also what may be right for the world.

You seem considerate, unselfish, and down to earth. I hear strength and resilience in your voice.

I agree with most of your politics and I love your perspectives on the word "fun," which I agree seems kind of shallow sometimes. I really prefer contentedness or joie de vivre as benchmarks rather than fun.

The time whizzed past without either of us feeling awkward.

Thanks for saying you thought I was cute in my online photo. I can be cuter in person, although occasionally, before coffee or tea in the morning, I resemble a friendly but freaky Thing from Outer Space.

Anyway, mostly just to say hi,
Marc

```
   _o
 _ \<,
(_)/ (_)
```

---------- ---------- ----------

And that was the whole, ultimately fruitless correspondence. Lisa called over to Marc, "I see I got a shout-out as a wonderful daughter, thanks for that...But what happened? Did you meet Melissa in person, or not?"

"Yeah, we met," he answered over his shoulder as he troweled up a clump of weeds. "And...?"

"And I was a little too old, and was also informed, gently, that I didn't have the right chemistry for her."

"What about her?"

"...too young, I guess, and...she didn't have the right chemistry, either," he said, finally settling the score.

"You are such a geek! Your little strategies in these emails are so transparent." She kidded, "And do you really think women would be turned on by javelin throwers?"

"Depends on the woman, I guess," he answered, as if seriously. "But DU doesn't have a javelin team, so there's nowhere convenient to practice, really..."

A little embarrassed by his brashness in the emails, he rationalized, "The thing about these dating services is that your profile HAS to be puffed up with hype and self-promotion, because you're one little minnow in a busy, sometimes very cutthroat pond." (He felt smug about his secret. Although he hadn't heard directly from Kerrie, she probably had her phone on the table, flipping anxiously through a magazine, painting her toenails. It had only been a few days, after all. He decided to call her that evening or the next day. Maybe she'd invite him over....)

"We need to get to work, Casanova," Lisa said, in the get-it-done tone she'd probably picked up from her mother in the early days. "Let's start in the attic and work our way down, okay? What do you have stored up there?" Although her first priority was to help create a more organized and functional house in this stressful time, she also hoped they'd discover a box or trunk of artwork and jewelry that her mom had packed away before her illness, labeled, "For Lisa."

"I don't really remember what's up there. Let's go have a look..."

Father and daughter sat cross-legged on the attic floor, flattened cardboard boxes under them and a barrage of full boxes stacked in front of them. As they sliced through the packing tape on the first few boxes, the mission was clear: to see what to keep and what to take to Goodwill. Lisa couldn't resist blurting out, "I have something I want to tell you, Dad!" Her face was flushed with excitement, like a teenager who'd just been accepted to Stanford. "Brad and I are trying to have a baby!" The look they exchanged was a treasure chest of emotions. Tears of pride and joy came to his eyes. "It seems like the time is right for you, Lisa," he said, impulsively putting his arm around her shoulder.

"Yeah, I'm not getting any younger—the clock's ticking," she said, immediately sorry she'd chosen those words. "We're making decent money from the shop and from his accounting business. And we have lots of love to share..." Marc nodded emphatically. "I know that!"

Lisa and Brad seemed to treat each other with great respect and admiration, and they'd weathered a few money-related storms like skillful sailors. He knew the inter-racial aspect of their marriage was sometimes a challenge. Brad was African-American and proud of it. Though Lisa had high hopes that having a mixed-race child would work out fine, especially in liberal-leaning towns like Boulder and Louisville, she wasn't naïve about the overt and covert racism that prevailed not only in America, but all around the world. She didn't mention that concern to her dad.

"I'm so happy for you both!" he said, with an uncontrollable smile. "No pressure, but can you please make that happen within the next year or so?"

92

It was Marc's unsuccessful attempt at anything-goes humor, to demonstrate that he was unafraid of his own ticking clock. "Oh, you mean because you *think* you're going to die? Well, you're NOT going to!"

Here it comes, Marc thought: *The lecture.*

"I want to hear you say you're going to start taking the drugs!" Her forehead was wrinkled with emotion, and now the dam did burst, as never before. She shouted, "You idiot! If you die, I'm an orphan!" He was touched by her vulnerability and intensity and reached over to caress her neck and shoulder, a gesture she'd known since childhood. He was going to bring the discussion down a notch, but he went in the wrong direction. In his own mind, he was a counterculture desperado, tilting at society's morbidly neurotic fears. "I went to a seminar the other night, a session on how to die with dignity, *whenever* it happens."

With exaggerated calmness, he explained, "The presenter—a minister— gave us twenty-five index cards, asking us to each list the five closest people in our lives (and of course you're at the top of that list), the five most treasured possessions...five traits we like best about ourselves, five favorite activities, and five places we love the most. Then every time you showed symptoms that your personal world or your health was slipping, you had to lay down another one of the cards, until you had essentially accepted the loss of your favorite things and your own mortality." He met her gaze straight on, insisting, "It's not a bad idea to be prepared for whatever is coming."

"It's your *life*, Dad!" Lisa's face was still flushed, and now she was also annoyed by that nerdy, condescending voice of his. Maybe a small, subconscious part of him was testing her love. If so, it worked: now tears were streaming down Lisa's cheeks. She could probably have filled out each of those cards for her father, she knew him so well. Aren't people so endearing, so precious, because of the crazy little habits they have, and the connections they've made? She was terrified to the core that her father would—way too soon—become a collection of memories, habits, and routines, sortable on three-by-five-inch index cards. A cardboard castle, sucked unceremoniously back into the ocean.

"Daddy, don't talk this way," she begged, grabbing his arm.

They sat in frozen silence for a moment, aware that this was one of the most poignant moments they'd ever shared. A fly buzzed overhead between the ceiling studs, smashing futilely against the paper backing on the pink fiberglass insulation. Awkwardly, Marc dug deeper into a cardboard box, pulling out a worn leather and wool purse of Karen's, purchased from a craft guild in Costa Rica. They both recognized it but didn't comment. "You're right, I know that," he said, trying his best to calm her down. He wanted to honor her deep concern. Nodding his head, he opted for negotiation and made a proposal: "The world's foremost authority on this virus lives in San Francisco, and I'm going to make an appointment with him—go ask him face to face if *he* would take the drugs if it were him, even though he's probably not allowed to tell me that. Still, I'm going to try to get his honest opinion." He stood up and swatted the tiny trumpet-playing fly, wielding a carefully folded collector's item: a December 1963 issue of *Life* magazine— KENNEDY SHOT DEAD!

And fly-buzz silenced forever.

Nine

The Language of Soul

Lisa was relieved by Marc's proposal to see a specialist in San Francisco. This new agreement was a tangible action they could take as a team. She suggested, "Maybe you could go visit Uncle Rock and Ellen while you're in the area. They're only a few hours north of San Francisco." As an act of good faith, Marc told her he'd call the doctor's office sometime that week. "Call right now. What's his name?" She quickly searched her iPhone, found his number and handed the phone to her dad. "It's ringing."

Marc explained his situation to the receptionist and requested an appointment. "Dr. Pilcher is just back in town from traveling," the woman told him, "but I see he has a canceled appointment for next Wednesday." Marc had the phone on speaker mode so Lisa could hear, and he grabbed the appointment for six days later. With the call completed, he asked her, "Why don't you come with me? Like you said, we could drive up to see Rock and Ellie, and you haven't seen your cousin Sara since she and Greg got divorced, have you? She and Zak are living in Willits now, at least temporarily."

"I'd love to come—that would be fun. But one of our buyers is coming back from Thailand and we need to see what she found." She suggested they could keep in close touch by text and phone. Then she remembered an important thought she'd had that morning: "You know, Dad, they told you that only five percent survive this disease...but you know what? You're IN that percentile. You've always exercised and eaten well, avoided stress... You're the one in twenty who's going to beat this!" Marc nodded, wanting to acknowledge and support his daughter's pragmatism and insistence on hope. She had a good point.

Lisa lifted an old Maxwell House coffee can out of the box. "What's in there?" he asked, still a little numb from their heated discussion. She pulled tissue paper out of the heavy can.

"It's a bunch of coins...?"

"Lemme see," he said, bending closer to the coffee can and shaking it. He dimly remembered a can of coins Karen's father had saved—pocket change from various countries he'd visited in the Navy. But they were surprised and delighted to discover that these were not pocket change—not by any means! They were gold fifty-peso coins from Mexico, each of them an ounce of pure gold. "Wow!" she said, "It looks like there are ten or fifteen of them! What do you think they're worth?"

"We can look it up. I know the value of gold is down right now, but it was up near $1,300 an ounce not too long ago. Put them in your safe at the bank and sell them when their value's up again—usually when the stock market's down. Start an IRA account for your baby's education."

"Thanks, Dad!" Their eyes met, and he could see that he'd been temporarily forgiven for his delinquency, as long as he got on the stick, pronto. "So you didn't know the coins were up here?" she asked, in an excited voice. "No, not at all! Your Grampa may have given them to Karen before he died, and that was at the beginning of her dementia, so even she may not have really known what they were. Maybe she just packed them away mechanically with the rest of her stuff. Or maybe she thought they were just more pfennigs and shillings from Grampa's travels. Anyway, what a nice surprise, huh? From your Mom."

"Totally!" On an impulse, she handed one of the coins to her Dad. "Give this one to Zak, from Aunt Lisa, who he may not even remember since he was two when I last saw him."

"Nice idea!" It made him feel good to know he could gift this small treasure to Lisa and Brad—and to Zak, too. It would give him a tangible link to Lisa's child and also to his grand-nephew Zak, even if he *wasn't* around as they grew up. Each of them were mentioned in his will, but this small gift felt more immediate, especially if Lisa was right about his chances and he survived. "Grampa was a character, wasn't he? He did all right in the world—a second generation German immigrant, started his own successful hardware store. Your Mom loved him and feared him at the same time, I think."

"Yep," Lisa said, putting the coffee can in a place of honor on a small, dust-coated table. Then she went back to unpacking the box. They were each curious about what else they might find, and the sound of tissue paper being stuffed into plastic bags was the only sound for a few moments, until Lisa spoke—slowly and with perceptible anguish. "I'll never forget what Mom said, a few months before her CT scan: 'What's the name of that disease where you can't remember?'"

"Hmmm...That was a tell-tale question, wasn't it? I think we both were expecting a signal like that, because she'd been slipping for a while and we both knew it."

"I remember I was home after my internship in Ecuador and I saw that she was becoming distracted, distant. Frankly, I was hoping she wasn't becoming an alcoholic or opioid addict or something."

"She was reworking a manuscript that winter, which her agent had rejected. In fact, the agent called *me* to ask if there was something wrong with Karen. The work was disjointed, she said, and the characters one dimensional. She couldn't believe Karen had written it, and told me that there was no way she could sell it in its current state. What a scary feeling that must be, to feel your brain slipping away." Lisa, a glass-half-full person, liked to remember her mother's better moments, like the energy she'd poured into Lisa's Open School, where parents were a primary resource. She became a mentor to many students, including a gifted young man who'd later published a few well-respected books on American history. And she'd volunteered as the guiding light of several school plays, insisting that the students call themselves "the producers."

"I was so happy for Mom when *Earth Rising* became such a good seller. We knew how much work she'd put into that book, even though most people think books just *appear*, like Easter eggs."

"You and Mom were close, weren't you?"

"Sure, but it wasn't always easy. There were times when I guess she was tense about a deadline or something and she became kind of controlling. You remember that huge argument we had about me going to Santa Fe with Becky? She thought I was too young to leave home for a long weekend. You tried to stand up for me, but she was convinced I'd buy drugs, or whatever. I was so angry at her. I called cousin Sara in L.A. and she told me, 'Go for it!' So I did."

"You snuck out, leaving a note on the kitchen table. Oh boy, did that cause a tsunami!"

"Yep, but nothing bad happened to me, did it?"

Marc nodded, with a smile. "I think that was the moment when you asserted your right to be *you*. Everybody needs to have that turning point, that reaching-out moment, if they want life on their own terms. That's why I supported you. But you know, she was really just trying to make sure you were safe and didn't get into any trouble. She loved you so much!"

"You know, I believe Mom was somehow there for me about a year ago, in a very critical moment—even though she'd already been gone for more than a year. Brad and I were having kind of a hard time. We were really getting on each other's nerves and we'd both threatened to call it quits. I did a meditation where I asked Mom what she would do in my shoes, and it felt like she responded. She told me to go back and apologize to Brad, hug him and tell him I supported his job changes, and that I was there for him. It felt like that's what Mom would have done, if you and she had a bad fight."

"And what happened?"

"Oh, he apologized, too, and asked me if I was ashamed that he was just an accountant. He was so open and vulnerable, and lovable, and...So, things have been pretty good since then. I needed my Mom, and she was there, at least in a way." Lisa fought tears, looking away.

"I had a few similar thoughts the other day," Marc said, after a short silence. "What if spiritual energy really is transmitted? Maybe, when a call for help is heartfelt, urgent, and unselfish, a certain frequency stimulates support from your ancestors or other spiritual...advocates?"

"Sort of like spiritual crowd funding?"

"Exactly. Maybe the request has to have "soul" to be understood and received. The requester is in darkest depths, doesn't know which way to turn. He or she, speaks in a vulnerable, primal voice we might call the language of Soul."

"Is that language down-loadable? Might come in handy, for all of us," Lisa kidded.

Marc shifted from whimsy (or was it?) to straight talk. "There have been times when I've really, really missed her, too. I remember how supportive she was when I had problems with a colleague at DU. And so many times over the years she was a strong, quiet force in our partnership—always authentic, always level-headed, and always completely independent." He paused, then summarized, "We were both lucky to spend so many years with her." His eyes teared up as he said this.

"I think, of all my friends' parents, you and Mom treated each other the best."

"That's a beautiful thing to say."

Marc was thinking, *Lisa doesn't have much of a clue about her Mom's last years, because she was traveling so much for her internship and work. And I'm not going to share that part, either.* Truthfully, he wished he could just delete Karen's last year from his own memory. At the age of fifty-seven, she'd been diagnosed with early-onset dementia, a finding that Marc knew was coming. One of the first indicators was only mildly troubling: when she and Marc played Scrabble together (they'd always been an even match despite Marc's nerdy competitiveness) her words had shrank to four letters, then to a childlike three. She gradually lost her ability to speak descriptively, in stark contrast to her years and accomplishments as a writer. After she'd taken a fall, they'd done an MRI. Although her brain wasn't hemorrhaging, they found something even more ominous: some of the light green lobes on the images had faded to gray, like once-colorful coral reefs fade to a murky white. Diagnosis: dementia, untreatable. About that time, the repeated phrase, "all right, all right..." began to dominate her sentences. She could still receive and understand much of what others were saying, but she couldn't form sentences to transmit her own thoughts, not even on paper.

Fortunately, Marc and Karen had a good insurance policy through DU, but this kind of luck felt like a pebble in a bucket. Watching her rapid downward spiral had shifted Marc's basic understanding of life. He kept up with medical discoveries, reading about how the memories of a person with dementia or Alzheimer's are still *there*, just buried under gooey layers of plaque. This left Marc pondering a Zen-like question: What exactly *is* a memory, like a chemical photograph?

When Karen had walked into a new neighbor's house—maybe thinking the old neighbors still lived there—she'd scared the bejeezus out of the new neighbors, and Marc knew even a sub-normal life was no longer possible. After trying for a year to cope with Karen's steady decline, watching his class enrollment fall and his weight drop from the stress, he decided, with the doctor's and Lisa's input, to move her to the memory care floor at Golden Years retirement home, a large old Denver mansion where she was the youngest among an ever-changing cast of six or seven others. As a social scientist he couldn't help but wonder what happens to a demented person's self-esteem. Was it relief or pangs of sadness she felt when reminded that she'd written a bestseller and had a beautiful, loving daughter? Did she worry about what she was missing, sitting day after day on a community room couch in the Memory Care wing, staring at a huge flickering TV screen, or walking up and down the long hallway? Did she still have a sense of purpose, so critical for human happiness? Then it hit him: *Of course she has a purpose: showing her fellow patients and the rest of us how to be strong.*

Marc and Lisa sold Karen's rental property to finance three visits a week from professional caregivers. One of them lived on a little farm in Wheat Ridge and would take Karen to see the horses, even ride one of them while she still had the balance. Though Karen's spoken vocabulary had by that time slid to less than two dozen words, "horse" was still one of them.

Another time, after he signed her out of Memory Care to be in the 'real' world for an afternoon, they were in a Target store and he turned to see by her expression what she thought of a shirt he was holding. Presto, she'd magically vanished! He frantically hustled up and down the aisles to intercept her before she wandered out the front door, oblivious to traffic. He alerted store managers, then the huge mall's security police, finally standing at the interior exit from the store into the mall, imagining a mass of marching shoppers sweeping her along in the currents like a piece of driftwood. After ten or fifteen very long minutes, a security guard returned with an oblivious, smiling Karen by his side. As she and Marc walked out of the store—his hand firmly grasping hers—he wondered what had been going on in her mind as she wandered. Maybe something like, *Those swimsuit colors are so bright...Something about a red bicycle I'm riding but Mom is calling me...Look at that huge, stuffed-animal dog, standing next to those laughing kids. The dog seems so soft and happy and I want to pet him...I like the shape of that little building, made out of those plastic blocks. Legos. I want to touch it and feel all the raised dots...I feel something, is it hunger?*

After the mall incident, he realized he could never again leave her alone in a public space, not even to go to a public bathroom—a critical challenge if he'd been drinking coffee or a glass of beer. A few times he'd even resorted to taking her into a men's room with him, after first calling inside. Unconcerned about how they must look to others in the automatic, everyday world, he was determined to enhance her quality of life no matter what. When they held hands, he knew that hand like he knew his own name. Just after her crushing diagnosis, he'd asked her what he could do to help her through this darkest of tunnels. Hanging her head, then looking him right in the eye, she'd replied, "Just be there for me." He'd honored that request, protecting her as if she were the most precious, exotic, wounded bird in the world. In his world, she *was*.

As Marc and Lisa continued to sort boxes in the attic, he very attentively unwrapped a piece of pottery from Costa Rica. Lisa's eyes opened wide when she saw the pot: terra cotta with dark lizards and other symbols of strength and fertility painted on it.

"Chorotega pottery! We have some of that in the shop, it's very popular." Costa Rica was a special place for the Blake family. They'd spent several "working vacations" together in the small country, researching indigenous cultures and advocating for their rights. One group was descended from the Chorotega culture, which fled in the 6th century from southern Mexico where they'd endured slavery and sacrificial rituals. Though their language and much of their culture was lost, the pre-Columbian pottery techniques had survived, still exquisitely vibrant.

Lisa would never forget the epiphany she'd had in a biological reserve in central Costa Rica. "*Rara Avis,*" she said with a bright smile and a sigh. Her father nodded, knowingly. The family's week-long adventure in this high elevation reserve north of San Jose had transformed all three of them. They'd stayed in a two-room rustic casita without power—only kerosene lamps for light—absorbing the nocturnal sounds of cicadas, tree frogs, owls and howler monkeys as they performed an interwoven symphony, each animal occupying its own unique audial niche: "taca, taca, taca...sissit, sissit," like a smoothly running printing press.

By the third day, Lisa began to understand things at a gut level that she'd somehow forgotten, or never known. The rainforest slowed her metabolism down to the speed of life, filling her lungs with the planet's very purest air. Her skin began to glow and there was an awestruck involuntary smile on her face. "It felt like the rainforest was painting itself. The red, green, yellow, and turquoise of a toucan, the dark purple of a morphos butterfly, the dappled red of a stained glass palm." Lisa was transported as she recalled the forest's damp trails, thick with pheromones and fragrances that communicated invitations, warnings and celebrations throughout the ecosystem.

"Remember the cuckoo clock?" Marc asked, smiling.

"Of course I do!" She'd awakened early one morning to the sound of a cuckoo clock and counted the hours as she slowly woke up. Only when the calls reached thirteen and fourteen did she realize it was literally a cuckoo *bird* calling, right outside the cabin. That call was a kind of life-alarm, rousing her from an addictive American Dream that made crazy seem normal. She'd realized, more deeply than ever before, that humans need to absorb nature's colors and cries of distress into their hearts, or face bitter existential regret as life continues to decline.

Far from being a tourist mecca, the reserve's access was limited to a few biologists, birders, and hardy vacationers willing to brave the muddy, three-hour trip by tractor-drawn wagon that yanked passengers over boulders, some the size of blue-ribbon pumpkins. Visitors clung to the wagon's side rails, standing up and bending their knees to become human shock absorbers—the women folding their arms tightly across their breasts and the men wishing they'd worn athletic supporters.

But what a payoff! Within minutes of reaching the summit, the guide had pointed out a Strawberry Poison Dart frog in the foliage, his bright red skin so toxic that no predator would ever mess with him. He'd probably die of old age, surrounded by a harem attracted to his brightness! A little further up the trail, the guide pointed to a boa constrictor wrapped around the trunk of a large bush, relying on camouflage and evolved musculature for protection. But the most amazing show of all was watching the commerce of the leafcutter ant—provider of sunlight, soil and protein for their home territory. Climbing in service formation high into the canopy, the ant colonies prune tons of leaves, allowing sunlight to reach the forest floor. Then the colony's millions of workers carry the leaf fragments back to underground fungus gardens, like a parade of surfers toting bright green surfboards. The leafy compost nurtures fungus, the ants' primary food source, and ultimately, deposits rich soil to replace what the trees have used.

"Why can't human life be as interconnected and purposeful as ant life?" Lisa had asked.

"Human industry is infantile. We've only had hundreds of thousands of years, but 160 million for the ants."

Marc and Lisa finished their work for the day, scheduling more time early the following week so the house would be clean and organized when Marc got back from California. "Do you have time to start a game of chess before I go home?" she asked, in a far better mood than when she arrived. Chess was something they'd done together for years, with completely different strategies. He knew every gambit and every endgame, while she played spontaneously, winging it from start to finish. And sometimes she won.

"No, sorry, I have softball practice tonight," he answered, feeling a little inconvenienced by his coaching responsibilities. But then remembering how good it felt to let everything else go and just inhabit the diamond like a schoolkid. He loved the camaraderie, the sound of the ball hitting the bat, and the possibility of putting together a championship team this season.

"Well, then, see you Monday at 9, okay?" He watched her get into her car, so grateful she'd come. "*Not a bad day's take for her! She not only achieved her goal about the drugs, she also carried fifteen- or twenty-thousand in gold out the door.*" He thought of Lisa, asking her mother for advice even after Karen was gone. He should have told her that he sometimes reached out to Karen, too.

Ten

Karen's Waltz

There were two events in Marc's adult life when the universe had opened up, gifting him eternity and profound emptiness at the same time: Lisa's birth and Karen's death. Now, with his health a huge question mark, he was trying to prepare himself, if necessary, for a third event in the series: his own death. It was true that he didn't have pain or discomfort at that moment, but the prognosis wasn't promising.

In high school, a phrase from Albert Camus' *The Stranger* had completely amazed him: The book's protagonist laid his heart open for the first time to the benign indifference of the universe. It was the word 'benign' that opened the door just a crack, supporting his belief that the universe can be trusted, that it knows the way. We're welcome to come along without fear and we don't have to have all the answers, either. We just have to ride the currents as skillfully and joyfully as possible.

Karen and Marc had attended natural childbirth classes for a few months and thought they were well-prepared for bringing a new life into the world. Not even close! "Remember, breathe, breathe, breathe, then exhale," Marc coached, leaning over a Karen he'd never seen before, panting like a marathoner: groaning, growling, laughing and cussing. Of course, everyone has seen the birth of a bison or wolf pup on nature shows—but when a man witnesses a tiny human bursting into the world, especially one he's fathered, his whole life shifts. Suddenly he understands at a gut-level that the universe *does* know the way! That all the disappointments and celebrations are small peanuts compared with this one preposterous, mind-blowing event.

"You did it, you beautiful woman!" Marc said, kissing Karen's salty cheek and wiping the tears from his own face. In a state of shock, both waited for the doctor to bring Lisa to her mother's breast. If there are angels, this is when they shine through a mother's ecstatic face. Flooded with peak-moment hormones, Karen and Marc felt every emotion all at once: relief, pride, outrage, joy, and giddiness. After months of hard work and with help from the universe, mother, daughter, father had produced a living, miraculous masterpiece.

Years later, a little tarnished and dinged-up but steady on his feet, Marc once again saw and felt the Power of the universe. He'd held up pretty well during Karen's illness—loving her no less but exhausted by her poignant decline. Now he sat with Karen at another sacred crossing. In her last waning days, life seemed to compress twenty-four years into each shimmering moment.

The day after she was gone, he wrote down in amazement what had just happened:

> Karen, my love, it was such a mind-opening, soul-stretching honor to be with you as you took your last breath yesterday. You hadn't spoken in years and you couldn't say good-bye out loud, but we found a way to do it, didn't we? Thank you so much for your courage!
>
> Even though I always chattered as if you understood, I wasn't sure you did. But I never asked you, "Squeeze my hand if you understand," I just went with tone of voice, knowing you'd get some of it. A few years into your long residency in Memory Care, just after we'd gone to see the delightful movie *Cinderella*, the heavy security door opened slowly and I announced to the

caregiver, "We're back!" I gently handed you off so he could walk you down to dinner.

"I love you," I said in a deliberately upbeat tone, kissing you on the lips and giving your arm a squeeze. With a stammer both heroic and poignant, you spoke your very last words to me: "I, I love you too."

Then you went completely silent for the rest of your life—four more years of walking resolutely up and down the long hallway, studying each carpentered detail on the railing, each little smudge on the wall. You were always the artist, visually in sync with geometric patterns and accidental art. In fact, you unintentionally became a professional when your brightly-colored abstracts from the Tuesday afternoon painting class went to the national Alzheimer fund raiser, and sold! (To Kai and May, who still exhibit the art on their wall). On my twice-weekly visits, I had a mission: to get you out of the building and into the sun. Find beautiful places where children were playing, and have quiet little picnics. Or go to the mall and eat ice cream. (What a pair we made!)

Another adventure was your silent but steamy cat fight with Carol for the attentions of Don, a smiley-faced old guy under a cowboy hat. That sweetly comical feud was resolved in fairly short order when Don disappeared like a wisp of smoke. But you and Carol became buddies for about a year before she too died in her sleep. Each of these dear but very temporary friends had valiantly wrestled what I call nature's dirtiest trick: the slow decline of once-vibrant humans—like juicy, fragrant peaches collapsing into something almost unrecognizable.

At least you missed the grisliest of the decade's news. I remember telling you gleefully that we were going to have the first woman President! Not long after that you must have heard me grumble, "Trump," but it wasn't your responsibility to worry. You'd told me bravely right after the diagnosis, "It is what it is," and you carried that Zen-like banner all the way to the end. You would help the staff fold laundry, escort wheel-chaired compatriots, and gratefully share the books I brought, collections of Best Instagram Photos and brilliant National Geographic images. You loved it when Lisa was home and spent time with you and when your old friends dropped by!

Your final descent was all too familiar. I knew it from my father's last days and later, my mother's: the stumble, then the collapse. The oxygen tubes and continuous mechanical drumming of the machine's bellows. Mucous pooling in the throat, and the lungs gamely soldiering on, though really designed for half a century at most. Then Hospice-prescribed morphine, every two hours. Your time had come. We had maybe seven days left, so we had to get busy. I was hopeful you would have a peaceful departure, you sure as hell deserved it. I couldn't decide if I should tell you that you were dying, but then you told me by putting your wrist in front of your mouth when I offered a spoonful of yogurt. You'd somehow booked your ticket, and I wanted, more than ever, to honor that. I wanted to be a fear-slayer, for both you and me.

I focused on what was still available to us: music. Like Mr. Green Jeans on *Captain Kangaroo*, I'd pop in as the music guy, equipped with iPad, Bluetooth speaker and a whole ensemble of musicians-in-a-phone. Van the Man Morrison opened the concert that first day, delivering his gutsy, primal anthem, *Into the Mystic*. Then Sting, Mr. Cool Guy, offered *Fields of Gold* as a blessing. We held hands, alternating squeezes and caresses, your eyes sparkling from the morphine, the extra oxygen, the fasting, and our twenty-four years together. Debussy wafted *Prelude to the Afternoon of a Faun*, and Chopin followed with *Nocturne in E Minor*, one of the most delicately sublime pieces of music ever written. I remember commenting, "Wasn't that beautiful?" and then being overcome by a shudder of helpless, humble tears. In this wide-open, peak moment we were savoring the beauty that life offers, choosing to ignore the certainty your bed would soon be empty. We were conspirators, and the only reality that mattered was *right now*. Each moment, each song, began to feel like a precious slice of eternity. (When experiences are so heightened, does the universe actually slow down for us?)

Without a doubt, your favorite song of all was the swaying, unpretentious *Margaret's Waltz*, flowing out of Bryan Sutton's acoustic guitar like a hand-held bouquet of wildflowers. If anyone else had been in the room, they might have thought we were getting ready to arm wrestle, but no, just slow-dancing the waltz with arms and hands rather than legs and feet. It felt like you and I were so small and the ocean so outrageously vast!

A few days later, December 15, your fever had come back. You looked god-awful when I walked in. With a cool washcloth on your forehead, you gazed unblinkingly, crook-necked, at something I couldn't see, up toward the ceiling. Was there some presence hovering over us? Your own soul, separating and rising away? Your mouth gaped open and your breathing was desperate. I'm not sure you even knew I was there, until I put on *Margaret's Waltz*— loud enough to drown out the oxygen machine. Your breathing suddenly relaxed. Maybe those rich bass notes had settled into your being. Come to think of it, maybe we'd been rehearsing for this very moment. Your leg shifted one last time ("kicking the bucket," I suppose) and your breathing was fading away, I watched it go. As the waltz ended, and without further ado, you hitched a ride on our last song together—the playful Fleetwood Mac tune, *Never Going Back Again*.

After whispering a fervent prayer I stumbled in shock into the hallway and told a caregiver that you'd just passed. I wanted her to make sure, but I do wish I'd stayed with you a little longer in that moment of transition. You marvelously mischievous lady! I learned so much from you in our life together! Your heroic efforts and exploits will never be forgotten, I promise. I'll keep a candle lit for you for in the next week, and in my heart forever.

Good-bye, Karen Amelia! I'll always be here if you need me.

Marc.

Eleven

In Spite of Everything

Rocket's phone rang, and without looking he knew who it was. "Hey Rocket Man," came Marc's familiar voice, very similar to his own. "How you doin'? I'm within striking distance now. After my doctor's appointment yesterday, I spent the afternoon and evening with Peter Klein walking around the Japanese Gardens, then grabbing dinner. You remember Peter, don't you?"

"Yeah, sure. So what's up?"

"Well, I'm looking forward to seeing you guys! I'll be in Willits by early evening if there isn't much traffic...and if that works for you."

"Absolutely, we'll be here, counting all our money. Great to hear your voice, buddy, how'd your appointment go?"

"Well, it's hard to figure out exactly *what* I heard," Marc said with a laugh. "He was a San Francisco kind of a guy, you know, tellin' it like it is. He listed the known side effects of my prescriptions, and they really don't sound like much fun: fatigue, disorientation, incontinence, and possibly the deadly droops—impotence—so, the whole nine yards."

"Bummer," Rocket said, in a low growl, the disease square in the crosshairs of his imaginary hunting rifle.

"I asked him, if he was in my shoes, would he take the drugs? I call one of them *Fuckitol.*" Both laughed at the cynical humor. "It turns out the doctor has *cancer* and he's trying to decide if he'll do chemo or not. Not the usual comment from a doctor, is it? He told me—emphatically off the record—that if he were me, he'd try the drugs and see whether they were improving his vital signs, and how severe the side effects were. Then make up his own mind about whether to continue. They'll have the results of another blood test in about 10 days to compare with the current levels."

"So, you've started taking the drugs. How are they working so far?"

"Well, I just started yesterday, Rock, so I don't really know yet." Then with a lame attempt at humor he added, "I know that I haven't peed in my... ooops, wait a second..." Rocket ignored the comment, well aware of the say-anything humor the brothers had staged over the years.

Abruptly, Rocket asked, "You think you're ready to jump out of an airplane?"

"Huh?" Marc responded, not sure where that particular joke was going. "My good friend John is this rich dude. Well, you met him last year when you and Kai were here. He's talked me into skydiving next week, from about 12,000 feet up." Rocket didn't say that he and John had planned the tandem-style skydiving event for the two brothers to have some fun together, like when they were kids—even though Ellen was concerned it might tire Marc out.

"And you want ME to do that? Jump two miles onto hard ground?"

"Yeah, why not? It'll be fun. And the ground's not that hard at the drop zone, according to John. It's got sand and marsh grass as a cushion."

"Small comfort. Well, I don't know anything about it, for one thing. Don't I have to be certified to jump?"

"No, you'll have a certified skydiving master strapped to your back. Not a problem. You don't have to tell me right now, but think about it!"

"I'll think about it.... Maybe I could skip the dying part and go directly to dead." Rocket mentally reached for some way to shoo death away from his brother, as if he were sweeping a black widow spider out of a bed. "Those meds will do the trick, I know it, even if you might have some crappy side effects."

"Well, look, Rock," Marc said, abruptly changing the subject: "I do know this: I'm going to hang out with Peter this afternoon, then head up to *Willitopia* to be with you guys."

"...'Gateway to the Redwoods,'" Rocket added, echoing a local slogan. "I should be there by seven or eight at the latest, depending on traffic."

"After Santa Rosa traffic, it's a piece of cake," Then looking at his watch, he told Marc, "I've got things to do, big guy, so I'll look forward to seeing you tonight."

"Sounds good, don't start any trouble, crazy man. And hey, could we minimize the talk about diseases and drugs and side effects? I'm already sick of it."

"10-4, copy that." Rocket had first uttered 'code words' like these with Marc almost sixty years earlier, maybe after watching *Sky King* on a first-generation television set. Or while climbing over beaver-felled tree trunks at the swamp next to their housing development in the suburbs of Cleveland. Or riding bikes downtown to get baseball cards and candy, or winging baseballs to each other in the vacant lot just down the street.

As Marc wound up the driveway to Rocket's and Ellen's cabin, he drove past a huge garden plot of multicolored snapdragons, a few just coming into blossom. In the dusk, the pinks were magenta and the yellows gold, but it was the white flowers that stood out like iridescent little lanterns. The place was impressively well maintained—no dead cars, no broken furniture, and not many weeds in the landscape, either. He thought, this looks like a rural version of Kai's and his parents' Japanese garden—always neat and beautiful.

Then, around a bend in the long driveway Marc saw John's house, completed! Bam! He couldn't believe how awesome the new house looked—the landscape fully leafed-out and colorful even in the twilight. And his own little brother had helped build it! As the last sun of the day filtered through the trees on the little homestead, he could just make out a few animals grazing in the pasture—llamas or alpacas, it looked like. When he'd visited the previous year, John's house was just a motley collection of poured concrete walls and huge mounds of dirt. Now the project was a done deal, tucked neatly into a gentle rise in the land. The most unique feature of the house was a short tower with a domed ceiling, poking through the tiled roof. Rocket had told Marc what a bear that room was to build—lots of cutting and fitting—but that it had come out great. John's 'man cave' was complete with sunny pastel walls, sturdy Scandinavian furniture and a walk-in closet. According to Rocket, the acoustics under the dome were incredible, and John, who played clarinet for a hobby, liked to riff on jazz tunes in the room.

The outside of the house featured terraces, off both the main floor and the lower level, enabling access to a courtyard where John liked to read and make phone calls. As Marc pulled into his brother's parking area, he recalled that John's house was a platinum-certified LEED project, a pinnacle of efficiency.

Rock's and Ellie's house looked pretty much the same as the previous year, although the tiny barn and studio space had been painted a tidy-looking, dark shade of red. On the other side of the barn sat the large chicken yard where the free-range, organically-raised hens were still pecking and grumbling, a few of them strutting up the ramp into their roost for the night. Widget and Willie—the laid-back household dogs—were lying on cushions on the front porch—just too comfortable to get up, let alone bark. But their carrot-shaped white tails batted back and forth in greeting, and finally one ambled over for a sniff.

Without knocking, Marc walked in, immediately seeing the whole crew sitting at the dinner table playing Scrabble, light jazz music wafting in the background. "Hey, mister!" Rocket said. "We didn't hear you come up!" The brothers executed the secret handshake followed by an extended bear hug and back-tapping. "I'm driving a rented Prius and it was in the electric mode, so it was pretty quiet. I wanted to test-drive a Tesla but they were all taken."

"Our neighbor John has a Tesla," Ellen commented, with a welcoming smile. "Hi Ellie! Great to see you! And you too, Sara...you're both looking great!" Marc hadn't seen Sara and Zak for a few years. "Zak, you remember Uncle Marc?" Rocket asked. "He's the one who should teach us how to play Scrabble. He's a champion!"

"Well, I bet Zak is too," Marc said, putting one hand on Zak's shoulder while giving Ellie a quick hug. He quickly scanned the board and saw an assortment of longer words, with three-letter ones sprinkled in. "Who made 'perplexed?'" he asked Zak, impressed with its score total.

"Zak and I made the 'per' part," Sara said, coming around the table to hug Marc, "and Mom added the 'plexed.'" Marc's niece gave him a warm hug and kiss on the cheek. "You're prettier than ever," Marc told her. "Thank you," she said. Then impishly, "So are you."

"Thank you, I *feel* pretty." Zak looked up at him saying, "You're not as pretty as my Mom," just making sure this guy didn't have any illusions.

"Well, I know that much..." He looked around the circle at his family. "Hey, I don't want to interrupt your game..."

"Oh, we're just about done," Ellen said. "Do you want a cup of tea or lemonade?"

As the rediscovered uncle sat at the table sipping his tea, Zak grilled him. "What's your best Scrabble word, ever?"

"I did pretty well with the word 'quartzite'" in one tournament. I grabbed two triple word scores at the same time by building quartzite around the word 'art.'" He pointed out the red squares. "See? Here, and here: 350 points for that word."

"Wow, that's a lot," Zak said, though clearly without a clue. Establishing a rapport with the boy, Marc said, "Most words that have a 'q' also have a 'u,' right after them, you know that? Those two letters really like each other. But there are a few Q words that don't need the u..." The banter was clipped short as Ellen told Marc, business-like, "We have some work to do. You want to help me make up your bed?" She wanted Marc to have his own space for whenever he was tired. "Not really, but I will. Let's see, the last time I was here I stayed in the tree house."

"Sorry, no vacancy," Sara said, then turning to Zak. "But I'll tell you what, little man, we have to get you over to your magic tree house before it gets totally dark, and get you into bed."

"And close the door in the chicken yard, right?" Zak added, taking his new chicken yard assignment very seriously. "It sounds like you must be the Chicken Chief," Marc observed. As Sara steered him out the door, Zak politely recited, "Well, good night everybody. I'll bring the eggs for breakfast. See you then!"

Sara turned her cell phone flashlight on so Zak could see the gate into the chicken yard. "There's still one hen that hasn't gone in," he called over his shoulder. "Just gently herd her up the ramp." With an inner laugh, she watched the hen resist. Zak's legs were bent and his arms outstretched as he tried to scoot the hen along, but the bird questioned his authority, squawking at him with ruffled feathers. Then the portly hen turned to peck at the boy's hands, flapping her wings for emphasis. Finally she grudgingly agreed to go up the ramp into the roost and okay, lay another egg. (Always more work...) Zak closed the dormitory door and walked back toward his mom.

As she flipped the light switch and climbed the circular stairway through neatly pruned tree branches, Zak was safely right in front of her. She gave him the usual warning, "If you get too close to the railing on the deck, you'll be grounded for a whole month!" The wrought iron railing was securely bolted onto the hardwood deck and she knew it wasn't really any more dangerous than their old LA condo, but still, Zak was one thing in her life she *treasured*. She loved what living in a tree house and the homestead in general were doing for him. He seemed much surer of himself—less whiny, less dependent on his iPad and video games.

"All right, you can play one of your games for a while and I'm going to call my friend Jasmine in Los Angeles, but we have a big day tomorrow, so you have to get some sleep, okay? Turn off the lights in a few minutes. Sweet dreams, cowboy." At the bottom of the staircase, she phoned her friend for a quick catch-up. She missed having her confidante right down the block. "Hey girlfriend," she began, picturing Jasmine in her cushy little condo. She confided, "Life seems so *vivid* right now. It's as if I'm waking up from a long dream filled with little challenges. There are so many new possibilities—and maybe traps—like with the guy I told you about, John."

"It sounds like you really like the guy."

"Well, I do want changes in my life...but I'm kind of afraid of losing control. John is interesting, no doubt, but does he value me for who I am, or just how I look?"

"How old is he?"

"He's older than me and he's got his own software business, and he's a really nice-lookin' guy...but would he have to be in charge, if we got together?"

"I know the feeling. You want your independence *and* your prince, right?"

"I don't want another Greg, that's for damn sure. And, as you know, I'm looking for a job, but I'm wondering if architecture is really the right profession for me. Do I have the right aptitude or was it just something I chose after high school because it seemed cool? Can I really imagine myself sitting at a computer every day and working with clients—some of them all full of themselves and grumpy?"

"I don't know, it might be less stressful than having to get dressed up like a black Barbie Doll, in my case, and be ordered around...Okay, a little more...seductive, even naughty...Now the profile..."

The two women talked for a few more minutes, and Sara felt much more grounded after they hung up, but she still felt unsettled enough to want to connect with her mom, too. She felt anxiety about her uncle's illness. She'd always admired Marc—a guy similar in many ways to her dad, but less impulsive and maybe less...goofy. Marc had always seemed so balanced and wise, although he *could* be kind of a know-it-all sometimes, too. On the other hand, here was a man who'd known early on what he wanted to do with his life, and she now had great respect for that. She wanted to get his thoughts about her future, too, but she didn't want to bug him. He seemed healthy enough, but she'd heard the disease might be increasingly severe.

Going back to the house she noticed the light on in the workshop and heard her dad and uncle laughing. Maybe this *would* be the time to talk with her mom. Closing the front door of the house behind her, she told her Mom, "I got him tucked in."

"That's great," Ellen said, looking up from a seed catalog. "Well, the men went over to see the totems and 'shoot the shit.' They seem like a couple of teenage boys tonight."

"Buddies for life. We should let them have their fun. Would you have a few minutes to talk?"

"Sure," Ellen said, sensing weighty topics on her daughter's mind. She'd been hoping her girl would open up to her a little more. Although their relationship had sometimes been volatile over the years, the bond was strong.

"I wanted to apologize for my little tantrum about the cake. I...."

"No apology necessary." Sara smiled at her mom. "I did think you were a little severe with Zak, though—he's just a typical six-year-old, you know. But I understand—and I think it's great that you expressed your feelings rather than holding them in."

Ellen thought with amusement, *I feel like I'm being lectured to...And talk about holding things in*...Still, she smiled back at Sara and said, "Yeah, I guess I needed to unload a little." She waited for Sara to open the conversation.

"Can I ask that this conversation be confidential?"

"Of course," her mother said, intrigued by the idea of a mother/daughter *tete a tete.*

"I love Dad, but sometimes he's a little bit...dense. So I want this to be between you and me."

"So, I'm not dense?"

"Well, sometimes. But I guess you guys are the best I can do at this point." They both laughed, wordlessly entering a safe, comfortable zone. Sitting cross-legged on the couch, Sara jumped in: "I just don't know what to do about John."

Ellen was relieved that the discussion would be girl talk, and mentally repositioned herself as a sage confidante, always ready to dispense female wisdom-of-the-ages. "It's not a bad situation to be in, is it? You have a very interested, very confident 'suitor,' and it's your move now, to express whether or not *you're* interested. Frankly...it seems like you've been a little...well...*bitchy* toward him." Ellen laughed awkwardly, hoping her frankness wasn't inflammatory. "Do you agree?" She was relieved when her daughter also laughed slightly. "I guess." Trying to get literally to the heart of the matter, the mother asked, "Do you have...feelings for him?" The directness of the question bumped Sara off balance. As Ellen knew, it was her daughter's nature to guard her privacy, but here she was, sitting on the couch, vulnerably asking for advice. "I do like him...I guess I'm trying to figure out *how much*. But he just seems to be pushing and pushing."

"You want him to slow down," Ellen said, not daring to report that he'd already announced to her and Rocket that he planned to *marry* her. "Exactly! There's a lot going on in my head right now. I just want to figure out what's next for me, and here's this guy, older than me—all set up and so sure of himself, who just won't let me alone."

"I don't know, they talk about 'love at first sight', but I'm not sure that's a very common occurrence, really—especially if it's the *real thing*. Your Dad and I had a two-year gap after college before he came to California. But maybe John just feels an honest connection. Maybe he just really knows what he wants, and that's *you*." There was a comfortable silence as Sara processed this flattering and secretly thrilling notion. "So you think I should tell him, maybe sort of indirectly, that I *am* interested, but that I don't want to hurry into anything right now?"

Ellen nodded, trying to guide Sara toward her own decision. "Yes, if it was me, I'd want to just be direct: 'I'm interested but I need you to slow down.'" She looked up at her unusually attentive daughter, hoping the maternal encouragement was useful. "Spend some time with him, joke around a little but let him know you're his equal. Be a friend first, then see how you feel."

"What if he tries to kiss me?" Sara blurted, which seemed to Ellen like a question an eighth grader might ask. But she knew what her daughter meant. "Hold your own sense of power. Wait for the right moment. But maybe have the courtesy to let him feel a sense of hope...if it's there. After all, if this potential romance is 'destined' to go anywhere, both of your hearts will have to be open so the feeling can *blossom*. Am I making any sense?" Ellen wondered if she sounded too much like an old-fashioned TV mom—Donna Reed or Carol Brady. And did her suggestion to protect John's feelings reveal a biased thumbs-up for John?

"Yes, you're making sense. You're helping me sort things out in my own head. What about the skydiving thing? What should I do about that? He wants me to jump with him in tandem and it just feels kind of...constricting." Ellen took a guess, asking carefully, "Are you afraid that if you let yourself go, you'll be kind of falling, in a couple of different ways?"

"Oh, you mean mutual trust...in this together...let's go get married, all that?" Sara's voice began to have a different tone, and her mother sensed the possible reappearance of the *edgy* Sara. The mother shrugged. "No, I just mean letting your guard down and literally *falling* in love. Am I getting the feeling you *don't* want to go there?"

"I don't know. But I suppose I should do the jump, since he's a certified jumper and everything." Sara shrugged. "I mean, he's a pilot with his own plane..."

"So, do the jump, but have the direct conversation first." Now Ellen felt like she'd just rolled a strike—she could almost hear the thundering pins. "Okay, thanks Mom!" Now the *angelic* Sara sat up straighter and summed up in a lighter tone, "I do like him. I just want to make sure he knows who he's dealing with."

"Good for you!" It seemed the two confidantes had wrapped up Sara's dilemma in short order and Ellen couldn't resist bubbling a little. "I love you, sweet pea." "I love you too, Mom. In spite of everything." Her devilish smile reminded Ellen of Rocket.

Meanwhile, another heart-to-heart talk was playing out between the two brothers. Their indivisible sixty-three-year bond was still peppered with sibling teasing and sparring. They'd always sharpened each other's skills, like two fox pups wrestling in tall grass. They went into Rocket's studio with a few beers and two dogs at their feet, Marc admiring the craftsmanship of a carved oak and copper sign over the threshold: *Not All Who Wander Are Lost.*" The studio had double-wide barn doors with antique hinges and latches, enabling large projects like Rocket's totems to fit into the shop. One of the massive poles was perched dramatically on Rocket's 15-foot-long workbench, propped up at one end by a sturdy antique steel jack. Though the studio's main source of heat in winter was hot water radiators from solar panels on the barn roof, there was also a classic wood burning stove at the far end of the shop for burning scraps as well as diced-up fallen branches from the property. Leaving dead brush on the forested ground was an invitation for fire—a threat that lurked in the dark shadows of hell.

The workshop's floor was brick, with sawdust tightly packed into the seams from Rocket's sweepings and footsteps. The workbench was lit by adjustable track lighting, trained on an almost completed Indian figure. "This is a Pomo Indian woman, a basket maker," Rocket explained as his brother bent closer to see the fine detail of the carving.

"It's beautiful!" Marc said, giving his brother's shoulder a squeeze. "A *lot* of work has gone into this project, hasn't it?"

"Yeah, a lot more work than $1,500 usually buys," he confided, tapping on the huge trunk.

"Fifteen hundred for one, or for both?" Rocket answered, "Fifteen hundred apiece, but I consider this project kind of a community service." It was obvious to Marc that Rocket had earned far more than money: the real rewards were creative satisfaction, the civic feeling, and the ongoing mastery of his craft. The pole had a diameter of about sixteen inches and had been planed and sanded as smooth as a table top. Each figure sprang to life beneath Rocket's chisels, razor-sharp carving knives and creative focus. Here a mountain lion's lanky body, here a great horned owl's rounded head and beak, there a humpback whale.

Pointing at his creation, Rocket continued, "The basket weaver's status in the group was—and is—powerful because the energy of the living environment flows through her into the baskets." Rocket picked up a narrow-bladed chisel and mallet to demonstrate. "The Pomo were traditionally acorn eaters and salmon fishers, but they also ate small game, wild greens, mushrooms, even grasshoppers," he said, tapping his mallet gently on the chisel. Marc loved how his brother's work was interlinked with the work of the Pomo artisans. Energy that flowed through their baskets—adorned with willow shoots, woodpecker feathers, and shells—had its origins in Pomo cultural traits and beliefs, then was expressed by Rocket's own hands, and finally felt by viewers of the totems.

Rocket suggested, "When we go over to tour John's house, let's ask him to show you the baskets he bought from a Pomo woman who still uses traditional techniques."

"This cultural story you are telling in the totems reminds me of a beautiful nature story I've told in a class or two, about the forests further up the Northwest coast, literally built by salmon. Fingerlings no bigger than fat pencils are born upstream in the forests, then migrate into the ocean for three to six years where they grow into mature fish weighing up to sixty pounds. When they return to their birthplaces their bright silver scales turn deep red and purple. After their chosen mates dig out a little hole, the females bury their eggs, then quickly die, leaving behind all the rich nutrients they've amassed."

"Nice."

"Black bears, insects, fungi and plants distribute those nutrients, and four-fifths of the nitrogen in the forest was shown by research to have come from the ocean." Rocket said, "There's so much magic that goes on in the natural world that we're clueless about. I love thinking about cycles like that!"

The conversation fell silent as Rocket deftly sharpened the basket maker's facial features, then recalled, "Ellen and I got involved in a political skirmish between Caltrans and The Coyote Valley Band of Pomo Indians a few years ago. As you know, they've now completed a six-mile bypass around Willits, but in the process they destroyed Pomo cultural sites in Little Lake Valley, along with mature oak woodlands and the headwaters of salmon and steelhead habitat. We came close to shutting the project down by protesting and hellraising, but a Federal Judge rammed the project through."

"You were always such a trouble maker."

"So were you! I was so proud of you when you decided to be a conscientious objector rather than go to Vietnam. That volunteer experience in Africa really launched your career, didn't it?"

"Yeah, I guess it did. And you were a pretty ballsy draft dodger yourself," the younger brother said, remembering that Rock had intentionally ruptured an eardrum to avoid being drafted. If a person talked with their back to Rocket, he sometimes didn't hear. "Does your hearing deficit piss you off sometimes?"

"Naa. Sometimes it's an advantage, like when Ellen is telling me to clean the rings in the bathtub..." The brothers laughed, having no words to express their mutual admiration. Although Rocket and Ellen seldom made time to watch TV, they'd once turned on *60 Minutes* and caught the interview with Marc, just by accident. It had been a big moment for all of them! Though Marc hadn't made a big deal out of it, Rocket had told everyone in town about his super-intelligent brother.

"You've done all right, haven't you?"

"Well, I guess I'm progressively less of an asshole," Rocket said with a smile. Taking a swig of Scrimshaw Pilsner, he seemed to be winding himself for a little speech: "You know, people sometimes think that a rural life like ours is 'dropping out,' but in our minds, it's dropping *in*. It's not about just getting away once a year for a package vacation, but being away, for your life. We're not out of it, or disconnected. We're *in* it—connected to the things that really matter."

"I hear you," Marc said, nodding approvingly.

"I was always hoping I'd find a way to stay out of the mess that America is becoming. Since you and I were kids, the U.S. population has more than doubled, I'm sure the professor knows that. All the megamalls, viaducts, suburbs and warehouses have just about destroyed America's wild spaces. Do you remember when we'd take family vacations, how the grill and windshield of our car was always covered with insects? They're not here anymore in that kind of abundance, and neither are the fireflies, the songbirds, the bears...And what do we have to show for it? An epidemic of anxiety and addiction. Confusion! When I drive down to San Francisco or even Santa Rosa, everybody's got their face buried in their cell phone, even while they drive. They're cutting me off or shaking their fist at me for going too slow."

"You're right. We're finally seeing the side-effects of the American Dream. Now we see that the emperor has no clothes."

"That's a terrifying image," Rocket said, laughing. "Don't get me started about Trumpsky." Their laughter felt like small revenge for the social and environmental damage the accidental president was perpetrating. Marc considered all the hirings, firings and fake news small potatoes compared with crimes against life on Earth committed by Trump: dismissal of climate change, cruel disregard for people of color, and premeditated, profitable destruction of the world's species as mining, development, and careless agriculture continued. The two shook their heads in wordless frustration about the mainstream definition of progress, and all the destruction it had caused in America— a magnificently, pristinely wild continent just 400 years earlier.

Marc joked, "I think it's kind of pathetic that we worked so hard as a species to *stand up* and now, all we do is *sit*." Rocket added, "Nobody thinks they have enough money. Either they can't pay the bills or at the other end, their yacht isn't the biggest one in the bathtub. No matter who you are, it's dissatisfaction guaranteed." Marc shared some *good* news he'd read about:

a new course at Yale University on the psychology of happiness had the largest enrollment of any course in three centuries—1200 students, or one-fourth of the undergraduates. "It seems like making money is not the only thing the next generation is studying. They want something meaningful, something that makes them feel *alive*."

"Nice. I guess there are some exceptional Americans," Rocket said, gesturing with both hands toward his brother, who immediately reciprocated. "If we were benevolent dictators, we'd fix this world up, wouldn't we?" Rocket held out his fist for a fist bump, then took another swig of beer. "You know how I would define happiness? Having the energy to do good work—work that's useful, not destructive. And having strong ties with a few others. That's what makes me happy."

Twelve

Best Friends for Life

The two brothers fell into a comfortable silence in the studio. Reaching over to the back of the workbench, Rocket pulled out a small pipe and handed it to Marc, "You want a toke or two?" Marc smoked pot only infrequently but wanted to accept his brother's hospitality. (Being the kid brother, he'd always had to measure up.) "We grow our own stuff—Sativa," Rocket said, reaching over to light the pipe. Then, looking down at the two white dogs snoozing on the bricks, "Whichever one of you barfed in the kitchen last night—you got me in big trouble." Widget sensed he was being addressed and looked up with sleepy eyes, his little Westie ears—pink on the inside like a bunny's—always erect. But since the word barf was not in his vocabulary, he didn't reveal a trace of guilt. Rocket explained his blunder to Marc: "I was up before Ellie this morning and somehow failed to take charge of a pile of barf by the back door, which Ellie later *slid through*. So, first I was negligent, then inconsiderate, then condescending...kind of a downward spiral." Knowing that the foundations of his brother's marriage were unshakable, Marc opted to just throw out a platitude: "Love is spending your life with someone you want to kill, but you can't, because you love 'em too much."

"I hope she remembers that," Rocket joked, as if his life might be in danger. Still focused on the dogs at his feet, he told his brother, "The man who developed this breed was allegedly a Scotsman who used terriers to flush out game. One day he shot his own favorite reddish-brown terrier, mistaking it for a fox. That's when he decided the world needed a snow-white terrier breed."

"Good idea," Marc said, kneeling down to stroke each dog. "Some friends of mine have a Lab with a well-developed sense of humor: they ask the dog if he'd rather be a Republican or a dead dog, and he immediately drops and plays dead." They both laughed, Rocket recalling still another dog tale involving their own family's Springer spaniel, notorious for retrieving ducks. "You remember when Alfie was getting too old to hunt and Dad took him out one last time?"

"Yeah, he put a dead duck on the shore of the lake, then fired a shot so Alfie could still feel like he was in the hunt. That was kind of the way Dad was. Was it him who got you interested in hunting? You still hunt wild turkeys, don't you?" Rocket nodded. "Turkeys, quail, pheasant. We got a few plump gobblers last year—good, clean meat. Yeah, I was familiar with hunting through Dad, but it was my friend Mitchell who really got me into it here. We go out a few times every year. I'll never forget what Dad told me the week he died." Marc was curious, knowing that Rocket and their Dad sometimes had skirmishes. "'Dennis,' he said, 'you're a very smart man with a lot of creative talent'—he didn't just use the word potential, but *talent*—'You're living life on your own terms, and I respect that,' he said. 'Keep mastering your furniture making, that's a very special skill.'" Talking about their father brought up another memory for Rocket—the time he'd gone with his Dad at the age of five or six to the 'swamp' and transplanted a cottonwood sapling into the front yard. 'I wonder if it's still there?' the ol' man asked me when he was in Hospice care. I had to find out, so I drove a few hours to the old house and took a picture of the cottonwood—now towering three stories above our little post-war bungalow. When I showed the picture to Dad, he said, 'Wow, well done!' We'd done something together that had been hugely successful. That meant a lot to me."

Marc recalled, "In my last conversation with Dad, he grabbed my arm and told me, 'Be the best damn teacher you can be, the world needs you.' Then I'll never forget what else he said, even though he'd always been such a skeptic: 'Climate change is real, keep telling people about the science of it.'" The brothers were swept into an unavoidably tender moment; each with tears in his eyes. "I'm not ready to lose you, big guy," Rocket said, hugging his kid brother as if there was power enough in it to heal Marc spontaneously. "I'm not ready to lose me, either." And for a change, deep in his gut, a tiny, tenacious voice asserted, *I* will *beat this virus. Of course I will.* Looking at Rocket's teary-eyed face, a face he'd known all his life, Marc suddenly became a kickboxer, ready to show the virus what defeat felt like.

After another silence, Rocket asked, as a college pal might, "How's your love life? You gettin' any?"

"What love life? Actually, I did have some luck with a young lady just last week, but it may have fizzled out. Looks like she went back with her old boyfriend after all."

"Movie star kind of babe?"

"No, but she's a babe all right—twenty-eight years old and really growing up fast."

"You sleaze ball," Rocket said, shaking his head, but with a smile on his face and a twinkle in his eye. "Not one of your students I hope?"

"Not anymore."

"That's way younger than our daughters, dude." Rocket said, in a mock-scolding tone. Marc felt duly reprimanded, but still, he was betting his brother was a little envious, and he knew Rocket understood that their situations were completely different. The older brother had been married for many years without a single transgression—at least nothing Marc had ever heard about—but what do you do when luck takes your wife, then comes after your life?

"So what's next?" Rocket asked.

"Open season. Kai dared me to go after any attractive, unattached woman I like." Although his encounter with Kerrie still stung, Marc played the role of the heartless stud for his brother's benefit.

"Go for it, Maverick," Rocket said, shrugging his shoulders. "You're the man. As for me, I just feel lucky to be settled in. Toward the end of any given week, I start craving two things: sex, and bacon." He paused, then added with a smile, "...but really, the rest of the week is pretty good, too."

The two fell silent for a moment—neither had anything in particular to add. After another swig of beer, Marc said, "It seems like Sara and Zak are doing great."

"Absolutely. She made a good decision, leaving LA. Now maybe she can get some kind of a career going. I think she just needs to open up a little, trust her instincts. I have a theory about why she got into modeling, besides the money. I'm guessing it was a subconscious attempt to reveal who she is, inside."

Marc nodded, though he wasn't sure what exactly Rocket meant. "By the way, Lisa says hi to all of you, and she had some news she wanted me to tell you: She and Brad are going to start a family!"

"Very cool!" Rocket said, giving Marc a high five. "She's a great one—always so interested in how things work, and the history and story behind everything. I think you and Karen brought her up right."

"Thanks, man."

As Rocket continued to work on the fine details of the basket weaver's face, he explained that the two poles (one of which was already finished, under a tarp outside) had matching totems. The basket weaver would match the Pomo shaman on the other pole, the eagle and owl were a match, the whale and salmon, and the mountain lion and coyote—all strong icons of Mendocino County history. "And you thought I'd end up in jail," Rocket joked, looking over wistfully at his brother as if this could conceivably be their last year together. The track lights highlighted Rocket's face, and for the first time Marc noticed the deepening crow's feet around his brother's eyes.

"So, what about this skydiving idea?" Marc asked. "You're not really serious about that, are you?"

"Of course I'm serious. It's all planned. Are you in?"

The two men smiled at each other as if they were seven and nine again, getting ready to jump off the garage roof onto a huge pile of leaves. "Hey, if you can do it, so can I."

"That's what I was waiting to hear," Rocket said, grabbing his brother by the shoulder and giving him the familiar little shake. The brothers may have taken different paths but they'd somehow ended up in the same place philosophically.

Walking back to the house, they met Sara just coming out the door. "I'm going back to read my book," she told them. "Good night, guys."

"'Night, butterfly," Rocket said. "See you in the morning. We have peas and strawberries to pick tomorrow, right? And I got you and Zak some gloves."

"We'll be there."

"What are you reading?" Marc asked as she walked away.

"*1491*. It's really interesting."

"Great book. Enjoy it."

"See you tomorrow," she repeated, moving through the warm, moonlit darkness.

"It's my bedtime too, in my time zone," Marc informed Rocket and Ellen as he walked toward his room. "I'm really looking forward to seeing your place in the daylight. I'll probably go for a walk before you guys even get up."

"There's a good little trail at the far end of the pasture," Ellen said. "It takes you up through the forest to an overlook. Pretty nice view up there."

"I'll check it out. Then I'm going to help with the peas, strawberries, and whatever else. Rock, you keep working on your totems, I'll cover for you," he said, closing the door to his room.

"Thanks, Marc, that'll really help!"

As he got ready for bed, Marc reflected on his final encounter with Kerrie. The cavalier way he'd summarized it to Rocket was not really the way it had *felt*. Six days earlier, the sweet little fantasy had popped like a get-well balloon.

At the first practice of the new softball season, Marc had felt great, quietly assuming his leadership role and clowning around with his teammates. If he was thinking about Kerrie at all, it was with anticipation. After some small talk and catching up, the players formed parallel lines and tossed balls back and forth with a lot of chatter. Then each player took ten or so pitches from Arnie, the team's ace fast-baller. Marc stood behind home plate surveying both batters and fielders. There were more than a few swings and misses as they cycled through the roster, although a few players smacked solid line drives. Each player was curious when Marc came to the plate, and one of Marc's buddies needled from the field, "No batter, no batter," as the coach assumed his familiar, relaxed batting stance. Sure enough, although he fanned once himself, two of Arnie's devilish fastballs cracked off Marc's bat into deep left field. Now, a few other teammates called, "Nice hittin' slugger," and "Still got the juice, Blake!"

Marc found himself recalling the time, years earlier, when he'd driven from Columbus to Indianapolis to be at Rocket's first pro ballgame. Although his brother had struck out, grounded out, and made a fielding error in the early innings, he'd whacked a double in the 8th inning that drove in the two game-deciding runs. "You had me thinking they were gonna drum you right out of the minors," Marc had joked, sitting in the dugout with Rocket and his date after the game. "You save your mojo for when you need it," Rocket had replied, always Mr. Cool.

A little before eight, as it started getting darker, Marc had called out, "That's good for tonight. You're lookin' damn good for this early in the season! Next practice is scheduled for the tenth, but I'm going to be out of town." Arnie volunteered to coordinate the practice, and Marc made a mental note to ask him if he was also willing to be the next team manager.

He fished his cellphone out of his pack and saw that Kerrie had texted him. "Marc, can you come over tonight?" she'd written—exactly the message he was hoping for! But after reading the words that followed—"I'm feeling kind of confused"—he thought, "Uh oh."

"Jimmy came over, uninvited. We had a fight. Would be great to talk with you—maybe get a cup of coffee?" Marc didn't like the sound of Kerrie's words. He'd decided not to pressure her after their afternoon adventure, other than a few short texts wishing her a good day—but it had been six days since they'd been together. Now, the text carried shadows. Maybe she hadn't called him because...she wasn't really interested. Or because it was risky business, considering his illness. Marc's felt his sense of comfort drop like a shooting star.

A few teammates walked by, one asking, "We're going to the U for a beer, you comin'?"

"I can't. I just had a text from a friend, and I need to go see her."

"Oh, a *friend*," one man teased, knowing that Marc was still the very eligible bachelor. "I guess we can't compete with that." Marc played it straight, smiling and responding, "Good first practice tonight. By the way, nice diving grab on that long ball, Micah. You got some authentic grass stains on your pants, man—proof of your hustle."

Marc texted Kerrie back. "Are you okay? He didn't hurt you, did he? What's your address?" As he walked back to his car with a full load of equipment, she replied, "No, I'm okay. 2713 Platte Circle, apt 3. White bldg, fake stone lions in front. c u soon?"

At the apartment building, Marc pressed the smudged doorbell button, waiting anxiously to hear Kerrie's voice through the intercom to assess which way the evening might go. Truth is, at that moment, the more he doubted her affections the more he craved them. Her voice was light, the tone inconclusive: "CIA, can you hold?"

Her little prank caught him off balance. He went with, "No, this is code red. Requires immediate action."

"Roger that...proceed through the metal detector in the elevator and report to the third floor, door #3." She sounded cute and kind of flirty, but was there also a hint of steeliness?

"Yes, ma'am," he responded, the dutiful subordinate. He floated up to the third floor at the speed of a low-geared elevator, part of him regretting he hadn't brought flowers. But another voice countered, *You're here to support her, idiot, not romance her.* When she opened the door, he immediately felt the physical connection. There were little folds of stress under her eyes, but she stood straight and seemed self-assured. "You're okay?" he asked as he gave her a hug.

She hugged him back, but then gently broke away. "Yeah, I'm okay, I just felt like I needed to see you." The uh-oh feeling was back. "I should have called you sooner," Marc said. "I can't stop thinking about you."

"I've been thinking about you, too...But then Jimmy showed up again..." Marc's instinct was to grab her and kiss her before it was too late, but she sensed that and took a few steps back, walking into the living room. Now he had to play defense. "But he didn't get physical with you?" Marc asked, immediately realizing these words were way too ambiguous. "He didn't hurt you?" he corrected.

"No, he would never hurt me, although we did shout at each other...a little." After a short silence, she blurted, "I was waiting for you to call."

So he was right. "My daughter and I have been getting my house a little more organized." She nodded, deferring to his higher priority, survival. "I should have called you," she said, lowering her gaze. "You did. You texted. So what's up with...Jimmy?"

She cut to the heart of it: "He wants to get back together."

"And what about you?" Marc asked, meeting her bold response beat for beat. He wanted to hold her, to confirm his claim on their relationship. She invited him to sit on the couch as she sank into an armchair, then immediately got up. "Do you want something to drink? A glass of wine? My roommates are out, so we can talk here."

"Sure, what kind of wine do you have?

"Cabernet or Pinot Grigio."

"Pinot Grigio, thanks. That's one of my favorites."

The apartment had an open floorplan and as she opened the refrigerator, she looked over her shoulder telling him, "Jimmy and I have been together for almost two years, and I thought it was going well, until..." She turned and poured the wine. Both of them were wearing shorts and T-shirts and somehow, it felt like the evening's probable outcome was linked with the air-conditioned chill in the apartment.

"Until what?

"Until he cheated on me."

"Oh. So now he wants to slither back, that snake," Marc said in a protective tone, trying to draw clear battle lines. She surprised him by saying, "Well... I cheated on him, too." Marc was speechless, his emotions careening downhill like a sharp-bladed sled on an icy hill.

"So, that's what our connection was the other day...*revenge*?" She handed him his wine glass. Its chilliness made the situation feel even less hopeful.

"No!" she said, emphatically. "I'm very attracted to you, and I feel like we have a strong, primal connection, don't you?"

He relaxed a little when she said that, but only for an instant. "The thing is...what kind of a *future* do we have?" she asked bluntly, reciting a line she'd apparently already rehearsed. If he was a rollup bug, he could have rolled right off the couch. Suddenly he felt discarded—no one's favorite feeling. "So you're going back with him?"

"Well, he told me—and I think I can believe him—that he'll never, ever do that again. And that he would quit smoking pot and vaping cigarettes, and...he called back today and told me he really loves me."

"And what did you tell him?"

"Well, I told him about you—how attractive and what a great person you are, and how we were...together, last week." Marc waited for the wrap-up. "And I told him that even though I really love being with you..." She hesitated, then got up the courage to say, "...that I wouldn't have sex with you again." The expression on Marc's face morphed involuntarily to that of a high school boy, whose hopeful invitation to the prom had just been rejected. Into a heavy silence came the unexpected words, "After tonight."

Her facial expression was deliberate, but he chose to skip over her intriguing words for the moment.

"I understand. I do." Now he retreated to a more formal, fatherly manner, realizing as he spoke that he really had no claim on her at all, that he couldn't lose something he'd never really had. He admired Kerrie and was drawn to her frankness, and the way she was moving decisively through her life. As a onetime mentor, hadn't he played a role in her successes? That was *something*.

"I told him, 'after tonight,'" she repeated emphatically, raising her eyebrows suggestively.

Should he go there? Should he take her offer—in a way, a sweet consolation prize? He knew he shouldn't. Couldn't...and, okay: wouldn't. The offer seemed to perch like a crumpled trophy on the glass coffee table as the two sat in silence, smiling genuinely at each other, trapped in a situation neither knew how to play. Standing up abruptly, he said with a sigh, "Kerrie, you're terrific! I don't want to screw things up for you. You're right, a long-term relationship probably isn't in the cards, and it sounds like you can make things work with your guy."

Relief and hurt appeared simultaneously on Kerrie's face, like Siamese twins. He held out two hands to Kerrie and she stood up supported by his grip. She waited for him to say something else, now deferring control of the situation to him. In effect, she was gratefully honoring his seniority, and chivalry.

He put his arm around her shoulder as they walked toward the door. There wasn't any reason to stay and make small, awkward talk, was there? "I'll keep up with you on Facebook and Instagram, okay? We know some of the same people. We like a lot of the same things."

"I'll keep up, too," she said, beaming honest emotion that made Marc go shy again, just a little. She added carefully, "And I didn't promise that I wouldn't *see* you again, just that I wouldn't have sex with you. Let's meet for lunch sometime." It was clear that their connection was real, it just wasn't possible, so *go home, dude*. But his emotions, and accompanying hormones, still hung in the air. He tried to reel them in even as he opened the door to leave.

"Hey, Kerrie, you beautiful person, good luck with everything!" he said, running his hand across her smooth cheek a final time. "I hope you get that grant you applied for. Maybe you'll let me know about that?"

He saw tears in her dark green eyes as she said, "Of course. Good luck to you, too, Marc. I think you're a wonderful guy, I always have! Let me know how I can help, I know this is a challenging time for you." He nodded gratefully.

The last thing he saw was that radiant face, glowing faintly like a hazy sunset. Getting into his vintage Toyota Corolla he thought seriously about going back in, but he'd already been the Lone Ranger, hadn't he, strong and virtuous? Maybe she'd open her door and coax him back in? Nope.

Okay then, acknowledge and move on. Get ready for a good visit with Rock and his family and just keep on truckin.'

The rest of the Willits clan may have called it a night, but Rocket and Ellen still sat in the living room, winding down. "Are you going to bed?" he asked, as Ellen met his gaze. After so many years together, she easily interpreted his facial expression and tone of voice. When she didn't answer right away, he ventured, "It's a nice, warm night. You want to walk down to the road and back?"

"Maybe."

"Let's bring the rest of the wine."

"Okay, I'll get some cups." *Maybe we can get things back on an even keel*, she thought, grabbing her flashlight and a tube of citronella repellent just in case the mosquitoes were on the warpath.

"We don't need cups, I'm not afraid of your germs. Your germs are my germs."

"And damn good germs they are!"

Walking down the gravel driveway they noticed a light on in John's office. "I need to tell John that Marc's going to do the sky dive, but I can call him tomorrow." He took Ellen's hand as they walked. She was open to romance, he sensed that, but he went with her apparent preference to just walk a little without talking. After her chat with Sara and her cathartic tantrum over the chocolate cake, Ellie actually felt a lot less anxious. It was such a warm, pleasant night. The stars were coming out, the moon was rising and the crickets were chirping, "No worries, no worries, no worries...." All this was evidence that life on Earth wasn't so bad, despite all the dictators, droughts, extinctions and broken hearts.

They heard distant music coming from the yurt—probably Jessie playing reggae or bluegrass on his guitar. Of the three interns then in residence, Jessie seemed the most interested in learning how to create a self-sufficient lifestyle. He was especially interested in mastering the skill of market gardening, and he'd spent the day planting 200 ever-bearing strawberry starts in the plot that paralleled the road. Always the organizer, Ellen wanted to see if he'd done a good job on the spacing, shining her flashlight over the electric fence into the bed. "Looks pretty good," Rocket said.

"It does. Maybe they can finish mending the fence around the orchard tomorrow, then help us with the harvesting and more planting. We need to pick strawberries from those three-year-old beds, quickly, before they peak."

Making his move, Rocket said, "You look so beautiful in the moonlight." In these cherished moments, he sometimes attained the status of Sir Lancelot, a significant rung up from the jester role he sometimes trapped himself in. Running his hand tenderly down the inside of his lady's arm, Lancelot then pulled her into a warm, familiar hug. Ellie thought it was liberating—even a little naughty—to be romancing outside on a summer evening. *What a lark, to be in our twenties again, cavorting in the moonlight!* With a heightening sense of anticipation, they found their way through the shadows, around the strawberry bed ("Watch out for the electric fence!" he reminded her), and into the small gazebo that served as a shady resting place on hot workdays. Sitting on the redwood bench, worn smooth as ivory over the years, they each savored a fruity gulp of wine.

First came the full-bodied, reconnecting kiss they each sought, melting away the emotional hiccups of the previous week. They began slowly caressing and teasing each other's hands, expressing through these ingenious fingertips and smooth palms how incredibly rich life is. Ellen whispered in a breathy tone, "This feels so *sexy!*" Their hands tingled as if they were cradling a thin, sparkling slice of moonlight. Ellen demurely pulled up her T-shirt, allowing her warm, radiant skin to bathe in the mild evening air. *No one can see us,* she thought, *and I probably wouldn't want to stop even if they could.*

Thirteen

Chicken Goggles

Marc's bio-clock woke him at about five o'clock, six Denver time, but he didn't feel any need to roll out of bed for another half hour, just daydreaming as streaks of light filtered through the east-facing window. He was anxious to explore his brother's little farm and couldn't think of a more pleasant way to get some exercise. Putting an apple in his day pack he quietly got dressed and tiptoed past Rocket's and Ellen's bedroom, where he heard the trace of a snore. *I hope those two are working things out,* he thought, pouring coffee into a thermos.

Marc always loved the clear feeling of being up before the rest of the world. He knew the pace and vibe in rural Willits would be completely different than metropolitan Denver where the droning of traffic and the smell of chaos on a weekday morning had become standard fare. The two dogs invited themselves along and the pack headed around the ravine toward the pasture. Approaching its gate, Marc heard the first sound in the deep silence of the morning: a woodpecker mining a tree for ants and beetles over in the woods. Looking in the direction of the loud tapping, Marc felt lucky to catch sight of the bird's bright red head, pecking on the trunk of a dying white oak. An even more unexpected sign of wildlife was the sudden appearance of Sara, running on the access trail around the pasture, her long slim legs accented by tight running shorts. She loped toward him as if running was more natural than walking.

"Good morning!" he called as she approached.

"Nice day!" she answered, putting on the brakes right in front of him. Her shoulder length hair was in a ponytail she'd pulled through the back strap of a Dodgers baseball cap. "Welcome to the ranch! I love mornings here!"

Marc had noticed the dairy cow grazing at the edge of the alpaca herd and asked her if she was going out to milk it. She smiled and said, "Nooo. The interns milk her every morning, maybe one of them already has. But if not, maybe *you'll* have to take over this morning!" she joked, still a little out of breath.

"Well, I guess I could give it a try. So you left LA, huh? What's next for you?"

"I'm looking for a job in architecture, but I want to make sure it's really the right move for me."

"Try it out, maybe do an internship," suggested the helpful professor familiar with encouraging young women and men to jump in. Sara nodded pensively as Marc continued, nodding in the direction of John's house. "What do you think of it? Is it good architecture?"

"It's pretty nice. I'm proud of my Dad for his role in building it. He even *designed* parts of it, like the solar carport."

"That's what charges John's Tesla? I saw it in the driveway."

"Yeah, it also powers some of his landscape lighting."

"I think architecture could be a pretty interesting line of work. Super creative, unless you're designing cookie-cutter houses."

"I'd never do that."

Nodding and looking into Marc's eyes, Sara felt it would be an omission not to mention his challenge. "I was so sorry to hear about your illness."

"Thanks, Sara," Marc said, returning her clear, unguarded gaze. She had light brown eyes the color of coffee with a splash of cream, and her tanned skin was only a little lighter. "I've decided I'm going to beat it," he said, for the first time saying these words out loud. He knew that "fighting" was the socially accepted response, but that wasn't why he said it. "I've had my few weeks of doom and gloom, but hanging out in this healthy place with you guys is giving me a different perspective, it really is." He paused, then broke through the awkward moment. "Hey, Lisa says hello. She really wanted to come with me, but she's got a sales meeting she had to go to. She asked me to give Zak a little present from her—it's back at the house."

"Oh? What is it?"

"You'll find out. It's something we found when we were cleaning the attic the other day, and she wants Zak to have it."

"That's so sweet!" Sara said. "I'll give her a call to say hello, and thank her."

"Ask her about their recent decision: they're ready to have a baby!" he said.

Sara let out a joyful little shriek. "That's so awesome!" The bond between Marc and Sara was subtle and undefined. They knew each other mostly from family gatherings when the girls were younger, from sporadic updates and holiday phone calls. He recalled the two high-energy cousins playing together years earlier at a family reunion. He'd been wary that Sara might be a little bold, even back then—whether it was swimming in deep water, talking to strangers on the beach, or wearing outfits that were a little too grown-up. But for the most part, Lisa had chosen which of the older cousin's traits she found compelling, and which traits were not her style.

"Well, I'd better get back and check on Zak. I know Mom worries about leaving him up in the tree house by himself."

"Okay, I'm going to check out the trail through the woods." Looking around for the dogs, he discovered that one was busily chewing little pellets of alpaca poop. "Good probiotics," Sara said, laughing.

"Probably knows what his body needs," Marc said, relieved he wasn't really responsible for the dogs. "That reminds me: I'm taking a poll. Are you in favor of a dog's face on Mt. Rushmore?"

Smiling at Marc's whimsy, she answered, "Why not? We've already got a dog's face in the White House." They shared a smile, then Sara looked at her watch and took off. Marc called out as she ran toward the house, "I'm going to help with the harvesting today, are you?" Looking over her shoulder, she called back, "Absolutely."

Near the end of his walk, Marc saw John in front of his house, weeding the edges of his "rock garden"—actually a small collection of beautiful marble and granite rocks of different shapes and colors, artfully mounted on thick steel-rod stems. "Hey Marc, long time no see! Good to have you back in the Golden State."

"Good to see you too, John. Hey, your house looks incredible!"

"I want to give you a tour anytime it's convenient. I imagine Ellen's already got you scheduled."

"Thanks, I'd love the tour and yes, Ellen's a tough task master, but you've gotta love her ability to keep everything together."

"Yep, she's a strong woman with a beautiful heart...and I trust she's declared a holiday for our sky dive tomorrow morning?"

"I'll be there. I was reluctant at first but, hey, what have I got to lose?"

"You'll love the free falling. I do. See you then...enjoy the day!"

"I'll do that, you too!"

As he walked toward Rocket's cabin, Marc's phone rang and it was Lisa, finally making contact after a few back and forth messages. "Hey you, what's up?"

"Just calling to say hello, and tell you I think you'll be impressed with the work I've done at the house." "You shouldn't have done that, you're busy!" (Though in secret he was he was uttering a silent "YES!")

"There were no critters with sharp teeth lurking in the closets, were there?" he joked. "Nothing bigger than a wombat. So how did the appointment go? What did the doctor say?"

"He said I should be completely cured by next week. Actually, he said we could watch now to see if the drugs reduce virus populations. We should know within a few weeks. So, yes, I'm on it, and also taking a Super Greens formula three times a day that Kai recommended."

"Terrific! I know you'll have good results. I'm really glad, Dad. Give my love to everyone there. I wish I could be with you guys."

Marc had chosen not to tell his daughter about a traumatic incident in the doctor's waiting room: a teary-eyed woman had confided that her vital signs were not looking good after fighting a disease similar to Marc's for six months. She'd taken the prescribed drugs faithfully, exercised, eaten exclusively organic food, but because of disappointing recent blood tests, she was panicking. Marc was shaken: she was about his age, had similar symptoms and, like him, had done a lot of international travel.

At breakfast, Marc sat at the kitchen counter with Sara and Zak while Ellen made omelets. Ellen seemed calm and energetic, ready for another productive workday. Marc had noticed a large whiteboard by the back door that listed the day's activities. Under "Harvest" were strawberries, peas, and snapdragons. Workers and approximate hours of duty were assigned to each crop. After strawberries, Ellen had written: Sara, Zak, Jessie, Marc? 9 to 12. Ellen assigned herself the responsibility of cutting, bunching and packing the flowers, 9 to 11. Other tasks for the day included planting, to be done by the three interns, Ellen and Rocket.

"I see Rock is listed as planting winter squash seedlings this afternoon," Marc said. "I want to fill in for him so he can keep working."

"He'll appreciate that. He's already out in the studio. Just meet us out by the long beds at 1, behind the bed where the strawberries were planted yesterday."

"I know where that is, along the driveway. I also want to volunteer as head chef for tonight's meal, if that will work? I brought some curry that I mixed up, dry, before I left. It might go pretty well with some of your fresh chicken."

"Sure, that'll work great! If you make chicken curry, I'll make strawberry cobbler."

"I'm hoping Zak will help me cook the curry. What do you think, Zak, can you be assistant chef?" Zak had a cowboy hat on that was almost as wide as his shoulders, so it was hard to know for sure, but it seemed like the boy was on board as sous chef. Sara quickly volunteered to assist (and manage Zak).

But Zak had a more pressing issue in mind: "Every day, cowboys wear the same thing."

"You mean they never change their shirts?" Marc asked, wondering if Zak had noticed that he was wearing the same shirt as the night before.

"Nope, they always wear the same shirt," said the boy, quite certain of his cowboy lore.

Ellen looked over from the sink and explained. "We watched a documentary from the library about cowboys. Sometimes the cowboys travel light, don't they Zak, when they're out on a roundup in Montana or somewhere?"

Marc asked Zak, "You ever seen a rodeo?"

"No, but I've ridden a horse, a *lot*. (Actually three times.) John has two horses, and he's teaching me how to be a cowboy."

"I'll bet you know how to round up the alpacas and the cow," Marc commented, raising his eyebrows. "Do you ever ride horses with your Mom?"

"Yeah, Zak and I rode the other day, didn't we, partner?" Sara smiled at Marc about the young cowboy's huge frumpy hat, a favorite of Rocket's when summer afternoons were killer hot.

"John's going to take me to the State Park to ride," Zak said.

"You are one lucky guy," Marc replied, looking in the direction of the moving cowboy hat. "And I have something in my room that I think will make you feel even luckier." He went back to his room, dug in his suitcase and brought out the shiny mint-condition gold coin. "This is from your Aunt Lisa, you know, my daughter. She lives in Denver and she wanted you to let your mom put this away in a safe place. Some time when you need money to buy something *really special*, or when you want to go to college, you can sell it."

"Wow!" Zak said. "Is it *real gold*!?"

"You bet it is."

Sara told Zak, "We have to make sure we never lose it!" She knew better than to grab it away immediately, instead letting Zak feel every ridge on the coin to get a full appreciation of its value. "Let's make a thank-you card for Lisa. She's one of my best friends, even though I don't see her as often as I'd like."

Zak asked, "What can I get with this?" Sara looked over at Marc for help with that question. "Well, it's worth about $1300 right now, so if you were old enough to drive, you could get a used car with that."

"Or you could fly all the way to France and back for that," Ellen added. "Or buy some bonds as an investment, so your money would grow."

"Money grows?" Zak asked, getting ready to deposit the new treasure in his pocket, which may or may not have had a hole in it.

"Yes it does grow in value, if you don't lose it," Sara said, holding out her hand for the coin. "Let's put it in our special little travel bag, so we'll always know where it is. Okay?"

A keen observer of human behavior, including body language, Marc studied first Sara's face then her Mom's, noting the physical resemblance as well as the personality differences. Ellie was down to earth, spontaneous and comfortable, while Sara was more reserved and deliberate. While the mother wasn't conscious of her movements or her words, Sara moved with a practiced dancer's poise, like the model she'd recently been. The daughter seemed to weigh her words before she said them, as if the wrong words would spoil the precise effect she wanted. And as for another character in the family, Rocket, you never knew which way he'd play it. He was capable of altering his personality right before your eyes, whether to tell you a joke or forcefully stand up for you in a jam. Marc remembered the time Rocket had taken the blame for the two of them getting home late after a double-date, and how Rocket's dramatic skills had saved the day. Marc had gotten a speeding ticket he didn't want his parents to know about, but Rocket bent the truth just a little by explaining to their father—still up watching a Johnny Carson re-run—that they'd offered to drive a friend home because he'd been drinking.

"And that took an extra hour?" their father had asked skeptically. Rocket improvised, "Well, then Emma had kind of a meltdown because she got an F on an exam, so we had to kind of talk her back up." Marc had been impressed by Rocket's inventiveness. The guilty brother had added a few fictional flourishes of his own to his brother's tall tale, but mostly he focused on just keeping the ticket tucked deeply in his pocket.

After breakfast, Zak ventured into the earthy-smelling chicken roost carrying three egg cartons. He'd replaced the cowboy hat with a baseball cap, also extra-large on his small head, but he was still quite certain of his coolness. A few minutes later he came out of the shed excitedly, carrying two and a half cartons of multicolored eggs: white, brown, and even light green ones laid by the South American Araucana hens. Marc and Sara stood outside the chicken yard, impressed by the Chicken Chief's enthusiasm. With a smile on his face, Marc told Sara about an article he'd read. "In the experiment, they used red lights in chicken roosts to increase egg production. Even midlife hens became super layers, and a few companies even tried outfitting their hens with red-lensed chicken goggles." Marc suddenly broke out laughing as he once again imagined a whole flock of free-range chickens with goggles on, bumping into each other like cartoon chickens about to watch a 3-D movie.

"What's he laughing about?" Zak asked his mother, proudly holding up the eggs he'd collected. "He's talking about a farm where the chickens wear goggles, like swimming goggles except with red lenses, so they'll lay more eggs." Maybe Zak found Marc's laughter infectious or maybe the idea was just the funniest thing the boy had ever heard, but he started laughing so hard that Sara had to grab the egg cartons before the boy lost control of them.

It was one of those rare moments: Marc and Zak had the giggles, and it felt so liberating! Between peals of laughter, Marc suggested, "If you wear goggles with red lenses, maybe *you'll* start laying eggs." The silliness of people laying eggs took Zak right over the edge, and he fell to his knees laughing uncontrollably, slapping his hand on the path. He looked up at Marc with tears rolling down his cheeks. "Maybe *you'll* start laying eggs," Zak shot back, as he stood up.

"Buck-baawk," Marc replied, flapping his elbow-wings.

After taking the eggs into the barn and washing them, the three headed to the south-facing strawberry beds on the slope of the ravine. Two of the interns, Jessie and Sam, also reported for duty and immediately began weeding the rows—a task always in demand. Ellen brought over a wheelbarrow piled high with a half-bale of straw, a few hoes and large plastic baskets—shallow so the berries wouldn't get bruised or smashed. She demonstrated how to pick the berries, and how straw should be packed under each cluster of immature berries so they wouldn't droop onto the ground and rot. Largely for Sara's and Marc's benefit, Ellen demonstrated how to hoe deeply, both to chop the weeds and aerate the soil. She watched as Zak became mesmerized by the wriggling earthworms that her hoeing had revealed. The boy grabbed one of the worms and felt it tingling in his cupped hands, a strange and slightly slimy miracle.

"Can you please put aside a few pints of berries for strawberry cobbler?" Ellen asked as she left to cut and bundle flowers. "Zak and Sara and I will get after the chicken curry late afternoon," Marc told her, popping a plump berry into his mouth after biting off the green tip. He was so impressed with the loose richness of the soil, and he knew the sweet yet tangy flavor of the berries was directly related. As they continued to pick, placing the berries carefully in the flat baskets, the experience felt like a dream to Marc. What a pleasant, stress-free way to spend time!

Sam had opted to be the hoer and straw mulcher, working by himself at the far end of the bed, but the long-haired Jessie worked down the rows with Marc, Sara and Zak. Before long they'd picked 5 or 6 gallons of fragrant bright-red berries. Marc noticed that Jessie seemed to be flirting with Sara and that she was responding to him, but apparently only as a chum. Really, she was only a few years older than Jessie, and they faced a similar challenge: what to do for a living. Jessie explained that he wanted to either be a farmer or maybe a chef, but he didn't have the money to buy or even lease land. "If I can save up a little by working in a restaurant, maybe

I could buy some land with a few friends and grow vegetables and...pot," he said with a laugh.

"What about your music?" Sara asked. "You have a really good voice. You should keep working on that, too." Marc watched Jessie's face as she said that. An embarrassed, involuntary smile came across his face. "It's pretty hard to make any money playing music," he replied. "Well, maybe studio work, if you keep getting better." Jessie remained silent, picking berries and absorbing Sara's flattering words like a sponge. Then he asked, "How is your search coming?"

"I may have a few leads." She had a degree and a decent resumé and he didn't, but she seemed to accept him as an equal, a fellow seeker. As they were talking, Marc noticed John, the neighbor, climbing into his car on the other side of the ravine. As he drove past, he beeped his horn and waved. All five members of the strawberry crew waved back, but Zak's wave was the most spirited. Marc suspected the boy was dreaming about how he would become a cowboy someday...that would be *his* work. It was easy for Marc to empathize with Sara's and Jessie's plight, having watched hundreds of students make their way into a world where people were being replaced with machines, unions were largely powerless, and the federal minimum wage was not even close to livable. Wanting to encourage them, he repeated what he'd told Sara earlier: "It's not easy finding the perfect job, but one metric is to choose work that makes the time fly by, and that gives you a sense of *connection*."

"For me, it's this," said Jessie in an earnest voice. "I really like to be in the flow of a natural cycle like this, growing food that makes me and other people feel good."

"Well, if you can find work that satisfies you, you've just given yourself five days a week," Marc said. Sara chimed in, "For my parents, the work is more like seven days a week. But they're happy, or at least they *seem* to be."

"I have so much respect for them," Marc said. "Your Dad's really become a master woodworker and carver, and your Mom seems to thrive as business manager. I haven't talked with her about her teaching, but I'll bet that's pretty satisfying too."

"They do like the life they've designed, but they've had to earn it. It's not an easy life," Sara said, shaking her head as if to say she wasn't willing to be a market gardener.

Sam, now within range of the conversation, reported that one of the drip irrigation lines was leaking. Sara turned to Zak and said, "I bet Grampa would be willing to take a short break. Can you run up and tell him there's a leak?" She'd seen her dad repairing the tiller and tinkering with the pump. She knew he'd be the right person to mend the leak, although the interns could probably have done it too. Zak ran up the hill and in a few minutes he and his Grampa rode the laughably slow iron lift down together, for fun. Rocket was wearing a tool belt and carrying a coil of irrigation line. Zak watched as Rocket quickly clipped out the leaking section and spliced a new piece of tubing into the line. As he finished, Rocket turned to Marc and said, "Thanks for volunteering for some of my chores today, guy."

"My pleasure."

Rocket added, "I'm making good progress in the shop, you want to throw a ball around after lunch?"

"Sure, man, maybe at 12:30 or something, before I plant squash seedlings? I brought my glove, by the way..."

"Terrific!"

Fourteen

Marching in Thunder

At her little urban homestead in Denver, May looked through the kitchen window at the flourishing landscape she, Kai, and his parents had created over the previous nine years. She was intently watching a Bullock's oriole fledgling learn to fly. The tiny multi-colored juvenile flapped earnestly from one shrubby branch to another under the watchful eye of papa, mentoring from the limb of an adjacent dwarf cherry tree. Each attempt demonstrated a narrow victory of instinct and physiology over gravity. Although the trajectory of each flight was steadily downward, by god, it was flight! Then the young aviator would hop branch to branch back to the top of the mountain mahogany shrub, like a ski student riding a chairlift back up the bunny slope. This was a huge moment for both birds, May realized. The fledgling had dropped instinctively into an exciting new phase of its life, a proud moment for papa, whose brilliant plumage of gold-yellow, orange, and black was among the showiest in Colorado.

It's flight school! she thought, feeling lucky to witness such a formative moment. A careful observer of nature, she'd seen a sudden increase of brightly colored finches, warblers and hummingbirds visiting the yard. Since the Bullock's orioles wouldn't come to the feeder, May usually set out high-energy grape jelly to attract that species, at least into July when they migrated a little further north. She loved the idea that the maturing gardens and landscape were increasingly attractive to these colorful birds, and she'd now seen more than thirty different species in the yard, including rare nocturnal glimpses and hoots of the great horned owl that patrolled the neighborhood for rabbits and rodents. But the colorful newcomers' presence was also ominous. She worried that it was partly the world's steadily warming climate that had brought them. Colorado was now just as inviting as their native territories, at least in the warm months.

When we spot the bright red plumage of the Cardinal, we'll know we're in deep doo doo, she thought. She was a proud member of the Citizens' Climate Lobby, a worldwide, 80,000-member organization whose mission was to build nonpartisan political support for a carbon tax. Back in late April, she'd joined ranks with other climate activists from all over the world for the People's Climate March in Washington, an event she described to friends as "marching in thunder." A quarter of a million outraged yet remarkably nonviolent activists had converged on the Capital, marching in ninety-five degree heat to advocate for prevention of human-caused climate change.

Amid the pounding of Native American drums and rallying, determined chants, there was a giant papier mache Donald Trump, swinging a golf club at the teed-up Earth. Floating in a torrent of faces were activist/actor Leonardo DiCaprio and one-time VP Al Gore, whose 1992 book *Earth in the Balance* had sounded an early alert about climate change. Tens of thousands of brightly-colored signs splashed raw pride and conviction into the emotional, politically-charged event, flowing from the Capitol building past Trump Tower to the Washington monument. Some of the signs were peppered with defiant irony and humor, such as "If 99 percent of doctors said you were dying, would you believe in science then?"

"Keep the Earth clean—it's not Uranus," read another irreverent sign, and another pleaded "Save the Earth—It's the only planet with dogs." May's artfully homemade sign warned, "Respect Existence or Expect Resistance." There was a jubilant smile on her face that whole day, starting with the celebratory mid-morning convergence of activists from all corners of the city and all states in the country. She'd returned home with a sense of hope that the peoples' voices would now be heard. The resistance was building!

Alas, exactly a month later, the President had stood in the Rose Garden and stunned billions by announcing that the U.S. would pull out of the historic Paris Climate Accord, agreed upon by 195 nations of the world. All week long, May had felt defeated and infuriated by this apocalyptic blunder. Standing in the kitchen, with sunlight streaming in the window, she thought indignantly, "Why can't we humans understand that nature is all we have? That nature isn't *subservient to the economy* but the economy is obviously *inside nature*?" When Kai walked into the kitchen, May had just begun to cry, leaning over the kitchen counter on her elbows. He placed his hands gently on her shoulders, surprised to see her crying; she was generally so upbeat and strong. "Tell me, what's the matter, love?"

"That fucking Trump!" She burst into unrestrained sobs, a fountain of rage and disillusionment.

"Oh, that. I understand."

"I wish all these obese, oil-drooling goons would just shrivel into mummies!" Complicit in her spirited anger, Kai marveled at the strength of her convictions. He turned her around to give her a big hug. With her head nuzzling his shoulder she hissed, "We don't need their ignorant, droopy-faced arrogance." Pulling his head back to look her in the eye, Kai urged her, "Let it all out."

"Future generations will demand to know where we were on this," shaking her head and now blowing her nose forcefully. "China's going to take over world leadership on climate change."

"Maybe, but I know U.S. states and cities, and the progressive billionaires will keep going anyway, and all the European leaders have said they absolutely won't abandon the agreement. There are dozens of U.S. cities that have already committed to 100 percent renewable energy."

"I hate to say it, but I'm ashamed to be an American right now. We've forgotten the real meaning of patriotism. It's not about the military and *Gross* Domestic Product, it's about taking care of each other, and nature. Or it should be."

The two looked into each other's eyes, beaming mutual strength and support. Kai would never be able to express how much he loved this remarkable woman. He loved her spirit, her empathy, as well as her silver-blonde hair, sharp blue eyes and pinkish, so-kissable lips. He felt very lucky to be her partner! Then Kai remembered he'd told his father he'd work with him in the greenhouse and gardens that afternoon. "I need to find my dad. I'll see you later, okay?"

"You know what? I love you. You keep me in balance," she said putting a warm hand on his shoulder. "And you do the same for me." With a quick but supportive thumbs up, he left. Watching him leave the room, she wondered, *How does Kai stay so solidly on his feet? He is such a decent, honorable guy, a little grumpy sometimes, but aren't we all? Sure, sometimes he lets his parents upset him. In their eyes he'll always be the boy. And sometimes he seems so earnestly nerdy, so idealistic. But then, so are Yukio and Michiko, and, I guess, me too.*

She also thought about what her life might have been if she and Marc had stayed together back in their twenties, when they'd broken each other's hearts. Each thought they had been rejected, but neither knew the full truth. He had felt physically and emotionally isolated from his long-distance girlfriend, since most of her emotional energies went to her dying mother. And because of the breakup, she'd carried a secret all those years, like a message in a bobbing, unrecovered bottle: separated by a third of a planet and with her feelings of abandonment, she'd decided never to tell Marc that they'd almost brought life into the world together. That somehow she'd survived a jet black mood-swing after the miscarriage that sent her life into a tailspin. True, she'd lost an earlier chance at motherhood at the age of 20, but at least that one had been her choice. Buoyed by confidential sessions with a very empathetic and perceptive Danish counselor, she'd realized that she couldn't be a good mother at that stage in her life, and the accidental father probably wouldn't stand by her. So she'd ended that pregnancy with great sadness. The later pregnancy with Marc wasn't actually intentional either, but that didn't make it any easier when nature swept it away. What if she had come back to Colorado before Marc met Karen?

When May did come back, she'd chosen to be friends with Marc and his new partner rather than discard a relationship she highly valued. Years later, when she'd met and fallen in love with Kai, she again felt guilty for not telling *Kai* about the miscarriage. She didn't want to upset him or let it come between their deepening friendship with Marc and Karen.

Kai was childless too, for several reasons. He believed there were already too many humans on this tiny planet. And despite his original intention to be an infiltrator and culture-changer in the world of high finance, he'd actually become addicted to the high life, which hadn't left time for a family. After getting a scholarship to Columbia for a Masters in Economics, he'd scored a job with Lehman Brothers, where toxic mortgages and tainted employee bonuses enabled a self-indulgent yet ultimately unfulfilling lifestyle complete with fast cars and pretty women. But he'd finally acknowledged the gap between his convictions and his actions and come back to Denver. Like a lightning strike that somehow disinfects the past, he'd met May.

Out by the greenhouse, Yukio enthusiastically explained horticultural techniques. Although Kai was already very advanced in vegetable growing, Yukio's mission was to excite his son about the herbs and ornamentals, too. The father's energy level always shot up whenever he explained details of the work to his son. Bent over a bed of sky-blue gentian, he would instruct, "This plant, *Gentiana scabra*, promotes good digestion and a healthy liver. It grows well in Colorado, but we don't want to baby it with too much water. When we water most of these herbs, we water deeply, but then we let them dry down for up to a week or even two, depending on the weather and the richness of the soil." He wanted to show Kai how challenging and rewarding it was to grow and market herbs that made people's lives better. Although Kai had watched him run the practice over the years, Yukio suspected his son hadn't paid much attention to the details.

Very energetic for an eighty-one-year-old geezer, Yukio had an outgoing personality and the dignified air of a master. He was a man you could trust, and Kai did, despite some rough stretches in their relationship in earlier years. And there were a few things about his father that really bugged Kai. For one thing, he sometimes wished his father would talk a little less! And, sometimes when Yukio laughed it was loud and sustained, as if he was breaking free of cultural restraints he'd grown up with. This dynamic, well regarded healer was not the stereotypical silent, enigmatic Japanese man.

As a child, Yukio had endured a few years of internment in the Granada Camp in southern Colorado. His own parents had been forced to sell their home in Colorado Springs at a loss, and he still remembered how suspiciously the Americans had treated first generation immigrants like his parents. But Yukio had risen above the indignity, as had Michiko, who was also confined as a child in a California camp. Somehow, each had found a path through a vengeful American culture that often denigrated them. After apprenticing and then practicing herbalism for many years, Yukio felt inferior to no one. In fact, from Kai's perspective, Yukio sometimes acted a bit *superior*. But then, maybe he was. There was some little piece of Kai's persona—like a sharp pebble in an otherwise comfortable slipper—that wanted to shrug off the compulsory traditions. He wasn't sure he could obey every instruction his father issued, like a good Japanese son. And yet, as the student, the understudy, wouldn't he have to follow instructions? Would the tensions that he and his father felt in earlier years resurface if they became full partners in the practice?

In the end, though, duty did pull at Kai from the deep well of Japanese culture. Although each of his parents was healthy at that time, they wouldn't be around forever, and he needed to take care of them as they had taken care of him. He'd recently decided to make the healing arts his new direction— a decision that had erased a lot of uncertainty and stress. Now in a comfortable chapter of his life, Kai had to admit he really *was* interested in learning how to grow, market, and prescribe herbs.

As his father's assistant in the vegetable gardens, Kai was well familiar with the care they took to maintain the soil. Together they had incorporated tons of amendments into the redwood-framed beds: kelp, greensand, compost, alpaca manure, feather meal, worm castings, rock phosphate and bone meal. The beds were arranged artistically in both back yards and less formally in the front yards, too. Over the years, Yukio had observed Kai's fascination with soil. As he incorporated oxygen and mixed nutrients into it, Kai always became very focused and absorbed.

Yukio explained, "We choose herbs that respond to a patient's symptoms, but we go deeper to find the *cause* of the symptoms. Our goal is to support the body's ability to heal itself. Sometimes we combine the exact three herbs we are hoeing right now—echinacea, astragalus, and agastache—to help a patient overcome congestion, coughing, low energy and flu symptoms. By adding in a decoction of fresh garlic, we've had good results with this formula. People come to see us every year right before flu season." Although Yukio and Michiko had the equipment to prepare formulas, salves and teas from their three-lot mini farm, their most marketable asset was Yukio's knowledge. The master continued, "I also use *Kampo* formulas like *Maoto* for flu-like symptoms. This is a well prepared combination of four herbs that you'll recognize as apricot seed, ephedra, licorice and cinnamon. If you work with me on the herbal side of our practice, I can teach you how to find the appropriate *sho* for each ailment, but you won't be responsible all by yourself!" Yukio laughed loudly, with a big smile and his hand on Kai's shoulder. "You're not certified yet, but I'll be here to work with you, and teach you."

It was a moment of truth: Yukio was putting the invitation right on the table—directly offering his son a partnership. Looking his father right in the eye, Kai said, "You know I've been thinking about this, and I'm almost ready to say yes, if you will be patient with me as I learn. I'm willing to put in the time to do the research, but I don't have a lifetime to study, as you did. I need a little more time to think this over, is that okay?"

Yukio took a deep breath and exhaled a barely audible sigh of relief. "You're very sharp, you'll pick it up." Sensing that he was very close to persuading Kai to be a partner, Yukio shifted gears, telling his son, "I want to give you a little tour of my cabinet of high quality premixed herbs. One of your first lessons will be to become familiar with the ten or twenty formulas we use routinely. Maybe you can help me keep that supply stocked, as well as help track the date we purchase them. We have to make sure we use fresh and powerful herbs."

"What's been your most challenging success? Is there one example that shows the capabilities of *Kampo* methods?"

Yukio thought for a few seconds. "A referral from a doctor whose patient had Stage IV cancer, where chemotherapy hadn't worked." Yukio paused, remembering the details. "First we built up the energy flow—the *ki*—with several traditional formulas as well as acupuncture treatments by Mr. Ogawa. A strict, emergency change in diet made the patient's body alkaline, then we used a strong herbal tea to knock out the cancer, which is still in remission." Yukio shook his head, confiding humbly, "We don't always have such good success with these kinds of advanced cases." Kai nodded, impressed by his father's knowledge as well as his humility. After a brief silence the *sensei* said, "Many people in this country assume that herbal treatments are a bunch of bunk—old fashioned and not as powerful as the expensive pharmaceutical drugs. *Kampo* is not about power, but *balance*. If a drug is *too* powerful, like many cancer chemotherapies, it can radically disrupt the body's natural flow. We want to help sharpen the body's defenses to rise up and *reject* the disease." He held up two fists and shook them for emphasis.

Kai mentioned the Chinese woman scientist who had received the Nobel Prize for rediscovering a cure for malaria in medical texts written sixteen centuries earlier. Yukio explained, "Her team found a brief reference to sweet wormwood—*Artemisia annua*—which has now been proven effective and has been widely used—though still resisted by the drug companies."

Each man liked how that story legitimized the practice of herbalism in the face of what Yukio sometimes called "the Casino" of high-tech, high-risk drugs. If botanical molecules had no health benefits, why were so many synthetic drugs based on them? Why were millions of people now relying on herbal teas and supplements for comfort and relief? Both knew that in nature, gorillas intuitively select from a palette of a hundred or more plant species depending on what their bodies need at that precise time.

Kai knew firsthand that a sick-looking tomato plant could be healed with a misting of rich compost tea, because of its natural antibiotics, enzymes and diverse nutrients. So fascinated was Kai by botanical benefits in both healing and nutrition that he was going to propose slight changes in the family business: he would agree to learn his father's trade if he could also become a salaried organic gardening advocate, promoting locally grown organic food from seedling to plate. The popular 1970s phrase, "You are what you eat" was far more than archaic pop-wisdom to Kai. Eating healthy food was wise, living herbalism.

Kai Sakata had been a rebellious son in his teen years, but he'd come through the challenges intact. He'd been the only Asian student in his junior high years in Colorado Springs, and sometimes he felt like he had to try harder than his classmates to fit in. When it came to grades he was always near the top. In those years, Yukio and Michiko didn't have much money and the appearance of Kai's outdated clothes, bikes and sports equipment were sometimes an easy target for teasers. The young man had gotten some guidance from the Japanese concept of *ikigai*, 'reason for being,' a guideline for how to create a healthy life. Its three key questions were: What do I love? What am I good at? What does the world need? He remembered the year in high school when he'd stammered noticeably, the same year that he and Penny started dating. She could have been hanging with the "cool" girls but considered them self-absorbed and went with her instincts. Kai's first shy kiss came after a prom date, foreshadowing secret, life-changing adventures, potentially hazardous to his grades. But who cared about that? With his speech far more normal and his voice getting deeper, he had more exciting things to think about.

He recalled a classic, wacky tale of teenage exhilaration. He and Penny were up in the third story of her house, a remodeled attic, after school. They were supposedly watching TV in her grandmother's apartment, which had the only TV in this hyper-literate household. Grammy was about 99 percent blind and two-thirds demented but could still get around, mostly by feel. She was away from the house with her friends, and both of Penny's parents were at work, so the opportunity for young love was far too compelling.

The curious, passionate high schoolers were stark naked and sweaty when they abruptly heard Grammy's high-pitched voice down on the street, calling goodbye to her friends and slamming the car door. Laughing, Penny said, "Hurry, get dressed!" But Grammy was making a beeline up to her apartment to take a nap. They heard her mumbling to herself coming up the last flight of stairs, hanging onto the banister. Penny, in the space between terror and hilarity, whisper-screamed, "Quick, get in the closet!" The naked lovers held their breaths, their hearts pounding and their clothes in their arms as Grammy came straight for the closet to hang up her jacket. In primal terror Kai watched Grammy's blind eyes looking straight at him but not seeing—or else choosing not to see. Mumbling to herself, she hung up her jacket, closed the door and slowly felt her way back down the stairs.

Naked in the eyes of the blind, Kai had called it, as if it were a Zen koan. When you survive moments like these, other traumas seem smaller. With Penny as his man-maker, he was suddenly way more than nobody. His scholarship to Columbia opened the door to intellectual pursuits as well as political mayhem, epitomized by the night he spent in a New York City jail cell nursing a black eye.

Yet he knew he was on the ethically correct side of human rights, and with the same intensity he'd thrown into the protest fight that got him arrested, he served as a firefighter for six years, then a down to earth, low-stress mail carrier for another six. At the ever-ripening age of thirty-six, he went back to Columbia to get a Masters in economics, determined to make his parents proud and his bank account more respectable. In interviews with Lehman Brothers, he was confident he could lead the charge towards ethical loans and investments. Money could be profitably allocated to build sustainable communities and provide useful, stimulating jobs. With financial incentives, renewable energy could stave off climate change. But he'd learned the disheartening truth in the Wall Street trenches: money could also become obsessed with reproducing itself, like marching broomsticks with switchblades. Fortunately, something better was waiting when he bailed at age forty-eight: a return to Colorado, where he met May— the crown jewel of his life.

Fifteen

Peas on Earth

Put a hardball in the hands of the Blake brothers and the sun would come out. Worries would wither and the universe would become orderly and comprehensible. As the two walked toward the pasture, Rocket threw the ball a few feet in the air, catching it without really even looking. He recalled a whimsical dream he'd had a few months earlier. "I was coming to the plate at Fenway Park and all the fielders started moving deeper because I was such a slugger. The outfielders were all back against the fence, and the infielders all backpedaled into the grassy outfield. The center fielder actually climbed into the bleachers—you know how dreams are—and all the fans assumed I'd probably just knock it out of the stadium no matter what. I took the first one, waiting for that sweet-spot pitch, and noticed the infielders backing up even deeper."

He paused, waiting for Marc to ask, "What happened then?" Both brothers exclaimed simultaneously—"I bunted/you bunted."

"Inside the park home run? Or actually, *infield* home run?"

"I don't know, I woke up laughing, after I bunted. But I know I would have at least gotten to second base standing, the infielders were so deep. I just needed to push it past the pitcher."

"That's using your head," Marc said in a teasing tone. Then, after a pause, "You know, some of the best advice I ever got came from you. You told me when we were still at Junior High to 'always be the one who wants the ball to be hit to you.'"

"I said that? That's pretty wise, isn't it? Don't just watch your life go by, be *in* it."

"Do you ever wish you'd played another year with the Indians, to see what life would be like in the Big Leagues?"

"Never."

"Even though the average salary in the majors is now over $4 million a year, with another $100 a day thrown in for meals?"

"Yeah, what's Clayton Kershaw making for the Dodgers, $30 million a year or something? No, I'd rather be a farmer-peasant than some rich asshole signing autographs."

"Bullshit!" Marc replied, and they both laughed as they walked. Beyond the pasture gate, Marc tossed the bat down, defining an imaginary home plate. He ran through the six-inch-tall grass, then abruptly turned and held his glove down as a target. Rocket winged a bullet toward his brother's feet and Marc deftly caught it, sweeping his glove across the ground to tag out the invisible, sliding runner. Then Rocket started hitting out fly balls, lofting them a little deeper each time; challenging the outfielder to show his stuff. Rocket knocked one twenty-five` feet deeper than Marc, then intently watched the play unfold: from the very heartbeat of his uniformed years in college, Marc turned his back to the batter and sprinted ecstatically, right through a crack in reality. Rocket watched what felt like a slow-motion clip, there were so many things to observe. Marc was precisely in the right position as the ball came down, catching it over his right shoulder with an adrenalin rush he hadn't felt in years. It didn't even faze him when he slipped on a mostly dehydrated cow pie, stumbled forward, and acrobatically somersaulted back onto his feet, victoriously holding the ball aloft in his glove.

His brother hooted at the top of his voice, "OH MY GOD, that's the *Willie!* I got to see you do the *Willie!*" He was referring to a mythical catch once executed by center fielder Willie Mays almost a lifetime earlier. You just turn your back and race like a cheetah is three steps behind you, your exact response based on split-second analysis of the contact between bat and ball, volume of the impact, wind conditions, reputation of the batter and, of course, thousands of hours of practice. Marc's catch wasn't *quite* as dramatic as Willie's (except in his own mind) but the bottom line was, he'd *caught* it, at the age of sixty-three, laughing as he ran and risking a back wrench as he gave it that extra ninth-inning effort. A smile stretched from one side of his face to the other. He was giddy that he had a brother like Rock to hit a fly ball just the right distance! Compared to what he was feeling right at that moment, a potentially fatal virus was no big deal. Tossing the ball back to Rock nonchalantly (you always had to "aw, shucks" it), he imagined as any schoolboy does that the fans were on their feet, cheering insanely.

After planting, fertilizing and mulching twenty-five butternut squash seedlings, Marc, Sara, and Zak went in to cook the chicken curry. Marc got out his container of dry ingredients—turmeric, chili powder, paprika, ground ginger, cardamom, cloves, cinnamon, bay leaf—and a jar of ghee. He had already discovered that Ellie and Rock had the other ingredients—a few red onions, garlic cloves, tomatoes (still in the pantry from the previous year's canning), some fresh cilantro, olive oil and, most importantly, the chicken. They set up a mixing area on a extra-large hardwood cutting board, inlaid in the counter near the sink. Marc asked Sara and Zak to dice up the meat while he began to combine the curry ingredients in a large skillet. Zak's chicken boycott of the previous night had slipped Sara's mind, but when she referred to it as 'chicken," a mutinous look came over the boy's face. "This is *Goldie* again?" Zak asked in an accusatory whine.

"Of course it is," his mother said, "but Goldie always knew her job was to help feed our family." Marc said, "I understand why you feel bad about eating meat that comes from one of the chickens in the yard. But let me ask you something: do you like hamburgers?"

"Yes…" Zak answered, squirming a little on the stool where he was kneeling. "That comes from an animal that was once alive, too…like the cow that lives out in the pasture."

"Caroline," Sara added. "Except she's a *dairy* cow...for milk, not meat," she explained to Zak.

Marc was hoping he had some leverage with the boy since they'd picked strawberries and even had a laughing fit together. Zak fidgeted, a crimson scene of slaughter in the foreground of his thoughts. He asked Marc, "Do you think it's fair to eat animals that were our friends?"

"Yes, I do," Marc answered. "If we treat the animals kindly when they're alive and end their lives quickly so they don't suffer, it is fair game." Sara came at it from a different angle, appealing to Zak's emerging work ethic: "You're the Chicken Chief, right?" Zak nodded, hesitantly. "Well, there's never been a Chicken Chief who didn't eat chicken, it's just part of the job," she said in the conclusive tone of a prosecuting attorney. But Zak didn't buy it. "What if he was a vegetarian Chicken Chief?" Both Sara and Marc laughed. The boy was finessing their best arguments. "Well, you're right," Sara conceded, "There may have been a few vegetarian Chicken Chiefs somewhere, but none here. Here, the Chicken Chief needs to *eat* the chicken to ensure its quality." Thinking on her feet, she went on, "Because if the meat tastes good, that means he—or she—is taking good care of the chickens. Feeding them well, making sure they have clean water and that the hens don't peck at each other."

Marc, always a repository of lame jokes, tried to steer the conversation into harmless absurdity. "Why *didn't* the cannibal eat the clown?" he asked, looking directly at Zak and waiting.

"Because the clown was his friend?" Zak guessed. "No," Marc answered. "Because he tasted...*funny.*" Bingo! By the time Zak got and then repeated the punchline, Marc knew they'd won the battle, at least for a while. It was bench-scale anthropology: If both his mother and his great uncle were okay with eating Goldie, the boy had no choice, if he wanted to be cool—especially if his job description demanded it. "I'll tell you what," said Marc, "Why don't you and I work on the curry sauce, Zak. And Sara, maybe you can do the dicing? Cubes that are about an inch and a half on a side, please?"

"You got it," she said, picking up the butcher knife.

A few hours later, forks and knives were clicking and tapping like a chorus of well-oiled machines. Marc's mild but flavorful curry was a big hit, even with Zak who requested a second helping. And of course the strawberry cobbler also drew kudos. "What a team!" Ellen said. "We got the strawberries and peas picked, the squash seedlings planted and with the help of Wanda's son Tommy we cut and bundled all the snapdragons well before bloom. Perfect! What about you, Rock, did you get a lot of work done?"

"The basket weaver figure is complete, and now only the mountain lion and eagle need finishing touches. And, I might add, the irrigation line repaired, Giants back in first place." (He'd listened to the baseball game on the radio as he worked.) Tapping a fork on his wine glass, Rocket stood up ceremoniously and raised his glass in toast. "To the best chicken curry I've ever eaten, or ever *will* eat." Marc smiled, bowing theatrically from his seat, then held up a bowlful of dark green peas. In an earnest tone mimicking his brother's toast, he proclaimed, "And may there always be...peas on Earth!" Sara teasingly booed Marc's pun, but Ellen and Rocket pretended to be earnestly in support of the toast. As if they'd rehearsed it, they held up their glasses, simultaneously repeating, "To peas on Earth."

Then Rocket reached under the table to grab an item he'd stashed, waiting for this very moment. Confident of his brother's reflexes, he flipped a baseball across the table and Marc one-handed it. "That's a present for you, big guy." Marc turned the ball around and read, *'For Rocket, a future hall of famer—keep swinging! Mickey Mantle.'*

"That's a helluva present, Rock! Thank you so much!"

A few minutes later, Sara excused herself and walked away from the table toward the living room, her phone in hand and texts to be answered. Ellen asked her, "Would you consider singing a few songs tonight? I'd love to hear your voice again."

"I'm a little out of practice. But I guess I could sing one or two...with another glass of wine." As she went to get her guitar, Ellen told Marc, "She's been playing music for quite a while now, including an appearance in a TV commercial. Get a front row seat for this."

Rocket added, "Her guitar once belonged to Don Henley of the Eagles." Marc was impressed but a little skeptical. "How do you know that?"

"I got the guitar as payment for drywalling work I did for the Eagles' manager, remember?" Now Marc remembered the story. On his way home from LA with the prize, Rocket explained to the United Airlines check-in clerk that he needed to carry the guitar on the plane rather than checking it. "It's a gift for my daughter and I don't want to take a chance with it." But the man at the counter told him, "You need to check it. You can't carry it on." After Rocket requested to speak to the supervisor, he could feel the other passengers' impatience in the line behind him, but still he refused to check it. The supervisor said, unimpressed, "Yes, I know who Don Henley is—*Hotel California*, but you still can't carry a guitar that large on the plane, this is a full flight." It was the authority in the man's voice that made Rocket come unhinged. "I won't check it. I'm carrying it on board." Now his fellow passengers were getting agitated, too, like cannibals gathering around a cauldron of boiling water. "You're off the flight," the supervisor informed him with tight-lipped, power-obsessed satisfaction. The upside was, his trophy was safe! He searched the Departures screen for other options and found another flight to San Francisco a few hours later. The woman at the Frontier counter had glanced at his driver's license, seen that his birthday was coming up and told him, "Sure, you can carry the guitar on board, and Happy Birthday, Mr. Blake!"

Sara came back to the living room with her Don Henley guitar, looking a little distracted. But since she'd told her mother she'd play, she was determined to carry it off. While the others continued to talk and eat strawberry cobbler, she positioned a stool in the empty space in front of the tall book shelf, where Zak sometimes performed puppet shows and Rocket and Ellen did yoga or sorted packets of garden seeds. Sara tuned her guitar and warmed up in a low, private voice while Zak, who'd heard his mother play many times—*too* many times—sat in the back of the room on the floor, teasing the two dogs by tickling the fur on the bottoms of their twitching feet.

Sara took a sip of wine and looked directly at Marc, who she didn't think had ever heard her perform. "You've probably heard this Dylan song before. A lot of people have covered it, including Joan Baez years ago. It's called *"Forever Young."* Ellen said, "Oh, I love that one," and Rocket nodded his head, anticipating the emotion his daughter always poured into that song. Sara cleared her throat and began fingerpicking the intro, not perfectly but with growing confidence. Marc was relieved when she began singing. In any amateur performance, the first few words can either make a listener squirm in his seat or eager to hear more. Sara's voice was strongly connected with the music and, although she didn't hit every note pitch-perfect, she had a stage presence, which didn't surprise Marc. She didn't sing to the floor but connected directly with her tiny audience, her brown eyes meeting first her mother's eyes, then Marc's, then her father's. Although Zak was preoccupied, she deliberately sang in his direction, silently dedicating the song's benediction to her cherished son.

Marc felt a pleasant shiver of emotion as she performed. It was so refreshing to listen to an intimate live performance rather than some hyped-up *America's Got Talent* competition booming through a metallic TV speaker. Clearly, Sara's motivation was to express herself and create a beautiful moment, nothing more, nothing less. *This music is real,* Marc thought, leaning back in his seat. As her daughter sang the words about always knowing the truth and seeing the light around you, Ellen finally lost it. Her face was tight as she tried to hold back the tears, but unsuccessfully. She sniffed as silently as possible. Looking over toward Rocket's seat, wearing a smile of pride, she was surprised to find that he had gone into the other room and was talking on the phone so quietly that he couldn't be heard under the music.

"John, Sara has her guitar out and it seems to be kind of an open moment. You should bring your clarinet over."

"That's a coincidence. Jessie is over *here*, and we're playing some music, too. What's she playing?"

"Folk music...Dylan. Come on over."

"Okay to bring Jessie too?"

"Sure, whatever. See you in a few."

Rocket was back in his seat just as Sara was finishing the song. She got the unconditional applause only a family can deliver. "Beautiful job, Sara," uncle Marc declared. "Dylan had, still has, an amazing career. He became a cultural icon, didn't he, like Picasso or Frank Lloyd Wright or...Meryl Streep."

"I agree," Sara said, "but I wish he'd gone to Sweden to receive his Nobel Prize for literature. It seemed kind of ungrateful of him to just continue his tour and blow it off."

"That's Dylan," Marc said, shaking his head, "enigmatic and always reinventing himself."

"I realized years ago I'm not a professional singer, you all know that, but maybe I'm good enough to play in living rooms and backyards."

"*Maybe*? Of course you are! Music isn't just about making money or becoming famous, it's about making people *feel* something." Sara nodded in agreement, "After all, the word amateur comes from the Latin word 'amor'—to love."

"Absolutely! We need more amateur *everything*—art, and cooking, sports, debate...Rather than letting advertising create us, why shouldn't we create and express *ourselves*, like you're doing?" Energy was zipping back and forth between the niece and uncle.

Rocket chimed in. "I'll never forget the scene in the movie *Titanic* where the musicians play together for the last time as the ship is going down. True story, they did play."

"'Gentlemen, it has been a privilege playing with you tonight,'" Ellen recited. "That scene still gives me the chills." Marc thought, *literally,* then asked, "Can you play another song or two...or three?"

Sara thought for a moment about what to play next, choosing another classic folk song, a difficult one to sing: Joni Mitchell's vintage *California*. Fortunately, she'd long ago adapted Mitchell's dulcimer instrumentation to a guitar and lowered the key an octave to make its high notes accessible. The song described Mitchell in Paris, reading about the peace movement back home. As she continued to play, Marc understood what Rocket meant about Sara's comfort in the spotlight. After getting warmed up, she was confident and radiant. He felt so lucky to be spending time with his family! He wished Lisa were with them. With the last notes still lingering in the air, Sara offered, "I could sing another one that's a lot different, that Jessie and I were playing the other day over at the yurt. Do you know Gillian Welch's music?" she asked, looking at Marc—both because he was the special guest and seemed so interested.

"Sure. I saw her at a concert hall in Denver. She's great—completely pure, with that spare, gutsy voice." Sara shifted her weight on the stool and threw her springy brown hair back over one shoulder. Just as she was ready to sing, John and Jessie walked in with their instruments, catching Sara off-guard. She made a joke: "It seems like all I have to do is mention Jessie's name and he magically appears." Jessie was barefoot and wore his shirt with several of the top buttons unfastened. "Don't tell me you're a witch."

Jessie didn't have a case for his guitar, so he carried the well-used instrument in his hand. John's clarinet was held in a black hard shell case. The family's only nearby neighbor looked like a college kid on a date to the diner. Had he quickly jumped into a clean polo shirt, shorts and sandals? Sara took an involuntarily breath when she saw him. He seemed so amiable, so sure of himself, and so strangely...familiar. Although she'd only heard John play from a distance, she felt butterflies at the prospect of playing music for him, let alone *with* him.

"We don't want to barge in," John said. "We'll just be audience for a while, does that work?" Sara was curious, looking around the room before she spoke. "How did you know we were playing music?" She glanced at John and Jessie, then quickly examined her father's face. Rocket knew he was in trouble, *again.* "Well, I thought since you were playing music, maybe we should have a little jam session."

"Nice of you to run that past me," Sara said without a follow-up laugh, in a husky voice that stunned everyone in the room except Zak. (The boy was now harassing the dogs with a battery-powered Lego truck, staging a clacking assault on Willie's snout despite the napping dog's obvious annoyance.)

As he pieced together his clarinet from its velvet-lined case, John assessed the sudden awkwardness in the room, taking a private, intuitive survey of what the group *needed.* He looked directly at Sara, with a jovial smile still on his face. She tried to interpret the smile. It felt safe and a little dangerous at the same time—a feeling she *typically* relished. In a split-second decision, she opted to accept John as an ally and friend, at least for the moment, while at the same time shutting the door on her father, whose unilateral invitation she considered obnoxious. *"I know this guy, John,"* Sara thought, surprising herself. *"Maybe I should be nicer to him."*

"Jessie was telling me that you and he have been practicing a few songs together. Can you play one of them?" John asked. Sara snuck an opportunity to study his handsome face when he looked at Jessie. Then she turned to her musical chum and fellow strawberry harvester, Jessie. "I was just about to play our Gillian Welch song, but I'd rather sing it with your guitar and harmony." She felt ready to shift emotional gears and dig a little deeper. It wasn't the song's words she liked but the edgy way they *felt*—a lively country tune about the harsh realities of life when you can't even afford a bag of groceries, and your next door neighbors might be opioid addicts. In the song, a woman "buys the farm" and puts a needle in her arm. She could be less sentimental and gutsier with this one.

A vein stood out on Sara's neck as she sang, and Jessie's bass runs in the background and strong harmony in the chorus amplified her own intensity. She knew the performer's strategy of converting nervous energy into excitement and leaned into the music, completely charming everyone in the room. As the song ended, Rocket caught her looking up at John first, for his reaction. "Dynamite!" John said. He liked everything about her, even the barriers she stubbornly put between them. Here was a woman who connected with life directly. He wanted her for the right reasons, but he wouldn't gush over her, that wouldn't be cool. "You guys are really getting that song down."

"Thanks. I like the pacing, and the bare bones feel of it. You do a great job with that on the guitar," Sara told Jessie. "What songs were you and John playing together?"

"*Three Little Birds*," Jessie said, fingering a few reggae chords. Looking over at John, he asked, "Why don't you sing the lead?" It was as if Jessie, too, were a matchmaker, ready to give John the spotlight. "Okay," John said confidently, looking around the room, "It's a singalong. Everybody sings lead on this one." Marc, Rocket and Ellen nodded, and any remaining uneasiness in the room had melted away as Jessie's reggae beat began. Since they had just practiced the song, it was in the right key for singing, and John sang out in a clear alto voice.

A man comfortable with being in charge, John addressed the audience with a smile as he sang, making sure that everyone was having fun. Even Zak settled in next to Marc on the couch, pretending he knew the words too. The boy studied and filed away each gesture and nuance of John's performance. Although Sara was focused on playing guitar, she kept sneaking glances at John, who threw himself into this feel-good song as if he'd written it. When their eyes met, John thought he felt an emotional agreement, making him all the more enthusiastic. After a few verses, he picked up his clarinet and played a simple, lighthearted instrumental break. He was not a polished musician either, but no one in the room cared. His energy was infectious. When the song ended, everyone applauded, happy they'd sung it together.

By god, every little thing *might* be all right after all. In a movie-scripted world, Rocket and Ellie would get their finances under control that year and finally buy the cabin. Somehow Marc's immune system would rise up and send the Q virus to hell. Sara would find a job and also connect romantically with John. Jessie would become a chef and grow much of his own produce.

And Zak would become a cowboy, or at least be *rich*, like John. President Trump (that title was still such a shock!) would change his mind about climate change being a "hoax" and immediately begin to lead the country and the world into peaceful, pro-environmental action. For the moment, happy endings all around, why not?

John picked up his clarinet again, telling Jessie and Sara that his next song was in the key of G so they could play along if they wanted. He played the old jazz standard *My Blue Heaven*, written in the 1920s and made famous by Fats Domino. Jessie was quick to pick up and support the beat and Sara followed along, mostly pondering her new resolution to talk with John. *That should happen tonight, after we play music,* she thought, with a twinge of excitement. She was still inclined to tell John she wasn't ready for romance, but given the way she felt right at that moment, maybe she *was* inclined. And then again, maybe she wasn't.

John's solo performance of this one was polished—he'd probably been playing it since high school. With his eyes closed and his clarinet first horizontal, then tilting skyward, he had everyone in the room tapping their feet and nodding their heads rhythmically. When he'd played a few variations, he wrapped it up, taking a facetious bow and blushing just a little before sitting down. Sara leaned over and asked him in a low voice if they could talk later that evening. Rocket and Ellen both noticed Sara and John conferring. With their heads close together, so he could hear her voice, John nodded with raised blond eyebrows.

Rocket, the de facto MC, pointed out that they should probably make it an early night since the Big Event was scheduled for the following morning. He asked John what time they should leave for Cloverdale, where the drop zone was. "We agreed that 10 o'clock at the site would be about right," John responded. Does it work for everybody to leave at 7:30 or so?"

"Maybe we could grab some breakfast at the Maple Cafe in Ukiah," Rocket suggested. As everyone got to their feet, Ellie answered, stretching, "Good idea. I love their breakfast burritos."

"It's not too late to back out, is it?" Marc joked,

"Way too late, brother, we're *doin'* this! This is my first time, too, man." Ellen drifted into the kitchen as John packed up his clarinet. Sara said, "I need to get Zak over to the 'Sky Lodge.' It's bed time. I'll be back in a few minutes." The message was for everyone, but she looked directly at John when she said it.

When Sara came back from the treehouse, John was standing in front of the cabin—looking, listening, and feeling the darkness descend. Inside, in the yellow rectangle that was the kitchen window, he saw Ellen's and Marc's silhouettes as they finished the dishes. He did not, however, have any idea that Rocket was secretly in the dark bedroom peering out the window. Sara felt it was more appropriate to have their talk in front of the cabin, rather than wandering further off in the darkness. She didn't want to send a signal that this was 'romantic' talk. They stood facing each other, the casual distance between them more like friendship than rendezvous.

The light in the kitchen eliminated Ellen's ability to observe the twilight meeting, but Rocket had it covered. Feeling guilty, or at least stealthy, he peeked into the darkening yard as if he was just looking out at the waxing moon, just in case he was seen. Here's what he took in, as he tried to interpret their body language: Sara, who after all had convened the summit, was saying her piece, her hands palms-up as she spoke. John stood listening and nodding, one arm wrapped casually around his clarinet case. It seemed to Rocket like the conversation was one-sided. "What's she doing, a frickin' filibuster?" His daughter stood straight and strong, defining her personal space and not yielding a square inch of ground. Finally it was John's turn to talk. An inch or two taller than the woman he was courting, he seemed to be speaking slowly and maybe inching up to her just slightly. For a moment, neither of them talked, then he spoke again, with his head high. Was there something more animated than usual in his posture, and more receptive in hers, or was Rocket just imagining that?

It was a four minute negotiation, total, ending in a quick, polite-looking hug, then a quickly widening gap between them. "It's all about the final gaze," Rocket thought, but now it was too dark to make out their faces. Through the glass panes, he heard their voices calling goodnight, maybe offering mutual support and excitement for their tandem jump the next morning. As John walked back toward his house, his stride was neither victorious nor dejected. Rocket noticed Sara turning on her flashlight as she walked back toward the tree house, but he couldn't pick up any clues there, either.

Sixteen

A Leap of Faith

As Marc lay in bed the following morning, he replayed a dream he'd had about jumping out of an airplane, of all things! He wondered if being so far out of his comfort zone had rekindled dormant courage because, after dream-jumping out of the plane, he'd experienced a deep sense of tranquility, even after both the primary and the backup parachutes failed to open! When the panicked jumpmaster loudly announced over Marc's shoulder that they were going to crash land, Marc had replied calmly, "We're going to be all right," and instead of smacking the ground at 150 miles an hour, they coasted in for a soft landing, just as if the canopy *had* functioned.

He got up and started getting dressed, hearing Rocket's and Ellen's first waking murmurs down the hall. There were also signs of life elsewhere on the homestead: over in his bachelor pad, John stumbled sleepily toward the room with the domed ceiling to ride his exercise bike. Sara, in sweat pants and a fleece top, scanned news headlines and managed texts and emails in the treehouse. After seeing the light from his Mom's phone in the other room, Zak had pulled a pillow over his eyes, and similarly, Jessie's alarm had gone off but had been silenced by two successive clicks of the snooze button. The other interns, Sam and Cynthia, fully intended to join the entourage, but were also snoozing.

Marc opted for a walk out to the road by the light of dawn, his feet crunching quietly on compacted gravel. He was still charmed by the music shared the night before, and amused by the whisperings and covert strategies going on between Sara and John. As a curious and protective uncle, he wondered if he would witness merger or meltdown while he was there. Although he planned to return home in a few days, he wished he could stay another month. After his recent years as a workaholic widower, it felt great to be with family and without major obligations. His brother's world was stimulating and relaxing at the same time. He really cherished the sense of rhythm and purpose at this little homestead.

Shortly before 7:30, the bold skydivers and their support crew began to assemble in front of Rocket's and Ellen's cabin, yawning, stretching, and snacking on a bowl of strawberries Ellen had put out on the front porch. Rocket made sure that as John's car came around the ravine, two of the interns and Marc were quickly ushered into Ellie's Subaru, leaving John's car as the only option for Sara and Zak. Jessie would ride his motorcycle because he wanted to stop and see a girlfriend after the jump. All three interns were grateful they'd been invited along, partly because it meant at least half a day off for a change.

"It looks like we're ready to go," John said, climbing out of his Tesla. "Who's coming with me?" he asked, just to be polite. "You get the pleasure of our company," Sara answered in an upbeat voice, determined to maintain the agreement they'd made: friends, possibly moving at an undetermined pace toward "something else." Sara added as an obvious point of information, "Jessie's riding his motorcycle."

"Do you think she'll make it?" John called out to Jessie, teasing him about the bike's missing muffler and wired-together parts.

"Of course, this is totally a lean, mean machine."

Zak climbed into the back seat of John's steel grey car, carrying a small backpack, a pillow and a toy drone Rocket had given him. He was erroneously confident he'd soon be riding in an airplane, learning how to be a skydiver. Sara, wearing a pair of white shorts, swung her long, tanned legs into the passenger seat, sending John into a secret swoon. As the little caravan pulled away with Ellie's car in the front and Jessie's very noisy vehicle in the back, John tried to create a comfortable ambience, plugging his phone in so they could listen to his playlist. "Did you sleep well?" he asked Sara over the drone of Jessie's motorcycle. She preferred not to acknowledge whether or not their conversation the night before had kept her awake, so the quality of her sleep (or in fact, lack of it) was really none of John's business. But she politely said, "Yes, pretty well, how about you?" John wore a khaki short sleeve button-down shirt and his tanned face and arms matched the tan of her legs. "I slept great!" Her words had been a gift, he believed, now the rest should be an exhilarating inevitability. And it was this very assumption of John's that simultaneously attracted and repelled Sara. She liked men who were confident, but hated when they crossed over into arrogance.

Before attaching her own seatbelt, she made sure that Zak's was fastened, and encouraged him to fluff his pillow and take a nap. "We won't be having breakfast for a while, so just close your eyes and I'll wake you up when we get there." As they drove down the long driveway, John turned on Brazilian samba music, sung by the sweet-voiced Rosa Passos, with Stan Getz on a lilting tenor sax. Sara wondered, *Did he hear what I said last night about going slow, or does he just automatically go into the flirt mode?* From the car in front of them, Marc's hand appeared out the back window making little puppets in the air—now a snapping crocodile, now a long-eared jackrabbit. Then, as they turned onto the main road, he stuck his head fully out the window, making a goofy anything-goes face. "What a motley crew," Sara said, shaking her head. In the rear-view mirror, she saw Jessie's jacket flapping in the wind, his long hair cascading out the back of his helmet. He seemed calm and independent as usual, despite the noise, the wind, and his junior position in the motorcade.

"We need to get you ready for the jump," John said, looking over at Sara confidently. "I haven't shown you the 'insane mode' yet, have I?" She couldn't believe he was going to show off for her, but she went with it, curious what the Tesla's insane mode actually did feel like. John signaled for Jessie to pass him, and the motorcycle noisily motored a hundred yards ahead. John asked, "Is Zak strapped in? Hey Zak, want to see how fast this car can accelerate?"

"Yeah!" Zak said, fully awake in less than a second, anxious to experience anything John thought was cool. John waited for a car to pass in the other lane, then pressed the insane button. Both passengers were stunned as the car lurched from zero to sixty in *three seconds*. Each felt a little like an astronaut ascending into orbit, G forces and all. "690 horsepower," John said, laughing. "It can travel a quarter mile in about ten seconds."

"Get many speeding tickets?" Sara teased, as the car quickly decelerated.

"No, I don't really have any need for the insane mode—except of course as a skydiving prep. But I think it's really cool that cars like this are way beyond 'granny-mobiles.' We need zero emissions cars, especially when they're charged with renewable energy."

"That was totally awesome!" Zak said. Then, seeking survival information, he asked, "When are we going to get to the restaurant?"

With a careful watch on the time, the gang sat at two tables, drinking coffee and tea and gabbing about who was scared and who was not. Not everyone gorged himself. Better to be on the safe side, just in case. When they were done, John said, "This is on me." Rocket pulled out his own wallet, insisting the check be split in half. He joked, "If this is our last breakfast, who needs money anyway?"

"You got it, but remember the sky dives are free—part of a deal I made when my friends borrowed my plane a few months ago."

In Ellie's car, the talk was largely about politics. After only 5 months in office, President Trump and his still loyal Congress had already bullied and shunned a wide spectrum of minorities, hired and fired many poorly-chosen federal agency officials, trashed key environmental safeguards and ripped up international agreements, including the Paris Climate Accord. Cynthia, Sam's girlfriend, said she was glad she lived in California, where Governor Jerry Brown was standing up to the White House. "But it's scary to think how care-free our country's leader is, in the *bad* sense of the word. He doesn't care about people, doesn't care about the planet."

A few car lengths back, John was explaining the fundamentals of tandem skydiving: "When you first jump, you won't see the ground but the sky instead, because your head will be facing up. When I tap you on the shoulder, you'll open your arms and extend your legs so you fall face down, without tumbling out of control. It's a clear day today, so we may have a pretty awesome view. After the parachute opens, I'll spin us around a few times to get a full view." Sara was impressed with John's knowledge about skydiving. Impressed enough, she realized, to trust him with her life.

The caravan arrived at the Cloverdale airport, with clear skies and hardly a breeze, just in time to see a tandem team hitting a bull's-eye, landing on their feet right in the center of the drop zone. It looked about as dangerous as a walk to the 7-11. Ellen, Zak, and the three interns went over to sit at a picnic table near the office while the divers-to-be went in to meet the jumpmasters. John was surprised not to see his friends, who owned the business and had offered the free dives. When he commented that he'd arranged to meet them at 10, one of the instructors said, "Oh, they had to cancel work today. Molly's dad is sick or something."

Richard, the instructor, had an upbeat, Marine-like attitude, prepared to answer any and all questions. As Rocket, Marc, Sara and John signed paperwork acknowledging the risks and waiving their legal rights to sue, Rocket joked, "What happens if the parachute doesn't open?"

Richard explained, "Well, as you probably know, both a main parachute and a reserve parachute are provided. If the main 'chute is malfunctioning at 5,000 feet, the jumpmaster will deploy the reserve, and if he or she is somehow unable to make that happen, an AAD—automatic activation device—deploys it."

Marc said in a joking tone, "I think for some *twisted* reason my brother wants to know what happens if *neither* of the parachutes opens. Maybe that's his way of asking if he's gonna live or die." John, the only experienced one among the Willits Four, nonchalantly preempted Richard's reply. "That's about as likely as getting hit by lightning or winning the Powerball lottery, isn't it Richard?"

"I want to know my odds before I sign on the dotted line," Rocket said with a laugh.

In a practiced, reassuring voice, Richard said, "You'll be surprised how smoothly everything will go." After a pause, he continued with a wry smile, "And if for some, almost unheard-of reason even the reserve parachute doesn't open, look at it this way: you'll be freefalling for the rest of your life." It took a few seconds for the joke to sink in, then Marc responded, "What a way to go!" at the same time that Sara commented, "Ouch!" Richard shared a quick, electric glance with this arrestingly pretty woman who he was hoping would be his tandem partner.

Sara turned to John, saying with a smile, "You'd better know what you're doing," and Richard, looking down at the paperwork, assumed she was talking to him. "Don't worry, we know exactly what we're doing. But since we're short-staffed today—we have three rather than our usual five—we'll have to ask you to split into two groups: two will jump on the first flight and two on the second." The others left it for John to explain that he and Sara would be jumping together. Very atypically, John looked flustered. "Caleb and Molly probably told you that I lent them my plane a while ago, and that when we arranged this, they knew that Sara and I would jump together."

Richard seemed speechless, finally asking, "Are you a licensed jumpmaster?" Sara looked at John, expecting him to pull out some kind of a license. "Well, since I've jumped a bunch of times—maybe twenty—I think they were comfortable letting me..."

"Twenty times?" Richard interrupted, "to get my FAA tandem instructor certification, I had to jump 500 times, and I have more than 3,000 jumps behind me now." As the two men gruffled at each other like alpha dogs, John's face turned pinkish-red. He was caught in a lie, enabled by his own arrogance. Sara stared at John with a look of disbelief, and Rocket and Marc, who knew nothing about skydive certification, were also stunned by John's blunder. John stammered, "Well, when we first talked about this skydive, we were just going to parachute onto my property—I have a six acre pasture, and...it was just meant as kind of an unofficial kind of thing." Richard arched his eyebrows, impressed neither by John's explanation nor his apparent station in life. "And they told you 'no way' to a homemade drop zone, right? I'm sorry, but I'm telling you there's no way anyone will ever do a tandem jump with an uncertified partner. Not here."

It was the first time Rocket had ever felt anything but admiration for John. How could his friend trap himself in such an embarrassing situation? And how could he risk Sara's life on some shaky agreement with the company's owners? Marc looked down, totally embarrassed, and Sara was right at the boiling point. "I thought you told me you were certified," she said to John, her eyebrows and forehead furrowed with both disappointment and rage. "Well, I never exactly said I was certified," John said, "but I am a licensed pilot, and I have done a lot of jumps. I...I'm sorry, I just thought it was something that might...bring us together."

"Never!" she said angrily. Sure, she was adventuresome, but when it came to security and trust there was zero tolerance. In this very awkward moment, Rocket tried to rescue the scheduled event from complete meltdown. "Okay," he said, trying to fast-forward from what had just happened, "why don't John and Sara each partner with an instructor on the first drop, and Marc and I will take the second drop?"

Neither John nor Sara spoke up. John was a zombie and Sara radiated red-hot anger. Finally John said, "You guys go ahead. I think I'm going to skip this one. I'm really sorry I screwed things up." As he started walking toward the door, Marc shared an eleventh-hour idea, looking at Richard: "What if John pilots the plane instead of one of you? Wouldn't that leave three tandem-certified instructors, one for each of us?" John paused at the opened door to hear Richard's response.

"Have you ever piloted over a drop zone?" Richard asked John, seeing a possible way out of this mess. "No, but if you guys work with me—with GPS data about location and wind conditions—I'm sure I could cut the engine at just the right moment. What's the target altitude?"

"Thirteen thousand, give or take."

"No problem. I've been flying for ten years—a plane very much like this one." Sara found herself questioning if John was once again stretching the truth. "I need to see your license," Richard told John, commenting in a low voice, "I shouldn't be doing this." But he probably rationalized that if John was not flying proficiently, he would take over. Rocket, still walking on eggs, said, "We appreciate it. That will let us all go up together." John seemed relieved, grateful that Marc had proposed a way for him to save face—at least a little.

After waving and clowning around for the moral supporters seated near the sandy drop zone, the whole bunch ceremoniously climbed the short ramp into the plane. John offered Sara his hand, which she refused—a porcupine with quills extended. Sitting in the copilot's seat, Richard explained the procedures and quizzed John on the plane's controls. Marc, Rocket and Sara made small talk, jammed onto the plane's benches as if they were at a crowded bus station. No worries...right?

Then the plane took off, ascending toward its target elevation, and Marc could feel a genuine grin on his face. He wasn't afraid! Examining the faces of his brother and his niece, he watched Rocket execute a gaping yawn fueled by thin air and adrenalin. Sara glanced only rarely toward John, who expertly guided the small plane skyward. One of the instructors explained that free fall would be about a minute—the closest they would ever come to being a bird in flight.

"You'll drop at the speed of a diving eagle—120 miles an hour." He added, for interest, "but slower than a Peregrine Falcon, which can slice through the air at twice that speed. At 5,000 feet, each of us will deploy the main parachute and each team will float to the ground under the canopy for another five minutes or so. Keep your goggles on tight so you can see well during free fall, which will feel like you're suspended on a cushion of air. So don't fight it, just relax."

"Remember to breathe," counseled another instructor designated as Rocket's partner. She was checking the buckles of the four contact points that would bind them together. "Don't hold your breath in free fall even though the air is rushing past you," she added. When Rocket told her, as quietly as possible, that the plane's open door freaked him out a little (would it suck them right out of the plane?) the instructor grabbed a carabiner and attached herself to Rocket's harness. "You're not going anywhere without me."

Richard continued to update John as they neared the sweet spot. "We're getting close," he told his jump partner, Sara. "Come sit on my legs, please, and I'll buckle us together." Then, as they lumbered their way carefully toward the open door, he reminded her, "Keep your head up as we jump." Sara looked around at her dad and uncle (and even glanced at John) saying simply, "This is it!" They disappeared into thin air, punctuated by a joyful yelp from Sara.

"You're next my man," Rocket said, beaming at his brother. Marc and his tandem partner shuffled toward the door like conjoined twins and, with a minimum of drama, prepared to throw themselves out of the plane. "Remember the Alamo!" John yelled at Marc over the sound of the engine. Rocket gave his bro the thumbs up and they disappeared, followed by Marc's bellowing, "Geronimo!" They fell straight toward the Earth but he was calm, surrendering his fears to the whims of the universe.

In the past few days—partly because of the warmth he was feeling at his brother's house and partly because he was sick of being the guy who might be dying, Marc was feeling stronger. And as he fell through the brightly lit space he was suddenly the guy who was living, the guy who might defy death after all. Seemingly rising up before him were the salt and soil from which his species and all others had sprung: ocean, mountains, river and grass. Way down below, Sara was hurtling toward the ground and, like Marc, she'd put her trust in humanity's ancient quest for knowledge: in Isaac Newton's rational mind and Leonardo Da Vinci's sketches of parachute-adorned humans with mechanical wings.

For these few minutes, the Willits gang was completely separated from the humdrum world of CNN, ROIs, and arguments with grumpy phone salesmen! From traffic jams, White House press conferences, undead movies, and the House of Pancakes. Sara needed to survive to be there for Zak, Marc needed to survive because life seemed incredibly *vivid* now and he wanted much more of it. Rocket needed to survive because he loved Ellie, Sara, Zak, and their little homestead.

Marc watched Sara's parachute open below and in another twelve seconds he felt the pull of his own canopy. The instructor offered to slowly spin the parachute for a panoramic view. Still mind-blown by the freefall he responded, "Yes, go for it!" He took in the foothills of the Sierra Nevada range, sparkling Clear Lake off to the east, the Pacific Ocean on the western horizon and below, the vineyards on both sides of the Russian River. You didn't get this kind of panorama in an airplane and, more importantly, in an airplane you were *contained*, shielded from the vast emptiness of the air by a high-tech composite membrane.

The instructor extended his forefinger to the south. It was a clear enough day to see San Francisco's skyline and Golden Gate Bridge! Compared with the exhilarating, ungodly freefall, the rest of the descent felt like a routine infield pop-up. And like a dream becoming wakefulness, the features on the ground became increasingly visible: over there were Ellie, Zak and the three interns, cheering and hooting as Sara got unstrapped, had her picture taken, and then let out a whoop as Marc landed. As soon as his outstretched legs touched the ground, Marc's first thought—like a kid on a sledding hill— was "Let's do it again!" As he looked up he saw Rocket and his jumpmaster winging mostly sideways toward the ground. Their parachute was not fully inflated, and they came in faster than the others, conversing loudly as they tried for a smooth landing. Unfortunately, they lost their balance, tumbling forward in alarm and then laughter as the wind-inflated canopy draped over them like a silk tsunami. Still, after their brief yet heroic exploits, all the divers were safely on the ground. Mission accomplished!

Walking back to the office, Richard told John, "Good job. Everything went smoothly."

"Good job yourself," John answered, still humbled by his earlier embarrassment. "And thanks for letting me pilot." He wrote Richard a check as they talked.

"I told her you're a damn good pilot," Richard said, with a knowing nod.

"Yeah. Hey, please give Molly and Caleb my best. You don't have to tell them how you kind of bailed me out...if that's awkward."

"Adios, amigo," Richard said, smiling. "Tell folks in Willits about us!"

While John was in the office, Sara had secured a seat in her parents' car. Jessie went on his way via motorcycle while Zak, Sam, and Cynthia waited at John's car. The boy delivered an insider's preview of the Tesla's "insane mode," and the interns were stoked.

B ack home, Ellen immediately mobilized the group to do some harvesting and bundling of vegetables and flowers. Zak collected the eggs, Rocket and Ellie planted potatoes with the interns, while John disappeared into his house.

After dinner, the family sat in the side yard debriefing about the adventure and watching Zak play with his toy drone, even equipped with a little parachute. Although Rocket had left a message for John, inviting him over for a glass of wine, no one had seen their neighbor since the return from Cloverdale. Both his car and truck were in the carport, and Rocket guessed he was catching up with his work. Or...maybe drinking a whole six-pack by himself.

"I'll tell you what, it was a great relief seeing those brightly colored parachutes falling out of the sky, one by one, carrying all my favorite people back down...alive," Ellen said, sipping a glass of Chardonnay. "Were you worried we wouldn't make it?" Rocket asked, still revved up.

"Well, I didn't tell you that a few days ago, I Googled 'skydiving deaths' and there were thirty or so in the U.S. last year."

"Safer than staying at home. There are probably a hundred times that many deaths from houses burning down." Sara, with cellphone in hand, quickly verified that fact. "Good guess, Dad—about 3,000 deaths annually from house fires."

"And what about traffic fatalities?" Rocket continued. "Cars are far more dangerous than parachutes, too, especially with everybody texting at the wheel, and with millions more old folks like us on the road," he commented, grinning at Marc.

"That's why we need self-driving cars," Sara said, and Marc rolled his eyes. "Don't get me started. What kind of humans are we when we can't or won't drive, walk, cook, repair a leaky faucet, or grow a carrot anymore? When everything is automatic, all that's left is watching...Watching the machines watch the last droopy Bengal tiger at the zoo."

Rocket spoke up in solidarity: "We're like a herd of inbred cattle, chewing our cuds when we should be stampeding."

"About thirty-five or forty thousand traffic deaths on average in the last few years," Sara reported. Rocket said, "See? Americans should be skydiving to work, for safety's sake."

At that moment, a bright red car came up the long driveway, bearing left toward John's house. From their seats in adjacent lawn chairs, Rocket and Marc craned their necks to see who was driving. It was a woman with short blonde hair, climbing nimbly out of the car in a tailored green pantsuit. She grabbed two items from the trunk—what appeared to be a laptop computer case and a small overnight type bag. Sara looked up from her cellphone to gawk, before the woman disappeared behind John's vehicles in the carport. They didn't see John opening the door but they did hear distant laughter as she went inside.

Rocket asked Ellen, "Who's *that*? Do we know her?"

"I didn't get a good look," Ellen answered. "Probably somebody he works with."

"You think so?" Sara had no comment. She got up without a word and ducked into the house.

Rocket said, "I need to get some more work done tonight," walking toward his studio. "Ciao for now. Great day, team!"

Seventeen

Breathless

M arc again woke up early to take his morning walk before life at the homestead went into high gear. This time, he'd follow the trail through the woods to its intersection with Highway 47, about a mile away, then follow the winding road back home. At 6:30 there wouldn't be traffic. He went over his to-do list for the day: answer a few phone messages, find out what needed to be done in the gardens so Rocket could stay with his carving project and if possible, tour John's house. Ellie had announced they'd be going to their favorite Italian restaurant on Marc's last night there, so Marc predicted it would be another rewarding day in Willitopia. Early the next morning, he'd fly to Denver. Back to bill paying, doctor visits and a barrage of troubling media about the rogues' gallery of political appointees in charge of "draining the DC swamp."

Fortunately, there were also many things he was looking forward to. The highest priority was spending quality time with Kai and May, who were having a dinner party later in the week. Marc could hardly wait to give his good friends an update about Rocket's and Ellie's lively homestead. He was eager to see Lisa again, too, maybe go to the Botanic Gardens or Denver Art Museum with her. He also had a round of golf scheduled with a few colleagues from the University who had just heard about his retirement but didn't yet know the reason for it. And, his softball team's first game was coming up, always colorful as well as comical.

As he started out, he couldn't help but notice that the red car they'd seen the night before was still at John's. *It's none of my business,* Marc thought, *but that damn sure looks fishy.* Then his thoughts drifted elsewhere, to the self-reliant lifestyle his brother had chosen. Since Rocket and Ellie provided many of their own needs—such as unprocessed food, clean well water, a rich life without the need for traveling, renewable energy, handcrafted furniture and homemade entertainment—their way of life had a far smaller footprint than the average American. To play the game of America as a typical consumer, the average American drew upon the equivalent of twenty or more acres of biologically-rich land and water a year. Marc guessed that his brother's lifestyle required no more than about twelve acres—six of them within a stone's throw.

As Marc told his students, the Earth was currently running an ecological deficit, since it took natural systems a year and a half to regenerate what humans consumed every year. Any region that ran a deficit met its demands by importing from other regions—cashing out its own ecological assets— fish, lumber, soil, plants, clean water—and in the process emitting more carbon dioxide than local forests, grasslands and oceans could absorb. Marc shook his head as he walked, wondering how many acres the Trump family required. Certainly far more than 100, and if every human lived at that vastly superfluous level, humanity would need the resources of about ten additional Earths.

Why can't the development of towns and cities be based on what a region can supply? Marc thought. *Denver's biological capacity should define how many people can live there, sustainably. But since Denver is perceived as a lifestyle mecca, its population will double by 2050.* Thoughts like these weighed heavily on Marc's mind, thanks to the sense of responsibility he sometimes felt *stuck* with. Yet, he had to admit, he would gratefully endure the stresses of this distracted, demented way of life if he could just have another twenty years of it.

After checking in with Rocket and Ellen about the day's to-do list, Marc accepted the job of delivering produce and cut flowers. He'd rely on his phone's GPS to guide the deliveries, and he'd also grab staples like coffee filters, toilet paper, light bulbs and mushrooms while he was in town. Looking at Ellie's shopping list, Marc was amazed at how few "imported" items were on it. In addition to their own products, the family often purchased or bartered for local products like cheese, shampoo and natural medicines.

Meanwhile, under the radar, covert actions were underway in the neighborhood. Midmorning—after the disappearance of the red car—John called Rocket to ask what Zak was up to. "Could you see if he can come over? Tell him he can earn a little money."

"I'll find out," Rocket answered, guessing there had been no thaw in communications between John and Sara or else John would have called her directly to find Zak. "You want him to come over now? I'm not sure if he went to town with Marc, but I'll check and call you back or else just send him over." Two or three minutes later, Zak was on his bike, darting over to John's like a pony on steroids. He was hoping John was going to take him horseback riding. On the front porch, John held out a bowlful of overripe apples. "Cal and Berta love to eat apples, you know that. You think you could go out to the pasture and give these to them?" Zak nodded enthusiastically. "Okay, take the apples over by the little stable, like we did the other day. Just climb onto the bottom rail of the fence and give each of them three small apples, one at a time. Can you do that? If you do it right, I'll give you a dollar." Zak went running toward the pasture gate, confident he could complete the mission and show John how capable he was.

Of course, John had an ulterior motive. He was finishing a Joe Humble note to Sara, and he wanted Zak to be his emissary when it was done. He was in a vulnerable position with Sara, and in the note he'd taken the lonesome road of total atonement. "I don't think I've ever done anything quite so thoughtless, and I'm writing to ask you to forgive me. I think about you all the time, and I'm just hoping we can at least get back to the agreement we made Tuesday night, as friends who might someday be more. I want you to know that it's not just "chemistry" I'm feeling but also deep respect. I want to know you better, at whatever pace feels comfortable to you. And

I'm hoping I can show you that I'm an honorable man, even if I did such an idiotic thing." His note continued contritely, all in very neat handwriting, on sky blue stationery with a drawing of his house printed on the letterhead.

Zak came back excited, reporting that the horses had crunched up the apples and didn't bite his fingers much at all. "Terrific! Can you take on another very important, top secret mission for me? It's worth another dollar."

"Yes!" the boy said, before even hearing the assignment.

John licked the envelope's adhesive and sealed the letter. "Take this to your Mom, right away. It's for her eyes only, and if you try to sneak a peek at it, it won't seal back up and you'll get caught," John said, with a warning smile on his face. "Can you do that?"

"Yes!"

John took two neatly folded dollar bills out of his pocket and pushed them into Zak's eager outstretched hand. "This is very important business, don't blow it, okay?" Zak jumped on his bike and pedaled up a cloud of dust. John was holding his breath and his chest felt heavy. He couldn't remember wanting anything more than he wanted her forgiveness. Though the letter was intended to be top secret, at least one person, Ellie, saw Zak clutching the envelope against one of the handlebars as he rode back, and with a mother's intuition she knew exactly what was up. Zak flew past the house and treehouse toward the large garden plot where Sara and the interns were planting potatoes. All morning she'd been exploring her emotions and thoughts. She felt a strange mixture of jealousy (who was that woman in the pantsuit?), forgiveness, fear, opportunity, and attraction. *Did I let my pride and need for security get in the way? Did I blow it? I'm sure I would have been safe jumping with John...He really did know the fundamentals, and he is a good pilot. And okay, a good house designer, clarinet player, and entrepreneur. And he's got a great smile, I have to admit. He didn't really lie about who he was, but just about a certain piece of paper he didn't have. Sometimes John seems larger than life, but maybe he's as large as he seems. Maybe he's not even interested after my tantrum yesterday.*

Zak jumped off his bike and laid it on the ground in one fluid movement, his sneakered feet still in motion. "This is for you, Mom. Top secret." Feeling very important, he added, "It's from John." Sara took a deep breath and told the other planters she needed to take a break. "Thanks, honey. Why don't you ride your bike back to the house and get some apple juice or something?" Marching over to the little gazebo, adorned with morning glories on the shady side and scarlet runner beans in full sun, she read the note, then carefully tucked it into its envelope and went back to work.

"John," Sara wrote in her response an hour or so later, "Thanks for your note. I accept your apology, and like I told you the other night, I'm flattered by your interest in me. I think you're an exceptional guy, and so does Zak." Then, needing to be as transparent as possible, she impulsively concluded with, "But what's on my mind right now is, Who was your overnight visitor, Blondie? Is she your backup girl, or would I be?" She'd left the door between them partway open, but a fatal slam was still quite possible. Once again, Zak was pressed into service as messenger. He informed his mom that the going rate was one dollar. Smiling, she told him she'd pay him later. She found herself acknowledging that she was going to compete for John if necessary, but if he was sweet-talking her while screwing Blondie, she'd never speak to him again, ever. Her head said, *Innocent until proven guilty*, but her heart added, *If proven guilty, it's the guillotine.*

Zak pounded on John's door like a pintsize FBI agent, discovering that Marc was now at John's house and the two were jabbering about politics or whatever. "Here's a note from Mom. Sorry to interrupt," he added, as if he'd get a tip for politeness. "Thanks, Zak," John said, trying to appear nonchalant about the contents of the return communique. "Here's a little something for your delivery services," he said, slapping still another dollar into Zak's hand. Then, saluting the boy, he instructed him to return to headquarters.

"Will you excuse me, Marc? I'd like to see what Sara has to say." He looked embarrassed, and nervous as a Forty-niners fan in overtime.

"Of course," Marc said, "Good luck, man." The two laughed slightly as John walked into the kitchen and as coolly as possible, slit the envelope open with a paring knife. Then came the audible sigh of relief. She seemed to forgive him! When John walked back into the living room, there was no doubt that the note had been a winner.

"Good news?"

"I think so..."

"Well, I should get out of your way, then," Marc said, even though he'd arrived just a few minutes earlier.

"No, no, I want to show you the house. Your brother did a great job on it. There's no great hurry," he said, now feeling relieved. "I'll call her in a while."

"Maybe you already know that there's a dinner out planned for tonight, including Ellie's parents? We'll be leaving at 5:30, I think that's the plan."

"Well, I don't want to get in the way of the *plan*," John said, in a voice twice as jovial as it had been the minute before, "but I want to at least spend a few minutes with you before you go."

John walked Marc through the house, impressed with Marc's knowledge about energy efficiency and architectural history. In addition to the solar panels incorporated in the roof tiles and carport roof, the house had a Tesla battery pack that stored excess electricity for overcast days. At the perimeters of the house, buried underground, was a network of pipes for a heat pump that fed coolness into the house in hot months, and warmth into the house with a radiant floor system in the winter. Marc was impressed with all the digital controls and solid feel of the house...a great demonstration that a mid-sized house could be completely off the grid.

But it was when John took him up to the room with the domed ceiling that Marc heard himself gasp. Completely covering one panel of the pentagonal wall was a huge photographic mural as vivid as a National Geographic scene, only many times larger, depicting an elephant herd cavorting in tropical surf. Completely amazed, Marc said, "Oh my god, I think I've been there! Is that Gabon?" John was stunned that Marc had somehow zeroed in on the exact location—the coast of this small West African country. "It is!" he said. "But how did you know that?"

"I did an internship in Ghana many years ago and I spent a week or so in Gabon. I'll never forget seeing that same scene. Most people don't associate elephants with the ocean, let alone splashing around in it like a family on vacation."

"Right! I've been there too, about five years ago. I was traveling with the guy who took that photograph, and when he sent me a high resolution image, I had to make a mural of it." Marc walked over to stand right in front of the mural. He could almost hear the surf! He looked over his shoulder at John. "Have you heard that elephants are starting to evolve shorter tusks, because the shorter tusked animals are more likely to survive?"

"That serves the poachers right," John said. "Hard times here on Earth. Too many humans. In a strange way, we've been too *successful*."

"Successfully what?" Marc posed, and John nodded.

Marc noticed a glass case in John's sunny leisure room—much like the one back in his own living room—containing woven baskets that Marc guessed were made by the Pomo Indians. "Wow! These are incredible!" There were three baskets in the case, one on each of the glass shelves. Marc studied a purple and beige basket about 18 inches wide, adorned with shells. "That one was made in the late 1880s, woven from sedge root and willow stems."

"I see where Rocket learned about Pomo culture. And what about this patterned basket on the bottom? It's so intricate. It really grabs you, doesn't it?" John opened the glass door and took the basket out of the case, handing it to Marc. "That's a more recently woven basket, by a living Pomo woman who's practiced the craft for 40 years or more. I want you to have it. I have a sturdy cardboard hatbox it will fit into." Marc was nearly speechless with gratitude. He knew better than to refuse the gift, sensing that John's offer was sincere. "Thanks so much John. It's beautiful!"

The two talked for a few more minutes, then Marc had to go get ready for dinner. John said, "If I don't see you before you go tomorrow, good luck with your recovery. And I'll see you next time, or maybe I'll be out in Denver one of these days." With his optimistic, nonchalant tone, he supported Marc in a way that couldn't be measured.

A few minutes after Marc left, John dialed Sara's number with a stomach full of butterflies. He tried to think of something witty to say, but when she answered, he let all pretense fall away and just said, "Thanks for your note."

"Thanks for yours," she answered, followed by a very emotional silence.

"Can I see you tonight?" he asked.

"You don't have plans with your...girlfriend?"

"Oh, you mean...'Blondie'? No, she went back to San Jose where she lives with her husband and two kids." John paused for effect. "She's my marketing director, Tanya. Sometimes when we meet here, she stays overnight in the guest room because traffic sucks in the evening. She's not my girlfriend," he emphasized. "I don't have a girlfriend.... But if I did have one, I'd want it to be someone exactly like you."

There was a noticeable change in Sara's voice. The high-pitched, accusatory edge was gone. All weapons were lowered, and both gleefully scrambled out of their trenches. "We're going out to dinner tonight, for Marc's last night here and my grandfather's birthday. We're leaving in a few minutes, so, I can't see you tonight."

"Where are you going?" he asked, suddenly in an exciting new place with her. "Mario's."

"I love Mario's. Have a good time! Maybe see you tomorrow?"

"If you're lucky."

"I *feel* lucky."

"Well, so do I," she said boldly. When she hung up, she realized that Zak had been eavesdropping. "He *is* your boyfriend, isn't he?"

"Yeah, I think he is," she answered, involuntarily beaming at her son.

The food was authentic Italian, and one person in the group was especially vivacious, a person who'd just made a life-shifting decision. Although

Sara wasn't usually one to laugh out loud, that night her laughter was infectious, and everyone at the big round table, except Sara's grandparents, knew exactly why. The elders soon got a clue when the waiter arrived with a platter of tiramisu desserts for everyone, "Compliments of John Bechard." Also on the platter was a small bouquet in a thin glass vase—several red roses intermingled with milk-white snapdragons, probably from the Blake homestead. "The bouquet is for Sara, and Mr. Bechard wanted us to say 'happy birthday' to Mr. Leonard."

Sara blushed, digging into her dessert, a specialty of the restaurant, as an escape from her embarrassment. "He's the king of drama," she said with a smile, looking around the table and shaking her head. Rocket thought, but did not say, *And you're the queen.* It was Marc who spoke up: "And you're okay with that, I think?" he said fondly, as charmed by Sara's lit-up face as the rest of the family.

Marc had an afternoon flight from Oakland airport but wanted to start early in case of heavy traffic. After breakfast, most of the gang, including John and Jessie, stood outside the cabin as Marc tucked his suitcase in the trunk of the rental car, along with the cardboard hatbox containing the well-padded Pomo basket.

"Call us when you get home," Ellie instructed, handing Marc a paper bag with a sturdy jute handle. "I made you a little lunch for the flight. And I found something else—a little surprise for Lisa." Peering into the bag, Marc saw a well preserved pair of miniature overalls, and knew immediately it was an early baby-shower present. "Whether they have a girl or a boy, those may fit pretty well when the time comes." Ellie continued, "I found them in a trunk in our bedroom closet. I don't know why I saved them. Sara looked so cute in them, years and years ago."

Marc was touched to the core. "I'm really gonna miss you guys. I wish I could stay all summer!"

"Come back when you get a chance, anytime," Rocket said, "We could use another pair of hands around here." Marc stood next to the car, comfortably ad libbing a personal farewell to each of them. Once he'd begun, the others let him run the show. "It's been great working in the gardens," he told Ellie, giving her a warm, grateful hug. Turning to his brother, he said, "Good luck finishing the totems, Rocket Man. And I'll expect to hear that you've skydived solo one of these days."

"No way," Rocket said, bear hugging Marc and shaking him by the shoulder. Then the older brother whispered something in Marc's ear. The younger brother exhaled through his nose, nodding emotionally.

"Don't forget to take care of those hens, Chicken Chief," Marc told Zak, lifting him up for a hug and discovering he wasn't as light as he had thought. "And if the hens aren't laying very well, I guess you'll just have to start laying eggs yourself." "No, *you're* gonna lay the eggs!" Zak bubbled, relishing an encore of their joke. "Sara, you've got a fine son here. It's been so great hanging out with you." (She rolled her eyes in reference to her sometimes-challenging boy). "Good luck finding the perfect job. You too, Jessie. And both of you: keep playing that great music." Looking over at John, "Thanks for the tour of your amazing new house! And for the Pomo basket. That's a real treasure. I promise I won't let Lisa sell it!" His nod signaled both respect and friendship. Blake and Bechard understood each other well.

Right before climbing into the car, he said in an elevated, emotional voice, "You've been a real inspiration for me! I'll be thinking about all of you, I really will!" The little delegation continued to wave as Marc pulled down the long driveway, totally invigorated from his visit. It was such a boost to be part of the life his brother had created with Ellie. He admired how each person in their circle seemed to grab a chunk of life and run with it. *"That's how we'll change the world, by living full and meaningful lives."* He definitely felt stronger than when he came. After all, he'd self-administered a pitcher of feel-good hormones while interacting with the Willits gang. Driving down Highway 1 toward the airport, he felt a heavy dose of irony: despite his very active and eventful sixty-three years, only now was life fully unveiling itself as a mind bending, multi-dimensional miracle. Never mind the suicide bombers, beltway bandits and charred but still-smoking, nutrition-free Pop-Tarts. He was ALIVE.

Eighteen

Greenhouse Passions and Poisons

A few days after Marc's return to Denver, Kai and his father were continuing their discussion about the business. Standing beside Yukio, Kai deliberately stepped in front of the older man to deliver The Pitch, face to face. "Dad, there's another thing that excites me as much as working with herbs and formulas." Yukio looked at his son with curiosity, but Kai's enthusiastic proposal was not unexpected: "I want to help urban agriculture become a *movement*. Organic growing solves so many of our problems." Kai counted the benefits of advocacy on his fingers: "1. We need to rebuild our soils because the food we eat doesn't keep us healthy. 2. Rich soil stores both water and greenhouse gases. 3. Gardening can slow people down and reconnect them with other people. Most Americans live in urban areas now. Wouldn't it be exciting to help create more organic gardens in metro areas—in backyards, school lots, church lots, and parks?"

Yukio looked at his son as if to say, *You don't think I know this?* But he waited for Kai to complete his thought. Having set the stage, Kai now went to the core of his message. "Our landscape design business can help create a fleet of productive backyard gardens. In addition to natural healing and the creation of beautiful landscapes and Japanese gardens, why can't we be activists for urban gardens? After all, Dad, aren't garden crops really *living* herbalism?" Yukio nodded and reading his father's expression, Kai sensed this might be easier than he'd thought. "Most of our designs already include *some* food production, unless a site doesn't have enough sun. But you want to amplify our focus on using cold frames, compost piles and cover crops, is that it?"

"Exactly. Artfully designed gardens. Something to be proud of and teach your neighbors about. We can show them how to grow organically and help make healthy food more popular in Denver than computer games, political scandals and shopping malls put together!" Both men laughed at the contrast Kai presented. One set of pursuits was about applied skill, natural connections and the satisfaction of working with one's body to remain healthy. In their minds, the other way of spending time centered on speed, insecurity and stress.

Yukio stunned his son with a simple, "Okay let's do it. I'm with you. We'll figure out the details as we go." At last, the deal between the two was finalized. Each man had what he wanted. They walked together toward the 'teahouse,' a tiny outbuilding in the southeast corner of the large lot, where Yukio showed Kai how he neatly dated and stored *Kampo* formula containers, and how the patients' response to the herbs was logged into a computer data base.

Then Yukio wanted to show Kai what needed to be done in the greenhouse the following day, which herbs needed to be harvested and which plots needed to be fertilized. They walked past a huge passion flower vine in the front entry of the greenhouse, perched regally on the top shelf of a wrought iron rack about eight feet tall. Pots of shade-tolerant herbs— mint, oregano, lemon balm, and sweet woodruff—were thriving on a chest-high shelf, peeking through the cascading vines of the flower, which were covered with magnificently intricate blossoms. "This passion flower needs a haircut," Yukio said. "The healthiest looking leaves get cleaned of debris and loaded into the dehydrator, and the dead leaves go in the compost piles. What do you think the dried herb itself will be used for?" Kai had subconsciously absorbed a lot information over the years and responded without thinking, "Anxiety and support for sleeping." He surprised himself, how did he know that?

As they looked up at the huge plant, Yukio noticed that one of the rack's iron posts was damaged almost to the breaking point. "That's a priority. It doesn't look very safe. Let's see if we can get Clint to come over and weld some steel splints onto it." Yukio's statement made Kai think again about how many different details were involved in running the business.

His father also wanted to emphasize a few things about the "poison garden" in a back nook of the greenhouse, protected from accidental contact by a hardwood gate that Kai had made. There were five different species that if taken in the right doses would be fatal: castor bean, rosary pea, doll's-eye, white snakeroot, and deadly nightshade. Kai's favorite among them was the rosary pea, a blood red tiny globe with a sinister black dot on one pole. Some jewelry makers were known to have died from a carelessly pricked finger while stringing the rosary beads. Although Kai routinely watered the poison garden, Yukio had sternly cautioned Kai, Michiko and others never to handle these plants without plastic gloves, which then had to be rinsed off in hydrogen peroxide.

"You see this?" Yukio asked, holding up a laminated sheet of instructions that hung from a support pole. "This tells you the lethal dosage for each plant. If your mother or I ever need to escape extreme pain or suffering, you'll know what to do." Kai wasn't sure if Yukio just enjoyed growing these specimens or if he truly wanted to go out botanically when the time came. The younger Sakata had read about the extreme discomfort that followed the ingestion of herbs like these. Kai responded as a joking colleague would: "You're talking murder, Dad. That's asking a lot."

"We'll make it look like an accident," Yukio came back, with a wry smile on his face. Despite his extroversion, Yukio was often mysterious, even enigmatic. "Wouldn't an overdose of heroin do the job more gently? That's an herb too, right, from poppies?"

"But it's an illegal substance that has destroyed many lives, even whole countries." Kai nodded but refused to shrink back to the size of a boy. He opted for collegiality, a more comfortable kind of relationship now that they were partners. Jokingly he said, "Well, if you're going to mentor me on traditional medicine, I need at least ten or fifteen more years of life from you." Yukio seemed confident it could happen. "I know I can give you a good ten years. Maybe I'll still be around in twenty!" After all, his grandfather had lived to the age of 105 in Okinawa.

Then Kai brought up Marc's illness again. He felt an urgency to have his father examine Marc and offer thoughts about natural cures. "Do you have time for that this afternoon?" Kai asked. He'd already checked with Marc about availability. "I have an order to fill—a case of severe arthritis. I hope to boost the patient's capacity to reduce inflammation with the *Yiyiren Tang* formula I've told you about. After I fill that prescription, I can see Marc."

When Marc showed up that afternoon, a few drops of rain were falling from the lighter half of the sky, with rumbles of thunder from the other. Marc remembered the hailstorm with its stinging, marble-size projectiles that had totaled Karen's old Volvo. But the sky wasn't that sickly yellow shade nor was there wasn't a spooky silence of birds. Despite the possibility of rain, dozens of bees both wild and domesticated eagerly perused flower blossoms as Marc followed the stone path through Kai's and May's front yard. The anthropologist had always loved the sculpture that distinguished the yard from all others in the neighborhood. It wasn't the Buddha—who instead was stationed in the backyard, humbly inconspicuous to neighbors—but a feature almost as iconic: a five-foot tower of miniature pagodas, stacked one on top of the other, made of molded cement and rustic wood. Years earlier, Yukio and Michiko had commissioned an Asian sculptor to create it. On a black slate bench behind the high-rise pagoda was a collection of bonsai cotoneasters trained to resemble craggy, ancient trees. Working with his father, Kai had already become adept at that craft. Walking through the gated pergola in the shady side yard between the houses, Marc saw Yukio working intently on trellises supporting espaliered peach and apricot trees. Their vigorous, artful limbs were trained horizontally to maximize both beauty and production.

Marc called, "Hi Yukio! We're not going to get hail this afternoon are we?"

"Oh, no, but we could sure use some rain." He was examining the tiny peach nubs that had emerged from the pollinated buds. Pausing to shake Marc's hand firmly, he opened the conversation with a favorite story. "A few years ago, we had very heavy crops of both apricots and peaches and I carefully wrapped the finest of them in little wax paper bags pulled tight with string, to protect them from birds, and—I was hoping—raccoons and squirrels." Marc nodded, smiling. (He didn't interrupt Yukio's story, even though he'd heard it more than once.) "The raccoons climbed along the horizontal branches at night, as easy as you or I walk on a sidewalk, and one by one they unwrapped my prize fruits...and *feasted*." (Now the frown became a half-smile.) "I could imagine them telling each other, 'They must really *like* us—not only growing the sweetest fruit in the world for us, but *gift wrapping* each piece.'" Both men laughed—Yukio loudly—and Marc added, "Let's hope they got bad stomach aches from overindulging and will stay away this year. Maybe try little wire baskets around them this time?" he suggested.

"We'll definitely use some thick-strand netting as a barrier." Then Yukio, always one for directness, cut to the chase: "I hear you're going to give me a chance to assess this confusion, this stubbornness in your body."

"I'm really grateful for your time and expertise," Marc answered, nodding, as if he were executing a slight bow. The older man led the way toward his summer office, bordered by a bamboo screen. Marc appreciated how this simple, artful feature conveyed a sense of separateness. Glancing around, he noted that the only grassy areas in the large yard were framed by rustic squares of grey and brown tinted concrete, creating a visually pleasing pathway between the espaliered trees and the long garden rows. There were four parallel rows in each 20-foot bed, a few of them covered by protective tunnels that retained humidity and protected crops from hail. All were easily accessible for planting and harvesting, and all faced a bright southwest sky. Spring crops like spinach, turnips, mizuna and

Daikon radishes were already being harvested and would soon be replaced by summer crops like eggplant, broccoli, shisito peppers and kabocha—Japanese pumpkin. The goal was to harvest three crops per square foot every growing season. Mulched by two inches of pine needles, none of the rows had more than the occasional weed, the meticulous Michiko always saw to that. The yard looked glorious—a cloistered slice of serenity in an increasingly chaotic metro area. All the landscape features were interconnected in this thriving, productive work of art. Marc admired how the landscape had been crafted intuitively to make the property feel like two cottages in the country.

Seated on a sturdy wooden cot in the office, Marc wondered if Western and Eastern medicines could and would be compatible against his virus. Kai had told him his father would use traditional methods of diagnosis including inquiry and intuition in combination with more technical, mainstream methods when appropriate. After asking Marc about his own observations of symptoms, discomfort, and changes in bodily functions, Yukio worked silently except for an occasional comment. "Our aim is to relieve the symptoms and restore harmony in the body," Yukio explained, taking Marc's temperature and assessing his general level of vigor. He observed Marc's reaction to sensations like pressure and coolness and also examined his pulse, tongue appearance, and possible abdominal palpitations. "This informs us about the amount and distribution of vital energy, blood, and body fluid." He looked quizzically at the most visible symptom of all—the rash on Marc's leg—and asked permission to take a picture of it. He'd never seen anything like these concentric circles, resembling a purplish tattoo of a tree's annual rings. Then, in a departure from traditional medicine, Yukio asked to see the blood profile Marc had brought. He read the diagnosis of the specialist who had delivered Marc's dire news, silently analyzing the puzzle pieces.

Kai stuck his head in the office after knocking lightly. "I don't want to interrupt but I'm back from the Harrison's yard, if there's anything you need me to do." Yukio seemed relieved that his son had returned in time to be part of the diagnosis. Each moment was an opportunity to educate and challenge his son, who had, just hours before, grown a *halo* by officially becoming a partner. Still deliberating about Marc's condition, Yukio was like a private investigator, examining a head full of clues. Then unhurriedly, he glanced at Kai before turning to address Marc. "You will recover from this condition," said the healer, nodding his head intently, addressing both the patient and in a sense, the virus itself. "If you insist," Marc said with a shoulder shrug, opting for feigned joviality with these two men he knew so well. "The last guy only gave me odds of one in twenty." Yukio, smiling slightly and eyes beaming energy, responded, "It's up to you. You are strong."

Marc assumed Yukio's words were partly meant to stimulate the power of placebo—a strong ally in any healing process. But now he listened to Yukio's more tangible prescription. "There are traditional formulas which can help kill the virus, such as *Hochuekkito* or *Juzentaihoto*," emphatically pronouncing each name with a careful Japanese inflection as he mapped out a strategy. "But I'm not sure they should be taken with the prescription drugs you're currently taking. What I would like to do is give you a two week supply of a powerful tea that contains five herbs to support your immune system, to be taken twice a day. Focus on gratitude rather than anger to keep your cortisol and stress levels low, and let's talk again in a week to see how we're coming." As they left the office, Yukio affectionately grabbed the arm of the man he considered a second son, repeating, "It's not your time yet," almost as if he were asserting, "the sun will come up tomorrow." Did he somehow have a window on the future?

Savoring the mild afternoon, the three men walked past the long, sunken picnic table that was already being prepared for the Solstice gathering that evening. A vase of purple irises and yellow coreopsis sat on one end, and a tray of unset tableware on the other. The table was a massive slab of red flagstone about ten feet long, perched on stone pillars at each end and the middle. Its connectedness with the ground and its comfortable intimate

211

seating made leisurely meals and discussions a unique pleasure. Even the long cushions on the sunken hardwood benches were subtly artful, with bold images of birds and trees over muted green backgrounds. The huge slab had been set in place with a small crane seven years earlier, about the time the Japanese grill and electrical outlets had also been installed, making the space a low-profile and very pleasant dining area in the warmer seasons. "I'm looking forward to dinner tonight," Marc told the two men. "I brought a fresh fruit salad, I hope that fits in the menu."

"Let's eat it right now," joked Kai, "then we won't have to worry if it fits or not."

Kai and Marc spent an unhurried hour in the gardens, harvesting Rocambole garlic—a violet-skinned, spicy variety that Kai had planted the previous fall. Because the soil was so loamy, the garlic plants pulled up easily, scenting the air with an earthy, pungent aroma. The men also planted broccoli seedlings and waxed bean seeds in some of the already-harvested rows.

Marc loved working with Kai, who personified the meaning of the Japanese term *genki*—"healthy enthusiasm." With a playful smile, Kai said, "I love to get 'down and dirty' out here. No question, gardening has become the ultimate passion for me, second only to time with May. I may never become the healer that Dad is—he's been working on it for many years— but I'm really excited about becoming a Colorado urban gardening 'guru,' and he seems okay with that. You know about May's connection with Grow Local, that promotes organic gardening, don't you? So now she and I can work on promoting gardening together."

May was immersed in the politics of gardening, an advocate for civic assets like food pantries, where local surplus organic food was distributed to those in need. Several of her friends were tenant gardeners with a spin— they planted and maintained gardens in clients' yards, both sharing and marketing the yield. May considered them role models for a different, more satisfying way to spend leisure hours. Kai's face lit up as they worked together, piling the garlic plants neatly in a wheelbarrow. He reminded

Marc of a skillful sailor in steady winds. "I need to take you back to see my brother's market garden in Mendocino County. The house he helped build for his friend John is done. It's awesome!"

"I want to see it, and see your brother and Ellie again. I also want to go back to the redwoods. Let's plan on another trip out that way. May will want to come, too. By the way, did you know that the scent of soil actually gets you high? Our endocrine systems release serotonin when soil is being worked, like right now."

"I'm feeling it," Marc said, certain that *something* was giving him a natural high. Kai added, "Beauty—like great paintings, or those Sand Cherry blossoms over there—releases feel-good hormones, too, you probably know that."

"Yeah, when you think about it, gardening meets so many of our needs. Humans love to use our hands and brains to create. We want companionship and leisure time in nature. We need exercise, and we thrive on healthy food. Gardening does it all, doesn't it?" Kai pulled and piled the last of the garlic plants. "Yeah, that was part of the conversation with my father: maybe the ultimate garden crop is enlightened healthy humans." Marc said, "I read this morning that carbon dioxide levels in both the air and the ocean sinks have become fully saturated. Soil is now our best bet for sequestering CO_2." Both knew that if the amount of organic material in farm and garden soil reverted to preindustrial levels, preventing a steamy planet would be a whole lot easier.

Though Kai had already accomplished a lot that day, there were a few other things on his list, like quizzing Marc about his work in Borneo. "Who did you work with when you went there?" He had a hunch that if Marc contracted his disease in Borneo, maybe natural healing was still practiced there. "That was three years ago. You remember I joined a delegation of ecologists and rainforest activists trying to reduce the catastrophic logging and palm oil harvesting. Our group worked with the Sarawak Conservancy. I had the pleasure of focusing on the lifestyle of the Penan tribe, one of the world's most gentle, sustainable cultures. They were forced to battle the developed countries' addictions to huge houses. *The Asian Invasion*, some called it, referring to China's, Korea's and Japan's appetite for Borneo's once-virgin forests. "

"I have a crazy idea," Kai said.

"What's that?"

"Let's pack our bags and retrace your steps in Borneo. If it's ground zero for the Q virus, let's go talk with the medicine men or women if we can find them, to see how they treat viruses like yours."

"That's an interesting idea, my friend. But it seems a bit far-fetched that we could find the precise person with the precise treatment. And, I need to stay on top of my new regimen of acupuncture and superfoods, including the tea formula your dad prescribed...it seems to be giving me a little more energy. I also have my softball schedule to think about, a golf game with DU colleagues next week, and Lisa's going to help me again with organizing the house. Besides, if I caught the virus three years ago, why hasn't it flared up until this year?"

"Viruses can go dormant. They hide in the human body as bits of genetic code, my dad says. But doesn't it make sense that's where you got it? And doesn't it make sense that the ecosystem that created the disease would also have a cure? How about this? Let me find out a little more about microbial genetics: it turns out that even microbes have unique "footprints," and the University of Massachusetts has a data base of infectious diseases and their geographic origins. Let's send a blood sample to them and see if your Q virus is traceable."

"I don't know what my rather conventional doctor here in Denver would say about this."

"Don't tell him. Let's go around conventional medicine, at least for the sake of research. We can have a blood sample taken at the Colfax Clinic, are you willing to do that?"

Marc looked at Kai with a mildly skeptical smile, but with a silent nod, he agreed to give it a try.

Michiko knocked on the kitchen door, where May was creating a Marzipan ring cake—a traditional Danish holiday dessert—for that evening's dinner party. Kai's mother was not much taller than the door's bottom pane of glass, and usually had an amiable smile on her face, her lips often lined with a light, ladylike shade of lipstick. Although slight in stature and by nature quiet, her sense of propriety and orderliness commanded the attention of family as well as friends. When she spoke, people either listened or risked subtle but unmistakable disapproval. Kai thought of it as "the silent stare," when her smile vanished like a sand painting in a sudden breeze, leaving a barren expression behind. Although Kai was casual and easygoing with May, and sometimes mildly rebellious with his father, he didn't mess with his mother. It could be psychologically painful.

May's relationships with both of Kai's parents were warm and respectful though not chummy. She shared Yukio's tendency to be a talker, but she was wary of establishing an open-door policy since the two houses were so close to each other. She made it clear that her partnership with Kai was not to be judged or altered by the parents. She'd requested that their dinners together, usually once or twice a week, be a balance between Asian and Western cuisine, not always noodles, vegetables and seafood (which she secretly considered "slimy"). Their shared landscape—back, front, and side yards—had a Japanese feel she loved, but she was proud of her own heritage, too. She was *Danish*. Still, she revered her in-laws' life wisdom and commitment to healing. These four Highlands residents were completely on the same page about the need for radical changes in America's careless lifestyle.

"What a beautiful morning," Michiko said, handing May a small paper sack as she came into the kitchen. She often had little gifts for May, maybe an implicit reward for May's commitment and devotion to her son. "Thank you! You know how we love Bing cherries!" The two women discussed details for the dinner. There would be ten people at the long table: Michiko, Yukio and their dear friend Mayumi, a widowed artist; Kai, May, and Marc; Lisa and Brad; and May's cousin Katrina and her friend Margo, if they arrived from their travels in time. Kat and Margo had been friends since college days, and even though Kat lived in Copenhagen and Margo in Washington, D.C., they'd arranged a 10-day road trip to California. At the end of that trip, May and Kat were anxious to spend a little time together before the cousin's return to Denmark. May hadn't met Margo but had heard from Kat that she was a "real piece of work."

In addition to baking the cake, either May or Kai would grill the salmon on the wood fired grill, and they'd also contribute three bottles of homemade plum wine. Michiko and Yukio would bring vegetable tempura, pickled vegetables, Miso and rice with wabi. A feast! It would be a nice warm Summer Solstice evening with a nearly-full moon, so they'd surely eat outside. "Let me know if you need help with the tempura," May said as Michiko quietly left through the kitchen door.

A little after seven, the pace picked up at both Sakata homes. Michiko was erecting a tower of fried tempura on a huge earthen platter in her kitchen. She had assigned Yukio the task of lighting a fire in the portable wood-fired grill out next to the table. A much larger gas-fired grill had a permanent spot nearby. With its built-in stainless steel griddle, it was perfect for grilling meat, stir fry and scallion pancakes. But that night—the longest day of the year—the salmon would be grilled over a flame of cherry tree twigs and limbs from a winter pruning, stored neatly by the garage.

In late afternoon, Yukio had soaked in the hot tub on the second story balcony that overlooked the back gardens and landscape. He was feeling refreshed and lively. He knew the company would be good, he loved fresh salmon, and *finally*, he'd officially brought his son into the business! Next door, Kai and May were getting dressed in Denver-casual style while Marc, still wearing his gardening clothes, swung gently back and forth in a sturdy hammock right behind Kai's house, reading *The Week* magazine. He wished he'd brought a change of clothes (maybe he should quickly go home and change?) But he was a hundred percent confident he wouldn't be asked to leave. *Gotta be nice to the sick guy,* he thought. There was something very peaceful, very purposeful, about this little compound. He felt grateful to have friends like these, and he was looking forward to seeing Lisa and Brad.

As Michiko carried the big platter of tempura out the door, Yukio relieved her of it, setting it on a warming trivet on the table. A few minutes later, Kai brought out another platter—twelve salmon fillets from the neighborhood butcher who always sold the freshest meats and fish in town. May soon joined the parade, bringing out the fragrant Marzipan Ring cake. She loved the idea of serving something familiar to her Danish cousin Kat, and she'd made the cake often enough to do it on autopilot.

Nineteen

Around the Table

After the guests had gathered in the Sakatas' huge backyard, chatting leisurely and touring the gardens, Michiko invited everyone to sit down and eat while the food was still warm. May's cousin Kat had called to say she and Margo were still on the road in the foothills just west of Denver, but the others took their seats according to the names neatly penned on colorful little origami umbrellas anchored in mandarin orange slices. Kai and Marc had just finished grilling the salmon—perfectly glazed and slightly crisp.

As Kai carried the platter of fish over, he was surprised by who was not sitting at the head of the table. Yukio sat at one end as usual, eyeing and inhaling not only the smell of salmon but the whole, delicious spread, pleasingly served up in a little fleet of bowls and pitchers. However, Michiko, who typically sat at the other end for these more familial gatherings, now sat catty-corner from Yukio, leaving her usual place vacant. Kai glanced up at his parents with a slight smile, inconspicuously checked for his name, then sat down without a word. He guessed that this new formality might include occasional hosting responsibilities, and a silent, slight nod from the father verified that.

After everyone's wine was poured by the person sitting next to them, Kai said in a clear, relaxed voice, "*itadakimasu*," meaning, "I receive this food." Then, in the manner of his father, he concisely noted where the food had come from, how it had been expertly produced, and how it would confer a sense of well-being to each of them. In a more formal tone, he said, "We are grateful to be joined by very dear friends tonight. We hope you will feel welcomed and comfortable at this table." May, very much aware of the honor Yukio and Michiko had bestowed, reached over and gave Kai's hand a squeeze.

Lifting his glass, Kai toasted, *"Kanpai!"* and the others raised glasses and repeated the word with genuine gusto, each familiar with life at the Sakata compound. The toast literally meant, "Chug it!" but everyone knew that would be a waste of great wine. In conversation right before the meal, May had touted her husband's wine-making skills and told guests the dry plum wine was Kai's best batch in eight years. In the persistent, slanted rays of the sun, each diner's wine glass cast an elongated magenta shadow, like a secret insignia of their Solstice evening.

Kai had always been amused—and at times a little threatened—by another traditional Japanese toast, *otsukare-sama*, or "Thank you for your hard work." While this age-old sentiment was meant to be appreciative and respectful, its modern connotation almost seemed to glorify the workaholic lifestyle led by many Japanese businessmen, including Kai in his previous life on Wall Street. He'd vowed that *karoshi*, or "death by overworking" would never again darken his spirits. With a quick glance toward the other end of the table, Kai knew he'd opened the meal appropriately. Yukio and Michiko were both beaming proudly.

Marc, Lisa and Brad exchanged smiles across the table, then Marc and Yukio also nodded slightly at one another, smiling. All seemed ready for another memorable evening. As the diners deployed chopsticks, forks and fingers to load their plates, May related a bit of Danish culture: "When sharing food in Denmark, it's not polite to take the last piece of any serving." (A few looked around to see if they'd already done something wrong.) "You can take half of it, but then the next person takes half of the half..." May started laughing a little, gesturing with a thumb and forefinger, "And you end up with a tiny crumb which no one will take."

After a measured pause Marc said playfully, "Unless it's a piece of your Marzipan Ring cake. When there's cake at stake, it's customary to wrestle for that last crumb, right?" Marc liked to bring a smile to May's face. Over the years their way of being with each other had become very familiar, genuinely amicable but without an overt hint of anything else—they were each mindful of that. She acknowledged Marc's whimsy with a smile, but good-naturedly corrected him. "No, in Denmark we don't fight, we cooperate, and *negotiate*." (Although she'd been a U.S. citizen for much of her life, she still used the "we" pronoun). She then instructed, in typical May fashion, "For example, our police officers walk the streets and ride bikes in their assigned districts to get to know the neighbors they serve and hear exactly what they need. There's a far greater sense of trust in *all* levels of government in Denmark than in the U.S."

Marc nodded, meeting May's sky blue eyes openly. She emphasized, "There's very high voter turnout, and citizens follow the issues, not the scandals." Everyone at the table knew that May's edginess was a slap at the current Trump regime. "...Partly because political ads on TV are banned!" Kai added, "and the campaigns last only weeks rather than months or years, so not as much money is needed to finance all the..."

"...mudslinging." Lisa interjected quickly, as if swiping the unsaid word 'bullshit' right out of the air. "I wish we had that here! I'm sick of all the black-and-white close-ups of an opponent's face, with a photo-shopped look of madness on it, like a devious vampire." The others laughed at her image.

"I haven't seen the vampire ad yet," Yukio joked.

May couldn't resist pushing a possible hot button, comparing the number of gun related deaths in the U.S. and Denmark. "Americans forget that when the U.S. Constitution was written, the right to bear arms referred to single shot muskets, not automatic submachine guns that launch a hundred rounds a minute." The thought of creepy, desperately insecure lunatics with machine guns sent a chill up her spine as she spoke. Marc noted May's slight shiver, suggesting with faux conviction, "We should change the Constitution to read, "The right to bare arms." He held his throwing arm up in an L and executed a quick bicep flex for possible comic effect. (Nothing.)

"Or the right to arm bears," Kai added, wearing his best bear-face (also not that great) and executing a slight growl, (or was he just clearing his throat?) It was apparent that the younger Sakata was feeling pretty good that warm summer evening. He was a natural host and enjoying it. "Yes, all bears should have guns, just in case," May said, in muted support of the two men's silly jokes.

Mayumi, a well informed and politically active elder, joined the discussion after internally checking her facts. "I read that in the U.S., there are about 30,000 gun-related deaths every year, but that in Japan, it's more like *six*. *Six!* It's almost impossible to get a gun there, in fact it *is* impossible to get a pistol. You can only have a shotgun or air rifle and you have to pass mental fitness tests, shooting skill tests and background checks. You're even required to tell police where in your house you store the gun and ammunition."

Brad observed, "So, more people were killed a few years ago at the Aurora Theater shooting than in all of Japan." Mild mannered and very articulate, he felt comfortable in the group, recalling how a friend of his had gone to a movie shortly after the Aurora nightmare and managers had announced on the PA that someone was seen carrying an unconcealed gun (legal in Colorado.) "They asked over the loudspeaker—'In the interest of safety and security'—if that person could please take their weapon out to their car, they would delay the movie for a few minutes. About ten people stood up and walked toward the exit." Kai added, "Last month during a robbery in Denver, everybody pulled out their guns and the police couldn't figure out which one was the thief."

Now May was becoming agitated. The conversation wasn't pleasant, and she felt to blame for bringing the topic up. She tapped on her water glass and stood up to interrupt the chatter about cops and killers. She looked casually attractive in her white V-neck sweater and designer jeans. "Now wait a minute, please. I want to offer another toast. Haven't we had enough in our lives about mass shootings and crooked politicians? I want to offer a toast to all humans who are resourceful, nonviolent, and active in their *politics*...those who do meaningful, beautiful things even if world events seem overwhelming. Here's to human creativity, and human empathy!" She raised her glass and said sharply, "Skol!"

After everyone raised their glasses and echoed her toast, she suggested that each of them might offer some short, positive story or thought— something that had inspired them recently. "No pressure or anything...and if you think it's too much work, we can skip it. But it *is* Solstice—another year around the sun—and maybe it's the perfect time to let more light into our politics." The diners all voiced or nodded buy-in, so May sat down to see what would come up.

Michiko spoke about the nonprofit organization where she and Mayumi volunteered. Several cooperative businesses, located in a challenged neighborhood, offered homeless people part ownership, with small deductions from their paychecks. The co-ops provided precisely what the area needed, in addition to jobs: contracted laundry services for several large hospitals and fresh, greenhouse-grown vegetables and fruit for neighborhood grocery stores. Michiko added that it takes planning and political will to put the pieces of a system like this together, the free market alone won't automatically make it happen.

Following up on Michiko's comments, Yukio observed, "I think the reason it's so challenging to create positive change is that our culture is looking in the wrong direction. Many of the things that add genuine wealth to our lives have "bad payback" so they're undervalued. It's impossible to *sell* things like long marriages..." (He looked fondly at Michiko.) "Or how about old growth forests, good conversation, amateur crafts and arts— these things make life worth living but they don't create economic growth. And if you think about it, lonely people—whether poor or rich—are great for the consumer economy because when you're feeling isolated or broken, you'll spend whatever you have."

Marc joined in. "I agree that a lot of our confusion comes from isolation. We're scattered geographically, separated from our families, constantly adapting to new workplaces." He checked to make sure he wasn't putting the others to sleep with his anthropology. "We sometimes join the wrong group because it's better than being alone, and maybe because their anger matches ours. Climate change deniers would rather ignore the dire truth than be ousted from their tribe."

There was a comfortable, contemplative silence, a brief break, while people processed Yukio's and Marc's thoughts. Despite the gravitas, they felt grateful to be pleasantly among friends, in a space that was sequestered and silent except for the twilight calls of insects and birds, and the melodic drip of a bamboo-pipe fountain by the entrance to the greenhouse. Healthy stands of herbs like oregano, rosemary and citronella throughout the landscape not only smelled great but also repelled the mosquitoes.

Lisa changed the subject a little by asking May, "There's a Scandinavian concept I read about of 'just enough'...what is it...la-...?"

"*Lagom.*" Then, noticing Kat and her friend coming into the yard carrying a large bouquet of wildflowers, May stood up to greet them, knowing they'd probably want a bathroom and a place to change after hours of car travel. "Lagom is almost a way of life," May said as she waved excitedly at her cousin. "It's about the pleasure that comes from moderation—the *perfect* amount. It comes from a Viking term meaning, 'Around the table.'" Then, walking toward the newcomers, she said over her shoulder, "A person should only take a *sip* of the mead that's being passed around, so no one will go without."

Yukio commented, "Trump wouldn't have a clue about lagom. With him, way too much is still not enough."

Michiko, who sat on a pillow so others could see her better, offered, "In Japan, the word *wabi* means not being trapped by material things, but finding ways to be content with artful design, symmetry and quality." Nodding emphatically, Yukio added, "Instead of 'doing without', it's more like doing within."

Marc immediately responded, "That's cool. I like that phrase, 'doing within.'"

After clearing her throat, Mayumi added in a light-hearted tone, "And the term *mottainai* is similar. It means a social obligation to feel guilty if you waste anything."

"There's plenty of guilt to go around," Kai said dryly, and the others laughed.

They were still talking about various cultural words and meanings when Kat and Margo stepped down to join them at the sunken table. "What does the Danish word *hygge* mean to you?" Lisa was asking the group. "I've come across that word a lot these days, maybe because Denmark keeps scoring at or near the top in happiness." May rolled her eyes and said, "A lot of journalists describe it as 'cozy and warm indoors,' with candles, coffee and sweetbread. But it's much more than that. It's a state of mindfulness, a way to make simple things dignified and satisfying. "Wouldn't you say, Kat?"

Kat, surprised to be immediately included in the conversation, responded, "Yes, satisfied with who you are, sheltered from cold weather and stress, connected with people you love. That's the way I think of it." Then, as she loaded her plate with salmon, fruit salad and miso over rice, Kat decided to risk a little humor, even as a newcomer. Looking first at Margo for moral support she said with a smile, "In Danish, the word 'gift' has two meanings: 'married,' and 'poison.'" The group was already laughing as she added, "And I think the double meaning is appropriate—at least in some cases." She again glanced at Margo, both of them smiling knowingly. The two women had each been married but were now either divorced (Margo, one child) or separated (Kat).

The conversation briefly became an update about the road trip the two had just taken to the California coast and wine country—San Luis Obispo, San Francisco, Sonoma, and back. It was clear they were still in adventure mode, although each traveler looked a little weary. Kat bore some resemblance to her cousin May, Marc thought, yet despite her younger age (56), she seemed less vivacious than May. Maybe the separation from her husband had been a difficult one. Despite the joke she'd just told, Kat was an introvert. A dinner party with mostly strangers was not her favorite situation. Back home, she enjoyed her solitary, focused work as a market researcher. Margo, on the other hand, seemed comfortable even among people she'd never met. She was attractive—not like a cover girl but in the audacious way she presented herself. Clearly, she was far from timid. It was impossible not to notice her prominent breasts, and she didn't shy away from wearing a fashionably tight long-sleeve T-shirt and brightly beaded necklace. In her career in Washington, D.C. she'd reached the senior management tier at the Department of Housing and Urban Development.

Glancing at May, Kat said, "I think renewable energy is an especially inspiring story. On one windy day last winter, all of Denmark's electrical demand was met with wind generators. And even on an average day, it's up over a third of the total, now."

Then Brad mentioned a story that had intrigued him, about an Illinois repo man who was sent to tow away an elderly couple's 1998 Buick. He was touched by the couple's humanness and by their challenges: the husband was in the first stages of Alzheimer's, and the two were stretching to pay their bills. The repo man had towed the car away but with remorse, and that night he went online and raised almost $4,000 through crowdfunding. He paid off the car and drove it back onto the couple's driveway—after first having the oil changed and a headlight fixed. "That's what any culture thrives on," Marc said, nodding his head: "Caring."

Margo blurted, "Caring? How many immigrants are getting their families torn apart right now by federal laws because their skin isn't white?" She caught the group off-guard with her brash tone of voice. Brad geared up for yet another diagnosis of the racial divide in America. As a black man, he'd heard so many! But Margo, aware that she had seized the stage, jumped to another pet peeve. "And what about the politicians who insist that abortion is the devil's playground, yet they adamantly support development that wipes out habitats and the species that live in them? Only *human* life has value? They also look the other way when bombing missions kill hundreds of civilians, and when the guns they fanatically support kill high school kids...The polar *opposite* of caring."

May was a bit stunned by Margo's addition to the conversation. Though spirited, the words seemed so full of anger. "I absolutely agree with you. But if politics has us tied up in knots, how can we untie them?" She was trying to accommodate her cousin's friend, now a guest at their house. "Well," Margo responded in a lighter tone, "we *were* inspired by a little band of backpackers we met in a café in Logan, Utah, on our way West. Five people of five different races, walking and ridesharing across the country...talking with as many people as possible about prejudice and inequality—in street discussions, in malls, on local radio, wherever. One of them used to be a skinhead, a white supremacist who'd never really known people of different races, yet was certain he hated them. His breakthrough moment, ironically, had come when he was beating someone, actually kicking him in the face. Their eyes met, and like a sudden strike of lightning, the man finally felt shame, and empathy. He became a peace and justice activist and had asked some of his past victims, in person, for forgiveness."

Brad said, "It seems like that kind of transformation needs to happen in millions of individual lives—but long before the violence..." May nodded. "Thanks for sharing that story."

Broadening the conversation a little, Kai offered, "So much depends on the *direction* of a culture, what the people consider meaningful and worth pursuing. The Japanese changed their cultural identity in the 17th and 18th centuries from warriors to peace lovers. When they ran out of resources like forests, metals and clean water, they shifted from an emphasis on power and wealth to a fascination with nature, art, leisure, quality products and experiences. All of a sudden, the material things in life were seen as demeaning, while advancement of crafts and human knowledge became the goals."

Again, Margo jumped into the conversation. "But what do you think the chances are of Americans giving up our conveniences, our *American Dream* in exchange for tea ceremonies and martial arts? And what about the people in poor countries, dying of starvation? Would you expect them to be satisfied with less?" Kai and Margo faced off, each animated by the debate.

"Isn't it really about meeting somewhere in the middle?" Marc asked, diplomatically. "If the rich countries continue to substitute time, health and connections for money and stuff...and if they cut their military budgets to provide real services like bridges that don't collapse and neighborhoods that are full of life, maybe the poor countries can catch up."

"But why should rich countries volunteer to have less?" Margo insisted.

May had a quick answer: "Because the old way of life just isn't working! More sensible ways of living are being substituted, piece by piece. They may look and feel unfamiliar, but they are the way of the future."

"I agree," Marc said, heartily. "Eventually, the rich countries will shift their worldview because the old way just doesn't make people feel secure, and *alive*. It's that simple. It will be a cultural shift more than a political one. Movies, books, and conversations like the one we're having right now will make moderation and 'lagom' seem very appealing, very obvious."

"And, at the same time," Yukio predicted, "the bubble will finally burst. The affluent lifestyle is just too expensive in many different ways. Social services, the insurance industry, colleges, and about half of the country's households are running out of money. And our true bank account, nature, has been drawn down to the point of collapse. We can't afford this fabled American Dream."

"Or is that 'nightmare?'" Margo added, predictably.

Marc said, "As we become increasingly agitated and addicted from all the stress, the poor countries will skip over some of the mistakes we've made. Seventy-five or a hundred years from now, we'll meet in the middle." He knew full well he sounded like John Lennon singing the song *Imagine*.

Lisa said, "One thing that confuses me about the current American way of life is all the envy and jealousy it creates. If competition is what drives the economy, how can we be happy? How can we wish the other person well if he's our competition? And how can we care about those we've left behind?"

"That's one reason that Denmark and neighboring countries keep scoring high on happiness," Kat said. "There's a cultural agreement that everyone is equal. If you brag about how rich you are, the group will turn its back on you."

Brad jumped into the conversation, recalling a neighbor of his who had worked with the Lego Company in Denmark for a year. "He'd started running with a co-worker after work, and only at the end of the year did he find out the co-worker was a national track champion. And he found out by seeing the runner's picture in the paper. The guy had never said a word, because it would have been bragging."

"Even a company's CEO doesn't make a huge amount of money in Denmark," said May. "She chooses work that challenges and excites her. Social status isn't based on your wealth but what kind of person you are."

"I play tennis with a guy who's a company president," Kat agreed, "and I also play with a guy who's a trash collector—and drives a Mercedes. He's paid well because his work is a critical service. He makes as much money as a lawyer and he only works twenty-one hours a week."

Margo couldn't remain silent, it all sounded too rosy. "What about the high taxes you pay? Doesn't that make you feel boxed in?" Now Margo and Kat seemed to face off, as if their road trip may have included some sparks.

"Yes, we have high taxes, but everybody pays them, no one is exempt," Kat insisted. "We get tangible assets by pooling our money: education, child care, health care.... six weeks of paid vacation, on average." Kat looked around the table at the attentive faces. "If your job disappears, you get two year's unemployment pay if you need it—at 80 percent of your salary. High taxes intentionally create a narrower gap between rich and poor, making the whole society less envious and insecure." She shrugged her shoulders almost apologetically, a gesture May also made when the facts spoke for themselves.

Kat's voice was becoming strained as she concluded, "There's a much greater sense of trust than here, I know that. I sure wouldn't leave my Principia bike—which I ride to work—in most American bike racks."

Marc had a sudden inspiration about how to sum up the conversation. "Denmark is *designed* to be happy! No wonder it always scores high on the happiness rankings. They've set up a *social infrastructure* that meets human needs and reduces stress." Lisa agreed. "Danes seem to know that after a certain level of income, more money won't make them any happier. The 'social infrastructure' you mention, Dad, is what has the real value. It's *cultural* wealth, held in trust, literally, for the whole society."

Before the spirited conversation and the evening began to wind down, Margo took one more swipe at Danish culture, asking how Danes could stay connected socially in such a chilly and comparatively dark part of the world. Once again, Kat and May teamed up to explain that in addition to being the land of Hamlet and Hans Christian Andersen, Denmark made a point of social clubs. For every possible interest, from painting through world history and badminton, there was an association, and there were social expectations that most people would find something of interest to keep individuals from becoming isolated and lonely. One national pastime, gymnastics, had become popular long ago for predictable reasons: the only necessary equipment was the body, so not a lot of consumption was necessary, and the outcomes were health as well as social connection.

The dinner group was a little relieved when Margo was finally tired of playing devil's advocate—or maybe was actually convinced of Denmark's socially successful experiment. She finally told Kat, "Well, it looks like I need to go with you back to Denmark, even though I hate cold winters."

"That's what *hygge* is for," May said, munching on one of the Belgian chocolates that Lisa had brought for dessert.

Twenty

Tickling the Bear

F our days after the Sakata's solstice party, a determined Marc sat at his desk finessing the daily to-do list. Things seemed to be going pretty well. He'd had a text from Kerrie (aka Wild Thing) saying she'd gotten the grant she applied for and wanted to thank Marc again for being a reference and a longtime mentor. She hoped he was doing well and urged him to join her and Jimmy some time for dinner (not high on Marc's list of fun things to do—or probably Jimmy's, either). He texted back that he'd given a gold-plated assessment of her proposal when the grantors called, and was glad it was working out.

Then Marc had called Rocket to say hello and ask if his free-spirited brother had met the solstice deadline for the totem poles. Bingo! Not only had Rocket met the deadline and received kudos for the fine work but, more excitingly, he'd been offered a job managing the construction of another house. "John's the gift that keeps on giving," Rocket told Marc. "A friend of his is building a house—a frickin' chalet, really—south of the town of Mendocino on the coast. John recommended me for general contractor! I'll have to pass an exam to get certified, but the project could be a financial *miracle*. We'll finally be able to pay off our cabin, it looks like."

"High-five, big guy! Good luck with that exam! So, tell me, has the liaison between John and Sara blossomed, or withered?"

"Well, they're on a long-tail boat in Thailand right now. That should answer your question."

"That was quick! I bet you feel good about that." Marc remembered his own feelings when Lisa and Brad had found each other. "Yeah, I do," Rocket answered, a quaver of pride in his voice.

"What about Zak?"

"Zak's with us. Or maybe we're with him. Either way, that kid is really on a roll. We're going fishing together this weekend. He was asking about you, wondering when you'd be coming back." Marc felt a warm twinge of appreciation. "Well, ask the Chicken Chief if he'll teach me how to fish sometime!"

Feeling energized by the catch-up with his brother, he felt hopeful that his latest lab results would be good news, too.

Still on his list were:

- DU guys about golf game
- get blood test results
- talk to Kai about the other blood sample (U Mass, Stanford)

When he texted several DU friends about the upcoming golf game, his cellphone's auto-correct outdid itself with a double-whammy. *Looking forward to seeing all your faces at our little tournament* became *looking forward to seeing all your feces at our little torment*...He tried his best to see the humor in it, but the unfolding universe of Artificial Intelligence was really getting on his nerves. He cynically imagined the day when a classified digital message like "replace the missiles" autocorrects to "release the missiles" or urgent attempts to dial 911 are idiotically routed to a phone-sex chat line.

Allowing himself a minute or two to check the news online, he got sucked into an article about 'happy hormones'—a topic they'd discussed at the Sakata party. When study participants are shown images of kids playing soccer or a climber summiting a mountain peak, brain scans of their reward centers pop like fireworks. Images like a love-radiant mother nursing a baby light up the ancient brain like the ding-ding of a casino jackpot. Marc was hopeful that the reward center might still be humanity's ace in the hole, capable of collectively choosing peace and the restoration of nature because, quite simply, they make humans happy, and healthy. He thought about *un*happy hormones like cortisol. No wonder dangerous neighborhoods aren't seedbeds of upward mobility. Stress levels paralyze positive emotions and human energy. What if we allocated more of our taxes to these neighborhoods for community gardens, meeting places and job training centers? Wouldn't we see happiness soar in inner cities, along with incomes and civic engagement? Marc knew full well that some of the world's finest teachers, inventors and political representatives often remain undiscovered on these desperate streets.

Now he understood the biochemistry of Denmark's happiness: there were many intentional opportunities in Denmark that trip physiological sensors and directly meet needs. Cultural assets like amiable bosses, free education and child care, equal opportunity—all these release happy hormones like juice dispensers in a health-conscious restaurant.

M arc finally turned his attention to his health history. By now he knew how to interpret the results, and if he had questions he could call the doctor's office. Getting his latest lab results was a little scary since the results *could* be bad news. Still, the meds had been in his system for a few weeks and they should be working by now.

"Incorrect Password," the website informed him. He reentered. "Incorrect password." After checking his password file he finally surrendered, clicking on *"Forgot password*?" The prompt implied, "You idiot!" and Marc always felt degraded and shamed for being so disorganized. But the computer follies were only just beginning! Abruptly, like a smoke alarm in the hallways of hell, his computer began beeping insanely—something he'd never experienced before. A flashing red box popped on the screen and a civil defense-like voice warned, over and over, "IF YOU CLOSE THIS SCREEN, ALL THE CONTENTS ON YOUR HARD DRIVE WILL BE DELETED!" He had five minutes to call the telephone number on the screen before the computer would crash and burn—really bad news for anyone whose computer files were crammed with decades of collected wisdom.

Although he suspected it was just cyber-theater—some kind of malware—it was also very freaky...Where did these voices come from?! (Were there also snakes wriggling inside the hard drive?) Panicked, he grabbed his cell phone to call Lisa, a whiz on computers. When she answered, he gasped, "You're my lifeline! There's this weird voice coming out of my computer, and a flashing pop-up that tells me to call a number for Windows Tech Support. Is it safe for me to...?"

"I can't hear you," she interrupted in a loud but nonchalant voice that floated in a stormy sea of static. "We have a bad connection," she continued from behind the steering wheel of her car. He raised his voice so she could hear him and said, a few words at a time, "I have an emergency on my computer. Can you hear me? Mayday!"

"You're breaking up," she said. "I'll call you when I get home, okay?"

Luckily, by the time Lisa got home half an hour later, Marc had rallied. First, turn down the insane volume on his desktop. Second, go to a security-related website on his cell phone to find out what kind of a virus this was, and how to punch back! He was relieved to find out it was the "Zeus" virus, a scam alarm that tried to scare you into calling the "experts" to buy their bogus consulting services.

Was humanity being anesthetized by this new generation of ad-popping devices? It felt so much like a carnival with an evil undertone, like Ray Bradbury's story *Something Wicked This Way Comes*. A few months earlier, as Marc was chatting with a colleague at the university, a voice had arisen from the conference table. It was Siri, queen of the iPhone, asking paranoically, "Are you talking about me?" Each man realized this was just the beginning. Shaking his head, Marc commented, "This brave new digital world is like a small wooden ship arriving in a South American bay about 1540, right? At first, the ship seems magnificent to the indigenous folk: the arrival of a long awaited, very benevolent god!" Marc still had the attention of his friend, speaking faster as he narrated, "Then the conquest begins: the swords, the horses, the guns, the rapes...the passwords, crash dumps, Russian hackers, Hillary Clinton to the scrap heap of history, cyber-warfare, Transformer militia, and yes, dystopia, just like in the movies..."

"We could just change the script..." the colleague had said.

"Exactly."

With great relief, Marc exited the screen with its fake time-bomb and gang of hackers, having just lost about an hour of his day. Then he quickly accessed the lab results and...wished he hadn't. His white blood cell count had shot up as his body tried to battle a rapidly rising virus population. It wasn't a huge difference, but his campaign was going in the wrong direction, despite all his diligent efforts. Leaning back in his office chair, looking woefully at the floor, he felt his bicycle calling to him.

It was a mild, pleasant day and he made two loops around the park's perimeter, feeling a bit more optimistic. A little lunch would help him too, wouldn't it? About two blocks from home, he felt an urgent need to pee! He started cranking on the pedals like he was in the Tour de France, even cutting in front of a car at the intersection, which elicited an extended, angry honk. He knew he had to make it home!

But he didn't.

Could this day from hell be any worse? Leaning his bike against the backyard fence, he snuck into the house, urine dripping over one kneecap, and a warm, wet circle under the zipper. In that dark, humiliating moment, he felt like an eagle with a sudden case of vertigo.

"I need to speak with the Director of the Sarawak Conservancy, please," Kai said clearly, hoping for someone who spoke English. He'd found the number of the nonprofit organization that Marc had mentioned, in Kuala Lumpur, and he mentioned that his friend had been part of an American-led project several years earlier.

Kai was determined to confirm his suspicion that Marc had indeed contracted the virus on the island of Borneo, parts of which are in Malaysia, so he'd also spent several hours reading online research papers that described commonly contracted diseases in Borneo, and possible herbal cures for them. He talked with the Bureau of Traditional Medicine after finally finding someone who could at least speak Japanese, which Kai spoke a little. He poured over satellite maps of Borneo to see where the Penan tribe lived, and watched a BBC documentary about their way of life. "This is our homeland, where we've lived for thousands of years, where we know how survive. We don't know how to survive in areas that are logged and barren."

Marc had absolutely no idea what Kai was doing. He wouldn't have believed that Kai was currently checking on flights to Malaysia and planned to leave ASAP. Although Kai knew the mission to Borneo would be a long shot, he had a hunch and he was going to follow it. His father agreed that the most precise and successful herbal cure for Marc's disease might be a local one, a proven folk remedy for an illness familiar to the local population.

A few days after Marc's pants-staining dance with the devil, Margo called him, suggesting a spontaneous get-together that evening. Both she and Kat were leaving Denver the following afternoon. Kat was returning to Denmark, and Margo to Washington, D.C. They really hoped to see Marc before they left. "We're both interested in getting to know you better. You made quite an impression on us. We can bring takeout from Little India restaurant..." Although Marc wasn't feeling especially sociable, he didn't want to be rude to them, and frankly he liked the idea of a convenient dinner after a few miserable days.

"Yes, that *was* a nice evening. I was interested in your comments, too, and Kat's." He wavered about inviting them over but finally said, "Sure, let's get together, but it needs to be a short night, OK? I want to get a little extra sleep. Would seven work for you?" He gave Margot his home address, glancing around the living room as he spoke. Compared with its landfill-like appearance a few weeks earlier, the house was looking shipshape, he thought, mostly thanks to Lisa. "It looks like a grown-up lives here now," Marc said aloud, poking fun at himself. He was pretty good at making samosas, a favorite Indian dish. He had some leftover, already-boiled potatoes and some fresh ginger and frozen peas, so he could crank out eight or ten little beauties in short order.

As he cooked, he half listened to the latest NPR reports about ongoing chaos in Trump's office—abusive remarks the President had made about his own staff members, more chatter about a secret meeting with a Russian lawyer who had offered *dirt* on Hillary Clinton before the election. He clicked off the radio, not wanting to get sucked back into it.

Kat and Margo arrived on time with a huge platter of warm, sweet and savory food. The two women were impressed with Marc's crispy looking samosas, and Marc suggested they eat informally at the long coffee table in the living room. Kat studied the tools and hunting weapons on display in Marc's glass case, remarking, "Wow! This is an awesome collection!" She carefully studied the labeled descriptions of each implement.

"And what a comfy living room!" She added, in a joking tone, "So... hygge," Marc thanked Kat, noticing that she seemed more relaxed than she'd been at the Sakatas'.

"I can assure you it didn't look so cozy a few weeks ago but my daughter helped whip it into shape." Both women were dressed a notch above casual, maybe indicating a high regard for Marc or at least hopes for another stimulating evening, even if it was to be a short one. Margo stood on the other side of the room admiring an elongated wooden mask on the wall. "It's beautiful!" she said, looking over her shoulder. "So simple, and graceful."

"Thanks, I got that when I was an intern in Ghana way back in the 70s."

The three sat down to eat and chat, the two women on the couch and Marc in a large, comfortable easy chair. "Kat," Marc began, "I'm really interested in the social clubs you'd mentioned at the dinner party. What clubs do you belong to?"

"Well, a few different ones. Adventure Club, where we hike, rock climb, even sky dive..."

"Sky dive?" Marc interrupted, "I just did that a few weeks ago! I loved it!" The two compared their experiences, talking directly with each other while Margo became absorbed in her cell phone.

"What other clubs?" Marc asked.

"European history, which recently has been about people showing great, culture-rich slideshows of their travels. Sometimes we go on trips together, too. Last January we went to Portugal for a week."

"Very cool!"

Nodding, Kat added, "Then there's Tennis Club."

"That's where you play with the rich garbage collector?" She laughed, "Yeah, we're pretty evenly matched." Marc nodded and asked professorially, "Do you think these clubs are a significant reason why Danes are happier?"

"Absolutely. When people talk to each other at work or church about their activities, those who haven't joined a club feel like they're missing the fun. Most people join at least two clubs."

"I'd love to visit Denmark...when I get well again." He hung his head just a little, trying to forget the frantic bike ride home a few days earlier, and a few other urgent nature calls since then. He put on a background recording of songbirds in their natural habitats as Kat reached over and turned the bright lamp down a notch. The conversation became leisurely, each of them finding a pillow or relaxing into a more comfortable position. Rummaging through her purse, Margo pulled out a pill bottle and announced unexpectedly, "I have some Molly. You know, Ecstasy. We could take some and just see what happens." This caught Marc *way* off guard. (He wondered, *What does she* think *will happen?*) But given the kind of week he'd had, he was tempted. He'd tried MDMA back in his undergraduate years and really enjoyed how it both amplified feelings of trust and heightened sensory perceptions. Wouldn't it be perfect for his current frame of mind? From what he remembered it's not necessarily an aphrodisiac, but it definitely makes people want to be *near* each other, both physically and emotionally.

"I can't do it, but I wish I could. I'm taking prescription drugs. I don't know if they would react with Ecstasy. You know what? Let's just talk, eat some dinner, and maybe smoke some pot."

Sensing Marc's mild discomfort, Kat asked politely, "Do you want us to go, after dinner? You said you wanted this to be an early night."

"No, I don't want you to go. I'm glad you came. I've had kind of a challenging week, and it's nice to have the company." When he said that, Margo seemed to sense an opening. "What drugs are you taking? We could see online if there are potential reactions with neurotransmitters like Molly." Marc reluctantly shared the names of the drugs, doubtful the information would be online anyway. "They told me to limit my alcohol consumption, and avoid antidepressants. But marijuana's not a problem apparently..."

Margo walked down the hallway with her cell phone in hand and Kat quickly seized the opportunity to apologize. "She's pretty domineering, sometimes. And she tends to be kind of tenacious, too."

"She's colorful, isn't she?" he responded, shaking his head slightly and smiling. He remembered her persistence at the Sakata's dinner party. "She had some traumatic experiences back when we were roommates in college, and since then, too," Kat explained in a low voice. By the severe look on her face, Marc couldn't help but be curious. But before their conversation went any further, Margo was back in the room, telling them she'd found a website with information about what to avoid. "Molly's not on the list for either of your drugs," she announced. Margo's face suddenly seemed softer to Marc. Somehow, knowing she'd had personal challenges let him see her in a different light. He had to admit he did want to experience the drug again, if only for the sake of *science*. Wasn't he bold enough—and old enough—to break a law or two in the sanctity of his own home? His brother would do it...

About half an hour later, all three were unable to contain broad smiles, each of them basking in an altered, elevated state. It wasn't a tingle exactly, but a heightening of the nerve endings, like flowers coming into blossom in a time lapse video. As the experience intensified for each of them, Kat invited Marc to sit on the couch with them. "No, I don't want to feel boxed in." It was so easy to just say what he felt. The chemical was a kind of truth serum. "How about if I pull this easy chair over and we can form our own little circle of silliness? Maybe we'll even become a force of nature." He had no idea what he meant by that, he was mostly just being playful. "A meeting of the Minds?" Kat asked, alluding to the mutual sense of wonder they were feeling.

"No, more a meeting of the *mimes*," Marc joked, his hands moving on an imaginary pane of glass like Charlie Chaplin. All three thought the pun was hilarious and it felt so good to share a laugh! There was no need to get up or go anywhere and, besides, the ground might not be completely sturdy under their feet.

"Have you done this before?" Margo asked Marc. "Only once. Back in college. About fifteen of us took MDMA at Mount Falcon, this great little park with a view of Denver in one direction and the Continental Divide in the other—snowcapped mountains under a bright blue sky. We had guitars and Frisbees, even a goofy costume or two, and we were sitting on each other's laps and running around in the warm sun, Then one guy, Bud, was climbing a large boulder and fell backwards with a dull *thunk* as his head hit a large, lichen-covered rock. I still remember that *thunk*...Obviously, we weren't expecting this sudden assault on our collective euphoria, but we kept our cool and did what we needed to do: we rigged up a stretcher out of long branches pushed through the sleeves of a few shirts. Bud was still unconscious, but someone stopped the bleeding on the back of his head with direct pressure, and someone else ran a quick half-mile or so to the phone booth to call 911. But when Bud came to, I've never seen or felt gratitude that strong. It was a miracle that he was alive, and that we *all* were!"

"So yes, I've taken it before...and I'll always remember this feeling. It sort of makes you feel like a happy-faced pumpkin with a small, warm candle inside."

"Is that what I look like, a pumpkin?" Margo asked, pretending to be self-conscious.

Marc lapsed into an explanation of how Ecstasy works, physiologically, but realized he was being way too factual for the occasion. "I know...I always end up lecturing about something."

"You're a *professor*," Kat said, supportively. As Marc studied her face, she was suddenly (even if temporarily) the most desirable woman he'd ever known. She seemed to understand him, and be attracted to him. The drug had taken ten years off each of their faces. Kat's face glowed like an excited girl's after her first legal drink. He saw on that perfectly imperfect face the same incredulity that he felt. The miracle was so obvious, why didn't people see it every moment of every day?

Margo felt the connection between Marc and Kat and struggled not to feel left out. In a vulnerable, childlike voice that caught all three by surprise, she told Marc, "You're really smart." Staring openly at Margo, Marc saw an incredibly strong woman. Her face was in high resolution, floating in front of a fuzzy background like a brilliant Impressionist painting. (Margo instantly became the second most desirable woman he'd ever met.) They looked at each other with uncontrolled smiles, dazzled by the beauty around them. It was such a privilege to see the world from a different angle, apart from all the static! Looking at each other's childlike faces, the three spontaneously started laughing again. Marc was puzzled by something: it wasn't physical attraction he felt with these two attractive women—who he may never see again—but something wider: a continuing connection with their pulsing, vibrating life energies. It made him feel grateful, always a welcome feeling when you may be dying.

Kat shared her feelings about being an introvert, admitting she sometimes felt misunderstood. "People may think I'm awkward because I don't talk, talk, talk. But usually, just as I'm getting ready to say something totally relevant (and extremely wise), the extroverts have stampeded on to the next topic. It seems to me like introverts process ideas in greater depth, while extroverts want to explore wider territory, to generate more stimulating ideas and personal experiences which, in turn, release 'happy hormones.'"

Marc beamed, delighted by Kat's insight. He assured her she'd been a very spirited, engaging talker at the Sakata party, as well as right at that moment. It was clear that she was both self-sufficient and intelligent. "I suppose I'm more of an introvert than extrovert," he told the women, "but I think what's happened in my life is I've been rewarded—psychologically and monetarily—for talking, and I've just gotten used to it."

"I'm probably somewhere in the middle," Margo added. "But right now, with my barriers down, I'm going to be super truthful. Here goes: It feels like I've created this alter ego, this mask to show the world how confident and self-assured I am." Marc and Kat both knew this intuitively and still received her frankness as a gift. All three felt their revved-up nerve endings ringing like miniature chimes.

Marc shared a recurring dream he'd had in his earlier years. "From about the age of three to my mid-twenties, whenever I was feeling especially stressed, this huge bear came lumbering out of the forest and straight toward my house. That monster was 600 pounds of snarling, drooling, razor-clawed mammal, its huge nostrils quivering hideously. I could hear its claws scratching on the hardwood floor upstairs, ever-closer to my bed, and there was nothing I could do to defend myself except wake up in a cold sweat. But then, somewhere in my late twenties, I began to get a grip in my life. Why be a hostage of my own fears? One very significant night, sick and tired of letting this intruder contaminate my life, I stood my ground and tried *tickling* the bear!"

The women, spellbound and holding their breath, laughed with relief.

"It's something you can only do in a lucid dream...break the spell. This ferocious animal chuckled like an amiable, apologetic teddy bear who'd rudely forgotten his manners. I watched him slowly amble out of my psyche forever. That moment, in that most-vivid dream, I found a life strategy:

finesse your fears and they shrink to the size of a harmless goldfish, just swimming in circles."

There was a long, appreciative silence as Margo and Kat processed Marc's story. Both wondered if this wasn't the underlying reason they'd wanted to see Marc before they left. There was a humble strength in this man, even though he had a life threatening illness. If he could be strong, why couldn't they? Emotionally boosted by the drug, each woman silently, instinctively transferred her most fervent well-wishes toward Marc.

"Well, in *my* dreams, the bear is still there," Margo confessed. She looked at Kat for moral support, hesitating a good four or five seconds. "Let it out," Kat whispered, sitting up and grabbing Margo's arm. With noticeable effort, Margo looked Marc in the eye and began, "Back when Kat and I were college roommates at Barnard, I was at a party that got kind of out of control." She hesitated again, then resolved to come clean. This felt like the right time. "A football player from Princeton...raped me." She sighed, so relieved that she'd found the guts to off-load this bitter memory to a man she hardly knew. Instantly teary eyed, Marc nodded supportively and stretched over to give her a brotherly hug. "Then, about ten years ago, *it happened again!*" she managed to say before bursting into a gasping squall of sobs. "I was just walking down a quiet street, about ten or so at night. He had a gun, and he ordered me to get into his car..."

Marc was devastated. In this moment of elevated empathy, he felt a complete spectrum of emotions, including gratitude that she had let it spill out. All three fell into a warm, unifying hug, infused with tears and magnified emotions. Spontaneously, Kat kissed Margo on the cheek, then right on her salty lips, startling Marc, who slowly pulled away. He wasn't withdrawing his support, not at all. He was just uncertain what was happening. Both women looked over at Marc, a little embarrassed but without any urgent need to explain.

"So you two are...together," he said with a genuine smile, feeling a little dense. (How had he not seen this?) But he was glad these two beautiful beings seemed to be sharing a loving relationship. Kat felt safe enough to just tell the truth: "Well, we've been experimenting," She told him that another of her social clubs was the LGBT club, emphasizing almost involuntarily, "With an accent on the 'B,' for me. We go to the museum together, we go on marches; we even toured a model neighborhood together—what you call cohousing here."

"That's cool. Yes, I have some friends who live in cohousing, and I knew the format was Danish." Still puffy eyed but purged, Margo prompted Kat mischievously, "Tell him about the *other* club you went to!" Kat blushed, saying defensively, "I only went once, or...twice...as something different."

Increasingly intrigued, Marc asked, "What kind of club...a...?"

"Sex club!" Margo blurted. "Where you give out invitations if some person or persons attract you, to see if they're interested, too." The energy in the room suddenly shot into space. Marc gulped, looking over at Kat, who was, at that moment, looking at the floor...waiting.

After a long pause, Margo urged, "We could have a sex club...right here!" She looked at Marc boldly, but he was completely flummoxed and couldn't respond. "I'll show you my tattoo," Margo offered flirtatiously, her face flushed and her breasts—from Marc's heightened perspective—about as prominent as the Grand Tetons. Marc still couldn't summon a response to this very compelling offer. Here, right before him, right in this moment, was an erotic opportunity he'd sometimes imagined. He knew he was by no means alone in having this fantasy, and he let his imagination wander. What harm could there be? But he also knew something else—something unspeakable, that the women didn't know: despite this rare opportunity, he didn't have even the beginnings of an erection. He was confused and a little...mortified! After the creepy events around incontinence, he'd already been feeling deflated. Now, this?

"He's not into it, Margo," Kat said, sensing Marc's confusion and wanting to give him a quick out. "That's not...really it," Marc said. "We're having a wonderful connection here, tonight. I feel very close to both of you, I really mean that. And I'm attracted to each of you: your strengths, your authenticity, and your...sex appeal. But I have a policy of not violating other peoples' relationships. I definitely prefer women, but..." He didn't continue, feeling too embarrassed to tell them the truth.

He leaned forward into this rich, intimate circle and gave each woman a heartfelt kiss on the cheek, then leaned back and said in a steady, unguarded voice, "It feels amazing how quickly we've kind of become soulmates." He got up to make another pot of tea and guessed, correctly, that when he got back the women would be playfully embracing. Seeing him come into the room, Kat slowly pulled away from Margo, repeating how glad she was that Marc had been open to having them over. "This is a very special evening," she observed.

Margo commented that Ecstasy affects people in different ways. Sometimes, she said, men aren't able to have an erection, but they still feel *intimate*. Marc stood holding the tray with the teapot on it, wondering how or if she knew. Had she seen in her web search that ED was a possible side effect of the meds he was taking? He neither confirmed nor denied anything, just returning to his seat in the circle of silliness. He found the courage to confide his current confusion about his illness, repeating the conclusive words he'd said to Kai, a few weeks earlier: "Somehow, I feel like I'm safe in the universe, whether I'm alive or dead. There are forces so much bigger than me. But if I don't make it, I'll certainly miss moments like these."

"Sometimes I wonder if life is an invention that enables the universe to admire itself," Kat commented, a notion that Marc found fascinating. In the next few hours the trio acknowledged and rose above cruelty, dysfunction, and mortality itself, talking and laughing until almost midnight, effortlessly forging a profound, unspoken pact. After all, whatever came next in each of their lives, they were fellow voyagers, safe in the universe! By the time a second round of MDMA had worn off and the women slowly stood up to leave, Marc felt like he knew them in a way he'd known few others. Walking them out to their rental car, his arms around each of their backs, he told them, "I'll always remember this night. I...love you two."

"Let's all meet in New York City next year," Kat proposed, as if laughing right in the face of doubt, fear, and dread. Wasn't that an underlying purpose of mutual support, to dress up unwanted emotions like these as ridiculous, powerless little pull-toys?

Twenty-One

Bareback

F ourth of July had never been a big deal for Marc, after the age of fifteen or so. Yeah, he was grateful his ancestors had fought for and won basic human rights 250 years ago, but the work wasn't done yet, and really, it never would be. It seemed to Marc like the brash festivities of the Fourth were born of war and meant to symbolize that America was an unassailably powerful empire. Just keep the beer and brats coming or we'll wrestle each other to the death, right on the back lawn. Marc thought it should mean so much more. *Democracy is a magnificent garden that quickly reverts to a weed patch if left unattended,* he thought. *Far more than "bombs bursting in air," coveted speedboats, and penthouses, the American Dream is an all-inclusive invitation to share decision-making. It's a rich seedbed of creativity, trust, and possibility—maybe humanity's best idea.*

This demonstrative celebration also made Marc reflect on the domination of men. He was so relieved that many of the world's countries now had women at the helm. Barbaric male behavior was becoming obsolete, just in time. Like fossil fuels, the divine right of males had to go. Still, despite the undertones, he did appreciate fireworks as an ancient art form, and in many previous years he'd hiked up the gentle slopes of Green Mountain right at dusk, where he and friends—dark silhouettes against the dazzling colors—could view dozens of shows at the same time. "Are you going up on Green Mountain again this year?" Lisa had asked. "Can we come too?"

"No, I'm just going to hunker down and watch the Ken Burns documentary on Thomas Jefferson, then watch the Denver Country Club fireworks from the Cohens' yard. They invited me over for homemade ice cream."

"All you can eat?"

"Absolutely."

He didn't tell his daughter how worn out he was from all the ups and downs of the past month. And he could never tell her about the odious side effects that were stalking him: the incontinence, erectile dysfunction, and fatigue—all so unfamiliar to Marc. He didn't tell Lisa that he'd felt feverish a few times recently, too, or that the rash on his leg was now a brighter purple. Although he'd fibbed to Lisa that his blood count was "holding steady," he wouldn't tell her anything more, not right now. She didn't have to know that he'd flung one pill bottle against his kitchen wall in existential bewilderment and tossed the other in the trash, goodbye. On Independence Day, he had proclaimed his independence from these imprecise, debilitating drugs. He contemptuously compared their side effects to an off-target airstrike that kills civilians. In that moment he'd decided he would give instinct and natural cures a try. He'd go bareback on a horse he hoped he could trust.

A few days earlier, he'd called his DU friends to opt out of the golf game they'd scheduled. He wasn't willing to wear Depends "adult diapers," dependable though they might be. And he had also talked one of his softball teammates into managing the July 2 game, claiming he had a really bad cold. It was time to see Yukio again, to tell him he'd stopped taking the drugs and to request the strongest natural formula Yukio had. Cutting the cord on the prescriptions felt scary and liberating at the same time, reminding him of a few weeks earlier, skydiving with his family. He was free falling, now.

Marc wished he could sit down and talk with his now-deceased father, the man who had named him after the emperor-philosopher Marcus

Aurelius. And the man who had once told him, "We find out how strong we are when strength is the only tool we have."

As Kai boarded an afternoon flight to Kuala Lumpur, he couldn't help wondering if he was crazy. The trip had come together so quickly. Tyler Morris, an Australian scientist with Sarawak Conservancy, had returned Kai's call, explaining that he not only knew Marcus Blake but he owed the bloke a favor, since Marc had helped his son get into college in the States. When Marc was in Sarawak three years earlier, he and Tyler had become friends, working on strategies to stop the ecological carnage in Borneo. Negotiations with the Malaysian government had not been successful, but the two men vowed to keep in touch as opportunities arose to shut down the runaway deforestation and cultural desecration. Meanwhile, Marc had helped Tyler's son put together a successful application to University of Colorado in Boulder.

Why had Kai decided to do it? For a whole suite of reasons, including his sense of adventure. He and Marc had gotten an unbelievably rapid response from Stanford University confirming that the Q virus did originate in Southeast Asia, with a high probability of Malaysia or Indonesia. Bull's-eye, since Marc had only been in one Asian country, Malaysia, in recent years. Marc had another appointment with Yukio, and the elder healer had confided to his son that Marc's condition was declining. The prescription drugs and immune system-boosting teas weren't working. Marc was hardly sleeping at all, and his vital *ki* was dwindling. Kai wasn't an overly compulsive person, but this report on Marc's health had prompted him to book the flight to Malaysia, leaving the date of the return flight open. The trip was propelled by both a depth of friendship and his fresh commitment to the family practice.

Marc wasn't strong enough to come with him, and besides, Kai was afraid his friend would try to talk him out of it, so he hadn't told anyone he was going except May and his parents. He told them to tell Marc, if necessary, that he'd gone to New York to see a few friends.

Using frequent flyer miles and travelers' advice posted online, he was booked, packed, immunized, and ready to go within twenty-four hours. He had the summer-weight sleeping bag, backpack, boots, rain gear, insect repellent and mosquito netting he'd need to bivouac through the jungle, though he was at a loss when the guidebook suggested "leech socks" to prevent the unwelcome visitation of blood suckers. However, looking at a picture of the socks he realized his lightweight ski gaiters would probably work fine. He also packed a tarp as a rain cover, which he would leave with the Penan tribe when he came home, a small steel kettle, and a few brand new, high quality "Colorado" T-shirts to give as gifts.

He was on his way to Borneo, no turning back now! He'd brought a few magazines and movies, but for the first part of the flight he found himself just mulling things over. His life was going to change with his new status in the family business, and he was ready to do something more challenging. Pondering the mission—to find the precise remedy for an obscure disease—he thought about how appropriate it would be if Marc's recovery was a blend of both age-old and hi-tech wisdom: the shamanism and wisdom of the ancient rainforest combined with the genetic foot-printing of microbial DNA. *Whatever it takes, we'll make this happen,* Kai told himself as he drifted to sleep. He'd taken a melatonin pill to help him doze through at least eight hours of the mega-flight, and it worked well in several ways: it carried him dreamily through the elbow-bumping snack carts, abrupt shrieks of laughter from First Class, and occasional, not-much-progress updates from the pilot. It also kept conversation to a minimum with the passenger next to him, coincidentally an oil and gas engineer with a map of Borneo on his laptop.

Tyler met Kai at the airport, holding a large cardboard sign that read, "Marc's mate KAI." Dressed in casual business clothes and with a warm smile on his face, Tyler seemed less of a hell raiser than Kai had imagined when they'd first talked on the phone. But the man soon revealed an untethered Aussie character beneath the beige sports jacket. "G'day," he said, shaking Kai's hand firmly, "I'm stoked that you're here!" The two sized each other up as Tyler continued, "I'll bet you're buggered from the flight." Walking down the concourse, Kai seemed more the adventurer of the two, with the large backpack towering over his shoulders and multi-pocketed khaki pants he'd worn for the long flight. He *was* weary from the flight, and although he could easily interpret Tyler's initial words of welcome, he wasn't completely sure what the man meant by, "I'm about as dry as a dead dingo, do you want to blow the froth off a few?"

Kai stopped walking and with a wide smile on his face asked Tyler, "Am I going to need an interpreter?" Tyler laughed, responding, "I guess they don't have dingoes in your part of the world, eh?" Kai shot back, "We have plenty of dingbats, including our current president, but no dingoes that I know of." It seemed liked the two were going to get along. "Well, I can translate: Would you like to sit down and guzzle a beer or two after your long flight so we can get to know each other? Is that more *American*?"

"You bet. Sure, I could drink a beer." After a pause, he added, "I really appreciate your offer to help me, Tyler."

"My pleasure. Any mate of Marc's is a mate of mine. Forty-five minutes later, Kai and Tyler were chums for life, with three bottles of Guinness in front of Tyler and two of Asahi Super Dry in front of Kai. There were also two empty plates of Pad Thai and two complimentary orangutan shot glasses, just barely worth taking home as souvenirs. The men had their phones out, showing each other pictures of their wives, their homes, and their vacations. Tyler's wife was a pretty Malaysian woman, and his handsome, chestnut-skinned son Logan was in a sense the person who had brought them together. "Logan's getting on well at CU in Boulder," Tyler reported. "A stone's throw from your home in Denver, is it?"

He also showed Kai shots of the longhouse where a notorious shaman, Jalang, was known to spend at least some of his time. "This is the resettlement area, Long Tengulu—our first destination tomorrow. Bulldozers, dams and oil rigs are bleeding the life out of this once-pristine rainforest, the river's about as muddy as the bottom of my boots, and wildlife is disappearing faster than your dinner." The man leaned forward and said in a low voice, "It's not cricket what they've done to the Penan and the other tribes of Borneo, booting 'em off their own land. These corporate and government deadheads have *shit* for brains." Kai shook his head woefully. "It keeps happening all over the world, doesn't it? To our nature-wise Native Americans; to the African princes stolen as slaves from their villages and... to your misunderstood, spiritually gifted Aborigines."

"Bloody oath," Tyler said in agreement. In that moment, Kai could see in Tyler's eyes that he was a man of conscience and conviction. It was clear why Marc had become friends with him. "I could really use some quality sleep," Kai said, "Can you drop me off at my hotel?" The two men made plans to get up before the sun and catch a 6:15 flight to Bintulu.

The small plane they boarded the next day reminded Kai of his smoke jumper days, and there were poignant similarities: Borneo was literally and figuratively on fire. Although much of the land below still seemed green, it was mostly second- or third-growth forest, palm oil plantations and weedy groundcover. Kai took in Tyler's colorful stories of Sarawak (the Malaysian part of Borneo) including one about the temporary return of the grisly practice of headhunting. "In WWII, a small band of U.S. Army airmen parachuted into the dense jungles of Sarawak after being shot down by the Japanese. Indigenous folk were loyal to the Allies, and the Yanks and Aussies persuaded a few tribes to form a battalion to protect their homeland. They scored more than a thousand Japanese heads," he said with a snort. (Unavoidably, Kai imagined what his own Japanese head might have looked like, dangling from a wooden rafter.) "So if anybody asks, tell 'em you're Korean."

Tyler kidded reassuringly, "Actually, the Penan tribe never got much involved with the headhunting, so you're probably pretty safe on that one, mate..." He told Kai about the Penan ethic of Molong, the practice of taking no more from nature than is necessary. "If they take care of the forest, the forest will take care of them. It's their sacred duty to bequeath the forest to the next generation..." With a sorrowful gulp, Tyler added, "And of course they also take care of each other. The most grievous crime in the Penan culture is see *hun*—a failure to share."

"I've been around these last hunter gatherers quite a lot, and I can tell you I've never seen them argue. The people we'll meet this afternoon— if the road's dry enough to get there—*should* be as angry as hornets in a bottle, but they're a humble, trusting people. They've been protesting non-violently for decades, trying to reason with the bastards who auction their homeland to the highest bidder, despite treaties the Malaysian government signed with them." Kai knew from his brief research that logging and palm oil plantation companies often hired armed thugs to push tribes further into the forest or into resettlement communities. Careless practices by huge logging companies, such as logging on steep slopes right above rivers, had caused a thirty mile-long morass of logs and mud in the Rajang River, the 'Amazon of Borneo.' After a rain, many tributaries and rivers were too muddy for drinking, cooking, or washing. To the logging companies, the sound of a chainsaw meant money; to these hunter gatherers, some of the last on Earth, it was the sound of apocalypse.

In Bintulu, the two men rented a Land Cruiser and prepared for their overland journey. They stowed a large red gas can in the back and, just to be on the safe side, Tyler packed plenty of Guinness Stout and Asahi Super Dry, along with a large plastic bin of meat pies and a bulging bag of oranges. He also tucked in a duffel bag filled with cleaning products, sheets and a few sturdy glass storage bottles, to share with his mates in the forest.

On the road, Kai was amazed how quickly the city of Bintulu became clearings of weathered, unpainted wood houses. Beyond the villages and oil palm plantations, the forest seemed to have swallowed humanity like a Venus Flytrap. The cracked pavement of the highway soon became a red dirt logging road and Tyler steadily morphed into a bushwhacking naturalist, grinning under a well-worn outback hat. Thirty kilometers down the road he suddenly slammed on the brakes, pointing at the moving limbs of an Acacia tree. "See the macaques?" At first, Kai saw only a blur of motion, then a troop of playful, gymnastic monkeys came into focus, swinging tree to tree. "These little devils pretty much own Borneo. They'll steal the biscuit right out of your mouth." Then accelerating on the shaded road through the forest, he said, "Maybe we'll see the Rhinoceros hornbill, a large crazy-looking bird whose bill is so long he's got to throw his fruit in the air to send it down his throat."

About midday they stopped for lunch, "elevens" in Tyler-speak. As they leaned against a bumper of the jeep, eating meat pies and drinking beer, he pointed at a tree with peeling bark. "That's the Paperbark tree— *Melaleuca leucadendra*, used by locals for soap, caulking for boats, and insect repellent. The Penan use the bark as flooring, to keep bugs out." Kai was impressed with Tyler's botanical as well as cultural knowledge. He was not an outsider really, but a native by association and choice. "Where are the mosquitoes?" Kai asked. "Did I put on DEET for nothing?"

"Oh, there are hundreds of species of birds and bats that keep the bloody mozzies under control, thank God." The Aussie was wearing shorts, which surprised Kai, considering the leeches he'd read about. Tyler explained that he'd rather see them and scrape them off than find them later feasting demonically under his pant legs. "You've probably read about the tajem tree?" Tyler quizzed as they drove. "That's the tree with the poison latex used in making blow darts?"

"Exactly, you've done your homework. That latex can put a man on his face within minutes. I've always wondered what happens if Penan hunters don't see where a stray dart goes down, and accidentally step on one with bare feet."

"I read that most of the darts find their target. Those long blowpipes work pretty well, it sounds like."

"I've got one of 'em back in my office. So far, I haven't had to use it on the boss man."

For Kai, the high point of the drive was seeing the world's largest (and surely most odiferous) flower. Tyler had parked the jeep at a crossroad explaining how, the previous year, he'd seen the Rafflesia not far off the road when he'd stopped to relieve himself. The two travelers had gotten lucky: the huge parasitic plant was still there, again in full bloom, an event that lasts only a few days a year. Also known as the "corpse flower" because it smells like rotten flesh, the blossom was more than three feet in diameter. Kai excitedly snapped a series of pictures, anxious to show Yukio what he'd witnessed in the wild.

Kai's and Tyler's short stay at Tengulu was poignant. Although the government insisted the resettlement would greatly improve the tribe's quality of life, the buildings they'd constructed reminded Kai of abandoned 1950s style Holiday Inn buildings. There were five "long houses," each building containing about twenty families. Tyler pulled the jeep up to one of the buildings, where kids played with a soccer ball on the ground floor deck. Women swept dust away from their front doors, and elders on the upper level gazed toward their cherished forest on the far side of the clearing. Refugees from the huge hydroelectric dam project that had flooded their ancestral lands, these once self-reliant villagers reminded Kai of forlorn vacationers who'd had their wallets and passports stolen. One of them, Ara, recognized Tyler and called down in broken English, "It's time we see your face." Ara's wife Tapi offered the two men a bucket of water and a towel to wash their face and hands, and also brought cups of lemon grass tea.

They talked for a few minutes about how the government had ignored continuing requests for reparations and land to farm. Then Ara and Tapi invited the visitors to join the family meal, sitting cross-legged on rattan mats: bowls of white rice, jungle ferns, tapioca greens, pineapple, and small river fish were laid out in front of them. Kai offered bottles of Japanese beer to the group, but the couple looked at each other, embarrassed, and declined. Ara explained why they had stopped drinking alcohol. "People like I and Tapi say alcohol is *'Ba' Setan'*, Satan's water, but others make bad decision."

With a scowl, Ara told Tyler and Kai that some Tengulu residents had to go to work for the very logging companies that were destroying the rainforest. Most villagers still relied on the forest for wild game—there were now several shotguns shared among the hunters—and also foraged for natural products to trade or sell: things like *gahara*, an aromatic wood used as an incense and medicine in China, edible birds' nests, also for Chinese, hearts of palm and wild mushrooms. Like other resettlement villages, they were trying to tap into the tourism market, but Tyler knew the truth: other well-established longhouse villages were just far more attractive than Tengulu, where the landscape was barren and villagers were still too outraged to be good hosts. Women like Tapi made exquisite mats and backpacks for the market, but received very little for their work. Pointing to a cleared area they called their farm, Ara explained they were trying to learn how to grow crops like rice, tapioca, lemongrass and sugar cane, but Kai could see that their horticultural skills were still very rudimentary, judging by the mottled and stunted leaves of a young banana tree. In truth, they were not yet "domesticated." Tyler assured the couple that the Sarawak Conservancy and other groups were actively negotiating with government officials for reparations, and hoped to have an agreement soon to make Penan lives easier. The Aussie then explained why he and Kai had come to Sarawak, asking if the shaman was currently in Tengulu. Ara replied that Jalang preferred life in the unlogged part of the forest—a full day and a half hike from the village—but that he came back sometimes to see if the extended family needed his medical help.

Tyler asked, "When was he here last?"

"At end of rainy season, about ten days ago," Ara said.

Kai tried to take this news in stride, but wondered how they would ever find him in the huge forest. Grasping for something tangible, Kai suggested to Tyler that they should show Ara and Tapi a picture of Marc's rash, on the off chance that maybe someone in the village had seen something like this. Kai held up his cell phone with a picture of the rash and the look on Ara's face was a turning point in Kai's quest: the Penan man nodded emphatically, and in Penan, he quickly instructed his son to go to the long house across the clearing and see if Paya was at home.

"Yes, I see this mark before. When Jalang treat he call sign of evil spirits." Tyler and Kai looked at each other in amazement, like they'd just chased away one of those retreating spirits. Was this coincidence really *happening*? A few minutes later Paya showed up, wearing western style clothes and smoking a menthol cigarette. He smiled, nodding respectfully, and when Paya saw the photograph he pointed at Kai, asking in Penan, "You?"

"No, his friend," Ara explained. "Aaah," Paya said, in a sympathetic tone as he solemnly pulled up his shirt to reveal the concentric rash on his belly, an unmistakable match with Marc's rash. Through Ara, Paya explained that when the rash first appeared he had such a high fever his family was certain he was dying. Jalang happened to be at Tengulu and performed a ritualistic chant with the community to dispel the evil spirits. Before going back into the forest, the shaman had given him a strong herbal preparation to drink twice a day—after dawn and before dusk—and showed Paya how to apply a poultice directly to the rash. He'd also posted healing, traditional totems at the entry of Paya's home. The fever had broken, and the rash was slowly receding.

Kai felt like a heavy backpack had been lifted off his shoulders. This trip to ground zero wasn't so insane after all!

Twenty-Two

Okoo bu'un—The Place of Our Origins

The easy part of Kai's journey was behind him, now came the real work. Backpacking about twenty-five miles would have been a breeze for Kai in Colorado, even at 9,000 feet, but in Sarawak, close to sea level, it was like walking through a steam bath. There was often dense, fallen brush on the trail that had to be scrambled over or under, and the sweat band he wore had to be wrung out all along the trail. After just a few miles, all his clothes were damp, and would remain that way for the next few days. Unlike Tyler, he had opted for long pants to be safe. Reluctantly, he slathered on another round of DEET repellent because the mosquitoes were now coming after them. Tyler guessed that the radical disruption of the ecosystem was increasing the occurrence of the whining, "blood sucking demons" whose predators had been eradicated. The three men—Kai, Tyler and Ara—hiked a sometimes-disappearing trail through the forest on the first day, knocking fourteen miles off their journey.

They set up camp a few miles north of Murum Dam that night, catching a glimpse of the huge concrete and earthen structure from their campsite. Before finally eating dinner, they strung hammocks from tree branches with rain shedding tarps above and mosquito netting suspended from the tarps. "I'm so hungry I could eat a horse and chase the jockey," Tyler proclaimed as he pulled the food bag out of his pack. Ara chuckled convivially but probably had no clue what a horse was, let alone a jockey. It wasn't a bad meal, though anything edible would have seemed like a feast: meat pies, oranges, and energy bars from Tyler's and Kai's packs; and roasted frog's legs and sago palm bread from Ara's leather and rattan pack.

Swinging gently in his hammock before drifting off to sleep, Kai marveled at the symphony of insect calls, and through the dense canopy on this relatively cloudless night, the stars twinkled like candles at a cosmic rock concert. Despite the ongoing decimation of the rainforest, this place still had a magical feel; it was easy to see why it had been sacred to the hunter gatherers for so many millennia.

The following day, crossing a tributary of the mighty Rajang River in a canoe, they caught sight of four crocodiles on a fishing expedition and, on the far bank, a small troop of orangutans gathered fruit. The further the men walked, the more abundantly wild the forest felt. Kai asked Ara if this land had been logged. "No, some trees here hundreds of years. Feel the difference—this place has cool breeze because trees tall." Ara related a few stories about Jalang, a man now in his mid-eighties who relied on his nephews to do the hunting and gathering. "When we made to move to Tengulu, Jalang try to live with us. He sit with us in Tengulu eating rice and meat from can, but he not looks happy. He get up and go to forest again, bring back deer meat the next day. Then he talk to people in community, ask some come with him back to *balei ja'au*—magic of the forest—where plants and animals speak to him and support him."

Jalang's wife had died a few years earlier, and her remains were now thirty feet below the surface of the reservoir. Like others in his tribe, Jalang had actively protested the dam's construction, insisting the land belonged to past, present and future generations of indigenous tribes, but one corrupt minister had commanded, "We don't want these Penan running around like animals. They have to settle down, give up their unhealthy living conditions and backwardness, otherwise they have no rights." Tyler said to Kai as they walked, "What these government and corporate nitwits (often the same blokes) can't comprehend is that the Penan have a deep emotional response to changes in light, sound, smell and temperature of their *okoo bu'un*—this place of their origins. They are woven together with this rainforest. To the twits in their shiny shoes, Jalang is a foolish old man with feathers in his headband and a loincloth over his privates. But to the Penan people, he is like your Thomas Jefferson."

As the three men approached the seasonal camp of the "unsettled" Penan tribe—largely a community of elders and their younger family members—Ara gave a birdcall to announce their arrival: a series of loud, penetrating clicks of his tongue against the roof of his mouth. He stopped for an instant, listening for the response before continuing up the path. Around the bend, Kai had his first glimpse of a hunter-gatherer village, not that different, really, from campsites he'd set up over the years. Six or eight people were busy with crafts their culture had practiced for centuries: blocks of sago palm paste—their source of carbohydrate—were drying on a hardwood rack near the fire. A few men were sorting game and wild produce into rigorously equal shares while others were weaving rattan mats or playing with the children. One man walked down toward the river with a pet monkey on his shoulder.

Earlier that afternoon, two men had gotten lucky, bagging several wild boars with a shotgun. Others had used traditional six-foot long blowpipes to kill smaller game—a squirrel and several small birds. Ara explained that the pork would be especially flavorful since the boars had feasted on acorns. There was a sense of purpose and calmness in the group, and members seemed receptive to the arrival of Ara and his friends. A few who had previously met Tyler regarded him as a friend and ally in their quest to regain official use of their own land.

Ara greeted them as extended family and several touched his hair and head in a traditional greeting. When Ara asked if Jalang was there, one of the men pointed toward the shaman's *selap* (large lean-to) telling Ara the shaman was sleeping. In a low voice, Tyler explained to Kai that the Penan are a quiet, somewhat shy lot, and proposed a strategy. Why didn't they settle into the camp activities, share dinner with the group and maybe share a few gifts they'd brought, *then* explain why they'd come? Ara took the liberty of showing Kai around, showing him how the *selaps* were made from thick poles tied together with rattan strips. Although roofs had traditionally been constructed from giant palm leaves, the common roof material was now durable brown nylon tarps. The wooden floors were four feet off the ground to keep the bugs out, and above a mud hearth were the kitchen cabinets—two rustic wooden racks for drying fire wood and storing cooking equipment. Each family had one open-air hut for living and a smaller one for sleeping, Ara explained.

Kai noticed that the cooking equipment in one hut included a cast iron pot, and was glad he could add to their equipment with the kettle he'd brought. He also noticed that one of the Penan wore a wristwatch (though probably not working) and another man even had a cell phone. In fact, to celebrate the arrival of the guests, he soon had an ABBA song bursting out of the tiny speaker.

With permission, Ara pointed out a few other typical possessions: a well sharpened ax, a clothesline supporting native clothes as well as Western, and a wok. They each admired a handsome wooden box with a hinged top that stored family treasures—things like matches, a flashlight, batteries, and maybe a few Malaysian coins. Kai deduced that these people were quite open to owning useful objects from the modern world, but since they were nomadic, they didn't *want* too many things. Kai thought about a few of his friends back home who were also nomads, traveling in trailers or on sailboats. They didn't have many possessions with them, either. In each case, the wealth was intrinsic in the natural and cultural surroundings: things like beautiful scenery, tree fruit, breeze-capturing sails, and quaint little towns with friendly residents.

Tyler asked one of the couples why they'd decided to marry. With a shy smile, the woman spoke up first as Ara translated. "I think he was handsome, good worker, and he makes good *selaps* and blowpipes." Added the husband, "We are happy for many years. Our son live in Bintulu. Has motorcycle."

When Jalang appeared, he was not in the traditional dress Kai expected; he wore a pair of loose-fitting cotton pants and Western style walking shoes. But his elaborate shirt expressed his standing in the community:

a beautifully embroidered yellow-gold shirt with the hypnotic pattern of peacock tail feathers on it. (Tyler whispered to Kai that in Penan culture, the shrill call of a peacock makes fruit trees blossom.) Jalang's single-most striking feature had taken decades to create: earlobes that stretched almost to his shoulders, with pierced holes but no jewelry at that time. The earlobes had been stretched by dangling weights, starting when he was a child. Possibly even then, Kai imagined, he was seen to have unique abilities and skills. In the piercings at the tops of his ears were small, sharp objects that Kai learned were the fangs of a clouded leopard, native to Sarawak but now rarely seen. Jalang's arms and neck were illustrated with tattoos, and though his skin was much wrinkled, there was a timelessness in his calm, piercing brown eyes. The shaman explained through Ara that his clan had been asking the government to stop cutting trees for years. "He says when forest is protected gives oxygen for everyone on Earth," Ara translated. Kai was highly impressed by the shaman's innate wisdom. Even so isolated from the world's evening news programs and the Internet, he knew in his heart, and with each breath, that the forest had far more value if left intact.

Shaking his head sorrowfully, Jalang continued, "Resettlement makes brothers and sisters weak. Nobody ask us, 'What do the Penan people want?' While we pray for the soul of the river and apologize to our sacred mountains for the destruction, the loggers and dam builders go with cold hearts to city to buy jewelry and motorcycles."

After listening to Jalang's thoughts and offering their support, Kai and Tyler decided it was appropriate to show Jalang the photo of Marc's rash. Ara asked if Jalang could help heal Marc, a man who had once helped the Penan tribe negotiate with government officials. "He has mark of Paya at Tengulu," Ara told Jalang. "You help bring Paya's soul back home."

Jalang paused, pondering his response. "I have medicine," he said, "but your friend needs to be here, at the center of the healing ceremony."

"He is too sick to travel," Ara translated to Jalang. "Maybe we can have the ceremony here and your power is so strong that even from far away, you chase the disease away." Kai showed Jalang Marc's picture as Ara explained, "This is Marc and his wife, who has passed over now." Jalang studied Kai's and Tyler's faces. "His wife is gone?" he asked, nodding solemnly. "So is mine." Kai explained that his own father was also a healer, and that they had come to Borneo to get a specific herbal cure for the disease, like the one Jalang had used for Paya.

"Your father is a healer?" Jalang asked, seemingly peering straight into Kai's soul. "Does he have the power of the clouded leopard and crocodile?" Kai answered, "My father is a *sensei*, a master, highly honored for his work. He has the power of the rising sun. And he is an expert in the use of herbs, like you, Jalang. I am honored to be studying with my father to become a healer, too."

"Maybe your father can perform the sacred healing ceremony when you go back. Do *you* have the power of the rising sun?" Without lowering his eyes, Kai answered humbly, "I am still learning, but I *know* the power and I have felt it." Jalang continued to study Kai's face and assess his energy. The younger man, moved by Jalang's presence, felt certain the shaman was reading his past, present, and future. Then Jalang asked, "Tell me about this man, your friend with the mark of *Setan*."

"In a way my sick friend is a healer also. He finds ways to make sure that all people are treated with equal respect, that no one takes more than their share. He studies the way people live and brings wisdom like yours to our Western world. He is a loving man, an *honest* man." Jalang seemed convinced that Kai's friend could be cured. He agreed to perform a healing ceremony that evening. The whole clan would participate in the ceremony, along with Kai, Tyler and Ara. After the ceremony Jalang would supply both a potent tincture as well as diced roots from the tree with the strong medicinal properties. Kai could take those with him for his friend.

Just after dark, several villagers lit a bonfire and beat hide drums to gather the small community. One of them mounted betelnut blossoms and small wooden carvings of crocodiles in branches overhead and the clan began to assemble, each individual wearing traditional clothing. One man announced that the hunters had seen a peacock in the clearing by the river, a sure symbol of good luck. When Jalang emerged from his *selap*, he was dressed in ceremonial vestments: a headband with hornbill feathers, a soft leather loincloth, and shells dangling from his long earlobes. His bare torso was oiled, tattoos covering both his chest and back. He set a machete on the ground next to him in a rattan sheath, in case the spirits threatened him. During the course of the ceremony, the healer was intensely focused, in complete control. Kai had never ventured this deeply into the supernatural, but a large part of him was open to the presence of a tangible energy that could somehow connect with Marc.

By the bright light of the crackling fire, Jalang went into a healing trance, calling on the creator god *Peselong* to chase evil spirits from Marc's soul, even from this great distance. About twenty villagers joined the ceremony, intently following Jalang's lead in rhythmic chanting and sipping from a wooden vessel that was passed around. Marc's picture had been placed on a large boulder, far enough from the fire to shine brightly from Kai's cell phone. But when Tyler took out his own phone to capture the moment, Ara grabbed his arm and explained emphatically, "You can't take picture, you steal Jalang's *balei ja'au*—his power. This is special moment."

The next day, as the three men hiked silently back toward the resettlement village, Kai relived the primal experience they had shared. Maybe it was the beverage they'd imbibed, or maybe the experience truly *had been* as powerful as it seemed. In fact, maybe it actually had touched Marc. Kai imagined his friend now feeling a glow of relief, dreaming peacefully at last back in Denver. He wanted to believe that Jalang's innate talents had not been stripped away by a skeptical 20th century; that they'd been nurtured and preserved in the sheltered rainforest by tradition and tangible results. After all, if Jalang's methods weren't effective, what had saved Paya from a feverish death in the resettlement village? What had begun to erase the graffiti that nature had scrawled on Paya's belly?

"That was one hell of a night," Tyler said, shaking his head. He turned toward Kai as they walked and said jokingly, "I think *I* was even healed by that ceremony." Revealing both hope and lingering skepticism, Kai answered, "It was powerful, wasn't it? The thing is, even if the ceremony was mostly theater—and I'm not sure it was—I have something very tangible in my pack: a few months' supply of powerful roots that have been used in these forests for centuries. My father knows how to turn them into medicine, so Marc's treatment can start almost as soon as I get home." Through an agreement the American embassy had arranged with the Malaysian government, botanical specimens could be express mailed to research facilities with precautionary measures. The raw herbs in Kai's pack—soon identified in Kuala Lumpur photographs as a type of Laurel—would be sent to a lab in Boulder where Kai would pick them up. Both Tyler and Kai felt like they had just completed Mission Impossible. At that moment, it was easy to feel like the rest was just follow-through.

In Kuala Lumpur, Tyler expedited the shipment of the herbal material to the University of Colorado labs, bending the truth just a little when he declared that those labs were researching herbal cures for viruses. The two adventurers parted company at the airport, resolving to get together when Tyler and his wife came to visit their son Logan in Boulder, probably the following spring. "You and Marc and I can drink some Champagne to celebrate Marc's survival. That virus of his is a goner after Blake starts taking the herb. Who knows? Maybe Jalang's ceremony already zapped it."

"Damn right, mate!" Tyler responded, shaking Kai's hand firmly.

Although the mission had been accomplished, it had been a huge effort and Kai felt completely drained. He could hardly wait to get in his seat on the plane and take at least a five hour nap. He'd decided not to call Marc until he got home, then reveal the whole incredible story as Yukio handed Marc a bottle of the decocted herb. On the seemingly endless flight, Kai tried to imagine what Marc must feel like, waiting and hoping for positive news from his blood tests. What must it feel like to be on death's doorstep? Did a person catch a break in the last days? Maybe when you're dying you don't feel so grouchy about all life's daily alarms and stale donuts. Who cares? No more screechy, scolding parrot voices in your head, either. "What's your password, what's your password? *Squawk*...Why didn't you try harder?" Near the end maybe you accept that Death happens to everyone, so what's the big deal? Still, Kai believed that the world urgently needed Marc's perspectives and care. He earnestly tried tapping into Jalang's "power of the clouded leopard" as the plane droned over the Pacific, beaming energy eastward to Marc.

As the plane passed over the Rockies within half an hour of Denver, a sudden blast of wind seemed to throw the plane sideways, so forcefully that a few passengers screamed and others talked in trembling voices as if they were praying. The plane bobbed up and down like the Devil himself was shaking the tail wing. Kai heard himself tell the guy in the seat next to him, "We'll make it," but inside, he secretly wondered if his own time was up. After a few more minutes on this bucking bronco of a plane, the pilot announced that they were beginning a bumpy descent.

Kai somehow sleepwalked through customs, picked up his luggage and called May. "I'll catch the 9:30 train, then call an Uber at the other end, so I'll be home by 12 at the latest," he told her. "You go to sleep and I'll see you in the morning."

"No, silly, I want to see you tonight! I want hear about your amazing adventure, love. I'm so proud of you!"

"All right. See you soon, then. I love you!"

When the taxi dropped him off at the house, he felt a little like a soldier returning home from an ungodly, ravaged front. The dismantling of the Sarawak rainforest still stung like an open wound, but at least he was coming back to the person who made his life feel complete. And, he was coming home with the goods! Maybe Marc's luck was about to change. As he opened the door, the house seemed dark, and he was glad May had decided to go to sleep. They'd catch up the next day, whenever he woke up from his exhausting 19 hours of travel, including a short layover. What was the flickering glow at the foot of the stairs? May had lit a series of candles-in-cups to guide him up the stairs and into her arms.

Kai slept until 11:00 the following morning, then got busy telling and retelling his stories to May, Yukio and Michiko, showing images of exotic plants, tropical birds, reptiles and mammals. One of his pictures showed the fading purple rash on the villager's chest and another showed details of the encampment where Jalang the shaman lived, taken while villagers weren't looking. His parents were especially interested in the healing ceremony, and Kai told them as many of the details as he could remember. Yukio had already found research about the herb, which corroborated its use as a potent anti-viral. As soon as Kai brought the herbs from the university, he and his father boiled the Laurel roots to make a potent decoction. Kai's family treated him like a hero, and the returning adventurer was especially moved when his father put his hand on his shoulder and said simply, "You've done very, very well, Sakata-san."

Kai's elaborate cover-up came full circle a few days later when he called Marc to suggest a follow-up appointment with Yukio. "How was the trip to New York?" Marc asked. "It was good. I saw some old friends." When the three men met at Yukio's and Michiko's house, Kai finally told Marc the incredible truth, watching Marc's jaw literally drop. The man was stunned, insisting at first that Kai was making up one helluva story. "You were in New York," he said, trying to comprehend that anyone would have traveled around the world for his benefit.

"No, actually I went the other direction and met up with your buddy, Tyler," Kai said with a huge smile. "And I brought something home that may help you beat the damn virus!" When he got out his phone and showed Marc the picture of Paya's matching rash, Marc was so shocked that he had to sit down. "You sneaky...son of a....!" Marc said, shaking his head with a wide smile on his face, his eyes tearing up.

"Dad has prepared a decoction of the treatment the Sarawak shaman used for the virus!" Kai told Marc. Then Yukio held up a bottle, telling Marc, "We've got enough of this material to prepare at least six weeks of treatment. Let's see if we even need that much."

"How can I...how can I ever thank you?"

"No thanks necessary, man. We're doing this for the sake of science," Kai said humbly. "The truth is, the trip changed my life. I got to experience the Penan villagers' simple but totally-connected way of life. You were right, they are beautiful people." Never in his life had Marc experienced anything so bizarre. Even in his low-energy state, this earth-shaking surprise instantly brought back a sense of hope. Marc walked over to Kai silently and gave this very special friend a long bear hug. Michiko, who had come into the room, very uncharacteristically joined the hug, and so did Yukio. "The shaman said we needed to have our own healing ceremony with Marc," Kai told them. "I think this is it."

The next day, at the same time that Marc was taking his second dose of the strong decoction at home, Kai was putting on his rubber boots and getting back to work, watering the herbs and exotic flowers in the greenhouse. Pulling the hose around a little pulley on the floor, he stepped up to the passionflower vine he and his father had talked about the previous week, perched on top of the wrought iron shelf. He made a mental note to follow up about the shelf's repair.

The vine was still magnificently in bloom, and Kai studied the complex design of its blossoms. As he meditatively soaked the huge plant, still lost in thoughts of the Sarawak rainforest, the damaged wrought iron shelf suddenly buckled. The huge potted plant slid forward on a slippery sheet of water and smashed directly into Kai's head. This man who'd always been able to nimbly dodge disaster didn't see it coming. He fell to the floor like a rag doll, his head receiving a second blow when it struck the brick pavement. The heavy pot cracked in half right next to his shoulder, the vines blanketing his body in a passionflower robe. Still in the man's loosening grip, the hose continued to gush water, but now it also carried an undulating rivulet of crimson blood and mucky soil into the floor drain.

Epilogue

Letters to the Future

For Yukio and Michiko Sakata, each day was as slow-motion as the one before. It had been three months since Kai's gruesome death, and more than once, they'd seriously considered harvesting lethal doses from Yukio's poison garden. Yukio couldn't stop blaming himself for not repairing the iron shelf in the greenhouse. "Kai would still be alive if I'd had it repaired while he was gone," he told Michiko.

But the Sakatas found a way to just keep going. They were so grateful that May and Marc had quickly stepped in to fill the emotional void. Marc helped plant the second crop of herbs and vegetables in late July, and routinely called to ask how else he could help. May wielded a rake and shovel throughout the growing season, too, though she told Yukio she would never, ever, be able to help with watering the greenhouse. Her suggestion to look for a young intern had brought about an unexpected development: a Naropa University student had jumped at the opportunity to be Yukio's apprentice, and she'd even moved from Boulder to an apartment in the Highlands neighborhood to get started. Another pillar of support for Yukio and Michiko was the Japanese trait of *gaman*—courage and stoicism in the face of great misfortune. The global family of Japan was culturally wide and historically very deep, and the two wore it like a life jacket.

As for the family business, Yukio was a man of service who wouldn't desert his clientele, period. They needed him, and he now realized how much he needed them. He'd researched conventional drugs with Marc, finding a breakthrough medication that prevented viral reproduction, at least keeping the virus from replicating while the herbs did their job. The two men had decided to use the Laurel root and the new trial drug concurrently, despite the slight possibility they wouldn't be compatible. However, as Kai had hoped, Marc's reliance on both ancient wisdom and high-tech science proved successful. By mid-September, the symptoms had almost completely disappeared. In addition to the treatments, Marc believed his willpower might have played a role, too: he simply would not let Kai's efforts be in vain.

But Marc hadn't yet found a way to deal with the empty place in his gut. He came across a quote from one of his favorite authors, Barbara Kingsolver, and found some comfort in it. *"It's the same struggle for each of us, and the same path out: the utterly simple, infinitely wise, ultimately defiant act of loving one thing and then another, loving our way back to life."* He emailed the quote to May, Kai's parents, and Lisa and Brad. It was a grief they shared for this unselfish man who was right there one moment brimming with life, and then instantly, gone. How do you thank someone for saving your life if he's not there anymore? Marc couldn't even imagine how empty May must feel and vowed to be there for her in any way he could.

At a dinner get-together with the Sakatas, May had said to Marc, "I hear you've found a powerful new experimental drug." Holding out both hands to Marc, she'd squeezed his, saying in a contemptuous tone, "That's going to be the end of this pathetic little *organism*..." At that moment, both knew that Marc was still in love with her, but both also knew she was unavailable. Her recovery from Kai's death was painful and slow and there was no perceptible energy coming Marc's way. Kai would have wanted her to be strong, and she'd sought refuge both in her work and with a psychologist. On good days—when getting out of bed hadn't felt overwhelming—she began to imagine running for state senator. Staying active and purposeful would give her life a sense of momentum.

Marc, completely amazed that he'd been among the five percent who survive the Q virus, acknowledged by early-October that there really wasn't a good reason to stay retired. And he also thought about reviving his time capsule project, *Letters to the Future*. Since the Smithsonian Institution was no longer interested in sponsoring it, he pitched the idea to colleagues and administrators at the University, emphasizing the prestige it might bring.

The weather started turning cooler and Colorado's high-altitude aspen trees were at their fall peak, boughs of yellow-gold suspended from snow-white branches, and white trunks with dark eyes, peering into the forest. Lisa called her father to suggest they share a long weekend in the mountains, and Marc, at home after guest-teaching a morning class, loved the idea. Why not drive up to Aspen, spend the night, and come home through Crested Butte, just for a little getaway? Always a take-charge person, Lisa had already called a hotel in Aspen to see about vacancies, finding two available rooms. She had it in mind to see if May wanted to join them, but naturally checked with her dad first. Marc thought the trip sounded like fun but balked at including May. He wasn't sure if it was appropriate to invite her right now. Besides, wouldn't they need three rooms to be comfortable?

Lisa was casual in her response, wanting to counter any hesitancy her father might have. "If she does want to come, she and I can be roommates. One of the rooms has two single beds. C'mon, let's do it, it'll be fun."

"I don't feel like asking her," Marc said.

"I can ask her," Lisa said. "She and I are buds."

Marc took a deep breath, thinking it over, then confided, "She went to a concert last week with some guy from the Governor's office. I don't even know if she'd want to..."

"Oh, come on, who knows what this concert thing was about? She probably just wanted to get out. Or maybe just picking his brain about the Colorado Senate."

"Well, I was surprised to hear her mention it. I mean, she's mostly kept to herself for the last few months."

"Of course, but life goes on, and we could each use a little diversion. It can't hurt to ask her if she wants to come, can it?"

"All right, if you want to ask, go ahead, but make it clear that it's just an outing, nothing like a..."

"Of course." Lisa's voice was light—so much lighter than three months earlier when Marc's life still hung in the balance. She knew full well that May needed time to accept the reality of Kai's death, but she also was certain that May and her father could help each other climb out of this pitch-black cavern. And she wanted to have a little adventure to escape her own routines. When Lisa called, May was just going out to lunch with a state senator, to find out how to run for office the following year. She liked Lisa's idea...she loved driving in the mountains, she loved fall, and she loved Aspen, too, despite its over-the-top lifestyle. But still she seemed hesitant. "Let me think about it and I'll call you back tonight or tomorrow, okay?"

Marc sat in his living room drinking a cup of green tea and thinking about the year he'd just lived through! He'd seen life at its naked core, realizing that no matter what luck we've had, what love we've found, or what mistakes we've made, in the end we all return to the same ocean. In a way, it had been an anthropology experiment: can an individual who loves life find a way to survive, with help from his clan? He felt infinite gratitude for what Kai had done, and he knew his friend wouldn't have wanted him to feel guilty, so he didn't. There wasn't room for guilt with all the other emotions he felt: pride, humility, and mostly, love. At least he could now return to his professional mission: be curious, useful, and have fun with his work. Thinking about his time capsule proposal, he drifted into his office and started writing a little essay from the perspective of a professor in the year 2220, reflecting on the year 2020. Marc imagined the essay as a sort of 'response' to the opening of the time capsule.

"To many people in 2020, it seemed that the human race had been wildly successful. With steady advances in technology and an ever-expanding appetite for 'the good life,' humans had out-competed most other species to become champions of the world, or so they thought. However, many scientists, clergy, and enlightened public leaders vehemently thought otherwise, praying that people of all nations would finally accept the truth: There were just too many humans on board, drilling, tilling, and spilling more resources than nature could restore.

Would our adolescent species–far less senior than crocodiles or ants—have the collective willpower to avert apocalypse as humongous chunks of glacial ice continued to crack into the ocean? Fortunately, the century's brightest minds were betting on it, knowing what a sweet victory it would be when the forests and seashores started coming back and people started trusting each other again. These bold ones had their sights set on an Age of Ecological Restoration and Design, and luckily, they had just enough energy, capital and imagination to take the first steps.

To those inspired pioneers of the middle and late twenty-first century, who began to redefine the very meaning of the word 'human,' we owe an immeasurable debt. Our forward-looking ancestors rose to the occasion, improvising a new way of being in the world, based on a slower, more creative pace of life and a newfound reverence for nature. They began the centuries-long restoration of living systems that has made our own lives more abundant. The historic Convergence of science and religion was first conceived in that time period, along with the planet-wide adoption of the Golden Mean, a key tenet a Chinese, Greek, and Indian philosophy that ritualizes tolerance, moderation, and equality..."

Marc's phone rang again, interrupting his essay writing. It was May wanting to get his take on the proposed weekend in the mountains. Was he really interested in Lisa's idea or was he just going along with it? "I think it'll be a breath of fresh air, for all of us. See the colors, eat some good food, and laugh a little." May's response wasn't immediate. "Well, that's why I'm calling. I think it would be fun, too, but I want to warn you and Lisa that I might not be too chatty...I'm mostly just trying to keep myself going."

"We know that. We understand. We'll just keep it low-key: three completely wonderful people just enjoying the ride."

"Well, okay, I'll call Lisa back and tell her yes, but I need to make sure there's no...there's no...you know..."

"Oh, you mean nothing...romantic about it?" he asked, bravely.

"I'm not sure if I'll ever be interested in dating another man. Our time together when we were young was very special, Marc, but in this part of my life, Kai was my guy. You understand." He heard her sniff, still so deeply grieving. Delicately changing the subject, he asked, "Did you hear that DU may be interested in my 'Letters to the Future' project?"

"Terrific! Would the letters themselves be published, or preserved for future eyes only?" Relieved to be talking about something other than their relationship, whatever it was or wasn't, he said, "Good question. I'm thinking of just publishing a collection of excerpts in an article for national or, hopefully, international news outlets. But first I need to find a sponsor."

"It could be a very useful project for people to think about the lives of our descendants, not just our own lives."

"There's one thing I want to make sure is included: Gary Snyder's poem, "For the Children."

"What's it about?"

Rather than describe it, he recited his favorite part: *"In the next century or the one beyond that, they say, are valleys, pastures. We can meet there in peace if we make it. To climb these coming crests, one word to you—to you and your children: stay together, learn the flowers, go light."*

"That's beautiful. I hope the people who open your capsule are caring, and happy."

They agreed on what time they'd leave the following Friday morning, and what they'd need to bring. As the call ended, Marc realized again how much he respected May: she was so resilient, even in the wake of Kai's death. Of course, he knew a little about that himself.

Marc had another call later that same afternoon: remarkably, DU had given final approval for Phase I funding of the time capsule: $10,000 to do a feasibility study on who would write the letters, and what the project's delivery date would be. If these initial questions could be answered satisfactorily, the University would commit $75,000 in philanthropic funding, given his standing in the field of Futures Studies. Marc was giddy. This project had so much potential, and with the anchor money he knew he could attract more if necessary.

The trip up to Aspen and back was exactly what the three needed: unplanned, spontaneous play. They took turns driving, telling stories about things they'd done—both heroic and embarrassing. They solved the world's problems before they even got as far as Vail, eating cardamom-ginger-applesauce muffins Lisa had made, and guzzling a drink May had mixed up from lemons, fresh cucumbers, mint and honey. Amazed by how quickly they'd gotten to Glenwood Springs, they unpacked their swimming suits and relaxed in the huge hot springs pool. Then they drove over to Aspen, downing a bottle of Chardonnay with dinner, laughing at anything. Though they had generally steered clear of talking about Kai because it was too painful, May recalled a hike the two couples had taken from Aspen over to Crested Butte, nodding her head with a little smile. Marc braved a brief recollection of the time he and Kai were camping in southern Arizona.

"Kai asked me, 'Have you ever made fire without matches?'"

"I told him no and asked if he was going to show me. Ironically, he'd learned to make fire-by-friction years earlier from a fellow firefighter. He cut a four-foot section from the tall, desiccated stalk of a desert agave. Working together, we drilled a hole into the soft-wood platform on the ground, creating both sawdust and heat. One of us would waggle the stalk back and forth from the top to bottom, then the other would start at the top again, giving the other guy a brief break." Marc tried to read May's expressionless face, hoping the story was warming rather than hurtful. "I remember one of us saying between gasps of breath, 'Think of our ancestors, hungry, cold, and desperate for fire.' We must have drilled for a good ten minutes sweating like crazy, our arms aching. Then finally, a tiny coal not much bigger than a grain of salt took hold in the sawdust. Kai grabbed a loose ball of dried grass, placing it right next to the tiny coal, and softly breathed fire into the tinder. I'll always remember that moment," Marc said, with a lump in his throat, "when we made fire together, then sat around the campfire drinking sake." Looking again at May's face, he wished he'd kept his mouth shut. Neither May nor Lisa said a word at first, but after a heavy silence, May said, "Kai and I made fire, too...thanks for sharing that."

The aspen trees in the Roaring Fork Valley were spectacular on the hiking trails and the weather was sunny and warm all three days. On the drive home, Marc mentioned the bike trip in Italy that he and Kai had always talked about. "You know, wouldn't it be great fun if the three of us did that trip together next summer?" Lisa was ready to commit to it, adding, "If I'm not pregnant by then." But May didn't say much at all, probably lost in thoughts about Kai's fanatical bicycling.

Winter was mild and breezy. Both Marc and May immersed themselves in their work, with a curious crossover: May became involved in Marc's Letters project. Because of her efforts, the first few letters in the collection were written by climate change expert James Hansen, who May knew personally, and Bill McKibben, another climate champion. May also sought out the participation of human rights activists, poets, artists, and politicians, including Barack Obama. The more Marc and May hung out together as friends, the more comfortable it felt. It wasn't unusual for her to call him with an idea for the project, and sometimes he talked her into a spring bike ride on the Highline Canal or a trip to the driving range to hit golf balls.

Spring accelerated, hesitated, and then lunged directly into summer, as usual. Meanwhile, Lisa did a little undercover work on her dad's behalf. Once, after having lunch with May, Lisa had casually leaked something potentially useful to Marc. May had told her, "Your dad is so generous, and so courageous. He deserves a partner who appreciates him." Marc's response was simply, "That makes me feel good." Her words weren't anything he could take to the bank but he did store them in his mind, and heart, imagining a possible relationship with May that was less about romance than unconditional support. They weren't kids anymore! As May's energy slowly returned, she began organizing her challenge for the incumbent's seat in the Colorado Senate, running on a higher minimum wage, renewable energy, and gun control. Marc was first in line when she began staffing her largely volunteer campaign.

One autumn afternoon, almost a year and a half after Kai's death, Marc walked briskly toward campus to teach his new course on climate change, *Forecasting the Future*. He got an unexpected text from May. Almost tripping over the curb as he crossed the street, he read and re-read her message: "Are you still interested in that bicycling trip in Tuscany, maybe next summer?"

www.ingramcontent.com/pod-product-compliance
Lightning Source LLC
Chambersburg PA
CBHW050230110726
47898CB00007B/2093